CLOUD WHISPERS

a novel by

SEDONA HUTTON

ISBN: 978-164255507-3

Cloud Whispers

Copyright 2018 by Sedona Hutton

Cover design © Lori Follett of www.HellYes.design

This is a work of fiction. Names, characters, places and incidents are the product of the author's imagination or are used fictitiously and resemblance to actual persons, living or dead, business establishments, events or locales is entirely coincidental.

For more information, please visit Sedona Hutton at www.sedonahutton.com.

ACKNOWLEDGMENTS

To my husband, Sean—This story wouldn't have been possible without your countless hours of help and encouragement. You're my "Liam"—my best friend, my greatest ally, my rock.

Laurie Sanders—Thanks for the topnotch editing, and also for sharing your inspirations and wisdom throughout the process.

BK—Thanks for your inexplicable, but much appreciated, expertise in grammar, and for your time and patience as my first reader.

CHAPTER ONE

"I'm Nathan Loncar, attorney for Gwendolyn Shelton," said the deep voice on the other end of the line.

With a heavy heart, Katie Callahan clutched her cell phone tight. She'd heard about Gwen's death from her father. Seemingly in good health, her cousin had suffered a heart attack and died shortly after. But why on earth was Gwen's attorney calling her?

"I'm contacting you because you've been named guardian of Ms. Shelton's daughter, Savannah."

The heavy feeling sank, settling in the pit of Katie's stomach as she sucked in a shocked breath. Why would her cousin, whom she had only met once, select her as guardian of her daughter? Mr. Loncar had to be mistaken. Sure, she loved kids. She had a beautiful step-daughter and she and her husband, Liam, had been trying to have children of their own. But Gwen wouldn't have known any of that. She was a distant cousin, her father's aunt's kid's kid or something like that.

"Ms. Callahan?" Mr. Loncar demanded. "Are you there?"

Another child for her to mother. An eager fluttering arose in Katie's breast, but she was also confused. Something didn't add up. Biting her lower lip, she dragged her attention back to the attorney.

"Yes, sorry. But why? Why me?" she asked, easing onto a chair at the kitchen table. "I've never even met Savannah."

"Ms. Callahan, I document whatever my client wants. I don't ask for explanations." He sighed heavily, and then proceeded to walk through the legalese. His words barely registered as Katie's mind raced. She and Liam both wanted more children, maybe this was God's way of granting her deepest desire. But how would Liam feel about taking on her distant cousin's kid? Unless....

Her head—and heart—flashed back to her days in Belize as a seventeen-year-old exchange student, to the child she'd given birth to there. Could Savanah be the child she'd given up for adoption twelve years ago? As light shone through the east-facing windows, shimmering and dancing on the kitchen table, hope unfurled in Katie's heart, bright and joyful as the rays of sunshine.

"How old is Savannah?" she asked interrupting the attorney.

Papers rustled. "She's twelve years old."

Katie's chest squeezed tight, but she would have to talk to her father to confirm what she already knew in her heart.

Mr. Loncar was speaking again, something about trust funds, but she wasn't paying attention. After years of wishing and yearning, she might finally have the opportunity to reunite with her daughter. The hope in her chest swelled, making her feel as warm and fluffy as the cotton-ball clouds floating past the French doors.

"That sums up the key terms," Mr. Loncar said. "I'll send you the documents, but do you have any questions?"

Still in shock, Katie couldn't come up with anything. Mostly because she hadn't been paying attention. But if Savannah really was her daughter, the rest of it was just a bunch of mumbo-jumbo.

"Ms. Callahan?" Mr. Loncar sighed again as if she were trying his patience. "Do you have any questions," he repeated.

She took a deep breath and forced herself to focus. "Uh, when, and what happens next?"

"Ms. Shelton stipulated if she passed during a school session, Savannah should finish the semester in Texas. She attends a private year-round school. Classes end on July 28th, so she can be placed in your care any time after that. Until then, she'll stay with her grandparents." Someone came into Mr. Loncar's office and he barked out orders before returning his attention to her. "Where was I?" He shuffled papers, muttering under his breath. "You'll need to carefully review and consider the material I'm sending you. It's critical that you call me back no later than next Friday to advise if the terms are acceptable. Otherwise, custody will be awarded to Gwendolyn's next of kin."

She agreed, ended the call, then dropped her phone on the table. She was so engrossed in thought that she didn't notice Liam had come into the room until he wrapped his solid arms around her from behind.

After a long moment, he pulled up a chair. "What's going on?"

Katie inhaled deeply as she looked up at her husband. Worry clouded his whiskey-colored eyes and a line creased between the brows of his ruggedly handsome face.

Even though she and Liam had been fighting a lot since her layoff, he was her best friend, her greatest ally, her rock.

"Oh, Liam," she said softly, resting her forehead against his.

"What's the matter?"

The truth ached inside her as if trying to force its way out, but she hesitated. She'd held her shame deep inside for all these years, unable to face her decision to give up her own child. How could she expect Liam to forgive her, when she hadn't forgiven herself? "It's... well...." Only half aware of her movements, she reached for a handful of hair that had fallen over her shoulder and twirled it around her fingers.

"Just tell me." Liam touched a large, warm hand to her cheek. "Whatever it is, we can fix it."

But this wasn't a normal fix. It would be a major change for their family. Still, they could handle it. Liam was capable of handling anything. The jittery nerves pricking her belly weren't because Liam couldn't handle the situation, he was strong and giving, and he loved kids. She was nervous because she hadn't been honest with him. She'd never told him about her child.

They were interrupted by the click, click, click of nails rushing across the hardwood floor. Their black Labrador retriever pushed between them and tipped his head up, his soulful brown eyes beaming hope. When he nudged against Liam's leg, Liam sighed and bent down.

"Hey, Pan," he said, rubbing the dog's head. "Not the best timing."

Pan's tail thumped.

Katie scratched Pan's back. *Perfect* timing, she thought.

Liam's cell phone rang. He wavered before pulling it out of his shirt pocket, glancing at her, then the phone. Finally, he answered.

"Damn it, we ordered six speeds, not five." Katie listened to Liam's side of the conversation, still twirling her hair around her fingers. "I know. Thanks, Seth. I'll be right down."

"Problem in the shop?" she asked.

"Yeah, I need to go help Seth with this order." Liam ran a hand down his short ponytail. "But first tell me what's wrong."

"I'm fine. Go help Seth and we'll talk later."

Liam's eyes narrowed to slits.

"*Really*, I'm fine. I'm gonna go visit with my folks. I'll be home in a few hours."

Liam continued to study her with a concerned expression. When she didn't budge, he sighed in resignation. "Okay then, tell them I said hi," he said on a low, half laugh, leaning in to kiss her cheek.

She shook her head at his sarcasm. They both knew her parents hated him.

A few minutes later, Katie jumped into her car and made the forty-five minute drive from rural Gem Valley to her parents' home in the bustling D.C. suburb of Bethesda. After pulling into the drive of her palatial childhood home, she tapped in the security code. The ornate wrought iron gate opened, and she drove up the long white gravel drive toward the house. Maybe she should have called before trekking the whole way up I-270, but her father usually worked from home on Fridays so he could golf in the afternoon and she needed him to shed some light on Gwen's request.

Pushing through the front door, she called out, "Mom?...Dad?...Hello!"

Her mother sailed gracefully down the long hallway with a bright smile on her face.

"Katie, what a nice surprise." She kissed one of Katie's cheeks and then the other. "Why didn't you call first? We could've had lunch."

"What's all the ruckus?" Katie's father rounded the corner. "Oh hi, Kathryn." The corner of his mouth ticked up ever so slightly, the equivalent of a smile for Mitch Patterson. "What brings you our way?" His eyes, a dark menacing gray, sharpened and narrowed. "You don't look well. Did you finally leave that no-good husband of yours?"

She rolled her eyes. "Dad, please. Give it a break."

"Mitch! Katie just arrived. Don't give her a hard time."

"Thanks, Mom."

"But did you?" her mother wanted to know.

"Ahhh!" she huffed, half regretting her trip.

Her father raised a dark brow. "Then to what do we owe this spontaneous honor?"

"I need to talk with you." She took a deep breath and tried to relax. "About my cousin Gwen." She watched for a reaction, but her father maintained a poker face. "Her lawyer called and—"

"Come with me," he said, grabbing her arm. "We'll talk in my den."

"But Katie just got here." Her mother's smile faded.

"I'll return her shortly," Mitch said. Without waiting for a response, he escorted Katie through the foyer.

She half-jogged to keep pace as they passed the grand, curved staircase and the social hub of the house, her mother's tea room. At the windows, they veered left and took the back corridor to her dad's office.

Katie flopped on the Chesterfield that had been handcrafted and shipped from Britain as her father made his way to the bar. The hardwood floors, mahogany shelving, and closed blinds cloaked the room in an uncomfortable darkness.

"Brandy?" he asked, holding up a crystal decanter.

"Dad, it's eleven o'clock."

"And your point is?"

Shaking her head, she got up and walked to the windows. "What I'd like is some light." She picked up the remote and pointed it at the blinds.

"I prefer it dark so people can't see inside."

"Who's gonna see?" She continued to raise the blinds, nodding at the enormous enclosed back yard. "The gardening staff?"

With a grunt of displeasure, her father made his way to the Chesterfield with his drink. "Come, tell me about this call."

Katie spun around and slapped her hands on her hips. "No, Dad —you tell me!" A sound of frustration escaped from low in her throat. "Why did Gwen leave custody of her daughter to me?"

Mitch took a slow sip of his drink. "I wondered if that might happen."

"And you never thought to tell *me?*" she demanded, stalking to the sofa. She wished she had a better relationship with her father, one that included two-way communication instead of his dictatorial, dole-out-information-as-he-deemed-needed approach. "Is Savannah my daughter? Tell me straight up."

"Calm down, Kathryn, and sit." Irritation pricked at every nerve ending in Katie's body as her father stepped over to the bar and poured a second glass of brandy. Pinching the bridge of her nose, she inhaled deeply. Why couldn't he just answer her question?

Her father returned and pushed the glass into her hand. "Drink up. It's good for you."

Used to giving in to him, and needing the drink to tamp down her annoyance, she tossed back a swig and then stared at him expectantly.

"Savannah is your child," he confirmed, easing down next to her.

Relief coursed through her veins even as anger and resentment squeezed the air out of her lungs. Why hadn't he told her? Maybe the adoption agreement didn't allow him to do so, but surely, he could have told her after Gwen's passing. Had he told her, she wouldn't have been shocked and blindsided by Mr. Loncar's call.

He could have answered her previous questions about the adoption instead of brushing her off with BS responses like, "that's best left in the past." She'd thought about her daughter every single day since she had given her up for adoption. He could have given her a little more information to ease her burdened heart. She clenched her jaw tight, biting back the angry words that had crawled up her esophagus. Still, she needed answers.

"Why didn't you tell me? All these years I've wondered, I've worried," she said. When she had given birth while living in Belize, she'd been practically a child herself. Scared and alone, with heavy coercion from her father, she'd made the heart-wrenching decision to give her child up for adoption. He had handled all of the details in his typical fashion—quickly, quietly, authoritatively. "You told me we didn't know the woman."

"Never said that." He swirled the brandy in his glass. "I told you the woman who adopted your child passed the requisite checks."

"*Insinuating* we didn't know her."

"I can't be responsible for what you inferred." He took a sip of his drink.

Even though it was a typical Mitch Patterson comment, exasperation shot through Katie. Why did he have to make her feel small? She wished her dad was more like her friend Vicki's father. The two of them had a nurturing, loving relationship, and Vicki's dad treated her like an adult, like an equal.

"What difference would it have made anyway?" Mitch said. "I kept my promise by arranging for your daughter to be adopted by someone with prominent standing and the financial means to take care of her."

Another knot of anger arose in Katie's throat, but she swallowed hard. Her father was right, at least in part. She'd heard that Gwen had been a big enchilada in high-end real estate so she certainly had the financial means to raise a child. Katie took another sip of her drink before pushing the glass aside. She had to drive home, and she needed a clear head to converse with her dad.

After all these years, she finally had the opportunity to unite with her daughter. Joy bubbled in her heart even as darkness hunkered in her gut.

Why hadn't she told Liam?

"What are you going to do?" her father asked, tossing back the rest of his brandy.

She raised her chin. "I'm going to go home, tell Liam, and we're gonna go to Texas and get my daughter."

"You have no job, no money of your own." Mitch Patterson let out a harsh laugh. "You think your husband, *the mechanic*, is going to support all of you? Gwen was a wealthy woman. Savannah's accustomed to the finer things in life."

Her father's words deflated her confidence, because the part about her having no job and no money was true. But he didn't give Liam enough credit. "Liam's business is doing well. I keep telling you that, and you know I'm looking for a job. Try being supportive."

"I've hired a top-end job agency to help you to find the right job. But you're going to have to do your part, too. You won't find good work in Podunk." He tipped back his glass as if searching for any last drops of alcohol before placing it on the table. "You'll have to commute and put in the hours to make a name for yourself. As we've discussed, you could stay here through the week to ease your commute."

Katie tried not to feel frustrated but it slapped at her anyway. They'd been through this before. She'd like to think her father was trying to help, rather than using her layoff as another ploy to drive a wedge between her and Liam. But it sounded like a ploy. Regardless, she loved her husband and had no intention of living anywhere but with him and her step-daughter, Cara. Besides, how was she supposed to raise Savannah, not to mention, Cara, if she lived in Bethesda during the work week? She opened her mouth to respond, but apparently her father hadn't finished.

"Do you really think that husband of yours will want your daughter?" he asked, his mouth set in a hard line. "He's just going to take in another man's child, no questions asked?"

Of course he would. Wouldn't he? Liam loved his daughter dearly, and they both wanted more children. Still, Savannah wasn't his and she'd never told him about her. What would he think now? Apprehension unfurled in Katie's gut, growing faster than the potato vines in her front porch flower pots. Damn her father for planting that seed of doubt.

Lifting her shoulders, she summoned up a confidence she didn't fully own. "Liam's kind and loving. Of course he'll want Savannah." She reached over and patted her father's cheek, a gesture he despised. "Thanks for your enlightening insights," she said, then scurried out of the house promising her mom she'd stop by over the weekend.

She got into her car and drove toward home on autopilot. Savannah was her child. The words reverberated through her mind, body, and spirit. She felt light, joyful, and free as a bird gliding across a serene sky. Soaring effortlessly through the clouds, bliss danced in every fiber of her being.

Until she got close to home.

Exiting off I-270 onto the less traveled I-70, her shoulders sagged, heavy with shame as the reality of her situation rose to the surface. She couldn't fully embrace her happiness until she eased her guilt by telling Liam the truth. She expected him to be supportive but the doubts her father had planted took root and grew stems of uncertainty. Even the purple rise of South Mountain and the green hills of her quiet community, which usually filled her with a sense of peace, didn't ease her troubled heart.

In Gem Valley, she passed by the neighborhood park with its charming walking trails. Even though it was a beautiful summer day, not a soul could be seen. Not surprising since most people were still at work like she would have been had she not been laid off. A full month had passed since then and Katie didn't miss her old job one bit. The only thing she'd enjoyed at American Security Bank was the community outreach program which had led her to Liam. She had only gone into finance to please her father. Given her druthers, she'd be in an altruistic field, but those jobs didn't pay well if they paid at all.

Absently, she rubbed her wedding band. Now that she knew Savannah was her daughter she had to tell Liam the truth.

She'd wanted to tell him before, and she had almost told him many times. But family was of the utmost importance to Liam, and more than once he had made comments like, "How can a father not want to see his daughter?" and "How could any parent give up their own child?" What would he think of *her* once she told him she'd given up her baby girl at birth without ever holding her, hugging her, nursing her?

In the past, she had justified her silence with the knowledge that her baby had been adopted by someone with the emotional and financial means to support her. But that was no longer the case. Her heart squeezed thinking about her daughter out there all alone grieving the only mother she'd ever known.

Pulling into her long driveway, she passed by the ancient sprawling oak trees, and her breathing slowed. When she parked next to the warm stone building that she'd called home for the last five years, her anxiety lessened.

She slid her gaze to the far end of the drive where Liam's business, Callahan Cycles, peeked over the rolling hills. An old barn converted into contemporary architecture, it had been renovated and expanded over the years as Liam's business had grown.

Liam worked hard, and he'd had a particularly busy week. She would tell him about Savannah, just not today. She'd tell him tomorrow because Saturdays were always good days.

The first thing Katie did on Saturday morning was check her emails. In her inbox, she found a response from the employment agency her father had hired with proposed interview dates and times for the position in D.C. they'd discussed earlier in the week.

Her chest puffed with pride—the second largest bank in D.C. actually wanted to talk with her—and then slumped with indecision. Did she really want another job in banking; one with more responsibilities and a longer commute? Her gut shouted *no*, but her head intervened. What choice did she have? She and Liam would need the money for Savannah and because she still wanted to have more children.

She hit print, and made her way from the computer nook to the calendar in the kitchen.

"What'cha got there?" Liam asked, glancing up at her over the morning paper which he had strewn across the farmhouse table.

Dangling the paper in her hand, Katie let out a heavy sigh. Liam wanted her to find a local job. Obviously, that would be her preference too, but there weren't many open jobs in their area, and none of them were in banking, the only field where she had any experience. It was an issue that had been a source of tension between them since she'd been laid off.

"Interview times for the investment banking position," she said wishing she could avoid the confrontation that was suddenly brewing between them.

Liam put down the paper. "The one in D.C.?" he asked, his voice incredulous.

"Yes." She lifted her chin. "I *need* a job. It's been over a month and things are gonna get tight."

"We're doing just fine," he said, with an edge to his voice. "We don't have bills piling up and my business is growing."

"Cara will be in college in a couple of years, and if we're ever gonna get pregnant we're going to need in vitro." Katie pressed a hand to her belly, the desire to conceive was so great she could feel the quiet calling. "Do you know how expensive that is?"

"You're only twenty-nine, we have plenty of time," he said in a calm, almost placating tone that plucked at her nerves.

She rolled her eyes. After almost five years of trying, it had become clear it wasn't going to happen by natural means.

"What we need is for you to be less stressed," Liam said in a tone that sounded almost accusatory.

A shard of pain jabbed at her heart. "So now it's all my fault?" Even though she'd had that thought more than once, it hurt to hear Liam say the words. "I need coffee," she grumbled.

"You know that's not what I meant," Liam said, rising. "Sit, I'll make the coffee. You want cappuccino?"

Lowering to a chair at the table, she nodded.

As Liam steamed milk, Katie tried to massage the frustration out of her temples. Why couldn't he understand? She was only twenty-nine, but he was thirty-seven and his daughter was sixteen, practically a young adult. How long would he be willing to try for another child? And now she had Savannah to consider. Granted, Liam didn't know about her yet, but she needed a job so she could support her daughter. Besides, at twenty-nine she couldn't quit working altogether. Even though her job at the bank had been stressful, she could hardly sit around and do nothing for the rest of her life.

"Here we go," Liam said, delivering two frothy mugs. Easing down, he handed her one of the drinks.

"Thanks." Katie placed both hands around the mug, and stared at the artful marble of coffee and milk. She took a couple of sips, allowing the warmth to soothe, the caffeine to rejuvenate. Then she put down her drink and lifted her eyes to meet Liam's.

Liam slid over, cupped his hands around her face, and kissed her long and tender until she was completely lost in him. When he drew back, they were both a little breathless. She wished she could encapsulate that lost-in-love feeling, hold on to it tight, and carry it with her. But when she came down from her Liam-high, her problems hadn't disappeared. Even so, she was a little calmer, a little less annoyed when she met Liam's gaze for round two.

It took her a full minute to remember where they had left off. "It's not that I want to commute to D.C., but there aren't jobs around here." She took another sip of her hot drink. "You know that, even if you don't want to admit it."

Liam reached for her hand. "That's why I'm suggesting you take a break to figure out if that's the kind of job you really want." This time his voice was gentle, encouraging. "Then, if you decide that's what you want, go back to finance." He rubbed the pad of his thumb over the top of her hand. "But things happen for a reason. Maybe you got laid off to give you this time to think.

"I'll think about it." She would, but she also had to think about Savannah. "But I should keep interviewing. It's a tough market and it'll take a while to find a job."

"Why don't you take a break and help me at the shop?" Liam suggested. "I hate office work and you're good at it. Marketing, too. I'm still getting business from that ad you ran in *American Biker*."

Katie's mouth formed into a yes, but she pressed her lips shut.

Sure, it was tempting. She loved helping Liam when she could spare the time. They were doing okay financially now, but eventually they would need another salary. For in vitro, for Savannah. "I love working at Callahan Cycle's, but I need a real job."

Liam raised a brow. "My company's not real?"

"You know what I mean. An important job. I mean…." As soon as she said the words, she wanted to take them back, but a lump of remorse clogged her throat making it difficult to speak. "I mean…."

Liam's eyes darkened and locked with hers. "I think that *is* what you meant, but that's your father talking, not you."

It most certainly was not what she'd meant. But was it her father's voice in her head?

Liam pulled her onto his lap, and wrapped his arms around her. She crumpled against him as a fresh wave of guilt squeezed her chest. He was so good to her and she'd been nothing but moody and snarky because she hadn't yet shared her secret. *Sorry, Liam.* She made the apology silently, but committed to telling him soon so she could get back to her normal self.

"Think about it," he whispered. "I don't want to fight, Katie-Cat. I just want you to be happy."

She allowed herself to relax in Liam's strong arms and came up with a plan. First, they'd take a motorcycle ride to blow away their negativity, then she'd tell him about Savannah. Maybe tomorrow she'd spend the day researching work options. She'd ask her sister to help. Liz was organized, resourceful, and had tons of contacts.

Liam pressed a kiss to her forehead. "How 'bout we take a ride?" he said as if he was inside her head.

Half an hour later, they were whizzing away from Gem Valley, their small town in the hills of western Maryland, edging toward the Pennsylvania border, passing corn fields and barns, houses with wide sweeping porches. Katie's body vibrated with new life as they roamed scenic country roads, her body snuggled tight against Liam's, the wind blowing her worries away.

Liam took a leisurely route, which suited her just fine. It was a beautiful June day with the Blue Ridge Mountains soaring in the distance, a bright yellow sun glistening overhead. She used the time to figure out how she would tell Liam about Savannah. Her mind and spirit were noticeably lighter when they headed toward home several hours later, twisting and turning down Bear Mountain.

As they neared the entrance to Beaver Falls, a massive pickup truck made a left-hand turn, barreling toward them. Katie sucked in a breath as her heart jumped into her throat. With a steady stream of traffic all around them, there was nowhere to go to avoid collision. Panic assailed her as the world shifted into slow motion.

She gripped her arm rests so tight that her knuckles turned white. The truck's driver slammed on the brakes, but it was too late. Her chest tightened, her heart froze. As the monster truck skidded toward them a million thoughts filled Katie's head in the seconds before impact. *We're gonna die! What about Cara? Savannah? Pan?* Her breath grazed her husband's neck. *Liam—my everything!*

She squeezed her eyes shut as she braced for the impending crash, fear paralyzing her body. The shrill, piercing sound of metal smashing into metal reverberated through the air, through her very bones.

Pain followed, throbbing and excruciating, shooting up and down the right side of her body. A split-second later, everything was black.

CHAPTER TWO

*K*atie awoke with a jolt, sweat beading on her forehead. Whooshing out a breath, she clutched the blankets to her chin. She couldn't remember her nightmare, but a feeling of fear lingered inside her.

"Let's try for a good dream this time," she murmured, slipping under the fluffy covers.

But she couldn't get back to sleep. Rolling to her side, she stretched and peeked out the window. The sun lifted above the horizon, glazing everything in hues of pink and purple. The sparkling ball continued to climb, transforming from orange to bright yellow, a dazzling contrast against the blue sky.

Rising, she leaned forward to take a closer look…and gasped.

She was *in* the sky, floating on a big, white puffy cloud.

She squeezed her eyes shut, then blinked them open again.

Nothing had changed.

Had she died in her sleep? Anxiety gripped her throat in a stranglehold, making it difficult to breathe. *I can't die! Who will take care of Savannah? Cara? And Liam….*

She sucked in a gulp of air. "I love you, Liam," she said in a rough whisper. Gloom and regret gnawed at her as she relived their last argument. She'd told Liam she would think about taking time off, but she hadn't told him she loved him. A single hot tear trickled down her cheek.

She wrapped her arms around her knees and rocked back and forth, taking in the surreal surroundings. Fear threatened to consume her, but suddenly her heart filled with a warm, comforting sensation that slowly spread through her entire being.

Her cloud floated effortlessly, occasionally passing other clouds, and she soaked in the tranquility as she hummed along with the birds that were chirping their morning melody. She passed by clouds shaped like a heart, a cat, and the silhouette of Starbuck's green goddess. The next cloud resembled her and Liam's Harley, and memories of the accident rushed back. The motorcycle ride. Beaver Falls. The monster truck.

Her heart pummeled. "What's going on?" she asked, even though no one was around to answer. "And where's Liam?"

Drawing in a long, shaky breath, she took in the implausible view.

Bright. White. Fluffy. Cloud.

Had she died and gone to heaven? That didn't seem likely. She hadn't seen the bright white light or pearly gates. Besides, if she was in heaven, surely there would be others here. Maybe she was in the hospital on some really good meds....

A loud pop sounded behind Katie. She jumped and whirled around in time to see a brown, furry head poke its way through the middle of the cloud. The head shook, flinging white puffs to both sides.

Bear! Her heart squeezed with joy at the sight of her deceased dog. What the heck was going on? Bear was dead...did that mean she was too? The panic returned closing in on her like a vise, squeezing the air from her lungs.

Across the cloud a paw popped out, then another, followed by the rest of his furry body. Bear shook again, sending more white puffs flying about.

Pulling in long breaths, Katie scurried over. As she scrutinized her dog, delight pushed her anxiety aside. He looked healthy, happy, and vibrant, not at all like the last time she'd seen him, when his body had been weak from the quick-spreading cancer, when she'd made the heart-wrenching decision to put him down.

"I can't believe it's you!" She threw her arms around the brown, curly-haired dog.

She smothered his head and face with kisses, and he lopped his tongue over her cheek with just as much enthusiasm. They hugged and rolled around on the cloud. Then Bear flopped onto his back, extending his paws straight up in the air.

Katie lightly scratched the dog's underside. "I've missed you so much."

The dog nuzzled against her and then stuck his head into the cloud. He popped back with a battered toy that he dropped at her feet.

Picking it up, Katie smiled. "Your favorite." She ran her fingers over the tattered material. The fuzzy puppy with long floppy ears and squeakers had been Bear's first toy. He had played with it, slept with it, and carried it to the door every day to greet her when she came home from work.

"You buried it with me." Bear gazed at her with his big, soulful eyes. "It's still my favorite—even up here."

Her mouth fell open in shock. "Did you just *talk* to me?" She half laughed at the insanity of her question.

Bear climbed onto her lap like he'd done thousands of times in the past. His front paws and chest lay across her legs while his back half flopped over her side. Although he had grown to be over eighty pounds, he'd always thought of himself as a lap dog. Lifting his head, he locked his brown eyes with hers. "Take a deep breath."

He's speaking again.

Then she realized her dog hadn't spoken at all. Not in the traditional sense, anyway. It was like the messages had just appeared in her head.

Bear gave her a doggie grin. "Now you're catching on."

Katie rubbed his soft ears. He was every bit as adorable as she remembered. How she loved his head, the way the flat brown hair on his snout gave way to curls mid-way across his crown, and the curly coat that covered the rest of his body.

She'd never seen a curly-coated retriever before Bear. At first sight, she had brushed him off as goofy-looking, with his oversized paws and milky eyes he had yet to grow into, and the mass of kinky curls. But after their first few days together, she'd decided he was the cutest dog ever.

"Aw shucks," Bear said.

She laughed. "Is this where you live?"

"No, I live in heaven." As she had suspected, this wasn't heaven. "I just came to keep you company while you're here."

She hugged her dog. "Where are we?"

"In Tranquility, a transition dimension." Bear met her gaze, his eyes wise and compassionate. "A place for people who are in between life and death."

What did that mean? Sheer black fear swept through her. Had she died? Was she in purgatory? "Did I die?" Her breath clogged in her chest as she twirled a long strand of hair around her fingers.

"You haven't died." Bear nuzzled his head along her arm as relief whooshed into her lungs. "But your physical body is in pain so this is a good place for you to be. Friends will join us soon and...."

Bear's explanation trailed off as two beings materialized on the cloud directly in front of them.

LIAM WOKE up feeling like a ton of bricks had fallen on his chest. Cursing under his breath, he batted his eyes open, taking time to adjust to the light. A sharp pain sliced into his ribs as he pushed up to survey his blurry surroundings. His arm got caught in a tube on the side of the bed, and he accidently hit the call button.

The door to his room flew open. A plump nurse with dark streaked hair dashed over to the bed.

"You're awake!" She smiled down at him. "How you feeling?"

He rubbed his aching right side. "Like hell."

"You sure look better." The nurse moved to his side and examined the machine next to the bed.

He ran a hand over his head and winced. He found his ponytail holder, and tied his hair into a short tail. What the hell was he doing in the hospital? Heart pounding, he closed his eyes and concentrated hard. A few seconds later, memories of the accident slammed into his already throbbing head. The massive truck barreling toward them, the knowledge that they were going to collide. The paralyzing fear and the horrific sounds of metal smashing into metal.

"Katie," he said, his voice cracking. "Where's my Katie?"

Preoccupied with his meds, or shielding him from bad news, the nurse didn't respond. Liam pressed two fingers into his temple, trying to get the accident out of his head. He'd tried to maneuver the bike out of the truck's path while at the same time avoiding oncoming traffic. He'd somehow managed to swerve out far enough to prevent a T-bone hit, but the truck had slammed into the back of the bike, and sitting behind him, Katie must have taken the brunt of the hit.

Damn it—he should've been paying more attention to the road instead of reliving his and Katie's last argument. Had he been fully focused, he might have been able to avoid the accident altogether. Guilt kicked at his chest, then fear ripped it wide open. Where was Katie now?

He must have been knocked out by the crash because he couldn't remember anything else. Now he had to find his wife. He gripped the bed rail, and sat upright.

"Be careful," the nurse said, turning to help him disentangle his arm from the IV tube.

"Katie...where is she?" he repeated, swinging a leg over the side of the bed. "I have to find her."

The nurse's eyes widened. "What are you doing? You can't get out of bed."

Dropping his other leg to the floor, Liam groaned. His right leg ached, but he couldn't let that stop him.

"Mr. Callahan! You're going to hurt yourself."

Ignoring the nurse, intent only on finding Katie, Liam pushed the rest of the way off the bed.

"I'll call for help," the nurse said, pushing a call button on the wall. "You shouldn't be out of bed."

Liam stumbled forward anyway, dragging the IV stand along with him. The nurse rushed to his side, and at the same time, the door swung open and his brother Shane entered.

Shane hustled over, and wrapped an arm around his shoulder. "Good to see you, but what the hell?" Shane took his arm. "Let's get you back to bed, bro."

A couple of nurses hurried into the room, but Shane held up a palm. "I got it."

"I have to find Katie." Liam snatched his arm back. "Where is she? How long have I been here, and who's watching Cara?" He blew out a long breath. "I don't even know what fucking day it is."

Shane rubbed a palm over his cheek. "Let's get you back in bed, then I'll tell you what's going on."

Liam didn't budge as fear closed in on his heart. He gave his brother a no-bullshit look. "Is Katie okay?"

"Mr. Callahan, you really need to get back to bed," the nurse said, waving her helpers over. "I'll call the doctor, see if he's willing to release you, but in the meantime, I need you back in bed."

A small muscle under Liam's left eye twitched in frustration. All he cared about was finding Katie. Why didn't they understand?

"If he goes back to bed, can you give us a few minutes of privacy?" Shane asked. "Maybe while you call the doc."

Liam's heart sank. If Shane needed privacy to answer his question it couldn't be good news.

"Deal," she said to Shane, then she crossed her arms and stared at him.

"Fine." He only agreed because it was clear he wasn't going to get answers—or any help—until he did as Shane had suggested.

He allowed his brother and the nurses to escort him back to bed even as worry snaked through him. If Katie was okay, wouldn't Shane have said so? How would he go on if she hadn't survived? An unbearable sadness weighted him down and he found it difficult to move.

Lumbering slowly toward the bed, he took a sidelong look at his brother. Shane's dirty blond hair, usually styled with every piece in place, an intentional tumbled look held together by a ridiculously expensive gel, was disheveled. Shane typically looked stylish even in his damn jeans, but today he had on wrinkled clothes. His eyes were pale and anxious, and his face closed, as if guarding a secret.

Liam finally reached the bed and eased to a sitting position.

Shane lowered next to him. "Give us a few minutes?" he asked the nurse.

She pinned a no-nonsense look on him. "Don't go anywhere," she said, wagging her finger in front of his face as if that would intimidate him, and then she disappeared along with the two younger nurses.

Clasping his hands together, Liam tried to prepare for what he was about to hear. It couldn't be good, or Shane would have blurted it out already. His brother was a direct, cut-to-the-chase kind of guy. "How is Katie?" he demanded, swinging his legs back and forth off the side of the bed. He was in a lot of pain, but the movement helped release some of his pent-up anxiety.

"She's alive," Shane said quietly.

Hope bloomed in Liam's chest bright as the sun rising over the mountains. Katie was alive! But Shane didn't look happy, he looked downright miserable. The sun formed into a hot ball of anxiety that burned in Liam's gut. Was she alive-alive, or hanging on by a string? Was she conscious or unconscious? Brain dead, paralyzed? He pressed his hands to his head to stop the madness.

Then he turned to Shane. "I'm going to need more fucking information," he said, his voice pure steel even as fear sliced his chest open with the endless bleak possibilities.

"I know, I know." Shane heaved out a breath. "But I'll start with your other questions first."

What the hell? Irritation welled up inside Liam and the muscle under his eye began twitching steadily.

21

"Cara's doing well," Shane said. "We were with you last night, but you were in and out of it. I took Cara to my place after we left the hospital so she wouldn't be alone. Liz drove up early this morning and she and Sabby are with her now. They'll be in later this morning"

Liam nodded, still irritated, but also grateful that Katie's sister and niece were with Cara.

Shane stared down at the bland linoleum floor—another bad sign. Shane never flinched or avoided eye contact. "It's Sunday, you've only been here overnight. They ran a bunch of tests, and I talked with the doc. Your ribs are bruised, your right leg is pretty banged up, but there's no real damage. You're lucky, Liam." Shane rubbed his hands over his face as his voice cracked. "Real lucky."

The knot in Liam's gut twisted as he glared at his brother, waiting for the rest. "And Katie?"

"She's here, downstairs."

Thank God. Relief washed through him like a spring river after a heavy snow melt, but when he turned and caught the look of tired sadness straining his brother's features, he crumbled inside.

"She's in a coma," Shane said quietly.

Liam felt an instant squeeze of pain as relief plunged into despair. A coma. Did she have any consciousness in her now? Would she ever come out of it, and if she did, would she be okay? He pressed both palms against his heart as a wild grief ripped through him.

"I'm sorry, Liam."

The door to his room opened and the doctor came in.

Shane rose. "I'll head to the waiting room at the end of the hall and wait for you there." He waved his cell phone. "If you need anything call." Then he disappeared.

Liam went through the motions with the doctor. Numb and grief-stricken, he insisted he be released so he could be with his wife. After the doctor relented and he got through the discharge paperwork, he changed into the jeans and T-shirt Shane had brought and then joined his brother in the waiting room.

"Sure you're ready?" Shane asked looking him up and down when he entered the room.

The tension in Liam's chest had spread to every pore of his body, but he nodded anyway. He had to see her.

He followed Shane to the elevator. On the second floor, they were buzzed into the ICU. Once inside, Shane spoke quietly with a young woman at the nurse's station, then they walked down a long hallway of patient rooms. Each step was agonizing and only in part because of his physical pain. Shane had prepared him for what he'd see, but Liam wished like hell for something else. At least she was alive, he reminded himself. He needed to stay focused on the positives.

But it was hard on this floor with patient rooms that all looked the same—bland and dreary. The smell of sterilized sickness, the dull expressions of nurses and visitors alike, and the occasional moans drifting on the stale air didn't help either.

Shane stopped at the end of the hallway and tipped his head toward the last door on the right.

Liam stepped inside slowly, his mind and body numb. When he saw Katie, still and lifeless on the hospital bed, he froze in place, paralyzed by the sight of her. Time screeched to a halt for several agonizing seconds before pain crawled up his right leg and into his ribs, jarring him forward.

Looming over the bed, he stared at his wife. Her right cheek was bruised, and stitches had patched a long gash above her eye. Tubes and wires connected her to monitors that seemed to be tracking her every function. Guilt and sorrow tore at his chest. He sunk onto a nearby chair and scooted it close to the bed.

"I'm so sorry, baby." Swiping away a tear, he lowered his head and repeated the apology.

Squeezing his hands into fists, he let out a long stream of curses. He cursed God, fate, and the world at large for hurting his beloved wife. Mostly though, he cursed himself. He should've been more careful. Then he put his head in his hands and let himself cry.

When he finally pulled himself together, he studied Katie again, this time taking in every minute detail. Despite the bruises and medical equipment, she was as beautiful as ever. Long brown lashes rested on closed lids concealing her eyes, the color of dark chocolate.

She had high cheekbones, the right side scarred from the accident. If he could blink away the scars and machines, he would have thought she was just sleeping. Rays of light drifted through the window, resting on her sandy brown hair, illuminating her golden highlights. He couldn't resist caressing his fingers through her long wavy locks, just like he did every night at home.

He pressed his lips to her hands. *Come back to me, baby.*

He hated that their last conversation had been an argument. Up until a month ago, he and Katie had rarely fought. In the five years they'd been married, their relationship had been full of love and a sweet tenderness that Katie had brought into his life.

Then, a month ago, she had been laid off from her job at the bank. Over the years, her work had become increasingly stressful as colleagues were downsized while Katie's responsibilities grew. Even so, after her own position had been eliminated, she'd begun searching for another job in the same field, which would entail the same level of stress and likely a long commute to Washington, D.C.

He'd encouraged her to take time off before rushing into the same job scenario. She'd been hesitant, mostly because her father had been pressuring her to find an *important* job. Liam was confident she would figure out what was right for her—if her father would give her the time and space to do so.

But now she was in a coma, and their last conversation had been a fight about it. If he could do it over again, he would support whatever she wanted. Guilt continued to claw at his insides. How could he have been mad at her—*fought* with her—over something as inconsequential as a job?

Please. He lifted his gaze to the ceiling. *Please bring her back to me.*

He returned his gaze to his wife. She'd be okay. She *had* to be okay, because he didn't know how he'd survive without her.

ON THE CLOUD, Bear woofed and thumped his tail, flicking white puffs here and there. He brushed his body back and forth against the man and woman who'd appeared in front of them and was rewarded with rubs.

Intrigued, Katie watched her dog interact with the strangers. While she was sure she had never met either of them before, they somehow felt familiar.

The woman bent down to kiss Bear's head, her long platinum blonde hair falling over his side and merging into the cloud. She rose gracefully, smoothing down the layers of her golden dress. Stunning eyes the color of the Caribbean Sea connected with Katie as a sense of calm flowed into her chest.

The man looked like an ancient warrior with his bronze complexion, chiseled jaw, and long, glossy raven hair. Wearing tan pants and cowboy boots, he knelt down to touch his forehead to Bear's, and his unbuttoned shirt flapped open in the breeze, revealing a sculpted chest. When he straightened, he directed his midnight eyes at Katie radiating warmth and welcome.

Bear waved a paw at the woman. "Katie, this is Posie, your spirit guide." He nodded at the man. "And Black Eagle, your guide and protector."

She had spirit guides? She had a million questions but before she could ask any of them, Posie approached her with open arms. "Welcome," she said, her voice soft and musical.

Katie stepped into her arms. Posie kissed each of her cheeks before moving aside to allow Black Eagle to greet her.

He took her hand and brushed his lips over it. "Katie, my dear, good to see you."

The warm vibrations emanating from her guides soothed her. Even so, she couldn't shake the niggle of fear slinking up her spine. She had no idea what was happening. Bear had said something about transition. Was she in the process of dying? Her heart twisted. What about Liam? Who would look after Cara? Savannah?

"It's a lot to take in." Posie touched a hand to her arm, and a calming sensation whooshed through her. "Let's have a seat and we'll explain."

Posie and Black Eagle sat cross-legged, and Katie joined them, forming a small circle with Bear in the middle, who rolled over to expose his belly. With a half-smile, Katie rubbed her dog. A lot of things were changing, but at least this was familiar—Bear had always loved his belly rubs.

"We'll begin by answering your questions," Posie said.

Confused, Katie bit her lower lip. "But I haven't asked any."

"We heard them nonetheless," Posie said. "Language is not required here."

"But you're talking now."

"I'm only using words to make you feel comfortable." Posie lightly scratched Bear's belly as she spoke. "Still, we know what you're thinking through your vibration, just as you've been able to understand Bear through his vibration."

Katie nodded, absently rubbing Bear's head.

Posie gave her an angelic smile. "With regard to us, like Bear said, we—" Posie waved a hand between herself and Black Eagle "—are your spirit guides."

Feeling extra special—because, wow, she had *spirit guides*—Katie tipped her head to one side. "What does a spirit guide do?"

"We help you along your path, provide guidance when you need or want it," Black Eagle said. "Throughout your life on Earth."

"Well, thanks. Do you help lots of people?"

"No." Posie touched a hand to her arm. "Black Eagle and I are entrusted to care for you and only you."

Katie's hand fluttered to her heart, humbled and awed that these angelic beings were dedicated to helping her. "I don't know what to say."

"No words are needed." Black Eagle tapped a fist over his heart. "We're connected to you, Katie. We feel your love."

Katie closed her eyes for a moment, awed and amazed that she could feel the connection too.

When she opened her eyes, she smiled at her guides. Then she thought about Liam, Cara, Savannah…her life on earth, and her heart tugged. How could she feel wonderful and pained at the same time?

"It's normal," Posie said, reading her mind—or her vibra-tions. "Tranquility is an in-between dimension where you can experience both the love and light of the spirit world and at the same time maintain your tie, thus your emotional connection, to your Earthly existence."

Katie nodded, understanding at least intellectually. "So, Liam... is he okay?"

"With the exception of minor injuries, he's fine physically," Posie said.

Katie breathed a sigh of relief that he had made it through the accident unscathed.

"But his heart aches for you." Posie gently rubbed her arm.

Katie felt the same ache so she shifted her focus to Posie's soothing touch. "Is everyone who comes here like me?"

"People come for many reasons," Posie said. "Some, like you, come because their bodies are in pain. They spend time here until it's determined whether they'll return to physical life or transition. Others have already transitioned."

Katie scrunched her nose. "What do you mean by transition?"

"We prefer the word *transition* over *death*," Black Eagle said, "because the soul never dies."

Die? Did that mean she was going to die, after all? Katie pressed a hand against her chest to stop the welling panic.

Black Eagle put a hand on her shoulder, and immediately, a sense of calm blanketed her.

Everything will work out as you desire, but you must believe. The words sounded in Katie's head and swirled through her heart. She didn't know where they came from or what they meant, but they lessened her anxiety nonetheless. When she glanced up, Black Eagle continued.

"Some come here before moving to their next phase because they have unfinished business. There are countless reasons why souls come to Tranquility, but I like to describe it as a holding place, a peaceful space between Earth and other dimensions like the spirit world."

Katie glanced at the empty clouds around her. "Where is everyone else?"

"There are other souls in this dimension." Black Eagle rubbed

Bear's armpit as he spoke, and the dog snorted in satisfaction. "But you don't see them unless there's a reason. This gives you the opportunity to be with your guides without distractions."

"Black Eagle, Bear, and I will be with you throughout your time here," Posie said. "Whether it's your time to transition or whether you return to Earth, we'll be here to guide you."

This time Katie maintained an inner calm despite Posie's mention of transitioning. She nodded, trying to take it all in, where she was, what her fate would be. She was grateful that her beautiful guides were here to help her.

"It's a lot to process." Posie gave her an encouraging smile.

"What does everyone think happened to me?" she asked, waving a hand at the green-blue ball rotating beneath them. "You know, down there."

Black Eagle placed his hand over hers. "On Earth, you're in a coma."

CHAPTER THREE

*L*iam awoke to the mouth-watering scent of bacon. His stomach growled, not surprising considering it was Monday and the last real food he'd eaten was Friday night's pizza. Rolling over, he almost crushed their dog, Pan, who was sprawled across the king-sized bed.

The black Lab had been out of sorts without Katie. He'd tossed and turned all night until he had finally tuckered himself out in the wee hours of the morning. Now Pan snored softly, his head taking up most of Liam's pillow. "I'm right there with you, buddy," Liam murmured, rubbing the dog's soft belly. "She'll be back soon." A knot formed in his throat, and he hoped like hell it was true.

He rose, took a quick shower, then headed downstairs with Pan at his heels.

Shane was at the kitchen table with the newspaper and a mug of coffee.

"Morning, Dad," Cara called out as she flipped omelets, her long blonde hair pulled up in a messy bun.

The sight tugged at Liam's heart. "My girl's making breakfast." He kissed the back of her head as he grabbed a mug from the cupboard. "Even bacon." He raised a brow. "That's very nice, Cara."

Especially since his daughter hadn't eaten meat of any kind since she was nine years old. She'd declared herself a vegetarian after falling in love with one of the pigs on the Collins' farm next door.

Cara glanced over at him. "You like it."

Touched, he nodded, and then searched his daughter's eyes. The blue sparkle had been clouded over by a grayish grief, but thankfully this morning there were no tears. He gave her a half hug, poured coffee, and then sat next to Shane. "Morning."

Shane put down the paper. "How you feeling?"

Last night, Shane and Katie's best friend, Jen, had tag-teamed and talked him into going home. Even though he hadn't wanted to leave Katie, in the end, he'd agreed. Only because he had been bone-tired. He had to admit he'd slept like a rock in his own bed. Even so, his body was still in pain.

He rotated his right arm. It hurt like hell. "I'm fine."

Shane narrowed his eyes, but he let the lie go. When he grabbed a piece of bacon, Pan scrambled under the table and thumped his tail. "The dog has ears like a rabbit," Shane grumbled, flicking a piece of meat on the floor.

"Pan loves bacon," Cara said, plating up the omelets, "so I made extra." She delivered food to the table, then sat in between him and Shane. "Eat up." Because her breakfast was an omelet filled with green stuff, she grabbed a slice of meat from Shane's plate and tossed it under the table.

"Hey," Shane protested.

Cara gave Shane an evil grin. "Pan's gotta eat too, yah know."

"It's delicious, Cara," Liam said after biting into the omelet stuffed with bacon, cheese, and onion.

"Second that." Shane shifted toward him. "You had a bunch of calls. Names and numbers are on the phone pad."

Liam grunted. "I don't have time for that." All he could think about was Katie. "I'm gonna drop by the shop, check on the guys, then I have to get back to Katie."

"Jen said she'd stay at the hospital till you get there," Shane reminded him. "You know we can count on her."

Liam nodded. He trusted Katie's best friend, but what if she had to leave? He didn't want Katie to be alone, and when she woke, he wanted to be there. His scattered mind returned to the phone messages. Surely Shane would have told him if the hospital had called. "Any important calls?"

"Yeah, Officer O'Connell," Shane said, "but I called him back. He wanted you to know he charged the kid who hit you."

Liam polished off his omelet. "What the hell was he thinking?"

"According to O'Connell, the kid didn't see you." Shane puffed out a breath. "Not sure how he missed your big bike, but he's eighteen, hasn't been driving for long. His crazy ass father bought him a monster-truck for his high school graduation."

Liam raised a brow. "How'd you get O'Connell to talk to *you* about the case?"

"Uncle Shane can get anyone to talk to him about anything," Cara said.

"Fuckin' A," Shane responded, pride evident in his tone.

Cara rose, grabbed the large glass jar from the counter, and shoved it in front of Shane. "Now you owe the swear jar."

"Damn it," Shane muttered, reaching into his pocket. "I keep forgetting."

Cara gleefully waved the jar, already half full of bills. "Now it's ten bucks."

Liam chuckled.

"Very capitalistic." Shane stuffed two bills in the jar. "You're gonna make a fortune off your 'ol uncle."

"And Dad too," Cara said with a sassy smile as she returned the jar to the counter.

Shane's mouth quirked. "O'Connell goes to Saint Rose of Lima. Said we Catholic boys have to stick together." He pushed his plate aside. "By the way, I had your motorcycle towed to your shop after the accident. I'm sorry bro, but it's totaled."

"I'm sorry, Dad." Cara turned to stare at him. "You and Katie loved that bike."

Liam ran his hands up his face. "All that matters is Katie getting better. I'll buy another bike or build one for her."

Shane retrieved the notepad from the phone table. "Liz called, too. Said she's at the hospital with Jen and asked if there's anything she can do."

Katie's sister had been with Cara yesterday, but he'd missed her since he'd gotten home so late. He wondered when she had returned from Dublin. Katie and her sister didn't see each other often because Liz traveled so much. Even when she was home, she lived in Georgetown—a one to two-hour drive from their place depending on traffic. Considering that Liz was nine years older than Katie, the sisters were surprisingly close, talking and texting on a regular basis. While he didn't know Liz well, he certainly preferred her over Katie's parents.

"Your monster-in-law also called," Shane said. He slid Cara a sheepish look, then cleared his throat. "I mean your *mother-in-law*. I touched base with her after the accident assuming you'd want Katie's folks to know. Even though they don't deserve shit from you." He raised a brow as if seeking confirmation.

Liam nodded even though the mere mention of Katie's parents made every muscle in his body constrict, awakening flickers of pain on his right side all the way from his big toe to the base of his skull.

Carolyn and Mitch Patterson were uppity, overbearing, and downright mean. And they hated him with a passion. He wasn't affluent enough for their likes, nor did he fit in with the Patterson's high falutin friends. They told anyone who would listen that he wasn't good enough for their daughter. That was probably true, but it was Katie's choice, not theirs.

He didn't have tons of money, but he provided for Katie and Cara, and they lived comfortably. Even though Katie's father had labeled him as white trash, redneck, blue collar, and many other less positive things, Liam was proud of the work he did. He'd built his motorcycle business, Callahan Cycles, from the ground up and it was doing well. He loved his work and he had established a solid reputation.

"I called her back so you wouldn't have to," Shane said, and Liam whooshed out a breath of relief.

"She was her usual stuck-up self, demanding more information than I had. Guess Mitch's money couldn't buy it from the hospital.

Assholes." Shane pulled a wad of bills from his pocket, moseyed over to the counter, and stuffed them into Cara's swear jar. He flashed her a quick grin. "I put in a little extra to cover me for the next one." As Cara shook her head, Shane turned back to him. "Carolyn said she hated to have to call *you* to get information about her daughter."

"Jesus." Why were they such assholes? They couldn't tone down the rhetoric, even with their daughter in a coma. Liam scrubbed a hand over his cheek. "Thanks for calling her back."

He carried his plate to the sink where Cara was already dealing with the dirty dishes. "Honey, I can do that. You cooked." That was their usual deal. Besides, Cara worried about damaging her fingernails and she'd just gotten them done to celebrate the beginning of summer vacation.

"It's okay, I wanna help. My nails don't matter today." She took his plate, put it in the sink. Then, as if losing a battle she'd been fighting all morning, she threw her arms around his neck and burst into noisy tears. "Daddy, is Katie gonna be okay?"

"She will be," he said, pulling his daughter in tight and once again, hoping beyond hope that it was true.

After Cara calmed down, Shane walked with him down the long drive to his shop. Along the way, he soaked in comfort from the land. He'd lived in Gem Valley his entire life. He loved the old stone house that had been his childhood home and the ten acres with beautiful views of the eastern Blue Ridge Mountains.

This morning the walk took longer than normal because his movements were laborious, but it gave him and Shane time to catch up.

He lit a cigarette and took a long drag. "Guess I'll have to deal with Katie's high and mighty parents at the hospital."

Shane scowled. "I don't want to see them any more than you, but they sure as hell better visit Katie."

"I want them there, but I don't." He took another long, satisfying drag, and let the tobacco feed his bravado. "They better not give you or Cara any shit."

"Don't worry about me," Shane said. "But I'll kick their asses if they even think about messing with Cara."

He nodded in agreement. Shane, his younger brother by just a few years, was protective of their clan and loyal to a fault.

He finally reached the walkway to Callahan Cycles and made his way to the door.

"Wait." Shane grabbed his arm. "While you're here, I'll check in with Cara, see what her plans are. You probably shouldn't be driving just yet." Shane gestured toward his leg which was throbbing like hell from the walk down the drive. "I can drop you off at the hospital, take Cara where ever she needs to go, then grab some stuff from my place. Figured I'd hunker down at your place for a while, help out where I can."

Liam didn't want to impose, but he could use the help, especially with Cara. And his brother *lived* to help. He had put Shane through college, and ever since his younger brother had the crazy notion that he could never repay him.

"That works," he said. "Thanks, Shane." Then he pushed through the doors to his shop.

His staff of five stopped what they were doing and made their way to the entrance like an army of obedient ants. The sign of respect made him smile, especially since his guys were all big and tough, at least in stature, with the exception of nineteen-year-old Seth, a beanpole. Without saying a word, Seth hugged him while the others looked on in solidarity.

"How's Katie?" Brandon asked.

His heart clutched. "Same."

The team muttered various versions of 'sorry.'

"All right, fools, get back to work." It was his way of saying thank you.

There was a big workload for his team to handle—a shitload of repairs and two custom cycle orders—so he needed to check in before going back to the hospital. But he was sure he could rely on his guys to deliver. He was in no shape to help—since walking hurt like hell. But even if he had been physically okay, he needed to be with Katie.

As his men scrambled back to work, he surveyed the large warehouse space with a sense of gratitude, and then touched base individually with each of his staff, spending the majority of his time with Seth.

Before leaving, he called his team together. "I'm not sure when I'll be back, so hold down the fort. I'm leaving Seth in charge." While Seth was his youngest employee, he'd been with Callahan Cycles the longest and was the person Liam trusted the most.

A short while later, Shane drove him to Good Hope Hospital. Jen had left, but Liz was still sitting with Katie. She rose when they walked in, and he pulled her in for a quick hug.

"Liam, Shane." Her eyes, usually shiny and vibrant, were a dull blue today.

Shane nodded at her. "How's our Katie?"

"About the same. Have you talked with her doctor?" Liz asked, pushing a long layer of dark, glossy hair behind her ear.

"Not yet, but the nurse is paging him," Liam said, leaning down to kiss his wife's cheek.

"I'm gonna take off, but I'll be back tomorrow," Liz said. She hugged him again. "Call if anything changes."

A few minutes after she left, Dr. Evans arrived and escorted them to a meeting room on the other side of the ICU. Once they were seated around a small table, the doctor opened his laptop and turned to him. "Your wife sustained many injuries on her right side, but there were no breaks, nor did we find internal bleeding."

"Thank God," he murmured. At least that was positive news. "But what about the coma?"

"It's not uncommon after a vehicular accident with significant force," the doctor said. "It's the body's way of responding to the severe impact."

"When will she come out of it?" he asked, half afraid of the answer. His mind flicked to every horrifying outcome as fear squeezed his heart in an iron grip. "What about brain injury?"

"Every patient is different," Dr. Evans said matter-of-factly. "I can't say when—or even if—she'll come out of it."

Shane rose, squeezed Liam's shoulder, and then paced the room as the doctor continued. "We can't know for sure whether she sustained a brain injury, but we ran a CT and an MRI. Didn't see anything disturbing on either." Relief gushed through Liam's body. "We won't know for sure until she comes out of the coma, but at this time, there's no reason to believe there's been permanent damage."

LIAM AWOKE with a jolt when his head hit the bed rail. It took a moment to get his bearings, and after he did, his heart sank. It was Tuesday and Katie was still in the hospital, still in a coma. Rising, he glanced at his watch—three o'clock in the afternoon. He stretched to work out the kinks in his body created by sleeping, and later napping, in that damn hospital arm chair.

He leaned over the bed and stared at Katie. She looked the same, motionless, lifeless. "I love you," he whispered, desperately hoping his words would create a miracle. When they didn't, a bleak despair closed around him like a frigid winter wind.

He hobbled to the table, rooted through his overnight bag, and retrieved a pack of cigarettes.

He stepped into the hallway just as Shane and Cara were buzzed into the ICU. His daughter sprinted over, her long blonde hair tumbling behind her. She threw her arms around his shoulders.

"Hi, Dad. Any change?" Her bright blue eyes sparkled hope.

He squeezed her in close. "No, honey. Everything's the same." He shot his brother an appreciative glance for staying with Cara.

As Shane nodded, Katie's mother, Carolyn, approached. She was dressed to the nines in an elegant pantsuit, her silvery-white hair perfectly styled. He removed his baseball cap and greeted her with a brisk nod. As he moved, pain shot up his right leg. Wincing, he shifted his weight to his left side.

Cara leaned over. "Are you okay?" she whispered.

He gritted his teeth. "Fine." Except he didn't feel like dealing with Katie's mom, which he wasn't about to share with his daughter. And *Jesus, Mary, and Joseph,* Katie's dad entered the ICU too, barreling toward them at a fast clip.

"Hello, Liam," Carolyn greeted, her eyes sweeping over him in a cool appraisal. Her thin, pear-shaped face and fair English complexion gave an air of royalty which matched her holier-than-thou attitude.

Before he could respond, Katie's father was in his face. Mitch Patterson was an imposing man with an innate aura of power. He was every bit as tall as Liam, with dark, angry eyes the color of wet cement.

"What the hell's wrong with you?" he roared. "Taking our girl out on that death machine. You could've killed her. You practically did!"

Liam clenched his mouth tight as Cara gripped his arm. Ignoring Mitch, he looked at his daughter. Her face was pale, her eyes wide. He removed her hand from his arm, and gently squeezed it. "Why don't you and Uncle Shane go visit Katie? I'll join you in a few minutes."

"But…." Cara's bottom lip trembled as she glanced up at Katie's father.

At least Mitch had the decency to zip it to give him the chance to send his daughter away. He kissed Cara on the top of her head. "Go ahead, sweetie. I'm fine."

"Okay." Cara spun around and linked arms with Shane. "C'mon, Uncle."

"You go ahead," Shane said. "I'll stay with your dad."

Liam locked eyes with Shane and tipped his head toward Katie's door. He knew his brother wanted to protect him, but he needed to do this alone.

Shane held out for a few beats, but Liam had far more patience than his brother. Eventually, Shane huffed out a breath and escorted Cara to Katie's room. After he shut the door behind them, a nurse suggested that they finish their conversation in the waiting room.

"Fine," Mitch snapped. Without waiting for his response, Mitch stormed down the hall, with Carolyn sailing behind him.

Liam considered ignoring Mitch's demand. He was pompous, pretentious, and a complete dickwad. But he was also Katie's father, and Liam owed it to his wife to try. He made his way to the waiting room, and the moment he stepped inside, Mitch laid into him again. Thankfully no one else was around.

"What the hell's wrong with you?" Mitch repeated. "I can't believe you dragged my daughter out like that. She never did anything dangerous or stupid before you. How irresponsible to risk her life for a hazardous joy-ride...."

Liam zoned out. There would be no point in telling Mitch that Katie loved riding or that she wanted to go out on the motorcycle more often than he did. It simply wouldn't matter. Mitch Patterson hated him with a passion and nothing he could say would change that.

Mitch droned on and on...he was low-class, blue collar, white trash...bad attitude, bad influence, bad apple. He'd heard it all before. Katie's parents weren't the least bit shy about communicating their feelings toward him, although Carolyn was typically milder than her husband. He glanced at her now, standing stoically at Mitch's side, her cheeks flushed. Maybe she had the decency to be embarrassed by her husband's behavior.

As Mitch continued his nasty, loud ranting, Liam's patience wore thin. Clutching his fists at his sides, he bit back the fuming, vulgar words that threatened to claw up his throat, spew out his mouth, and validate Mitch's every point.

Still, he had had enough. He took a step forward, not stopping until his face was about an inch away from Katie's father's.

Mitch finally stopped yapping.

"Enough," he said in a firm voice. "I've listened to your bullshit for long enough. I've tried to be civil for Katie's sake, but I'm done. Katie's out there—" he jabbed a finger toward the hallway "—fighting for her life. I'm not gonna waste my time in here with you. Katie's all that matters."

"If you really thought so," Mitch retorted, "you'd be doing something to support her."

Liam's jaw clenched. "What the hell's that supposed to mean?"

"She needs a *real* job. You can't possibly support her on your mechanic's salary. She needs a high paying job so you don't all end up in a trailer park." Puffing out his cheeks, the old man shook his head. The look of shocked disdain on Mitch's face would have made

Liam chuckle had he not been so pissed off. "Imagine. My daughter in a trailer park. *A trailer park!*"

He'd taken Mitch's bullshit in stride, but the dig about Katie's job got his goat. Katie's need to land an *important* job was the source of all of the recent tension between the two of them and Mitch was the driving force behind it. He and Katie weren't well off like her parents, but he sure as hell made enough to take care of his family.

He opened his mouth to respond but clamped it shut just as quickly. It didn't matter two shits what he said. In Mitch's mind, he'd never be anything more than a low wage grunt worker. It was frustrating as hell considering he'd built a successful business with nothing other than good, honest, hard work.

"You don't know how to manage her," Mitch said, his tone condescending. "If she doesn't get a real job, she'll turn out to be a lowlife, a nothing."

"You mean like me?" Liam said through gritted teeth.

"At least you get it. So do something about it." Mitch stormed out of the waiting room and stalked down the hall to the elevators, without even bothering to stop by Katie's room.

Jackass.

Carolyn gave him a look that was akin to a shrug and then hustled off after her husband.

Liam pulled in a long breath and ran a hand down his ponytail. He had a lot to be proud of. Besides creating and running a successful business, he'd guided Shane and Seth through their turbulent teenage years. He'd been a good dad to Cara, a good husband to Katie. So why did her parents make him feel like the worthless teenager he'd been in his youth?

Huffing out a sigh, he ran a hand over his stubbly face. For a man who valued family above everything else, he sure as hell had a lot of family troubles.

CHAPTER FOUR

$\mathcal{I}$n the ICU waiting room, Shane consoled Katie's friend, Jen, while he waited for Liam to wake up. Liam had fallen asleep again—not surprising considering his off-the-chart stress levels and the endless hours he'd been spending at the hospital.

Jen sniffled and he squeezed her in tight. "It'll be okay. I promise," he said. As he stroked her back, Katie's sister, Liz, entered. She took one look at him holding Jen and raised a brow.

He kissed the top of Jen's head. "She's going to come out of it," he said quietly. Jen moved aside to grab a tissue, and he greeted Liz.

"Hey, there." When he leaned down to kiss her cheek, a strand of her dark, glossy hair brushed along his jaw. Something stirred low in his stomach as he wondered what it would feel like to run his hands through all those silky layers. Curiosity, lust, or real interest, he wasn't sure. Maybe he was just feeling lonely because he and Trina had broken up again.

Whatever it was made him take a second look at Katie's sister. Because she traveled frequently, he hadn't seen much of her over the five years since Katie and Liam had been married. But he gave her a quick once over now. She wasn't drop-dead gorgeous, but there was something about her that spoke to him. Maybe those expressive eyes, a beautiful sparkly blue, with soft overtones. Her body was fit, but curvy. Because he typically dated model-thin women, he had no idea why that attracted him.

"You hanging out here till Liam decides to wake up?" Liz teased.

Shane's body constricted and his mind refocused on the issue at hand. He needed to get Liam the hell out of the hospital before he put himself back in a room.

"I was just joking, Shane," Liz quickly added, finger-fluffing her dark brown hair in a nervous gesture.

"I know, but Liam's gonna run himself into the ground." He ran a hand over his short hair. "He's here day and night. He wants to be with Katie twenty-four-seven, but he has Cara to think about, too. Not to mention a business to run." He pressed his lips together. "He'll never admit it, but he needs our help."

"I'm here to help." Jen dabbed at her eyes with the tissue. "Just let me know what I can do."

"Count me in, too," Liz said.

Nodding his thanks, he blew out a breath. "Let's try to drag Liam out of here, take him someplace where we can talk. Maybe we can come up with a schedule to take turns being at the hospital. He doesn't want Katie to be alone, but he might take some time off if we had shifts."

"Mom's on her way in now," Liz said.

Shane scowled. Liam's *monster-in-law* would only stress his brother out even more.

"I know she's tough on Liam," Liz said, "but Mom loves Katie and wants to spend time with her. I can ask her to sit with Katie while we go out. I think she'd love some time alone with her."

Shane was dubious, but in the end, he agreed. Mostly because he didn't have a better plan. And, Liz's idea actually worked. Right after Carolyn arrived, he convinced Liam to take a break. One look at Katie's mom had won Liam over. Despite all the bad blood between them, Liam seemed to recognize that she was grieving too—albeit in her own royal, pain in the ass way.

"Let's hit the road," he said, pinning a firm look on his brother.

Liam kissed Katie goodbye, and then surprised the hell out of him by taking Carolyn's hand and squeezing it. What the hell?

"Thanks for being with Katie," Liam said.

Carolyn nodded stiffly.

"Where we going?" Liam asked once they were in the hallway. "How 'bout The Coffee Grind?"

Liz's expression was pure disbelief. "You're kidding, right? Starbucks is practically across the street."

"Katie *adores* Starbucks," Liam said softly.

"Yes." Liz rubbed Liam's arm. "And there's one right across the street. How about we go there instead?" She flicked a glance around the group. "The coffee's better. Besides, we can't come back too quickly. Let's give Mom some time to sit with Katie."

Across the street, Liam and Jen snagged a back table, while Shane ordered drinks at the front counter. Liz stayed with him to place her order. After he ordered two bold blends and a non-fat latte, he looked at her with a raised brow.

"I can get my own," she said.

"I insist," he responded, and waited her out.

Liz ordered a cappuccino, then turned to him. "Thank you," she said, her gaze trailing down his body. When her eyes raised to meet his, Shane detected attraction in their depths. He slid her a lazy grin.

With flushed cheeks, Liz snatched up two of the drinks and headed toward the back. Chuckling, he grabbed the other drinks and followed her.

"Jesus, you expect me to drink all this?" Liam said with a half-smile, scooping up the Venti-sized cup of bold blend that Liz placed in front of him.

"You need it," Shane said, grabbing cream, sugar, and stirrers from a nearby counter and sliding them over to Liam. He sat next to his brother and eased into the topic of a schedule. Liam was resistant at first, but after some bickering, he convinced his brother that he couldn't disregard his other responsibilities. His daughter needed him and so did the guys at the shop.

The four of them mapped it all out, dubbing it "Katie's Care Calendar." The schedule included times designated for each of them, as well as Carolyn and Cara. They had everything figured out except for overnight stays. Liam—the stubborn ass—wouldn't budge on his determination not to miss a single night at the hospital.

"Damn it, Liam." He pounded a fist on the table. "You're being a moron. You know we love Katie too, so why can't we take turns? You can't get a good night's sleep at the hospital."

"I'll take your help," Liam said in his don't-give-me-any-shit tone. "But I'm going to spend every night with my wife. Non-negotiable, end of story."

Shane had a long, tense stare-down with his brother.

Eventually, as usual, he gave in. "Fine. But Cara shouldn't be alone, so I'll keep staying at your place for the next little while."

Liam clasped his hands in front of him. "Okay, thanks. I won't worry about Cara as much with you there."

He nodded. Damn straight. Cara adored him.

Liz cocked her head. "What about your work? Whatever that actually is—"

"I play the market," he said lifting a shoulder. "I can work from anywhere."

"You don't have a real job?"

"He doesn't *need* a real job," Liam said, quick to defend him. "He's like Warren fuckin' Buffet."

Shane chuckled. "Hardly, but I do okay."

Laughing, Liz shook her head. "Listen, Sabby's out of school for the summer," she said, shifting toward Liam. "I can bring her by every morning on my way to the hospital. She's worried about her aunt and about Cara too. It'll give her a way to contribute."

"That's great, but what about your work?" Liam asked.

"I'm going to cut back on my article assignments for the next little while. I can get my current projects done from the hospital, Starbucks, wherever." She shrugged. "I'll figure it out."

Liam nursed his coffee, and then lifted his gaze to Liz's. "Why don't you and Sabby stay at my place too? I've got plenty of space and it would be easier than commuting from Georgetown every day. You can work from the house in the morning, then head to the hospital for your afternoon shift. It would be easier for you and nice for Cara since she'd get more time with Sabby."

"Not a bad idea." Liz turned toward Shane. "Think you can handle two more women in the house?"

He flashed her a badass smile. "I can handle anything."

AFTER A LONG, restful nap snuggled up with Bear, Katie sat up wishing she could see her loved ones.

The thought had barely passed when a small cloud stopped directly in front of her. Bear rose on his hind legs, touched his head to the cloud, and a hospital room appeared in the center of the white fluff. A woman with long, dark hair lay on the bed, lifelessly still.

Katie sucked in a breath. It was *her*!

Liam was next to her, holding her hand. Her heart tugged at the sight of him slumped in the armchair next to her bed. She wrapped her arms around her body, tangling herself in Liam's blanket of grief.

Her arms dropped to her sides when an alarm pierced the air and the room came alive with activity. A doctor and nurse rushed in and checked her vitals. The nurse adjusted the meds in her IV while the doctor spoke with Liam, not that she could hear what they were saying.

She pressed a hand to her thumping chest to lessen the shock of viewing her body as an outside observer, detached from the activity around it.

As she pulled in a long breath, her guides appeared, one on each side of her.

"How can I be here *and* there?" she asked, her hand still pressed against her racing heart.

"You're not *really* there," Posie said, lowering next to her and taking her hand. "That's just your physical body."

Confused, she opened her mouth to ask another question, but Black Eagle answered before she could form the words.

"The body is just a covering. Think of it as a suit, something to keep your atoms and molecules together during your time on

Earth." He sat on her other side. "The real you is more than your body, more than your mind. The real you is eternal."

Katie glanced from one guide to the other. "Then why do you have bodies?"

"We can put on a body or not." Black Eagle's lips curved. "Here, we usually toss one on. If we're wearing Earth Suits, it helps orient those who are used to seeing bodies."

Earth Suits. Katie put a hand over her mouth, but a giggle popped out anyway. "If that's not me," she said, pointing at the body in the hospital, "then why do they think I'm alive?"

"There's just enough life force left in your physical body to keep it going," Posie explained. "What happens next is up to you…and God."

Katie couldn't begin to fathom what that meant but she was distracted when her gaze fixed on Liam in the hospital. "I can see, but I can't hear."

Sound instantaneously sprang forth from the cloud.

She latched on to the familiar tune. Liam sat close to the bed, his large hands wrapped around hers, looking sexy as ever. Broad shoulders, muscular arms, hard chest—a hot body sculpted through years of early morning workouts and physical labor. But his whiskey eyes were veiled with sorrow and heavy lines creased the muscles in his face. Even so, he was singing to her. Softly, almost in a whisper.

Her heart hurt. For Liam, for her, for their love.

"That song," she murmured, listening to him sing the words to "I Need You." "The Tim McGraw concert was one of our best dates. Liam sang it to me that night too, at the concert."

In the hospital, Liam sang the sweet, heartfelt lyrics, word for word. When he had finished, he tipped his head back. "Damn, God. You know I'm not much of a praying man, but I'd do anything if you would give her back to me. Absolutely anything."

"I miss you, Katie-Cat." Dropping his head, he raised Katie's hand to his lips. "I need you, I love you. Come back, baby."

A tear fell from his cheek to hers.

"I miss you too, Liam." Katie cupped her hands over her heart. "And I so want to come back."

She closed her eyes and remembered the last time he'd sung that song to her. They'd gone to an outdoor country festival where Tim McGraw had been the headliner. While concert-goers around them had been focused on partying, she and Liam had gotten lost in their love. They'd found a private corner in the campground and had created their own little world. Liam had held her tight, gazed into her eyes, and sang to her. Later, wrapped in each other's arms under a star-studded sky, they'd shared their most intimate desires with one another. And over the next several years, they'd made their dreams come true.

When she blinked her eyes open and glanced at the cloud screen, Liam's expression was pure euphoria. He pumped his hands in the air. "Yes!" he shouted, jabbing at the yellow button beside the bed.

A nurse rushed into the room.

"Katie squeezed my hand," he said. "She moved!"

A warm glow spread through Katie's chest. "What happened?" she asked Black Eagle.

"Good, old-fashioned love." He rubbed her hand. "You and Liam had the same thought at the same time. Despite being in different dimensions, your souls touched and it manifested physically when your hand squeezed Liam's."

When tears trembled on her eyelids, Bear nuzzled his head along her side. Absently rubbing her dog for comfort, Katie tipped her head toward Black Eagle. "I wish Liam knew I was here. Will I ever go back?"

"It's up to you," he said, his tone kind.

A tear trickled to her cheek. "I don't understand."

"Don't worry, we'll teach you." Posie wiped her tear away, and a soothing wave of warmth glided through Katie. "We're here to help you," Posie said. "We'll teach you how to achieve your desires."

Things were strange in this dimension. Here, Katie had loving guides who wanted to help her, and there had been an almost automatic response to her requests. She'd asked to see her loved ones, and a viewing cloud had appeared. She'd wished she could hear them, and sound had materialized. Was it coincidence...or were her requests being fulfilled simply based on her wishes?

"You've got it, Katie." Black Eagle winked at her. "Desires manifest based on thought."

Trying to take it all in, Katie glanced at the cloud again.

Leaning over the bed, Liam stared at her motionless body. He was alone again, and his joy had been replaced with sorrow. "Come back, Katie. I miss you." He shook his head. "So damn much I feel it in my bones."

When Liam broke down, Katie did too.

Warm, loving arms encircled her, and both Black Eagle and Posie held her tight.

"It's okay," Posie soothed. "Let it out."

"I can't die," she managed in between sniffles. "I left after a fight —" her sniffles turned into sobs "—after a bunch of fights with Liam. How can I leave like that? And what about Cara? Who's going to mother her? And Savannah?" Katie's gut twisted as she thought about Liam and her girls. "I just found Savannah. She needs a mother…I can't die now."

"Katie, my dear, you must focus on that which you want," Black Eagle said. "The universe doesn't understand the difference between what you want and what you don't want. It will hear—and deliver—that which you focus on."

Katie recognized that Black Eagle was trying to teach her something of importance. But in her frantic desperation to get back to Liam and her girls, she couldn't quite grasp what it was.

"I just wanna go home," she whimpered.

Bear locked his eyes with hers. "Now you're getting it!"

LIAM ROSE from his bedside vigil to greet Jen when she arrived right on schedule on Thursday morning.

He picked up the remote, pointed it at the TV and clicked it off with more force than necessary wondering when *The Wizard of Oz* had come on. He didn't need the damn Tin Man to remind him of the emptiness inside his chest.

Turning, he greeted Jen. "Thanks for being here." He kissed her on the cheek.

He wasn't ready to leave, but he'd agreed to the schedule. Besides, Shane had been right in that he had other commitments. He couldn't afford to let his business falter, and he needed to spend time with Cara who was also grieving for Katie. Reluctantly, he kissed his wife goodbye, then shuffled out of the room and down the hall to meet up with Shane who still insisted on driving him around.

He found his brother and Cara in the ICU waiting room, playing cards at the small table in the back. He'd barely said hello when Katie's mother sailed in.

Jesus. Just what he needed.

While he was pretty sure he looked every bit as scruffy as he felt, Carolyn looked her usual polished self, all put together in a trim black pantsuit.

She approached them slowly. "Liam."

He nodded in a silent greeting.

"Uh, Sam?" she said, glancing at Shane for confirmation. What the hell? She'd just seen Shane at the hospital a few days ago.

Shane's face twisted into a scowl.

Turning toward Cara, Carolyn's face softened. "And, Cara, hello."

Irritation pricked along Liam's spine. What kind of game was she playing? He didn't give a damn what she and Mitch thought about him, but he wouldn't tolerate them messing with his daughter. Katie's parents had rebuffed both him and Cara from the beginning, in hopes that Katie would 'come to her senses.' Over the years, they had regularly invited Katie, and only Katie, to holiday get-togethers and other family functions. Every time, Katie would respond in the same manner—she'd come, but she'd bring him and Cara along. Like clockwork, her parents would rescind the invite, then they'd have the nerve to get all pissy about it.

Assholes.

Cara smiled warily at Katie's mother. "Hi, Carolyn."

"Well, honey, you don't have to call me Carolyn. Not anymore," Katie's mother said.

Liam exchanged a fiery look with his brother.

Cara cleared her throat. "Um, what should I call you then?"

He wondered if Cara's question made Carolyn feel ridiculous. Her step-granddaughter—the child *her* daughter had raised for the last five years—shouldn't have to ask what to call her. But she had no one to blame but herself.

"Sabrina used to call me 'Grandma' but recently changed it to 'G-Ma.' She said that was more hip." Carolyn smiled at Cara. "You could call me either."

Cara glanced up and caught his eye, presumably looking for his concurrence.

Hell no was his first thought. But what if Carolyn wasn't messing with Cara's emotions? Maybe she was finally reaching out. He forced his head to bob up and down. It was the right thing to do, and it was what Katie would want.

"Then I'll call you G-Ma like Sabby," Cara said. The delight in her voice made him glad he'd taken the high road.

A low, dark sound rumbled out of Shane.

Aw, shit. Suck it up, Shane. He tried to communicate telepathically with his brother. Clearly, it didn't work. Shane's face was a glowering mask of ire. Drawing in a long breath, Liam plastered on a smile in an attempt to ease the tension.

But his brother wouldn't look at him. Instead, he fumbled for cash in his pocket, pulled out a wad of bills, and handed them to Cara. "Would you be a sweetie and get us some sodas? Then you can have your time with Jen and Katie. Okay?"

Cara shrugged. "Sure."

After she made her way out the door and down the hallway, Shane reeled around to face Carolyn. "I can't believe you!" he said, his voice full of contempt.

"Don't start," Liam warned in a low voice.

"Sorry, bro, but it's long overdue." Shane gave him a half-assed apologetic look before pinning a hard stare on Carolyn. "I'm Shane, not Sam. Since you never see your daughter's family, I'm not surprised you need a reminder." He snorted derisively. "Cara's been a part of Katie's family—of *our* family—for five years and you're *just now* offering to allow her to call you 'Grandma?' That's bullshit."

Liam leaned forward to grab Shane's arm, but his leg gave out and he ended up against the wall instead. Staring at the ceiling, he huffed out a breath cursing his weakened state.

Shane continued, full of steam. "Katie's fucking amazing, and she has fucking great taste. How dare you look down on our family, on my brother? You and your husband are a bunch of hypocritical assholes."

Liam pushed off the wall. "What the hell, Shane? She just reached out to Cara. That's a good thing." Not that he disagreed with his brother's assessment, but he couldn't let Shane continue to steam roll Katie's mother. "We have to pull together now. *For Katie.* Got it?"

Shane narrowed his eyes to slits, but as was typical, he ignored the question he didn't want to answer. But at least he shut up. "Oh, look," he finally said, pointing at the hallway. "Here comes Cara, and her hands are full. Better go help." Then he hustled away leaving Liam alone with Katie's mother.

Although he felt a twinge of guilt over Carolyn's shell-shocked expression, she was the last person he wanted to spend time with so he mumbled a quick excuse and headed downstairs.

Outside, he leaned against the brick wall and tipped his face to the sky, soaking in the light and heat. A few minutes later, he lit a cigarette.

His blood still pounded from Shane's unpleasant exchange with Carolyn. His brother always gave him a hard time about avoiding confrontation, suggesting he'd feel better if he said whatever he had to say unfiltered. He did so when necessary, but it typically made him feel worse, not better. Shane, on the other hand, indulged in altercations for sport. One thing was for sure, you always knew where you stood with him.

Carolyn was an entirely different story. Liam had no idea how to interact with her. She had ostracized him and Cara for so long it was hard to believe she was genuinely reaching out now. But maybe

Katie's condition had caused her to look deeper, to reconsider her mindset about them.

Taking a long drag, he wished like hell Katie was with him to celebrate the olive branch her mother had extended. But had Katie been well, Carolyn probably wouldn't have made the goodwill gesture. Maybe, something good would come out of this tragedy.

He finished his cigarette and lit a second, desperately wanting, needing, aching for Katie to wake up. She'd been in a coma for five days now, and the clock was ticking.

CHAPTER FIVE

$\mathcal{K}$atie drew in a long breath of fresh pine-scented air, which evoked happy memories of Christmastime. As a child, on the first Saturday of every December, she and her dad had visited a Christmas tree farm in western Maryland. Thinking about those trips, and the exclusive time with her father, filled her with a warm, fuzzy feeling. Her dad had spent most of his daylight hours working, but he'd carved out time for a few traditions. She'd looked forward to those hallmark moments, including Christmas Tree Day. They would make an entire day of it—selecting the biggest, best tree, then they'd have lunch at a country café. After, they'd cart the tree home and transform it into a beautifully adorned centerpiece for their holiday festivities.

Now, she strolled along a mossy path with Posie and Black Eagle. They were surrounded by tall, blue-green Douglas firs reminiscent of those grown at the Christmas tree farm, along with pines, oaks, and a myriad of other trees in various shapes, sizes, and hues. Above her, tree branches reached across the sky embracing one another in a canopy of green.

"How can we be in a forest *and* on a cloud?" she asked her guides.

Bear darted out of the woodland to join them. "We're in a different dimension," he said, his tongue lopping out.

Laughing, she bent down to rub his ears as a happy yellow glow formed around her body.

SUNLIGHT DANCED through open patches in the trees, glinting diamonds on the light green carpet below. Katie pressed her toes in the soft ground, stirring up additional childhood memories of playing with friends in the forest behind her house.

There'd been a soft mossy path through her woods in Bethesda too. Sadly, the trees had been cut down a long time ago, replaced with large estates like the one she'd grown up in. Still, it had been a magical place to play as a child.

"We thought you'd enjoy this throwback to your youth," Black Eagle said.

"But how...." Katie's train of thought was interrupted by a soft thundering. As they rounded the corner, she gasped. Fields of vibrant wildflowers gave way to massive red rocks rising jagged into the sky. Water cascaded hundreds of feet from the cliffs above into a paradise-blue serenity pool. She'd never seen anything more beautiful.

She ogled the picturesque scenery, her heart light, joyful, free. But as they ambled along the path toward the water, she was unable to maintain her bliss. The yellow glow she'd just glimpsed around her body had transformed into a grayish haze. The air in her chest grew dense as her mind returned to her problems.

She needed to go home so she could get Savannah. She needed to find a job because she and Liam would need the extra income after her daughter moved in with them. They'd also need money for in-vitro because after years of trying to get pregnant she was convinced it wasn't going to happen by natural means.

She twisted her fingers through a long strand of hair. Although she was surrounded by remarkable beauty, her brain wouldn't let go of her issues. "I need life guidance," she blurted out.

Black Eagle took her hand and led her into the colorful field of flowers. Bending down he touched a daisy. "Be the flower, Katie."

She choked out a laugh. "Uh, okay."

Her guide glanced up at her and chuckled at what was surely a look of pure bewilderment. Black Eagle eased to the ground and patted the space next to him. She and Posie sat on each side of him while Bear sprinted through the flowers, leaping gleefully in the air touching his nose to a monarch butterfly.

"The flower just is," Black Eagle said. "It knows its purpose and simply goes about it."

"What is its purpose?" she wanted to know, staring at the white and yellow flower for answers.

"To grow and shine and share its splendor." Black Eagle smiled at her. "Can you imagine a world without flowers? Without beauty, without growth? This little flower shows us the way."

"Look at its magnificence." Posie gently caressed the flower's petals. "It doesn't worry whether it's as pretty or as tall as the other flowers. It doesn't worry what others think. Instead, it effortlessly and joyfully goes about its purpose."

Studying the daisy, Katie nodded. Could life really be that simple? Was one's purpose to be like the flower, to grow, to shine, to share light with others? But if that was the case, how did one pay their bills? In the real world, people had mortgages, car payments, not to mention groceries, gas, clothes, and a boatload of other bills. Not everyone had as much money as Shane and her parents. While her brother-in-law and her father were very different people, both had worked long hours in crazy jobs to get where they were. Yet, both loved what they did. Maybe *that* was the point—to align with what you loved.

Bear trotted over and flopped down in front of her, resting his head on her lap.

Find your purpose, your joy, and live it.

As she rubbed Bear, the thought whirled around in her head and took root. But what did she really want? That was the question Liam had been asking her. Maybe he'd been trying to help her find her purpose, her joy.

They stayed in that spot for a long while, and this time, she emptied her mind of everything but the stunning scenery.

"It's all so beautiful," she murmured. The flowers, the red rocks, the cascading water.

"Come on." Black Eagle extended a hand and helped her up, then he slipped her arm in his. "Let's take a closer look."

They moseyed through the field of flowers toward the red rocks.

"How did you know I used to play in the woods?" she asked as they approached the waterfall. Gold light gleamed on the rocks, danced through the water, and created a spray of pixie glitter. Katie spun through the mists while Bear dove into the water for a swim.

"We know all," Black Eagle said on a low laugh.

"Guides are assigned to humans at birth." Posie sat cross-legged on the ground. Katie joined her, facing the dazzling view. "Black Eagle and I have been with you since the day you were born."

"Wow." She angled her head, wondering how it all worked. Her mind flashed back to her days in Belize, when she'd suspected she was pregnant. She'd been so scared, so alone. Her exchange mother had been kind, but Katie had only been with her for a month when she'd figured it out. She'd missed a few periods before she'd gone to Central America, but she'd chalked it up to stress after her boyfriend had broken up with her the day after they'd finally had sex. Her exchange father had been cool and distant, and her popular exchange sister hadn't wanted anything to do with her. She'd managed to make a few friends on her own, but their friendships were new and delicate. Then, seemingly out of the blue, another exchange student had appeared in their small coastal town. She'd come from Sweden, with fair skin and long, shiny blonde hair, and had been the prettiest girl Katie had ever seen. She'd looked a lot like…Katie lifted her gaze to Posie. "*You!*"

Posie's lips curved into a smile. "I thought you could use a friend."

Katie threw her arms around her guide. "Oh, Posie." She had no idea how she would have gotten through her time in Belize without Linnea, a.k.a. Posie. Linnea had stood by her side when mean girls had called her a whore and poked fun at her growing belly. Linnea had been her coach when she'd delivered, and had held her tight through her sobs after her baby had been taken away. "I can't thank you enough."

Posie let out a soft laugh, the sound sweet and musical. "That's what we do."

"So you just appear on Earth when I need you?"

"That's only part of it," Posie said, her eyes twinkling as she spoke. "Guides communicate in many ways—showing up is just one of them. We also send messages telepathically or through a dream."

"Sometimes we plant an idea with a friend or guide our humans to a book, magazine, or song," Black Eagle put in with an impish grin. "Like we did after you met Liam."

Katie drifted back to meeting Liam six years ago at the charity motorcycle ride her bank had sponsored. She'd been instantly drawn to his bad boy charm and the gentle kindness she'd detected underneath, so she'd jumped on the back of his bike and had spent the afternoon riding with him. Later, although completely out of character, she'd gone home with him and had spent an entire blissful night in his arms.

After, she had tried to forget him. They didn't fit in each other's worlds and her father would have had her head on a platter if she'd dated him. He was big on class and stature, and he'd been trying to fix her up with one of the top performers at his venture capital business. She'd met Curt at one of her parents' cocktail parties, but there hadn't been any chemistry. In fact, he had been—and still was as far as she could tell—a junior Mitch Patterson and she had no desire to date her dad's mini-me. Despite this, she'd considered agreeing to *one* date, if only to get her father to stop harassing her.

Then she'd heard a song on the radio that she couldn't shake. It had played on her country music station even though it had been a jazzy-soul song with a funky beat. The chorus had repeated over and over in her mind as if desperately trying to send her the message that Curt wasn't the man for her.

Black Eagle snapped his fingers and a bass guitar appeared. He strummed a few chords of the familiar song, then belted out the chorus. *"Follow your heart, it's a good start. You can't go amiss if you follow your bliss. You can't go amiss if you follow your bliss."*

His voice was identical to the singer she'd heard on the radio. It had been *him*! Katie shook her head as her guide put down the guitar and shrugged sheepishly. "I love my reggae music."

She'd desperately wanted to see Liam again. He had called her a few times after their night of passion, but she'd been torn. They were so very different, and then there was her father. She wasn't sure that she was strong enough to stand up to Mitch Patterson.

The day after she'd heard the bliss song, Liz had emailed her a copy of the magazine article Liz had been working on. It had been titled "You're Stronger Than You Think." She narrowed her eyes at Black Eagle, making him laugh.

He lowered next to her. "Guides bring people, events, and ideas into their person's life at the exact time they're needed." He picked up a small stone and skipped it across the water. "We don't interfere, but we respond to requests made, consciously or subconsciously."

"I planted the idea for the article with Liz," Posie added. "It was perfect subject matter for your sister to tackle and the right time for you to deliberate on the topic."

Leaning back, Katie rested her head on the ground contemplating this connection, the idea that help had always been available. Feeling awed, humbled, and a little larger than life, she soaked it all in. The grass was cool, the humming water relaxing. But then her mind shot back to her problems like a dying woman clutching to her last breath. Why couldn't she stay focused on the beauty, on the positives? She tried to be the flower, but her mind ridiculed the idea, and her head began to throb.

Posie scooted over and pressed a warm palm to her temple. The ache immediately subsided. "Don't let the ego voice in your head overrule your heart," her guide said.

"I'll try." Katie let out a muddled sigh. "But can you give me guidance, like what to do about a job?"

Posie cupped her hands around Katie's head. "Of course." Her guide's soft voice and soothing touch infused Katie's body with absolute serenity.

"Look inside your heart," Black Eagle said, "and that sums it all up," he added on a rumbling laugh. "Remember my song—*follow your heart, it's a good start.*"

"What I know is banking," she murmured in a trance-like state. Posie's hands were still on her head and tingly vibrations circulated through her body. "I didn't love my last job, but I was good at it. My dad found me a job search firm but Liam doesn't think it's a good idea."

"What do *you* think?" Posie asked.

Katie was stumped. Her face heated with embarrassment as a disturbing awareness unfurled and wrapped around her head like bright, flashing Christmas tree lights. She should know what *she* wanted.

"That's right, Katie. Look within," Black Eagle quietly urged. "Think about what *you* want, not what anyone else wants for you."

"I'm just not sure." Rolling onto her belly, she rested her head on her crossed arms. "That's pretty sad."

Posie lightly stroked her back.

Why had she gone into finance? Lulled by Posie's soothing touch, Katie reflected on her indecision after college. She'd majored in business, but had made the choice out of practicality rather than passion. After graduation, she'd considered joining the Peace Corps or starting a shelter for homeless animals. But those ideas weren't acceptable to her father, so she'd gone into banking instead.

"Think about what you want now," Posie said as her warm hands continued their magic. "If you quiet your mind and look within you'll be provided with the right guidance."

"But you must listen to your heart," Black Eagle put in, "not your head."

"I'll give it a try." She closed her eyes.

"Ask yourself: What do I want? What will bring me the greatest joy?" Posie said. "Then rest and receive."

"It sounds a little too easy."

"It works," Black Eagle assured her. "And not just with your job situation. Connect with your heart, then start with what's most important to you."

Drawing in a long breath, Katie did just that and Liam appeared in her mind's eye. *I want to come home, Liam, and make things right between us. I want us to get Savannah. I want you, me, Cara, Savannah, and the other children we'll someday conceive to be one big, happy family.*

Later, Katie realized that in the process of connecting with her heart she hadn't once thought about finding an important job.

FEELING RESTED after a long nap in his own bed, Liam lit a cigarette and walked down the drive to Callahan Cycles with Pan trotting at his side. He was finally starting to feel normal again. Good thing, because his business was busier than ever.

Over the last week, Seth had taken on more than his fair share of the workload. As Liam pushed through the shop's front door, he made a mental note to give the boy a raise. When he stepped inside, Seth jumped up from the shiny blue Road King he'd been servicing and raced over to greet him.

Seth asked about his and Katie's welfare. The two of them chatted for a few minutes and then he touched base with each of his team members. After, he retreated to his office with Seth for a more thorough debriefing.

Midway through their meeting, Cara waltzed in, wearing a lacy halter top, revealing a little too much cleavage, and ripped up jean shorts that were so short they didn't cover her ass. Damn it, he needed Katie. She'd long been in charge of approving Cara's wardrobe choices—he couldn't possibly talk to his baby girl about boobs and asses—and he was pretty sure Katie'd never let Cara out of the house in that get-up.

Cara carried a plate of cookies and two lemonades. "Figured you'd be with Seth." Smiling brightly, she set the goodies on his desk.

"Thanks, sweetie." He reached for one of the glasses while avoiding another look at his little girl who was far more grown up than his mind was willing to accept.

Seth, on the other hand, out and out gaped at Cara.

Cara started out the door, then paused and glanced over her shoulder. "Don't stay out here too long, Dad. You shouldn't push yourself." Without waiting for a response, she sailed out.

Seth flipped back his long bangs and watched Cara walk away until she was completely out of sight, his eyes gleaming with pure male attraction. Liam sucked in a shocked breath. He knew that look—it was same way he looked at Katie.

What the hell? He shifted his gaze from Seth's dopey expression to Katie's gardens outside his office window. With any other guy, Liam would have called him on it. But Seth was different, more important to him...maybe even the one young man who might be worthy of dating his daughter. But as he watched Cara strut up the drive flipping through her cell phone, he realized he didn't have to consider the possibility yet. Cara appeared to be oblivious to Seth's longing.

He cleared his throat, drawing Seth's attention back. "Good job covering for me."

Seth sat taller and Liam would've sworn that his chest puffed out.

"I mean it." Liam leaned back in his chair. "I have no idea what I would've done without you."

"Thanks, but I owe you. You know I'd do anything for you," Seth said, gulping lemonade. "Katie, too."

Liam slanted Seth a look. They'd had this conversation too many times. "You don't owe me anything." He took a cookie, pushed the plate toward Seth. "You're my right-hand man here, that's enough."

Sure, he'd hired Seth and had given him a chance, but his young understudy had more than paid him back.

Seth's jaw set. "If you hadn't saved me, my life would be shit. I'd be in prison...maybe even dead."

That was probably true. Liam drifted back five years. He'd taken a motorcycle ride and had stopped at the local McDonald's for a soda. When he made his way outside, he found young Seth eyeing his motorcycle.

"Hey." When he spoke, the boy jerked back and the green fuck-you monster on his T-shirt flipped Liam the bird. It was as if Liam had jumped back in time and come face-to-face with *his* teenage self.

When Seth lifted his hands in the air, a cigarette dropped from his mouth. "Hey man, I didn't do nothin.' " He turned to run, but Liam caught his arm.

"It's okay, son, you can look at my bike." He extended a hand. "I'm Liam."

The boy looked at him cautiously. "Seth," he finally said, and after a quick shake, yanked his hand back.

Liam had felt a desperate urge to reach out to the kid. Maybe it was the glimpse of wistful hope underneath all that attitude, maybe he saw himself in young Seth. Because he'd been a wayward rebel himself once upon a time, he knew how to talk badass. So he struck up a conversation and got Seth to stick around.

Seth had a keen interest in motorcycles, so he'd invited him to stop by his one-man shop the next day after school. A few days later, he had offered Seth a job.

"I don't know why you hired me," Seth said, drawing him back to present. "You weren't busy enough to need help. I was a fourteen-year-old pain in your ass, following you around, asking moronic questions."

Liam shrugged. "You needed guidance."

And it was no wonder. He'd quickly figured out that Seth's home life was dismal. His father had taken off before he could crawl and his mother's hippy dippy parenting entailed no rules, no responsibilities, and no expectations. She left him alone frequently, even overnight. How could she expect Seth to turn into a decent young man with no guidance, with no one around to set an example? Liam's own parents had never let him doubt their belief that he could do better. It was the one thing he regretted most in his life—he hadn't stepped up until after they'd been killed in an airplane accident and he had needed to be there for Shane.

He'd taken Seth under his wing, set clear expectations, and pushed him to do better—at school, at home, at work. He'd listened, offered guidance, and ultimately taught Seth everything he knew about motorcycles.

Seth had never once disappointed him. "Maybe I saw more in you than you saw in yourself," he said. "And I was right. Look at the great job you're doing here."

Seth's eyes misted.

Liam shook his head. "Now, get back to work."

As Seth shuffled off, a sense of pride unfurled and settled deep in Liam's chest. Blowing out a breath, he tried to shift his focus to the stack of invoices on his desk, but his heart and mind persistently returned to Katie. It was Saturday, the one-week anniversary of the accident. How could he not think about her and agonize over what had happened?

His heart physically hurt. What if she never came out of the coma? He put his head in his hands as fear snaked through his body.

LATER THAT EVENING, Liam and Shane took the girls out to dinner at Bonnie's Grill, a local eatery that had been serving home-cooked meals to the residents of Gem Valley for generations.

Sliding into their booth, Cara and Sabby yakked a mile a minute. Sabby was only a year older than Cara, but Liam didn't miss the subtle power she had over his daughter. While his niece was smart and polite, something about her—maybe the hint of unruly in her pretty hazel eyes—kept him on guard.

"How you feeling?" Shane asked, giving him the once over.

"Much better."

After implementation of the Katie Care Calendar, he had spent more time at home, including afternoon naps in his own bed. He'd also been working again, and while he wasn't putting in his usual long hours, it felt good to add some normalcy to his life. What's more, he was now having at least one meal a day with Cara and spending quality time with Pan who'd been a lost soul without Katie. And, he still spent every night at the hospital. He was willing to admit—even if only to himself—that his brother's plan had been brilliant.

"So, I'm finally gettin' time with awesome Uncle Shane," Sabby said, as if reading his mind about his brother's greatness. "I feel like I know you already. Cara's always saying 'Uncle Shane this,' and 'Uncle Shane that.'"

Shane laughed. "Well, I don't have any of my own, so Liam lets me share Cara."

"And Cara makes out," Liam said, sipping his sweet tea. "Like Paris last year."

Sabby ran a hand down the bright strand of burgundy in her otherwise dark brown hair. "I was soooo jealous. Mom and I had just moved back to the States. But even when we lived there, I didn't get to go to all those cool places."

"Paris." Cara sighed dreamily. "Hashtag beautiful."

Cara and Shane bantered about the things they'd seen and done in Paris, Milan, and Athens, while Sabby's expression turned green with envy. Liam drifted off in his own world, thinking about the trip he and Katie had taken while Cara had been in Europe with Shane. Katie had taken two and a half weeks off from work, much to her boss's displeasure, and he'd left Seth in charge of Callahan Cycles. They'd headed south on the motorcycle, partied like teenagers in Panama City, then followed the Gulf to New Orleans where they hadn't left their plush hotel room for two days. After, they had followed the Mississippi River before cutting east, exploring new parts of the country by day, making love every night. Gazing skyward, he silently appealed for many more years of trips just like that one...with his sweet Katie at his side.

"I even got to drink wine," Cara said, jolting him back to conversation at the table. "Dad would never let me do that."

Liam scowled at his brother, who was busy making hangman gestures across the table at Cara. But he let it go. He'd already chewed Shane's ass about letting Cara drink. Shane had insisted it was just a shot-sized portion, but his story and Cara's had differed greatly, and after Liam's misspent youth, he had a no-nonsense policy when it came to teenage alcohol and drugs.

Food arrived, and they dug in as the girls bantered back and forth about who'd said what on an array of social networks. Their chatter didn't let up, and they were still in a heated debate over which movie star was the hottest when they arrived back at the house. God help him.

On the front porch, Pan shot toward him like a speeding bullet, knocking him against the wall. Shaking his head, he bent down and hugged his dog. "I missed you too, boy." Pan was noticeably needier with Katie gone, but *he* was feeling needier, too.

"I know, buddy," he whispered in the dog's ear. "I know."

When he straightened, Pan moved on to greet Shane by pressing his head into Shane's crotch.

"Still has the manners of his old man," Shane joked as he rubbed Pan's ears.

"Blame her." Liam flicked his thumb toward Cara. "She taught him."

Cara grinned. "It's adorable."

"Yeah, it's especially great when we have guests," he said. "Who doesn't love a wet nose in his crotch?"

Sabby bent down to greet the dog. "Who's a cute boy?" she cooed, then tipped her head to one side. "How'd he get his name, ya'll into pots and pans?"

Cara snickered. "It's short for Panther. When I was a kid I watched Animal Planet 24-7."

"Nah," Liam said. "Pan's name is a nod to Harley-Davidson's classic engine."

At Sabby's confused look, Cara laughed. "Panheads. You really don't know anything about motorcycles, do you, Sab?"

Sabby primped her hair with one hand. "Nope, but I know lots of other things," her voice teased and her eyes glinted trouble. Damn, what was Sabby up to? He wanted to protect his innocent little girl, but felt completely helpless. It was impossible to shield her from the big bad world, even though he'd sure as hell like to. "C'mon Cara, let's go Snapchat." Sabby grabbed Cara's arm and tugged her into the house.

He followed the girls, along with Shane and Pan.

"Hi, Mom," Sabby called out as she passed the kitchen.

"Hey, Liz," Cara yelled, trotting behind Sabby. Even though Liz was Cara's aunt, she had never called Liz by that title. Probably because Liz hadn't been around much. Sabby and Cara had become close over the years, mostly through social media. This past year Sabby had stayed with them a few times when Liz had traveled for work.

Liam and Shane trailed the girls down the hall, but veered into the kitchen following the delectable scent of brewing coffee. Placing the stack of mail on the counter, Liam breathed in the rich aroma. He grabbed two mugs from the cupboard, sliding Liz an appreciative glance. She smiled at him from the kitchen table, where she was engulfed in magazines.

"I'm gonna go through the mail, then head to the hospital," he said, handing one of the mugs to his brother. "Any changes?" he asked Liz.

"No, but Mom, Jen, and I had a good visit. Jen's still there and she said you should take your time."

He sorted through the mail, poured coffee, and then settled in between Liz and Shane at the table. Gratitude flooded his chest. He had no idea what he would have done without their help with Katie, with Cara, with the house. After a few gulps, he cleared his throat. "You guys don't know how much I appreciate your help."

"It's not a problem." Liz moved a pile of magazines from table to the floor to make more space.

"Ditto," Shane said.

"Where do you live—you know, normally?" Liz asked Shane.

"A few miles west," his brother said. "I have a little place in the hills."

Liam chuckled to himself. Shane's *little* place was a custom-built log cabin that sat high in the hills. It boasted six bedrooms, eight bathrooms, and multi-level decks. It also had indoor and outdoor pools and a home theater in the basement, where Shane and Cara spent countless hours watching movies. His brother's *little* place was worth millions.

He guzzled the rest of his coffee, took his mug to the sink, and grabbed his iPad off the counter. "I'm heading to the hospital," he said with a renewed burst of energy.

"You need me to do anything at the shop in the morning?" Shane asked.

Liam knew his brother didn't know one end of a wrench from another but he appreciated the offer. "Thanks, but I don't think there's much you could do." He gave Shane a teasing grin. "You know, that would help anyway."

Shane raised his middle finger, then looked at Liz sheepishly. "Sorry."

Liz just smiled.

AFTER LIAM LEFT, Liz caught Shane's gaze and held it for a long moment. Damn, the man was attractive. He and Liam had the same solid bone structure, the same ruggedly handsome facial features. Both men were sinfully well-built, but Liam's ponytail and tattoo sleeves gave him a tougher look—Katie had always had a thing for bad boys—while Shane's style was more refined.

When the temperature in the room spiked, she rose to refill her coffee.

She didn't know Shane well. In fact, she'd only seen him a handful of times over the years. While she knew Katie adored her brother-in-law, she had gotten the distinct impression from some of the things Katie had said that he was a big-time player. The last thing she needed was to get involved with someone like that.

"Liam's building a bunch of custom motorcycles these days," Shane said, after she'd returned to the table. His gaze rested on hers with such intense scrutiny it made her wriggle in her chair. Was he looking for a reaction? "He's built quite a reputation. Just created a kick-ass bike that looks like the one Trace Gordon rode in Midnight Combat."

Her mind flashed to the last scene in the movie where Trace rode into the dark midnight sky on his post-apocalyptic chopper with the earth coalition empress wrapped around him after he'd taken out the entire alien warrior resistance, saving the empress and all humankind. "Really?" She took a sip of her hot coffee. "I just saw Midnight Combat. Loved it."

"Huh. I would've figured you as a romantic movie kind of gal." Shane leveled his gorgeous blues in her direction. The hints of mischief in their depths caught her attention—and to her distress— her interest. She wasn't looking for a man, and even if she was it certainly wouldn't be with one who lived a couple of hours away. Nor would it be with Katie's brother-in-law. Imagine the shit storm it would cause with her parents if she went out with Liam's brother. That thought swung her around full circle, back to considering the idea. She was always game for exerting her independence.

"You like action flicks?" Shane asked, drawing her attention back.

"Sure. Who doesn't? And by the way," she said, wrapping her hands around her mug, "you don't need to convince me of Liam's success. I may not see Katie a lot, but we talk. I think it's great Liam's doing work he loves."

She smiled into her coffee at Shane's bewildered expression. He'd probably expected her to be standoffish like her parents. She loved her folks, but she was nothing like them.

"Katie was always telling me how much Liam loves his job, and how she wished she loved her work." She flipped a layer of hair away from her face. "I don't know why she's been looking for a job in banking. She didn't seem to enjoy her last job."

Shane gave her another look she couldn't quite decipher. Even so, her heart picked up speed. She needed to get a grip. She was worldly and sophisticated, not a googly-eyed teenager. Let's blame it on lack of caffeine, she thought, guzzling the rest of her coffee.

"What do you think she wants to do?" Shane asked, rubbing a hand over his jaw, which had just the right amount of sexy stubble.

"I'm not sure she knows." She dragged her gaze away from Shane's five-o'clock shadow. "But she loved helping Liam last summer, especially with marketing."

Shane nodded, drawing her attention to the blond streaks in his deliberately tousled hair. Jeez, what was with her today? She probably needed to get laid. It had been entirely too long—a little over six months to be exact. Either that, or she needed to whip out her handy-dandy vibrator and take care of her needs herself. Maybe then, she'd stop having these wayward thoughts about Shane.

"Liam wants her to work for his business full-time. Although Callahan Cycles is doing well, it could grow even more with Katie's marketing magic." Shane leaned back in his chair. "She really doesn't need to work at all. I've offered to help them, but Liam won't hear of it. Stubborn ass," he muttered, but Liz could hear the love that laced his voice.

"Hmm." She had the sneaking suspicion that Liam wasn't the only stubborn mule in the family.

"I'm confident in Katie's marketing abilities too—" she angled her head toward Shane "—but I think she worries about what Dad will think if she doesn't get another corporate job." Her voice trailed off as she contemplated how she could help her sister.

"Hey, there." Shane reached over and put his hand on hers. Goosebumps pricked up and down her arm. "We'll all team up together to help Katie as soon as she gets well."

"Thanks." She glanced at Shane, at the genuine care and concern written on his face.

She was intrigued by him, even though she didn't want to be. He was a man of many layers. Today he was warm and open, practically oozing sex appeal, a stark contrast to the tough talk he'd given her mother earlier in the week at the hospital.

Shane's hand lingered on hers for a few seconds longer than it should have. The tingles intensified and spread to her other arm. His blue-gray heavy-lidded eyes gave off a sleepy, sexy vibe. They drew her into their spell, toppling her former vow of restraint. In its place was the desire to get to know Shane Callahan much, much better.

CHAPTER SIX

*K*atie closed her eyes and tried to connect with Liam. If she could just hold his hand or nestle her face against his neck....

When Posie touched her shoulder, she jumped.

"Didn't mean to startle you," her guide said, easing down beside her.

Black Eagle sat on her other side and Bear slipped into the middle of their circle. She reached over and rubbed her dog's ears. "I was just sending Liam love. I hope he felt it."

Posie's lips curved into an angelic smile. "Your thought will transform into a positive, loving vibration that he will receive."

As a vision of Liam formed in her head, Katie sighed. "I was thinking about how lucky we were to have found each other."

"Luck, schmuck." Black Eagle flicked his wrist. "Luck is a human-invented term to rationalize things that can't otherwise be explained. In truth, you create luck—" he used air quotes around the word luck "—through prayers, desires, intentions. Then, with a little help from the universe, synchronicity occurs and that which you desire is delivered to you."

That sounded really good. But if that was the case, why hadn't it happened in her life? Why wasn't she at home with Liam now preparing to get Savannah? And why wasn't she pregnant? She'd been praying about it and trying for years. While Black Eagle's idea sounded good, it wasn't working that way in her life. "There must be more to it."

Bear lifted his head. "You ask for something, believe in it, and *BAM*, the universe begins its work to make it happen!" With that, Bear flopped over to expose his belly.

Chuckling, Black Eagle stroked the dog's belly. "That's what I love about you, Bear. You're like—*BAM*—to the point!"

Bear's tail thudded, shooting white puffs of cloud onto all of them.

"I don't understand," she said, wiping cloud wisps from her arm. "If it's that easy, how come we can't think things into being on Earth?" In a way, it made sense. In Tranquility, everything was different.

"The vibrational concept works the same way on Earth," Posie said. "You can think things into being."

"Then how come everyone doesn't have everything they want on Earth?" she asked, still not getting it.

"Sometimes it takes longer on Earth," Black Eagle acknowledged. "It requires a greater faith, but it still works. That is, if you can overcome the greatest obstacle down there," he said, waving a hand toward the blue-green ball rotating beneath them.

Katie's brows knitted together. "What's the greatest obstacle?"

"The mind." Black Eagle tapped his index and middle finger on his temple.

Now she was completely confused. Her guides had just explained that she could think things into being. If that was the case, how could her mind be the greatest obstacle?

"I'll show you." Black Eagle rubbed his hands together as his expression turned gleeful. "Chair," he said, snapping his fingers together.

A chair appeared in front of him.

"I ask for it and it's delivered. Now granted, the pure love and positivity up here result in quicker manifestation of desires, but on

Earth humans could get things a lot faster if they didn't over think everything." Black Eagle's lips curled into an impish grin. "You see, I just thought 'chair.' 'I need a chair.' I didn't flip-flop, consider whether I deserved the chair, if I could afford the chair, or if a loveseat would really be better." He glanced at his backside. "I didn't wonder if this particular chair would make my butt look big."

Katie snickered, thinking about the many times she'd wondered the same thing about a dress or a pair of jeans.

"I simply asked for a chair and got a chair. When you ask for something the universe begins its work to deliver that request to you. If you start questioning it, the universe hears, 'I don't know if I want this,' 'I might not really need this,' or 'I don't deserve this,' Black Eagle said. "You must be clear and consistent with your request and believe it will manifest. If you do so, you will receive. It's universal law."

"The chair analogy was helpful." She smiled at Black Eagle. "I think I get how it works now, but I'll have to work on the over-thinking part."

"Good." Black Eagle winked at her. "Remember believing is the most important part of the deal. If you don't believe then you won't receive. It's really that simple." He put his large, warm hand over hers. "Now, I want you to think about this in context of your desire to go home."

She nodded solemnly. "I really want to go home."

"We're here to help you achieve whatever you want," Posie said, placing her hand on top of Black Eagle's, connecting the three of them.

Warm vibrations flowed from Katie's guides' hands into hers. "Thank you," she murmured. It was both staggering and humbling to have two beautiful guides whose sole purpose was to help her. Heart overflowing with gratitude, she drew in a long breath and contemplated what she wanted and what she needed help figuring out. "First, I want to go home. I need to tell Liam about Savannah, and we need to go get her. I'd like to have more kids. Beyond that, I'm not sure." She pushed a long strand of hair behind her shoulder.

"When you suggested I look in my heart, a lot of things came up, but nothing job-wise. Still, I need to find one…."

"Think about what you *want*, not what you *should* want," Posie said, in her soft, soothing voice. "The key is to find your passion. Think of the accident as an opportunity to reflect on your true desires, to reconnect with your soul intentions."

She absorbed Posie's wisdom. "I am—well, *was* enjoying life more after I got laid off. Except for the pressure to find a new job and arguing with Liam over it."

"External influences can exert a strong pull, but if you look within, you'll always find what's best for you." Black Eagle's voice was low and deep, a complete contrast to Posie's, but every bit as soothing. "When you allow your feelings to guide you, you'll find inner joy."

Use her feelings to guide her decisions? She heard her father's voice—*Impractical, reckless, absurd*—and while she wanted to align with Black Eagle's wisdom, it was a completely foreign concept. She couldn't move past the reservations that wrapped around her chest like a sopping wet towel. Growing up, her father had taught her to make decisions using her head, not her heart. In business school, she'd learned that sound decisions were based on logic and statistics, not on emotions. The heavy towel around her chest compressed, squeezing her body into a straight-jacket.

"It's a different concept," Posie said in a reassuring voice. "For it to work, you need to let go. Releasing family and societal expectations is not only freeing, but it also allows you to connect with what *you* really want."

Well…letting go of all those pressures sounded pretty good.

"Feels good too." Black Eagle winked at her. "As an added bonus, when you connect with your feelings, you can consciously guide your thoughts to that which you desire."

Choking out a breath, she broke free of the stranglehold of social burdens. The towel around her chest warmed, along with her harmony toward the concept.

Posie put her palms on Katie's back. Katie sighed contentedly as tingly vibrations shot out in every direction.

She stretched. "The bank probably did me a favor by laying me off. Maybe God was encouraging a change." She stretched again, vowing she would figure out what she wanted, and that she would do so by looking within and connecting with her feelings.

More relaxed, she sprawled across the soft cloud. "What's God like?"

"The best way to explain God is with one word. *Love*." Posie moved her hands to Katie's head. "God is simply love."

"On Earth, many religions portray God as a man in an attempt to describe him in human terms," Black Eagle said, still rubbing Bear. "That works until people add human qualities. God doesn't have human characteristics so it's hard to explain the God-entity in terms humans can fully understand."

Katie marinated on this information as Posie massaged her scalp. "Your fingers are like magic," she murmured.

Posie laughed, the sound soft and angelic. "God is love. Unconditional love that infuses everything, including each of us." As her guide continued to gently knead, warm vibrations flowed through Katie from head to toe. "God represents the highest vibrational energy, that of pure love."

Posie had barely spoken the words when Black Eagle burst into song. He belted out every word to "Love is My Religion," his vocals nearly identical to Ziggy Marley's.

When he had finished, she sat up and clapped. "That was amazing."

"That's my man." Posie leaned over and kissed Black Eagle on the cheek. "He can illustrate anything musically."

"You see Katie, everything in the universe is vibratory." Black Eagle extended a palm and she felt his positive energy even though he hadn't touched her. "If you put out loving vibrations, you receive vibrations of love back. If you give *any* kind of positive vibration, you get positive feelings in response. But, if your thoughts and actions are negative, that's what you will receive."

A ray of light shimmered from above, brightening their cloud and illuminating the Earth rotating beneath them as if in cosmic agreement with Black Eagle's words.

"God's rays." Black Eagle rose, then stepped over and fluttered his hand back and forth through the stream of light. "Simply beautiful."

Full of wonder, all she could do was nod. Posie took her hand and they made their way over to Black Eagle as the brilliant light painted the sky a rainbow of otherworldly colors. Hues she had never seen and could only describe as more vibrant reddish-orange, blueish-purple, and pinkish-white.

Flanked by her guides at the edge of the cloud, Katie took in the exquisite sunset while contemplating the nature of God and the dance of the universe.

SHANE OPENED one eye and glanced at the black ball of fur curled up next to him. Scratching Pan's ears, he glanced at the clock. Five after nine.

"Damn. Can't remember the last time I slept in this late," he mumbled. "Must've been the warm Pan blanket." The dog nuzzled in closer, resting his big head on Shane's chest. "Okay, ol' boy, we'll stay in bed for a while longer."

Half an hour later, he rose, showered, and then made his way to the kitchen. The girls were rummaging around in the pantry. Liz was at the table working on her laptop and guzzling coffee. She glanced up and smiled when he walked in.

"Morning, everyone," he called out in a raspy voice.

He grabbed a mug and filled it to the rim with coffee, then sat at the table next to Liz. Her layered hair was flawlessly styled, her make-up subtle except for her sultry red lips. His gaze lingered there for a few beats as he wondered what it would feel like to brush his lips over hers.

When she raised a perfect brow, he snapped his gaze up. "Sorry, I don't function until I've had at least two cups." He took a couple of gulps of his coffee.

Liz pushed her laptop aside and looked him up and down. Was

that interest flickering in her eyes? Wanting stirred inside him along with a punchy desire to pursue this further.

He guzzled more coffee and waited for the kick. "Tell me Liz, what do you do for fun?"

"I don't have a lot of time for fun. I work a lot." She took a sip of her coffee, leaving a siren red lipstick stain on the white mug.

"She dates a lot," Sabby yelled from the pantry.

He arched a brow in Liz's direction.

"That's an exaggeration." She wrapped her hands tightly around her mug. Her arms were toned—a trait he appreciated in a woman, given the care he took with his own body—and her teal top strained across her chest when she moved, hugging her generous breasts. "Of course I date. You know, occasionally. How about you?"

"Occasionally." Parroting the word back, he gave her a slow, lazy grin.

She angled her head, her dark, shiny hair a contrast to her light, shimmery eyes. "What do *you* do for fun?"

"I play the markets. It's like a chess game, you make the right moves at the right time and you win." He got up to pour himself another cup of coffee as the girls traipsed out of the kitchen with a handful of junk food. "I also travel—the islands when I want to relax, Europe when I'm in the mood for history." He lifted the pot of coffee toward her. "More?"

"No, but thanks," she said.

He returned to the table with his freshly filled mug. "And given my Irish blood, there's no place more beautiful than the Emerald Isle." He faded into memories of the trip he'd taken many years ago after the twelve-hour days in the trading world had taken a toll on him. He'd booked two weeks at a secluded cottage in Ireland and had soaked up every minute of rest on a quaint farm just outside the village of Terryglass, relishing in the break from the digital boards, noise, and competition of The New York Stock Exchange. He'd meandered in and out of old-world pubs, sailed in Lough Derg, and marveled at the Portumna Castle. The trip had restored his battered soul, and before returning to New York, he had committed to taking a real break at least once a year. And he'd kept true to his promise, taking a two-week break every year since then.

He surprised himself by telling Liz about the epiphany he'd experienced in the rolling green hills of his homeland. She was intelligent, easy to talk with, and she loved to travel, too. They spent the next half hour sharing travel adventures and comparing notes on places they'd like to visit next. The Galapagos Islands were high on both of their lists and for the same reasons—relative isolation, interesting landscapes, and rare animals.

Eventually the conversation shifted to Katie.

"Were you two close when you were younger?" he wanted to know.

Liz tucked a strand of hair behind her ear. "No. I mean I always loved Katie, but she was in elementary school when I went off to college. Then—"

"Wait." He lifted a palm. "There's no way you're that much older than Katie."

"Nine years."

His eyes roved over her. "You are one gorgeous, hot as hell thirty-eight-year-old."

"You are quite the flatterer, Shane Callahan." She let out a low laugh. "Despite your youthful age."

"You're killing me." He pressed his hands over his heart. "I'm only four years younger than you."

"How 'bout this?" A hint of a smile curved her red lips. "You're a young man, but a *sexy* young man."

He sat up a little straighter. She found him sexy? Now that was interesting. "I'll take it."

But before he could hike the flirtation up a notch, Cara popped her head into the kitchen.

"You ready, Uncle Shane?"

He wanted to finish this particular conversation before he left the house. "How about half an hour?"

"That works," Cara said, and then disappeared.

Liz shut down her laptop. "I need to get going, too. I'm heading to the hospital early today." She tucked papers, magazines, and her computer into a canvas tote bag, then grabbed a short-sleeved black sweater and shrugged it on. The cropped style ended just below her breasts, drawing his attention there. He wondered what it would feel like to hold her ample breasts in the palms of his hands.

"Since Cara and I are headed to the hospital too want to ride together?"

"Thanks," Liz said, "but no. I have errands to run after I see Katie. Oh, and in case Cara didn't tell you, she and Sabby are gonna eat at Chipotle tonight, then hang out at the mall." The corner of her mouth lifted even as she rolled her eyes. "To hunt down guys I'm sure." Rising, she grabbed her bag, then stepped into the hallway. "See you later, Shane."

"Go out with me," he blurted even though he hadn't intended to ask her just yet. And he sure as hell hadn't intended to ask her like that.

Liz wheeled around and gaped at him.

Now that the words had been said, he had to see it through. It was what he wanted anyway. He rose and met Liz halfway, leaning against the jamb in between the kitchen and hallway. His lips curved into his best how-can-you-live-without-this smile. "How about a dinner date?"

Liz continued to stare at him.

"You gotta eat, right?" He lifted a shoulder. "The girls are going out, so why not?"

Now she laughed. *Laughed.* "Be still, my beating heart," she said, fluttering a hand to her chest. "You need to polish up your lady talk, Shane Callahan!"

A laugh huffed out of him. He wasn't overly polished, but he didn't need to be because it was easy for him to get dates. Women tended to flock his way, but their interest was usually superficial and mostly based on his net worth.

He liked that Liz showed restraint, even a little indifference toward him. And now that he had a challenge, he was even more intrigued. So he changed his strategy. "You afraid? Think your daddy will view our date as a Hatfield going out with a McCoy?"

Liz quickly closed the space between them. Her sandal wedges gave her added height, and her sparkling blue eyes only had to tip up slightly to meet his. "As a matter of fact, that makes your offer all the more attractive." She gave him a cheeky smile that shot straight to his groin, and he found himself holding his breath waiting for her answer. "I'll think about it," she said, and then she sailed out of the house.

～

STILL HOT AND bothered from her exchange with Shane, Liz climbed into her Mercedes tugging off her sweater. Tossing it onto the passenger seat, she drew in a long, calming breath before backing out of the drive.

Up until now, she hadn't spent much time with Shane. In fact, the only occasions she could remember being around him was at Katie and Liam's wedding and during their annual Callahan Christmas parties. Based on the floozy-type women Shane always had with him, she'd dismissed him as Liam's arrogant, playboy brother.

She had no idea why she hadn't noticed him—really noticed him —before. About six-two, he had gorgeous smoky blue-gray eyes, a sexy five o'clock shadow, and a rock solid build with muscles that bunched and begged to be touched. Just thinking about him now caused a ripple of awareness low in her belly. Turning onto Main Street, she attempted to regain her composure.

Shane Callahan was not her usual type. She went for ethnic, passionate, creative geniuses. The last two men she had dated, both of whom easily fit her norm, hadn't worked out so well. Images of Frederic, the novelist, and Amir, the Persian rug dealer, pervaded her mind. Both men had been irresistible, yet the first had been a tragic Mama's boy, the second a Casanova who'd secretly juggled two other women at the same time he had been dating her.

Shane, on the other hand, was Irish, edgy, and confrontational. He had a tough exterior, but she'd caught glimpses of a softer, caring side, too. From what she could tell, he was loving and loyal to a fault, at least with his immediate family.

He'd looked so damn hot earlier, dressed in tight blue jeans and a plain black T-shirt that had looked anything but plain stretched across his sinewy chest. Pulling into the hospital parking lot, she considered his unique dinner invitation.

Should she or shouldn't she?

Every female part of her voted a resounding yes, but her mind had a different thought altogether: *Are you insane?*

Shane was a woman's man. He was arrogant and headstrong. He was also Katie's brother-in-law. If she agreed to go out with him and they liked each other, then what? After Katie woke up from the coma, she and Sabby would return to their own home, a two-hour drive from Gem Valley. Besides, after her and Shane's inevitable break-up, there could be awkwardness between their families.

The reasons to decline clearly outweighed her shameful lust, the only explanation for her strong desire to say yes.

She stepped out of her car and rested against it for a long moment. Now that she was at the hospital, she needed to focus on Katie. She offered up a silent prayer, like she'd done every morning over the past week. *Please help my baby sister to wake up, to be okay.*

Once inside, she quickly made her way to the ICU, then to Katie's room at the end of the hallway. After giving a quick knock, she walked into the room.

"Hey, Liam," she greeted, dropping her purse and tote bag next to the bed.

Her eyes roamed over Katie before she leaned down to kiss her sister's cheek. Straightening, she turned to Liam. "Any changes?"

Still holding Katie's hand, Liam rose, his eyes sad and distant. "No."

Her heart poured out to Liam. To all of them, but especially to Liam who loved Katie more than she had ever thought possible.

"I'm sorry." She reached over and squeezed Liam's hand. "She's gonna come out of this."

"Yeah." Liam rubbed his chin. "I keep telling myself that."

"Keep it up," she said in a reassuring tone, "Katie's a fighter."

CHAPTER SEVEN

*L*iam nodded. He had to believe Katie was coming back. It was what kept him going.

"I'm only gonna stay for a short while this morning," Liz said, fluffing her dark hair. "I have to run home to take care of a few things, but I'll be back later tonight. Shane and Cara are right behind me, then Jen and Mom will cover my early afternoon shift since I'll be in Georgetown." While the group had agreed on a basic schedule, it was Liz who followed up with everyone to make sure all shifts were covered and to coordinate any changes. He was eternally grateful for her help. It took all of his energy to put in some hours at his business, put on a positive face for Cara, and spend every night at the hospital. "Jen said she'd stay for however long you need her to this evening."

"Thanks," he said. "I really appreciate the help, Liz."

They visited with Katie together for a while, swapping stories. When he reminisced about their first Christmas party as a married couple, he would have sworn that Katie squeezed his hand. But when he looked down, it was motionless. He gently rubbed his thumb on her palm, hoping for a reaction. When none came, fear clogged his throat, making it difficult to breathe. Why was she still unconscious?

Cara and Shane pushed through the door, and he welcomed the distraction.

Cara rushed into the room. He nodded at Shane over Cara's head as he wrapped his arms around her. "Hey, there, what's wrong?"

"Bad dream," she said, sniffling. She wiped her nose on his shirt, and then glanced up, her eyes stained with tears. "Katie came to see me and I thought she was saying goodbye."

Liam's entire body stiffened as the mere thought tore at his insides. He stared at Cara blankly, unable to move a muscle.

Thankfully, Liz stepped over and pulled Cara into her arms. "Sweetie, Katie was probably just checking in." She gently stroked Cara's hair. "Did she actually say good-bye?"

Cara shook her head, and Liam whooshed out a breath of relief.

Shane nudged him. "You okay?"

He nodded and hoped it was convincing as Liz continued to talk Cara down.

"You know Katie's not shy," Liz said. "If she came to say good-bye, she'd have just said it. Don't you think?"

"I guess." Cara wiped away her tears with the tissue Liz offered.

After Cara had calmed down, Liz gathered her stuff. "I should get going." She hugged Cara again. "You remember what I said, okay?"

Cara smiled. "Thanks."

Liz stepped over to him next, and kissed him on the cheek. "You hang in there, Liam."

She made her way to Shane last. "Yes," she said, and then made her way toward the door.

"Yeah, baby!" Shane shouted, pumping his arm in the air.

Liz burst into laughter, but continued to make her way out of the room without sparing them a look.

After Liz exited, Liam glanced over at Cara. "You better now?"

She nodded.

"Then your uncle and I will go grab some sodas and give you a few minutes alone with Katie, okay?"

"Thanks Dad."

He bent down and kissed Katie on the lips, thankful for her breath, thankful that she didn't need assistance from a machine to breathe. He hoped it was a positive indication that her mind and body just needed rest, but that her systems were still functioning.

He squeezed Cara's shoulder, and then followed Shane out the door. In the hallway, he gave his brother a curious look. "What's going on with you and Liz?"

Shane's face split into a cocky grin. "I just got me a dinner date."

That was the last thing Liam had expected to hear. He'd gotten the distinct impression that Liz wasn't overly fond of Shane. "Well, good for you."

Shane must have thought so too since he whistled throughout the entire walk to the vending machines and back.

Inside Katie's room, Liam handed one of the Cokes to Cara. "You look nice today," he said, eyeing her skinny jeans, red top, and matching red wedge sandals.

"Sabby and I are going out tonight."

"Where you going?"

"To the mall, maybe the movies. So—" Cara turned toward Katie "—I don't wanna talk about my dream anymore, 'cause Liz is probably right. Anyway, remember Josh, the guy I was talking to?" She paused for a long moment staring at Katie as if she expected her to respond. "He's my boyfriend now."

Liam's jaw tightened. "What happened to Travis?" Not that he had particularly liked Travis, but at least he'd met him, and had had the opportunity to give him the don't mess with my daughter lecture. Much to Cara's chagrin, the talk had occurred when he just happened to be on the front porch cleaning his dad's old Remington rifle.

Cara spared him a glance. "He is soooo yesterday." She twisted back to Katie. "Josh is hot. Really hot. You'd like him, Katie."

"What would *I* think of him?" he asked, even though he already knew the answer. He didn't like him, sight unseen.

Cara rolled her eyes. "You don't like *any* of my boyfriends, Dad."

"Because none of them are good enough for my girl."

"See what I have to put up with, Katie?" Cara sighed dramatically. "Everything's easier with you around."

"Isn't that the damn truth?" he muttered, taking Katie's hand and rubbing it in between his. "We all need you back, Katie-cat."

Cara plopped down and scooted her chair close to the bed. "Let's talk more about Josh. First, did I mention—he's reeeaaaaaally hot?" Cara slid him an evil grin. "He has blond hair with this tiny, cute little wave in the front."

Letting out a long exhale, Liam ambled over to join Shane at the windows. "Talk to me, bro. I don't need to hear details about the newest boyfriend."

"Why not?" Shane's lips curved up. "This is fascinating talk."

Cara continued to prattle on. "He has the most gorgeous blue eyes." She let out a long, dreamy sigh. "Turquoise blue, like the Caribbean Sea."

Liam pinned a look on Shane. "What's happening with you, other than your upcoming date with Liz? Got something to take my mind off *Josh*?"

They chatted about his business, one of his custom jobs, and how the Yankees, Shane's team, had kicked the Orioles ass the night before.

Half an hour later, Jen arrived, and Liam, Shane, and Cara left. As they passed by the ICU waiting room, Liam peeked inside. Carolyn sat in the corner rocker, staring out the window with a faraway expression.

He and Cara exchanged looks.

"Why don't you go in and say hi?" he suggested. "We'll wait for you out here."

"What the hell?" Shane muttered.

"I don't know what to say," Cara said, scuffing her shoe on the floor.

Cara had a point. Had Carolyn made an effort, or hell, had she responded to any of Katie's attempts, she'd already know her granddaughter. But damn it, this was for Katie.

"I know you haven't been close with her," he said. "But she's hurting. Katie is her little girl, just like you're mine. She's feeling the same kind of love, the same kind of grief as us."

Cara's face lit with empathy, and she pushed through the waiting room door. Carolyn's expression brightened when Cara approached, and his heart warmed.

Shane cleared his throat. "What the hell?" he repeated. "Just because you have PAI doesn't mean you should push it off on Cara."

He raised a brow.

"You know, PAI." Shane flashed a wicked grin. "Parental Acceptance Issues."

"You made that up." Liam huffed out a breath. "That's not a real thing."

"It is for you."

He flipped Shane off even though they both knew it was true. "This has nothing to do with me. It's good for Cara, she's never had a grandmother."

A full fifteen minutes later, Cara strutted out of the waiting room, earbuds jammed in her ears, and the three of them made their way downstairs together. When they reached the first floor, Cara walked out of the elevator in front of him and Shane, her head bobbing to the music.

"So you and Liz, huh?" He nudged Shane. "Honestly, I didn't think she liked you."

"Guess you were wrong." Grinning, Shane stuffed his hands in his pockets.

Shane and Liz as a couple? Liam tossed the idea around in his head. Both had a less than stellar history of dating choices and they shared a fear of commitment. The longest Shane had dated anyone was just under two years, and it had been rocky at best. Liz had been married once, although only for a brief period of time. Maybe they would make a fitting pair, after all. He shared his assessment with Shane.

"I just haven't met my Katie yet," Shane said matter-of-factly.

"I think Katie would like to see the two of you together."

Shane's grin widened. "Anything for our Katie."

Liam chuckled.

In the parking lot, they quickly found Shane's Hummer. Once they were all seated, Cara nudged him from the backseat, and pulled out her earphones. "So, G-ma—it's still weird calling her that—wants to take me and Sabby for a mani-pedi tomorrow. Is that okay?"

Shane let out a low growl, but Liam warmed at the thought of Cara finally having the opportunity to connect with her grandmother. "Of course."

Cara stuffed in her earbuds again, and burst out words to the song, "Yeah Boy."

When they stopped at a traffic light on Main Street, he elbowed Shane and pointed at the fender of the bright yellow Jeep in front of them. The bumper sticker read: *If I wanted a Hummer, I'd call your wife.*

Shane eyed the back seat, presumably to see if Cara was paying attention. "I probably already did his wife," he said. "You know, before they got married."

"You do get around," Liam said on a laugh. "Problem is, they never last." He studied his brother. "Given your upcoming date with Liz, I take it you and Katrina are done?"

Shane turned left at the light. "She went back to L.A. a couple of weeks ago to shop her screenplay."

"I didn't know."

"Didn't want to bother you with it with everything that's going on." Shane blew out a breath. "Shit happens."

"I'm sorry." Trina was the first woman Shane had dated for any period of time since his live-in girlfriend had left him almost six years ago. Even so, Shane and Trina had broken up and gotten back together more times than Liam could recall.

"Don't be," Shane said, pulling into their driveway. "The on again, off again thing was getting old."

Cara jumped out, still jamming to her music, and strutted toward the house.

Liam climbed out slowly, circled the hood, and then leaned against the side of the Hummer staring at his home. Positioned on a hill angled to the east, both the front porch and the back deck had stunning mountain views. Shane and a few buddies had helped him renovate the house just before he and Katie had married, expanding the living room and kitchen and adding a master suite. They'd also put in another bedroom to make room for more children.

He'd been born and raised in the stone house and had lived there for his entire life. He loved the shit out of it, but now he couldn't imagine living there without Katie.

Shane gave him a sidelong look. "You okay?"

He puffed out a breath, thinking about Katie. It had been just over a week since the accident but it felt like it had been months since he'd walked hand-in-hand with her around their property or sat with her on the front porch swing watching the sun set. "Fine."

Shane's expression indicated he didn't buy it, but there was nothing else to say. There was no escaping the situation—he could only deal with it as best as he could.

But what if Katie didn't return? That dark thought ambushed him every morning, and even though he tried to push it aside, the gut-wrenching possibility lurked over him like a phantom waiting to pounce.

KATIE PALMED down the cloud mists that had built up around her even as Bear sliced through the fog flinging white puffs. "My silly Bear," she said laughing.

Bear flopped down in front of her, activating a blizzard of white.

"Bear loves his cloud play." Black Eagle reached over to scratch the dog's ears.

"Woof, woof." Bear thumped his tail and more white wisps flew about.

Katie brushed the cloud puffs from her shirt, and tipped her head toward Black Eagle. "Remember that dream thing you told me about? How guides can pop into a human's dreams?"

Black Eagle nodded. "Sure."

"Could you do that for Liam?" she asked, swirling a finger along the cloud base. "He needs help moving past his guilt over how he was before his parents' death. You know what I'm talking about?"

"All is known here," Posie said. "And of course we'll help."

"But we'll send Molly and Patrick instead." Black Eagle's lips ticked up. "That would mean more to Liam."

Katie's eyes widened in surprise. "You could send Liam's parents?"

Black Eagle squeezed her hand. "Consider it done."

Fluffing Bear's ears, Katie looked from one guide to another. "Any news on my status?" Her chest tightened as she thought about Liam, Cara, Savannah. "And if I'm going back?"

"It's all up to you, Katie." Posie's tone was soft, compassionate, and encouraging. "Remember our talk about intentions?"

"Yes." She absently rubbed Bear's belly. "And my intention is to go home. I mean it's wonderful here, but I miss Liam, Cara, and Pan so much." She let out a long breath. "And I need to get home for Savannah. Otherwise, what will happen to her?"

Bear nuzzled his head on her leg. "But I'll miss all of you." She cupped her hands around Bear's face. "That includes you my fluffy Bear." She kissed the top of his curly head.

"We'll be with you no matter what you decide," Posie said. "Always have been, always will be."

Black Eagle nodded his agreement. "And it will be different now that you know how to connect with us."

She tilted her head. "I do?"

"Sure." Black Eagle chuckled. "Now that you know we're here, you can just ask for help. We can pop into a dream or just drop by."

"That would be awesome." She pressed a hand to her stomach to steady the flurry of relief at the knowledge that she wouldn't lose this connection with her guides. "How will it work? Will I see you like this, in bodies?"

"We could, but there's lots of constraints in the Earth dimension." Black Eagle pressed his lips together. "Takes a while to don our Earth Suits to get in down there. Easier and quicker for us to come as energy."

She giggled over the term *Earth Suit*, and then wondered how she would know her guides were there if she couldn't see them. Before she could ask, Posie put a hand on her shoulder and it began to tingle.

"You'll feel us, just as you feel my energy now."

Katie smiled at Posie, her belly settling with her guide's reassurance.

"Bear too?" she asked looking down at her dog.

Bear lifted his head and lopped his wet, slobbery tongue on her face.

Laughing, she fluffed his ears. "I'll take that as a yes." She looked from Bear to Posie to Black Eagle. "So how do we do this? Do you have a spaceship that'll take me back?"

Black Eagle snickered.

"You just need to share your intentions with the universe," Posie said. "Just like we taught you."

Katie scrunched her nose. "That's it? But how do I get back?"

"That's the first part," Black Eagle said. "Then you must believe. It's the believing that will get you back."

"Remember believing is crucial." Posie took her hand. "Let's work on it now. Close your eyes and take a long, deep breath."

Katie did as Posie had instructed.

"Now think about what you want—in minute detail." Posie's voice was soft and nurturing, and it put Katie in a Zen-like state. "Visualize being at home and who's there with you. Liam, Cara, Pan. Pick up Savannah in Texas and bring her home." Katie did just that, and a warm, fuzzy feeling formed in her heart. "Create a picture in your mind that's so crisp, so real, you can actually feel it. Keep envisioning this scenario…and believe it."

As Katie focused, vibrant images spun and swirled in her mind's eye. Her beautiful stone home, walking hand-in-hand with Liam around their acreage, playing with Pan. Cooking with Cara, Shane coming over for dinner. A tender reunion with Savannah. Working alongside Liam at Callahan Cycles.

The more she reflected, the more she visualized. The more she visualized the more real it became.

Posie's soft voice drifted into her consciousness, offering new instruction. "Now, you need an intention to go along with your visualization. It will become your mantra. Something that embodies your intention to be at home. I'll offer up thoughts, but the intention needs to be yours." Posie gently massaged Katie's hands. "Something like: I'm home. I love home. Home is where my heart is."

An image of Dorothy and her glittery red shoes came to Katie. "How about, 'there's no place like home?' "

"That's perfect." Posie lightly stroked her hair. "Now, repeat your intention out loud or to yourself while you continue to visualize home, and then when you're ready, slowly open your eyes."

"How did that feel?" Posie asked after she finally blinked her eyes open.

Katie hugged her knees to her chin. "Warm, comfortable. *Real.*"

Posie smiled brightly. "That's exactly how it's supposed to feel. I want you to follow this process right before you go to bed tonight and again first thing in the morning."

"You can also put your desires out anytime simply by directing your thoughts," Black Eagle said. "And by repeating your mantra."

Katie playfully tossed white fluffs onto Bear's head while practicing her mantra. "There's no place like home. I want to go home. No place like home...."

Bear thumped his tail wildly, propelling white puffs all around them.

Katie shook the white cloud wisps from her face and arm. "What's is it, Bear?"

"Woof, woof." Bear gave Black Eagle a doggie grin, and the two of them shifted into play mode, dipping hands and paws into the cloud, packing cloud balls.

"Watch it, Katie," Posie warned just as a cloud ball hurtled through the air.

Katie scooped up white fluff and packed it into a ball, then she winged it at Black Eagle with child-like wonder. Posie joined her and before long they were in the middle of a good-natured cloud ball fight.

A short while later, a woman appeared. Katie laughed as the stranger ducked to avoid being hit by a fluffy white ball.

"Cease fire," Black Eagle shouted as he greeted their visitor. Posie and Bear stepped over to greet her next.

Putting down her cloud ball, Katie studied the visitor. She wore blue jeans and a flowery top, and she seemed oddly familiar. Medium blonde hair styled in sharp layers with deep blue eyes that reminded her of Cara's. *Rose—Cara's mother.*

"I knew Katie would recognize you," Posie said to Rose.

Rose extended her arms, and Katie stepped into the woman's embrace. After a long hug, they released. "I hope you don't mind a visit." Rose tipped her head toward Posie. "Posie thought you'd be up for it."

"Yes, absolutely." Katie wiped white fluffs from her body eager to spend time with Cara's birth mother.

"Great," Rose said as Posie and Black Eagle faded into the background.

Katie and Rose sank into the plush cloud while Bear sprawled in between them, tongue hanging out, clearly tuckered from the cloud ball fun.

"First, I want to thank you for raising Cara," Rose said. "You're doing a wonderful job, you and Liam both."

"Thanks." Her heart tugged thinking of Cara. "That means a lot, especially coming from you."

"Cara's a good girl. She's beautiful and strong, true to herself." Rose smiled. "And popular with the boys."

"Yes," Katie agreed, gently rubbing her foot on Bear's exposed belly. "I connected with her last night in my dreams and she told me about her latest."

"Josh." Rose scrunched her face. "Tell Cara that Seth is a better choice for her."

"Oh." Katie smiled. "I never thought of Cara and Seth, but I'll let her know. Liam and I love Seth, he's practically grown up with us." She glanced over at Rose. "I guess you know that."

Rose nodded. "He's turned into a fine young man thanks to you and Liam." Rose stretched her legs out in front of her. "On second thought, don't share my observation with Cara. Our mission is to guide, not interfere. Instead, why don't you tell her that we visited, that I'm well and I watch over her?"

Touched, Katie put a hand over her heart. "I will."

"While you're at it, tell Liam about our visit, too. That I'm doing great and he needs to stop the guilt trip."

Katie shifted awkwardly. She wondered if she should be discussing Liam's feelings with his former wife.

Rose reached down to rub Bear's ears. "I know he feels guilty because he didn't love me. But, our purpose wasn't to form an endless love. It was to keep him and Shane together, and to create Cara, and we did a fabulous job on both fronts. We weren't meant for each other beyond that." Rose waved a hand above her head, and Katie followed her gaze toward the sky overhead. "My guy's up there. After having Cara, I left Earth to reunite with him, which gave Liam the opportunity to find you. I understood that you and Liam would care for Cara."

It was mind-boggling...but before she could completely wrap her head around Rose's message, an intense longing for home nipped at her chest. "I miss Cara," she said on a heavy sigh. "Liam, too."

"I know you do. But remember, all of this is happening for a reason. To everything there is a purpose."

"That's what they say." Katie pressed her lips together. There were a lot of things that had occurred in her life that didn't seem to have a good reason. The motorcycle accident, her coma. Her inability to get pregnant, her parents dislike for Liam. "It's sure hard to understand."

"We have additional senses up here that enable a big picture view." Rose snapped her fingers, materializing a bottle of champagne and two glasses. "Join me?"

"Yes, please." Katie contemplated Rose's statement. She wasn't sure she bought it. What about the bad stuff that happened— starving children, people with cancer, innocent victims of war? And all of life's little frustrations...surely, they served no purpose.

Rose popped the cork, poured bubbly liquid into the glasses, then handed one to her. "Now, where were we? Oh yes, purpose. On Earth, you don't always have enough information to connect the dots. Regardless, there is a reason for everything that occurs.

Let me offer a few examples," she said. "Your bank's charity motorcycle ride. That particular event served a purpose. Liam signing up and filling in as ride captain, even though he rarely participated in group rides."

At the time, Katie had chalked it up as luck. But Rose's perspective was consistent with Black Eagle's who'd insisted there was no such thing.

"Now, I'll share a minor occurrence that avoided a major one," Rose said smiling at her.

Enjoying their visit and all that she was learning, Katie raised her glass. "Share away!"

"Remember last fall, when you decided to go to a yoga class at a different studio? You drove to Frederick only to find the studio locked up."

Katie nodded. "Yeah, it took me twenty minutes to get there, twenty plus to get home, and I didn't even get to do yoga. Very frustrating."

"Yet there was a purpose." Rose took a long sip of champagne. "That class would have ended at eight o'clock, and you would have left a few minutes later. At the exact moment you would have merged onto Falls Road, a car ran the red light. Thankfully, no one was in the intersection at that time. Had you taken that class, *you* would have been there."

Katie took a quick sharp breath, then drained her glass.

"Time for one more—the mall incident. Remember how you almost didn't go to the mall that day when you met up with Liam and Cara?"

She remembered it well. It had been the weekend after the motorcycle ride. Saturday, grocery shopping day—that is, until her favorite pair of jeans ripped—and she went to the mall instead. Liam had left her a bunch of messages throughout that week. While she had desperately wanted to go out with him, she'd hesitated, concerned over her father's reaction. Even so, she hadn't been able to stop thinking about him. After she heard the bliss song and read Liz's article on inner strength, she'd asked God for a sign. A couple of hours later, she went to the mall and ran into Liam and Cara. She had started dating Liam right after—because God trumped her father.

She let out a low laugh. "Are you telling me that my jeans ripped on purpose just so I'd go to the mall?"

Rose's lips quirked. "The universe works in mysterious ways."

CHAPTER EIGHT

On Monday evening, Shane took Liz to dinner at the Rock Springs Inn. Perched on top of scenic Thunder Gap, the long-standing building was hundreds of years old and had seen its share of history. Reportedly, young Lieutenant George Washington had stayed at the inn. In the late 1700's, pioneers had traveled past on their westward trail. During the Civil War, the structure had transformed into confederate headquarters…and just over five years ago, the inn had served as the gathering place for Katie and Liam's wedding reception.

"Brings back memories," Liz said as he held the door open for her.

"Sure does." Trailing behind Liz, Shane took in the view. Snug blue capris tastefully showcased her backside. His gaze flicked back and forth between her very fine ass and her shoes, white heels that were high, strappy, and very sexy.

At the hostess station, Liz twirled toward him and flashed a killer smile, her lacey top fluttering and dipping with her movement. He sucked in a breath at the unexpected quake in his gut. Although why he was surprised was beyond him. God hadn't skimped one little bit when he made Liz. She was lean and fit with generous curves in all the right places.

He cleared his throat. "Reservations for Callahan," he told the hostess, and then placed his hand in the small of Liz's back as they were escorted to his requested location in the newer section of the inn. Liz's sheer shirt, the same shade of blue as her pants, was silky soft, making him wonder if what she had on underneath was just as soft.

Their table was positioned next to the windows, facing Rock Springs Trail. He sat next to Liz facing the windows so they both had a view. He tipped his head toward the rolling hills and the small, quaint chapel across the street where Liam and Katie had married. "A good place for a wedding."

"Despite my family, it was a happy day." Liz blew out a breath, puffing her bangs. "I still can't believe my parents didn't go to Katie's wedding."

Shifting, he looked into Liz's eyes, which were the same shade of blue as her shirt, like a perfect summer sky.

"You're not your family, Liz." He'd been plenty pissed at her parents at the time, too. But it hadn't been her fault. "You can't take on their actions."

When their waiter approached, he ordered appetizers and a bottle of expensive red wine, waiting for Liz's nod of agreement to each before committing.

After Chad left, Liz glanced up with shimmering eyes. "That's a nice thing to say. Katie is incredibly happy with Liam. My folks need to get over it."

"Agreed on both counts," he said. "I remember you from the wedding. You came dateless."

Liz's long lashes flew up.

"What?" He shrugged. "I'm observant, especially when it comes to beautiful women."

"Your lady talk is improving." Her lips curved up. "But, I'm surprised you remembered, especially since you had a skinny, big-boobed blonde at your side."

"Ah, Barbie." He let out a low laugh. "That didn't last long. What about Sabby's dad? When did the two of you split up?"

"When Sabby was just a year old," Liz said on a sigh.

He shook his head. "Asshole."

That made her smile.

"Yeah, he really was. I married Phillip when I was twenty-one and pregnant. Young and naïve, I thought I was in love." She took a long sip of her wine. "Talk about family drama. My dad flipped out when he found out I was pregnant. Although part of that might have been because I didn't tell him as much as he observed my growing belly."

He laughed. "Liz, you're too much. Then what?"

"Dad made his usual demands—tried to talk me out of marrying Phillip, asked if I really wanted to have a child," she said, her voice tight. "So Phillip and I eloped."

"Wow." Controlling son-of-a-bitch. "I can't believe he pushed you like that."

Liz half shrugged. "He's a good man. He just likes things his way. I tend to stay under his radar except when I feel strongly about something—like marrying Phillip and having Sabby—then I have no problem standing up to him." She put a couple of stuffed mushrooms on her plate. "And he comes around. He was a lifesaver when I got my first job and had to travel. Mom and Dad helped me find and pay for high quality daycare and a nanny. I'm grateful for that, for the opportunity to advance my career, while at the same time making sure Sabby was well cared for."

"Well, that's something. Kind of like Liam helped me."

Liz titled her head to one side. "How did Liam help you?"

He took a bite of a mushroom. The crab and Italian cheese stuffing was so tasty he had to suppress a moan. There was nothing better than good food and good wine, other than maybe a good woman. He put down his fork and smiled at Liz. "Liam put me through college." He took another bite of the delicious appetizer and washed it down with wine. Even after all these years, gratitude for what his brother had done welled inside him. "*He* didn't get to go to college because he put me through; said he wouldn't have gone anyway, but I don't think that's true. My life would be so different if Liam hadn't come through. I owe him—big time."

Over salads, he shifted their conversation to lighter topics. Cara. Sabby. The break in hot weather which was expected to return early next week. Favorite Katie memories.

"Sabby mentioned that you lived in Paris," he said. "When did you move back?"

"We lived there for a couple of years. I loved it. We just moved back to Georgetown last year."

His lips curved up. "I'm glad you came back."

Liz tucked a lock of silky hair behind her ear, and tossed him a flirty smile.

Tipping the appetizer plate toward her, he offered her the last mushroom cap. "Tell me about your work. What's it like being a writer?"

Liz's entire face lit up. "I love it. Helping people experience new, exciting lands without ever leaving their homes, showing readers life in another person's shoes. I'm grateful I get to do what I love every day—" she looked at him with a modest, but proud, expression "—and make a decent living at it." She pushed her salad plate aside. "Now that I've developed a solid reputation, I have a lot of flexibility. I can work from wherever, unless of course, it's a travel assignment. I'm also at the point where I can take a job or pass on it, and I've been traveling less over the last year."

The waiter returned, cleared dishes and delivered their main courses. Shane thanked him before turning his attention back to Liz.

"I can appreciate the flexibility because I have that, too. Guess it's easy to take it for granted," he said. "These days I have just a handful of clients who followed me from my New York days."

Time to turn up the noise. "So, Liz, what would you write about me?" he asked, sawing into his thick helping of beef.

She took a long sip of water. "Shane Callahan, abrasive... smart...loyal...sexy."

He grinned, and they both laughed.

They deepened their conversation over Beef Wellington, his dinner choice and Liz's Amore Cavatappi pasta. He learned that she'd been published in most of the mainstream magazines, which ultimately had convinced her father that writing could be a lucrative profession despite his initial insistence that she go to business school.

"Hard to believe we've known each other for five years," Liz said giving him the once over, "but we barely know one another."

"Here's to getting to know each other better," he quipped, tapping his glass against hers. "Tell me something else I don't know about you other than the fact that you write for top magazines like *Playboy*."

She laughed. "Wrote for *Playboy*. One article. It's not like I'm on staff there."

"What was your *Playboy* article about?"

"It's in the December two thousand ten edition," she said, curving her lips into a wicked smile. "Get yourself a copy."

He chuckled. "Guess I'll have to. Well then, tell me about this Phillip."

"Not much to tell. I thought I was in love, only to later realize I was in love with Phillip's laid back style. Him—not so much." She swirled the pasta on her plate, took a bite before continuing. "He was a fledging artist, a year older than me. We were young, crazy kids."

"What happened?" he probed.

Liz put down her fork. "I thought he was a free-spirit, and with his art, he was. But he ended up being just another controlling man." She ran a finger around the rim of her wine glass. Shane understood that she was also referring to her father, so he didn't ask. "My career was on a roll, but Phillip had the nerve to say it wasn't creative enough or artistic enough or some such bullshit. He suggested I quit my job and write the great American novel instead." Her mouth set in a hard line. "Had I done that, the bills wouldn't have been paid since Phillip wasn't willing to get a job because it would—" she made air quotes "—*prostitute his art*."

What an asswipe. Maybe he was old school, but in Shane's estimation Phillip should have been more concerned about providing for his wife and child rather than worrying about *prostituting his art*.

He studied Liz and sipped his water in silence waiting for her to continue.

"When Sabby came along," she said, "I was thrilled, but things between Phillip and I got worse. I don't think he ever wanted to be a daddy; he paid no attention to Sabby. I'm not sure he wanted to be married, either. He actually said that Sabby and I stifled his creativity."

"Sir Richard Cranium," he grumbled.

At her puzzled look, he spelled it out. "You know, a royal dickhead."

Liz tossed her head back and laughed. "Well, lesson learned."

"And the lesson was?"

"I don't need any man telling me what to do."

"So now you steer clear of relationships?" he asked, leaning toward her.

"Maybe." She gave him a sidelong look. "But it's not entirely Phillip's fault. My independent streak runs as big as Texas, and I've always been a bit of a wild child."

"I like that about you." Topping off her wine, Shane thought about the wild, crazy things they could do together. But when his southern region twitched with readiness, he turned the conversation down a notch. It was too early in the evening to sport a hard-on.

"Sabby says you date a lot," he teased.

"She exaggerates. I wouldn't say a lot, but I date. Just because I'm reluctant about relationships doesn't mean I can't have fun."

Shane caught a glimpse of that wild in her eyes, and the twitch returned. He crossed his leg and willed it away. "No one's interested you enough to move to the next step? Not since you were twenty-one? And that couldn't have been seventeen years ago, not from where I sit." He eyed her up and down, and wiggled his brows.

Liz's lips curved. "You are quite the flatterer, but it *has* been that long. And no to your other question—no one has piqued my interest. I've had plenty of fun, but no lasting relationships. Not a great track record, I know." She touched a napkin to the corner of her mouth, placed it on her lap. "Enough about me. How 'bout you, Shane? Ever been married or in a long-term relationship?"

"Married—no. One long-term relationship."

"Yeah?" When he remained silent, she pushed. "You gonna make me pry?"

Leaning back in his chair, he studied Liz. Pretty blue eyes, and dark shoulder-length hair with long bangs and layers that came off as professional and flirty. The style suited her. It was both edgy and feminine. Eyes on hers, he nodded.

"Fair is fair. Ironically, my relationship track record is similar to yours," he said. "Jana and I dated for six months and then lived together for a year and a half. It was a while ago, back when I lived in New York."

"How long did you live there?"

"Nine years. I went to college in New York, earned a business degree from NYU."

The waiter returned to take their dessert order. They agreed to share a piece of carrot cake, and also ordered two cappuccinos.

"And after college?" she asked.

"I marched straight to Wall Street and secured a spot in trading," he said with pride in his voice. It had been a bold move, but it had paid off.

"Must've been exciting," she said, "but crazy, too."

"You can't even imagine." He flashed back to the pandemonium of the New York Stock Exchange. Traders in blue jackets, rows of high-speed computers. Huge electronic screens, big wins and big losses, shouting in the pit.

"What brought you back to this area?" she wanted to know.

"Cara and Liam. Gem Valley is my home and I guess it always will be. Liam had been raising Cara alone and I wanted to be around. I'd already made a name for myself on the street so I figured I could work from anywhere. My relationship with Jana had just ended, so that was a factor, too." He took a forkful of the carrot cake the waiter had just delivered. "Time goes by quickly; it's been six years since I've been back."

"Do you miss the city?" Liz asked, also digging into the cake.

"Not really." He took a thoughtful sip of his cappuccino. "I've fallen in love with this area all over again. Besides, I go back on occasion, mostly for client visits."

"So, tell me about this girlfriend," she said.

"We met through a mutual friend and I fell quickly. Jana was different from other women I'd dated. Intelligent, fun, attractive. Not gorgeous, but attractive in a sexy kind of way." He shook his head. "Sorry, probably TMI. Anyway, we dated for six months, although given my job that didn't entail a lot of quality time together. I worked like a dog, day and night. Probably why I asked Jana to move in with me." He guzzled more cappuccino to soothe the sting of betrayal he still felt all these years later. "It didn't work out."

Liz narrowed her eyes waiting for more. He thought she was going to push for more information that he had no intention of sharing. Thankfully, after a long uncomfortable silence, she changed the subject.

ON THE SHORT drive back to Liam's, Liz reflected on the evening. She'd been comfortable talking—*really* talking—with Shane. She was usually reserved with men, especially on first dates. Perhaps she shouldn't be surprised considering she and Shane had for all intents and purposes been living together for the past week. Together, they'd made meals, spent time with the girls, and handled basic chores. In the process, they'd gotten to know each other better.

Shane pulled into the drive and walked around the Hummer to open her door. Extending a hand, he helped her down and escorted her to the front porch.

Leaning against the door frame, he tipped his head toward the driveway. "Looks like the girls are still out."

"Yes." And wasn't that convenient? Her pulse thumped eagerly. Ever since Shane had asked her out, she'd been thinking about their date, about what they might do *after* their date. "I don't expect them back for a while."

"I had a nice time. A surprisingly nice time," he said.

Shaking her head, she let out a short laugh. "You sure have a way with words, but I'll let it go since I had a nice time, too." Underneath, she knew what he meant. A week ago, her perception of him had been shallow playboy. They'd both done an about-face over the course of a week.

"I'm usually more suave. For some reason, you get me all tongue tied." Stepping closer, he cupped his hands around her face. They were big and warm and smooth, and they made her cheeks tingle. "I wonder why that is," he whispered huskily.

He was so close she could feel his breath caressing her cheek. Her heart hammered in her chest, and her gaze settled on his lips, making her wonder what they would feel like on hers. The tingles moved from her cheeks to her breasts to her belly. She wanted him to kiss her more than she'd wanted anything in her life. Mindlessly, she leaned in closer.

Shane slid his hands around the back of her neck, and pressed her in close. He brushed his lips over hers, smooth and light. Her body came alive and pleasure pooled in all the good spots. He drew back to brush a finger over her lips, all the while holding her gaze as her entire being hummed with anticipation.

He kissed her again, slipping his tongue inside to tangle with hers while his hands trailed the outline of her breasts. When she let out a whimper of pleasure, he dropped his hands to her ass. She couldn't resist wiggling against his palms, and had the satisfaction of hearing a moan rumble from deep in his throat.

He nibbled on her bottom lip, her earlobe, her cheek, then licked the long expanse of her neck, and every nerve ending in her body sizzled. One hand plunged into her hair while the other slowly trailed south, hovering at the waistband of her capris. She sucked in a sharp breath when his fingers edged underneath and feathered her skin.

She moved her hands under his shirt and across his very fine chest. Shane's fingers dipped lower, trailing along the band of her pantie. She held her breath in sweet anticipation, wanting, *needing* his touch to alleviate the hot ache between her legs. But he didn't touch her there. Instead he whipped her around, pushed her against the door, and reclaimed her lips. His kiss was deep, wet, and needy. He kissed her until the earth moved and she saw shooting stars. When he shifted and pressed his hard body against hers, proof of his desire thumped between her legs, making her even hotter than she had been seconds ago.

She didn't usually have this strong of a reaction to a man. But it had been a really long time and her under-utilized girl parts were on high alert, craving the attention they so desperately needed. A little voice inside her head urged her to drag Shane inside and up the stairs where she could have her way with him, and damn it, she wanted to. Not that she normally behaved that way on a first date.

Normally, she asserted her independence. Made a guy *really* want her before she gave in. But she yearned for a different plan with Shane. She'd grown very fond of him during their week of living in close quarters. And now he had gotten her all hot and horny....

"Shane?" she managed in a raw voice that didn't sound a bit like her own.

Before he could answer, a truck rumbled up the drive and parked next to the porch.

Shane stumbled back a step. "Jesus," he muttered, running a hand over his short hair. "Bad timing."

She had to agree. Even so, she snorted out a laugh as her eyes flicked toward the beat-up truck. "I feel like a teenager who just got busted."

As Sabby and Cara climbed out of the truck's cab, she moved to the edge of the porch to regain her composure. When the girls lingered in the drive chatting with their dates, she turned and batted her lashes at Shane. "To be continued," she mouthed.

THE SCENT of her grandmother's tea wafted through Katie's dream. Rolling over, she inhaled the fusion of aromas—cinnamon, ginger, nutmeg.

When a tongue licked her cheek, she instinctively rubbed her dog's head. "Pan," she murmured, groggy from sleep. "I'm having a good dream. Go to sleep, dream with me."

Another lick. "Oh, Pan." Shifting to one side, she blinked her eyes open. But it was Bear lying next to her, not Pan. She shook off the dream. *You're not in Kansas anymore, Katie, not in Maryland...not even on planet Earth.*

She sat up and hugged her dog. "I might not be in Kansas, but I sure smell Grammie's tea."

"Then come on over and have a cup," a familiar voice called out.

Stunned, Katie spun around and found her grandmother on the other side of the cloud in a big rocking chair.

"Grammie!" Bouncing over, she threw her arms around her grandmother. "I can't believe it's you!" She held on tight, drawing warmth from the woman she'd adored from her earliest days. When she drew back, she kissed her grandmother on the cheek and gave her the once over.

A healthy build, bright smile, and positive energy radiated the same warmth and kindness Katie had remembered from her youth. Twinkling brown eyes connected with hers as her grandmother handed her a cup of tea. Katie took the mug and sat on the open rocker.

Bear pushed his head onto her grandmother's lap. "Howdy, Bear." She rubbed the dog's head. "Haven't seen you since the McGregors' festivities." Bear wiggled and wagged as she rubbed him, then he flopped down in the space in between them.

"Grammie—it's so good to see you." Katie took a sip of her tea. "Yum—this is every bit as good as I remember. I try to make it on occasion, but mine isn't as good as yours."

"You need to use fresh ingredients, not the jar stuff. Fresh cinnamon sticks, fresh vanilla bean, and a little more ginger wouldn't hurt, either."

"How do you know?" Laughing, Katie raised a palm. "Never mind, I keep forgetting everyone knows everything here. Oh, Grammie, I've missed you so much." She reached over and took her grandmother's hand. "I so wanted you to meet Liam. And Cara, too."

"I have, honey." Her grandmother squeezed her hand. "I'm with you down there. Quite a bit, actually."

"I've wondered," Katie said, picking up her drink. "Sometimes I smell your tea and your lilac lotion." She took a sip of the drink that evoked so many fond memories. "Mmm, so good."

"It's like nectar for the soul," her grandmother said with a wink. "Now, how's my girl doing?"

Katie sighed. "My life is kind of a mess." She had a child who needed her, but she couldn't get to Savannah. Even if she could, she had yet to tell Liam about her. She didn't have a job, didn't even know what she wanted to do. And she was in a coma, incapable of dealing with any of it.

"Phsaw!" Grammie waved her words away with a flick of her wrist. "Katie, girl, you're going through a growing patch, that's all. You'll figure it out."

"Thanks, Grammie." Tears trembled on Katie's eyelids. "I need to get home to tell Liam about Savannah." Anxiety unfurled in her belly, and she lowered a hand to gently rub and soothe. "Hopefully he'll be okay with us adopting Savannah. Then I have to figure out what to do with the rest of my life." She nearly mentioned her dream of having other children, but stopped short. On the highway of her life, that aspiration was like a lead car, always in sight but just out of reach. Regardless, she'd been putting her intentions into the universe like Posie and Black Eagle had instructed, but she was still working on getting her mind out of the way.

"It will all work out," Grammie said, taking a long noisy sip of tea. "As long as you follow the Law of Attraction."

The *what*? At her confused look, her grandma let out a low laugh. "It's what Posie and Black Eagle have been teaching you— Ask, believe, receive."

"Oh, *that*." Katie nodded. "I'm working on it."

"That's my girl. We need to get you home." Grammie reached over and patted her knee.

"Once you truly believe, you'll be back in a flash. But believing is the hardest part."

"You got that right," Katie said. "I'm putting out my intentions—I guess that's the ask part, and I'm sure ready to receive. But it's hard to believe what I want will happen just because I want it."

"It's a challenge because we've all been taught that reality is what we see. We've even made up sayings like, 'I'll believe it when I see it,' that go along with that kind of thinking. But that way of looking at it contradicts the Law of Attraction. To get it to work for you, you must believe that what you've asked for will happen. It requires an unflappable faith." Grammie finished her tea and put her mug down. "Either that or an understanding of quantum physics, but science was never your thing."

Katie let out a half laugh. "I'm gonna have to go with the faith option."

"I'll help you, then." Grammie rose, picked up the tea pot and refilled both of their mugs. "I'm going to share a few ways this universal law has already worked in your life. Once you understand that it really works, it will be easier to believe."

Katie nodded. "That would be helpful." She took another sip of tea, savoring the delicious spices in her drink, and appreciating this precious time with her grandma. Growing up, she'd spent as much time with her Grammie as her parents would allow. She had loved spending the night at her grandma's house, a stark contrast to her own formal home. Her parents had been—and still were—rigid and traditional, and Katie had felt like the black sheep of the family. She'd wanted to play with the collector dolls instead of looking at them; she'd wanted to wear jeans and climb trees instead of sitting at the table in her dress listening to her father discuss commodities. But at Grammie's she could be wild and free. They would eat dinner in the living room and mosey around in Grammie's gardens, uncon-cerned about the dirt on their clothes. It had been Grammie who had given her a glimpse of the universe beyond the conventions she had learned at her parents' Methodist church. Her grandma had taught her the basics of other spiritual traditions, like Taoism, Gnos-ticism, Buddhism, and Hinduism. Grammie explained that all reli-gions and spiritual traditions tied together, and that they were simply different approaches to connecting with God. While her parents had pooh-pooh'ed Grammie's ideas, they had resonated with Katie.

Grammie rocked back in her chair. "First, when you were pregnant and alone in Belize. You fervently prayed for a friend. For a few days after, you thought about how good it would feel to have someone to hang out with, and then Buddy showed up."

Buddy. The sweet black and white stray dog had shown up a few weeks after she'd arrived in Belize, and had disappeared about a week before she'd gone home. She'd snuck him food every day, and every night they had sat on the beach together listening to the waves. He had eased her problems with a nuzzle of soft fur or a sweet lick.

"Then Linnea appeared and you had two friends," her grandma said.

So she had attracted Buddy and Linnea-Posie into her life just by asking for a friend and thinking about what it would feel like to have one? Her thoughts filtered back to that disheartened seventeen-year old girl. Alone in a foreign land with a family who had taken her in only to showcase their prominence, and still grieving over her beloved Grammie's passing, Katie had found herself pregnant, miserable, and so, so alone. One night she had walked to the beach, plopped on the sand and pleaded with God, Grammie, her spirt guides, the angels...really, to anyone who had been listening, to give her the help that she so desperately needed and to find her a friend. Then sweet Buddy showed up, an angel with paws. Linnea came next, another angel, another miracle. She couldn't imagine making it through that difficult time without Linnea and Buddy. She pressed a hand to her heart to hang on to the deep sense of gratitude that she felt.

"Now you're getting it!" Her grandma reached over and rubbed her arm. "How about that Black-Tie affair you had to attend at American Security Bank? You couldn't find a date, so you attended solo. Later that night, feeling particularly lonely, you asked God not only for a date, but for your soul mate. At night, you dreamt about your soul mate and during the day you thought about how it would *feel* to have someone you deeply cared for in your day-to-day life. You imagined the things you would do together—talk, hang out, ride in your convertible. As you imagined those specific things, as you felt the feelings of love and joy those things would bring you, the universe began its work. Two weeks later, you met Liam."

"I'd forgotten all about making that request," Katie murmured into her mug, feeling a sense of wonder and awe that her personal plea had been answered. And answered with a man as wonderful as Liam, a man who kept her grounded and helped her experience the joy in life, just like her Grammie had done years before.

"Let me offer one more," Grammie said. "This one shows that your requests are answered, but not always in the exact way you anticipated. Sometimes it's even better. Once you learn to look for the manifestations you've been blessed with, it becomes easier to believe that what you've requested will occur in some way, shape, or form." Her grandmother gave her a loving smile. "You and Liam have been trying to have children for years. You haven't gotten pregnant, but your request was answered in a different way—Savannah."

Katie let out a soft gasp. Why hadn't she made that connection? Nothing would be better than reuniting with her *own* child. She'd thought about Savannah every single day since she had given her up for adoption. She'd prayed for her, dreamed about her, and secretly yearned for the chance to mother her. While she would still like to have more children, the ability to reunite with the child she'd reluctantly given up was a dream come true. She'd been focused on the lack of fulfillment of her desire to get pregnant when her request had been answered in an even more beautiful way. The opportunity to raise the daughter she had given up, but still carried in her heart.

"Thanks Grammie," she said quietly, wiping a tear from her eye. "Thanks for showing me the way."

"Remember that believing is crucial, here and on Earth," her grandmother said. "Believing will get you home. Once you get there, continue to believe in your dreams, big and small. Getting Savannah, getting pregnant, whatever it is that you desire. It can all come true, but only if you have the courage to believe it will happen."

As the magnitude of Grammie's words settled in, a weight lifted from Katie's shoulders. She wasn't at all limited in the way she had previously believed. Instead, she was as boundless as the sun rising over the mountain, illuminating the infinite universe.

Black Eagle, Posie, and Grammie had all told her the same thing. If she truly believed, her wishes would come true. She needed to get home before she could achieve any of the rest of her goals, so she would focus on that first. Now, she actually believed it would happen. With her strengthened faith, hope glistened in her heart bright and shiny as a pot of gold at the end of a rainbow.

CHAPTER NINE

On Friday evening, tired of take-out, Shane tossed some kabobs on the grill while waiting for Liam to finish work and Liz to get home from the hospital. Turning the gas to low, he took a swig from his water bottle to counterbalance the heat and humidity.

When Liz pulled into the drive and stepped out of her car, his breath caught in his throat. She had on a V-neck shirt that hugged her large breasts, capris molded to her fit legs, and high-heeled sandals that would make any red-blooded man drool. He hoped he wasn't doing so now, at least not visibly. He turned the meat over on the grill, his blood heating along with the food.

He hadn't seen much of Liz over the last couple of days. On deadline for an article, she'd spent yesterday and today in the D.C. area. Since their Monday night date, they'd shared morning coffee and dinners with the girls. They'd snuck in a kiss here and there, but they hadn't had any real alone time the entire week. Something he planned to remedy.

"Smells good." Stepping over, Liz peeked inside the grill, checking out the kabobs of all colors and shapes. "Looks good, too."

Shane yanked her against him. "*You* look good." He studied her bright red lips, and then unable to contain his desire to muss them up, he lowered his mouth and nibbled on her lower lip. "Taste good, too," he said, then he kissed her long and hard. Her curves molded against him so perfectly it was as if she was meant to connect with him. He feathered his fingers through her silky hair, slid a hand down her back, then crept even lower to palm her very fine ass.

Liz glided her tongue over his bottom lip, then slid it inside his mouth. All of the blood drained from his head to his southern regions. As they deepened the kiss, the outside temperature spiked and the air around them pulsed and sizzled.

When they finally came up for air, he wrapped his arms around her shoulders. "What am I going to do with you?" he asked, his voice a little uneven.

When his bulge twitched against her belly, Liz gave him a come-get-me look. He was just about to kiss her again when Cara called out from the house.

"Uncle Shane, when's dinner?"

He pulled himself out of the embrace and slid his gaze to the front porch where his niece stood with a hand covering her mouth.

"Soon." He moved behind the grill to take cover. Poking at the kabobs, he looked back at Cara. "Half an hour, okay?"

" 'Kay. I'll let Sab know, too." Cara shot him a saucy grin before disappearing into the house.

"Jesus, busted again," he muttered, turning the kabobs.

"I know." Liz huffed out a half laugh, half groan. "I'm beginning to think the God's are against us."

Shane cast his gaze skyward. "Cut us a break," he said, making Liz laugh again. He reached over and brushed a strand of hair behind her ear. "I missed you."

"I missed you, too."

He pulled her back into his arms and rested his forehead on hers. "Go out with me again," he whispered.

"Hell, yeah," she said as her lips ticked up.

As relief washed through him, Shane let out a long chuckle. "Okay, then."

A short while later, their clan—Shane, Liam, Liz, Sabby, Cara, and Seth—all gathered around the dining room table for dinner. The chicken, shrimp, and vegetable kabobs were a big hit. After countless compliments, Shane decided he would make homemade meals more often. They'd all been eating a bunch of junk food since Katie had been in the hospital.

Halfway through dinner, he raised his glass. "A toast to Katie waking up soon." He touched his glass to the others, hoping like hell it would happen and happen quickly. His brother was lost without Katie, and in some ways, they all were. She was the glue that kept the Callahan's together.

"More?" he asked Liam, waving the pitcher of sangria he'd whipped together.

"No thanks," Liam said. "I'm gonna drive to the hospital in a few."

"Liz?" He held up the pitcher. "Looks like it's just you and me to finish this."

"Sure, why not?" Liz extended her glass. "It's quite good."

After dinner, Seth headed home, Liam left for the hospital and Cara and Sabby took on clean-up duty. Shane topped off Liz's glass of sangria, then led her to the front porch. "Relax," he said. "I'll join you in a few." Then he made his way inside to feed Pan leftovers.

Rounding the corner to the kitchen he heard Sabby's hushed voice. "What's up with Uncle Shane and Mom? Did you see the looks they gave each other?"

"Yeah, it's adorable." Cara snickered.

"Finally Mom finds a man I actually like," Sabby said. "Uncle Shane's *all that*."

Shane's heart tugged. Sabby had started calling him *uncle* last week and he found it endearing. Every day he'd been growing more and more fond of her, right along with her mother. It both pleased and scared the bejesus out of him.

Pushing those thoughts aside, he fed Pan, then returned to the porch to enjoy the sunset with Liz. As they sipped sangria, the sun dipped, painting the sky shades of pink and orange and the mountains a shimmering purple.

"What happened to your parents?" Liz asked, moving from her wicker chair to the porch swing.

"Plane crash," he said, feeling a pang of fresh pain, even though it had happened a long time ago. "I was fifteen."

"Oh, Shane, I'm sorry." Her eyes clouded with sympathy. "That must've been devastating."

"Yeah." He rose, and leaned against the porch rail to watch the last rays of light fade into the horizon. "It was even worse on Liam."

"How so?"

He hesitated, not wanting to talk smack about his brother. But it was hardly a secret, even Cara knew the story. Liam had shared it with her years ago, hoping it would scare her into being a *good girl*. Seemed to have worked too, at least thus far.

He turned to face Liz. "Liam was a fuck-up in high school." He ran a hand over his scruffy cheek. "I have no idea why. We were a typical middle-class family. Our parents loved us and paid attention to what we did. Even so, Liam ended up with the wrong crowd and became a badass." He joined Liz on the swing, and to lighten the mood, he added, "And not the romance novel kind of badass."

Liz let out a low laugh. "Like you?"

He gave her his best badass grin. "You know it."

"So what happened?"

"Liam skipped school, smoked and drank, gave my parents a bunch of shit." His lips pressed tight at the memory. "They were on him all the time, but they couldn't reach him. Then we got the call that they'd passed." He pressed a palm against his gut which still ached over their loss. Shane remembered the scene like it had happened yesterday; where Liam had stood in the living room, how he'd stared out into thin air completely shell-shocked.

"Damn, Shane," she said, linking her fingers with his.

He blew out a breath. "My folks were taking our older brother, Sean—who'd just turned twenty-one—and his girlfriend to an island in the Caribbean, but the Cessna crashed before they got there. Liam and I were supposed to go too, but there was this school thing I wanted to do."

The corner of Liz's mouth curved up.

"Yeah, I know. School function or island vacation." He shook his head. "I was the nerd of the family." He rubbed his thumb over the top of Liz's hand. "Liam—despite his issues—adored me. He knew how much I wanted to go to the math competition so he promised he'd stay clean and stay home with me. Mom finally acquiesced, telling Liam, 'I swear to God, all the neighbors are watching you.' In her next breath, she told us she loved us more than life itself." He leaned his head back. "That's the last memory I have of her."

"Oh, Shane," Liz said, her voice compassionate. "My parents can be difficult but I couldn't imagine losing them, especially at such a young age."

"It was tough." Lowering his head, he puffed out his cheeks. "Then after my parents and brother died, all hell broke loose." He shut his eyes as his mind burned with the vivid recollection. "The school found out and called Social Services. They tried to take me away."

It took him a few long moments to bring himself back to the present. When he opened his eyes, he turned toward Liz.

"Then what?" she asked, her expression pure sympathy.

"Liam fought for me. He sobered up cold turkey and got a full-time job as a mechanic, but he had a reputation. My social worker told him that the courts tended to award custody to married couples, so instead of going to college, Liam married Rose," he said, snorting out a laugh of disbelief. "She was every bit as messed up as he was, and completely wrong for him." He picked up his glass and guzzled the rest of his drink. "In the end, we won but only because Liam made sacrifices. What he did meant the world to me...who knows what would've happened had Liam not cared so much." He pressed a hand to his gut to settle the competing emotions of gratitude and guilt. "I hate that it still haunts him."

"What does?" Liz tipped her head. "What he did was amazing."

"Yes, but Liam's messed up because our folks never saw him clean up or grow into the man he is now."

"Really?" Liz swirled the wine in her glass. "He seems okay to me."

"He has his moments." Shane sighed. "Sometimes I think he's over it, but then something happens."

"Like what?"

"He's been asked to coach baseball for both the middle and high school teams because he was such a kick-ass player in junior high and high school. Even when he was drunk or high, he somehow got his head together on the field. A couple of big colleges offered him scholarships, but he declined." Shane felt the familiar claw of guilt. Over the years, he had tried to repay Liam at every opportunity, but his brother was too damn stubborn to let him.

"Why won't he coach?" Liz wanted to know.

"He says the kids won't look up to him, parents won't respect him…or some such shit."

Cara strolled outside, and he was more than ready for the interruption. He'd already shared more about his family with Liz than he had with any other woman, including Jana—something for him to think about later.

Cara waved a deck of cards. "Canasta anyone?"

"I'm in!" He'd spent many evenings playing cards with Katie, Liam, and Cara after Katie had taught all of them how to play.

"Sure—why not?" Liz agreed. "But it's been a long time."

Sabby made lattes, oohing and aahing over Liam's high-tech machine while Cara set up the game, explaining the rules to Liz and Sabby.

"It's a shame about Dad and Katie's bike," Cara said, shuffling the cards. "They really loved that thing."

"Since your dad's in the bike business, I'm sure he'll figure it out," Shane said, laying a card on the table.

"Yeah." Cara sighed. "I miss riding, too. It's so much fun."

"Aw." Sabby picked up a card, put down another. "I wanna go riding."

"Dad'll take you sometime." Cara's eyes brightened. "Or Uncle Shane will."

"You have a bike, *Uncle* Shane?" Sabby asked, her eyes wide with hope.

"Yep. A sweet custom Liam built a few years back. I'll take you for a spin sometime this week, but first you need to try on Cara's equipment—make sure you have boots, a helmet, all that safety stuff."

"Coolage. Wait till I put this on Snapchat and Instagram." Sabby beamed at him. "I'll have to find something fitting to wear for Uncle Shane Cycle Day."

Chuckling, he turned to look at Liz, who was engrossed in her cards. "Liz…."

"Yeah, yeah. I know, my turn." She blew out a breath, puffing her bangs. "Gotta decide what to do."

He leaned over and peeked at her cards. "Okay, partner—" he pointed at a card in her hand and tipped his head toward the discard pile "—that pile's yours, baby!"

"Oh." She picked up the pile of cards and put down a few melds. "Yes!" Raising her hands in the air, she nudged him. "Thanks, partner."

"Anytime." He leaned in close to Liz and whispered, "You can repay me later," and then in a voice the rest of the table could hear, asked, "Have you ever ridden?"

"No." She gave him a spicy grin. "Let me correct that—yes to bikes, as in bicycles. Trains, planes, and rickshaws. Horses, camels, and elephants. But motorcycles? No."

"You wanna ride?" he asked, jumping at the chance of having Liz brush against him on edgy turns in the road.

Liz's eyes lifted, bored into his. In those heated seconds, the air around them charged and pulsed, and he found himself twitching.

"I'm game," she finally responded.

He grinned. "You got riding boots?"

"Why would I?"

He shook his head. "What size do you wear?"

"Why?" She crossed her arms. He had no idea why she was all pissy but she looked adorable. Jesus, he had it bad. "You have a closet full of motorcycle boots from ex-girlfriends?" she asked snidely. "No thanks."

He ignored her comment. Of course he'd taken other women on

rides but he wasn't about to share that with Liz. Nor was he going to give her another woman's wares.

"Shoe size?" he asked again.

"She wears an eight," Sabby offered.

He winked at Sabby. "Thanks sweetie, and you let me know if you need some too after you try on Cara's boots."

As they continued to play, Shane's gaze kept drifting in Liz's direction. They'd been living in close quarters for almost two weeks, and in that time, he'd developed strong feelings for her. His want ran deep, but that he understood. She'd also made her way into his head…and he wasn't sure what to do about that.

LIAM's dismal attempt at invoicing was interrupted when Shane sauntered into his office. Blowing out a breath, he grabbed a pack of cigarettes from his top desk drawer.

Pan awoke from his slumber under the desk, rose, and stuck his head in Shane's crotch. Flattening the dog's ears on both sides, Shane gave the obligatory ear rubs. After, Pan shook his head wildly and then flopped back onto the floor.

"Your dog's got it made," Shane said.

Lighting a cigarette, Liam thumbed at the seat in front of his desk. "Sit. Stay a while."

Shane grabbed a couple of Cokes from the mini-fridge, handed one to him, then took a seat.

"I'm taking Liz riding tomorrow," Shane said, popping the top on his soda.

"On the chopper?"

"Nope." Shane took a gulp of his Coke. "Figured she'd like a Harley better, to ride in comfort like Katie."

"Probably so." Liam took a long drag. "Katie rode on the back of my chopper once and said never again."

Shane put his hands behind his head and leaned back. "Seeing as your Harley is totaled, I bought one."

Shaking his head, Liam took another puff. "You bought a Harley for *a date?*"

Shane lifted a shoulder. "Why not? I had to stop by the house this morning anyway. Paid bills, took care of a few client requests, then I headed to Frederick to pick it up." He looked up with a shit-eating grin. "It's fully loaded, too. GPS, infotainment, one-touch saddlebags…." He paused as if trying to come up with the rest of it. "And a bunch of other shit, too."

"Jesus, Shane." His brother had just purchased a motorcycle on impulse, the way normal people bought a pack of gum. Only his crazy ass brother. He put his cigarette down and picked up his Coke. "Color?"

"Amber whiskey," Shane said still grinning.

"Nice." He took a swig of Coke, his body needing the caffeine as much as the tobacco. "How much did that baby set you back?"

"I got everything extra they could add without special ordering. Ended up just under thirty."

"Ouch." Liam let out a long breath, this time thinking of his totaled Harley and how much Katie had loved riding. "I'm gonna have to deal with that one of these days."

"Want me to get you one too?" Shane offered eagerly. "I can go back tomorrow."

Liam let out a strangled laugh. "Thanks, but no. I want to wait for Katie so she can help pick out our new one."

"You sure? I could buy another loaded bike and you could pimp it up, then surprise Katie with it when she gets better."

Liam shook his head again. "We'll wait for the insurance money. You're one crazy mama jama."

Shane looked as if he were going to press the topic, but thankfully he didn't. Liam knew Shane was trying to help but he didn't need his baby brother buying him a damn motorcycle.

After Shane left, he picked up one of the many pictures of Katie from his desk. "I miss you, baby," he whispered.

He was beyond blessed to have Katie in his life even though he had no idea how he'd convinced her to hook up with him, especially after he'd shared his past with her. He'd wanted her to know what she was getting into before he asked her to marry him. But she'd loved him anyway, in spite of it all. Putting the picture down, he heaved out a sigh. He hadn't shared everything with her. But he soothed his conscience with the knowledge that some ugliness was best left in the past.

Since he wasn't getting any damn work done, he booted down his computer. He'd only put in a meager four hours but he couldn't concentrate. It was Saturday, two weeks to the day of the accident, and he couldn't stop thinking about Katie and pining for her return.

He'd also promised to take Cara and Sabby out for dinner, to give Shane some time alone with Liz.

He took the girls to the mall to waste some time first—*you're welcome, Shane*—and then to Carrabba's since Italian fare was Cara's favorite. On the drive to the restaurant, the girls yakked a mile a minute. By the time they'd ordered their meals, he was practically caught up on all of their teenage drama. And he'd enjoyed every second of it.

His daughter kept him balanced. As the days wore into weeks, he sometimes slipped into bouts of doubt. But being with Cara reminded him that he had to set an example and he needed to stay positive. Even so, some days were easier than others.

Except for a brief discussion about Katie's condition, dinner dialogue was light and fun. The weather. Boys. Liz and Shane. Boys. Memories from summers past. Boys.

He glazed over during parts of their conversation because Cara and Sabby were knee deep in teen-speak, the kind designed to make anyone over the age of twenty-five scratch their heads in bafflement. They talked about ussies—what? How Brendan was totally marble-free and Mrs. Kent was a fright bat. The last one he could almost figure out. Something was goat, or maybe someone had a goat, hell if he knew. When talk turned to Mandy, who had Facebook diarrhea, he drifted into his own world, thinking about Katie and willing her to come back.

God, how he missed her.

He reconnected with Cara and Sabby when the conversation shifted to driving.

"You know Katie was gonna teach me how to drive this summer," Cara said, twirling pasta on her fork.

He sighed. "I know, sweetie, and Katie will as soon as she can."

"I really want Katie to teach me, but I don't want to wait. The summer's gonna fly by and I have to get my hours in so I can get my permit."

"I'll teach you," Sabby offered. "I've been driving for almost a year and I'm killin' it."

God, no. He didn't trust Sabby. "Very nice of you, Sabby, but Cara has to be with someone who's at least eighteen, until she's eighteen." Thank God for the Maryland DMV rules.

"Oh." Sabby pouted. "Well, I could at least come along and give Cara tips."

"Cool. Thanks, Sab." Cara leaned toward him with a puckish expression. "Josh said he'd teach me."

"I don't think so, young lady."

Cara's lips twisted into a scowl. "Why not?"

"Don't trust him." Seth's perspective drifted into his head. He realized Seth was biased, but Josh's character had been called into question nonetheless. Besides, he tended to agree with Seth's take—Josh had cheated on his last two girlfriends, thus he didn't deserve someone like Cara. "Don't really like him, either."

Cara glowered at him. "Dad! You don't even know him."

He shrugged. "What I know, I don't like."

Cara's expression turned from sweet to evil in the blink of an eye, forcing him to change his strategy. "*I'll* teach you, sweetie."

Cara sighed. "Daddy, you know I love you but I don't think you'd be the best teacher. You're not the most patient man in the world, you know."

Liam hid his grin. "I'll *try* to be patient...." His sentence drifted off when he recalled a recent conversation with Seth. "Maybe we could have Seth teach you."

Cara exchanged a look with her cousin. "Seth—really?"

"He just turned nineteen. He's been driving for years." Liam took a sip of his beer. "And I trust him."

Cara tilted her head to one side and flashed him the sweet look again. "Will you please just give Josh a chance?"

"It's Seth—or me," he said firmly.

" 'Kay 'kay." Cara held her hands in the air. "Seth it is. I'll talk to him tomorrow."

Nodding, Liam took another sip of his beer. As Cara and Sabby chatted about driving, he processed research data in his mind. The accident had occurred two weeks ago. According to both Dr. Evans and information he'd found online, most individuals who recover from a coma do so within a few weeks. After an average of four weeks, it becomes less likely that patients will wake up and more likely that they'll pass or end up in a vegetative state.

Earlier, Shane had pointed out that Katie's coma was simply a reaction to an event—the motorcycle accident—so she didn't have to recover, her body just needed to wear off the shock. While he liked his brother's logic, it wasn't based on any medical evidence. Shane was merely trying to make him feel better. Still, he appreciated the effort.

He needed to stay positive in spite of his growing concern that they were running out of time.

CHAPTER TEN

*B*ack at Liam's, Liz stirred red sauce in a stainless-steel pot. She hoped Shane liked this recipe that she had tweaked and perfected over the years.

Shane snuck up behind her and wrapped his arms around her waist. "Smells magnifico!" His breath was hot on her neck and gave her shivers.

"I make a mean marinara." She spun around to face him. "I love cooking when I have the time to do it right."

He tugged her close. "There are other things we could do that take time to do right."

Enjoying the dance, she batted her lashes against Shane's cheek. "And there are things we could do that are quick, hot, and intense."

Shane's eyes heated.

She laughed, patted his cheek, and whirled back to the pot. "But for now, I must attend to my sauce."

Behind her, Shane's lips skimmed the back of her neck, shooting shivers up and down her body. She forced her focus to the pot, even though the attraction between her and Shane simmered hotter than the sauce she was stirring. Maybe they should skip dinner…she could turn off the stove, toss Shane on the kitchen table and have her way with him.

But as she turned, Shane stepped away to retrieve wine glasses. "I brought a bottle of French Bordeaux from my wine cellar," he said, grabbing the bottle and popping the cork.

"Nice." The man had his own wine cellar? Shaking her head, Liz drained the linguine and plated the pasta while Shane finished tossing the salad.

Over dinner, they talked politics and religion, travels and traditions, and once again she found Shane to be an intriguing and enjoyable conversationalist. With mention of their upcoming motorcycle date, her voice rose an octave. Although she'd heard Katie speak of the exhilaration, she had never been on the back of a motorcycle. Eager anticipation bounced around in her belly.

After dinner, Shane insisted on handling cleanup since she'd cooked. He said it was the way his mama had taught him. While he cleaned the dishes, she topped off their wine and carried the glasses into the family room.

Sipping the silky, rich wine, Liz contemplated the many facets of Shane. He could be cool and confrontational or warm and easy and was seemingly comfortable with both. He was loyal to a fault and not at all sexist...and good Lord, the man was hot. She rarely saw him in anything other than blue jeans or khakis but even so, he exuded affluence and style. His clothes were of the highest quality and oh my, how he filled them.

Fanning herself to dissolve the small bead of sweat that had formed on her forehead, she thumbed through the music on her phone, selecting soft and jazzy Nora Jones. She put her cell in the iHome system and turned on the music. After, she flopped on the couch and flicked off her summer sandals.

Swirling the wine in her glass, she shifted her thoughts to Katie's progress, and offered up a silent prayer, pleading for her sister's quick and healthy return. As she finished, warm, firm hands began massaging her shoulders.

She sighed contentedly. "You missed your calling. You've got good hands," she said as Shane kneaded her shoulders one more time.

He circled around to the front of the couch and sat next to her. "I give better naked massages," he said, wiggling his brows.

She let out a low laugh.

"You seemed to be deep in thought. What were you thinking about?"

"Katie. How I hope to God she comes back soon." She took another sip of the delicious wine.

Shane waited until she was done, then he took her glass and put it on the table. He grazed his lips over her fingers, causing a zing in her belly.

"It's damn hard waiting," he said as he gently massaged her hand with his thumb, then tipped his head toward the sound system. "Nice pick. Who is it?"

"Nora Jones. I love her." Liz's lips curved. "But then again, I love most kinds of music."

"Me too. Except for rap," Shane said, picking up his glass. "Thankfully Cara doesn't listen to rap often. She and Katie mostly listen to country music." He put down his glass without taking a drink. "Listen, I know Cara puts on a tough front but I've heard her crying at night." He rubbed his palm over the top of her hand, the sensation warm and tingly. "I'm grateful you and Sabby are here. I've heard the two of you consoling her. This has been really hard for her because Katie's the only mom she's really known."

She knew Katie and Cara had a special bond. "Katie said Cara's mom died when she was very young."

"Cara was just three, so she doesn't have any real memories. Liam tells her how much Rose—her mom—loved her, but Katie came into Cara's life when she was ten, and the two of them quickly bonded." He took a few drinks of wine before continuing. "And God bless Katie, she made us a family again. She and Liam had just started dating when I moved back to the area."

"Weren't you a family with Rose?"

"I was fifteen when she and Liam got married, and he only married her so the state would let him keep me." He puffed out a breath. "She tried, he tried. After they had Cara, they both loved her to pieces, but they never loved each other. Where there's no love, there's no family." He lifted her glass. "More?"

"Sure." When Shane disappeared with her glass, she thought about what Liam had done. She knew Liam had married Rose just to get custody of Shane, but she hadn't understood the magnitude of his selfless gesture until now.

Shane returned a few minutes later with two full glasses, passing one to her.

"So you were in New York when Rose died?" she asked.

"Yeah. She was killed in a car accident after a party. Liam sobered up after our folks died, but Rose never did." He clasped his hands together. "It was a tragic accident, two others died along with Rose. I was gonna come home to help Liam with Cara, but he wouldn't have it. He insisted I stay in school." Shane rested his head against the couch. "Liam's always been a good daddy, but it was still a struggle for him. He and I grew up with lots of family—our parents, grandparents, our older brother, Sean. Even though Liam and Rose had issues, she was great with Cara. After the accident, Liam had no support system. I tried to get him to date, but he had no interest—absolutely none whatsoever—until he met Katie. Then he fell for her instantly. I never believed in love at first site, but after seeing them—" he shrugged "—it's obviously possible."

He turned to her. "But here I am jabbering away which I normally don't do. You bring out the…the…something in me."

Liz cocked her head. "Something good or something bad?"

Shane chuckled. "Probably a bit of both," he said, taking her glass and placing it on the table next to his.

He brushed his thumb over her lower lip, then gently claimed her mouth. She had been married once, had had her fair share of dates, yet somehow Shane made her feel like an awkward high school girl. Butterflies danced in her belly, desire pinged in her core, and her heart fluttered foolishly.

She needed to snap out of the teenage-like haze and lighten up. This thing between her and Shane was a fleeting dalliance. As soon as Katie woke up, she'd go back to Georgetown, and she and Shane would move on with their lives.

Separately.

Shane apparently had other ideas. He tugged her onto his lap and the want that had pinged low in her belly now skittered from her head to her toes. Even though this would be a short-lived romance, maybe she should focus on the now. Because the now felt pretty damn good. Shane's lips continued to worship hers, melting her worries about the future with slow, drugging kisses.

"This is better," he whispered when they finally came up for air. It *was* better, so why had he stopped? He framed her face with his hands and rested his forehead against hers which did nothing to impede her romantic notions. "Much better," he repeated, sliding his hands down her back.

He pressed open-mouthed kisses behind her ear, down her neck, across her throat, and then pulled her face to his again. This time his lips were hot, needy, and urgent. Her mind liquefied into fiery desire as Shane's hands cupped her breasts over the thin material of her blouse. When his fingers trailed underneath, she pressed her chest against his palms, desperately needing his warm touch.

She was so immersed in passion that she barely heard the click at the door. Girl's laughter followed, slicing through the thick, electrified air.

She flew off Shane's lap, snatched up her glass and attempted to act normal, even though she once again felt like a randy teenager caught in the act.

Sabby waltzed through the door first. "Hi, Mom. Hi, Uncle Shane." Her daughter stopped at the couch and gawked at her. No doubt her hair and clothes were mussed, her lipstick nearly gone, although some of it could be found on the side of Shane's neck if one looked close enough. She hoped to God no one did.

Sabby glanced between her and Shane as an amused grin played at the corners of her mouth. " 'Kay then."

Cara gave them the same once over. "Hey peeps," she said, giggling.

Liam, who trailed the girls, glanced over, shrugged apologetically, and then ushered the girls into the kitchen.

After they left, Liz let out a frustrated breath, then scooted over to kiss Shane's forehead. "Probably for the best," she whispered. It was likely fate's way of reminding her this was a short-lived flirtation.

Shane's frown suggested that he disagreed. He yanked her back onto his lap. "We're not done here," he said in a thick voice that made her insides flutter all over again. His lips lowered to hers, but this time his kiss was unexpectedly tender.

She'd been saved by Liam and the girls' arrival and she knew it would be best to put distance between herself and Shane before things got any more out of control, but her lips parted instinctively and her hands slid into Shane's hair. Somewhere in the recesses of her mind she remembered that the girls were in the next room. But that did nothing to stop her ass from rubbing against Shane's hard lap.

His soft sweet kiss moved her every bit as much as the hot hungry kiss had. The temperature in the room spiked, the air smoldered, and beads of sweat pricked across her breasts and between her legs.

"Not done," Shane repeated in a quiet, but firm voice. "I want you, more than I've wanted anyone in a long time." He brushed a strand of hair behind her ear. "You're one damn sexy woman."

Unable to help herself, she rewarded Shane with a smoking-hot kiss, and then hopped off his lap and out of the inferno.

"Guess I'll call it a night." She slipped on her shoes, kissing the top of his head. "What time are we riding tomorrow?"

"How about noon?"

"That works." As she inched away, she glanced over her shoulder. "Shane? I had a nice night."

In the hallway, she paused to catch her breath. Pan trotted past her and into the family room where Shane greeted the dog in a tight voice. "Trying to console me, buddy? For the best, my ass."

THE NEXT DAY Liz anxiously paced the front porch while she waited for Shane to arrive. Because she and Shane were both living at Liam's, they'd spent an inordinate amount of time together over the last couple of weeks. It was an odd way to start a relationship. If that's what this was…they hadn't really talked about it.

Regardless, the close-quarter approach had given her a better sense of who Shane was. She'd enjoyed watching him interact with Cara, who visibly adored him, and loved hearing about their various trips and crazy adventures. Her own daughter was also growing fond of Shane and had begun sounding like Cara, offering up new *uncle* stories on a regular basis.

This morning they'd had coffee together, then had whipped up pancakes for the girls. After, Shane had driven to his place to pick up the motorcycle while she had taken Cara to a dentist appointment. She'd been wearing out the porch floorboards for the last half hour and could hardly contain her excitement when he finally pulled into the drive on a big, shiny motorcycle.

She rushed down the steps sucking in a breath at the sight of Shane on that big machine looking all kinds of hot and sexy. Pushing that aside—she'd have plenty of time to check him out later when they were on the road—she circled the bike, scrutinizing every detail. She'd been thinking about their ride all morning and looking forward to it with a passion.

"Looks new," she said, touching the shimmering orange finish.

Shane climbed off the motorcycle, removed his helmet, and pulled her to him for a kiss. It was nice…light and flirty, but it ended way too quickly. After, he gave riding instructions but she had trouble concentrating with her lips still warm and tingly from his kiss.

Pulling in a long breath, she forced herself to pay attention. She'd already missed some of what Shane had said. Since she'd never ridden before, she needed to know what to do.

"Don't wiggle around," he said. "especially at stops. Also, do the wave. You gotta wave at the other bikers. And most important, sit back and enjoy the ride."

"Okay." Hopefully she'd at least gotten the safety stuff. But the only safety instruction she had heard was not to wiggle when he stopped. There was likely more to it. "Don't I have to lean into you on the curves?"

Shane's grin came quick. "You can lean into me anytime, baby."

"Yeah, I've got your number." She put a hand on her hip. "I mean to make sure we don't crash and burn."

Shane laughed. "Sure. Lean in the same direction I do especially on the turns." He brushed his lips across her forehead. "But I know what I'm doing. We're not going to crash."

Liz usually threw caution to the wind, but she thought about Katie and Liam's recent accident and all of the sudden felt a little tentative. "Have you ever crashed?"

"Well—" Shane scrubbed a hand over his scruffy cheek "—just the one time."

She chewed on her lower lip as unease pinged in her gut. Studying her expression, Shane lifted his hands in the air. "Wasn't my fault."

That was all he had? *That* was supposed to make her feel better?

An indulgent glint appeared in Shane's eyes. "Sure you're up to this, Liz?"

Damn him. In a very short period of time, Shane had learned her buttons and how to push them. Liz Patterson never, ever backed down from a challenge. "Of course." She forced her anxiety aside and flashed him a bright smile. "But do I really need to wave?" Holding up a palm, she slowly moved it back and forth.

"Jesus," Shane grumbled. "You're not in a royal parade. Like this —" he snapped his right hand to his side "— or this—" he flicked his index and middle finger downward. "Just a quick hey kind of wave. But you gotta do it, it's biker code."

"Got it." Flipping back her hair, she tossed Shane a playful smile. "I'm ready to roll."

"Not quite." Before she could blink, she was back in his arms. This time the kiss was longer, needier…and, oh so good.

When Shane drew back, he staggered. It was slight, but she was observant. Good. She didn't want to be the only one impacted by this explosive chemistry. Keeping his distance, Shane's eyes raked boldly over her figure.

"You clean down nice," he said. "You look like a real biker chick."

She'd gone shopping especially for this occasion. Wearing hip hugging black pants and a tight pink tank with the Harley logo, she felt the part. Pleased that Shane had noticed, she tugged him back for another sizzling kiss.

A rough groan tumbled out of him. "Keep doing that and we won't be taking a ride."

She laughed but took a step back.

Shane skirted the bike, lifted the trunk. He retrieved a box and several bags, then handed them to her. "You'll need these, too."

She reached into the box and pulled out a helmet. Trailing her fingers over the bold, hot pink design, her riding enthusiasm returned. "Look, it matches my top."

Scrutinizing the accessories, she ran a finger over the price tags. Shane had purchased these with *her* in mind; it wasn't crap left over from some ex-girlfriend. Grinning, she sailed toward the porch. "Be right back," she called over her shoulder, excitement mounting as she peeled the black fingerless gloves from the plastic wrapper and eyed the black-heeled boots.

KATIE'S HEART WRENCHED, and her eyes filled with tears of frustration, as she watched Liam grieve through the cloud screen. How she wanted to reach out and touch him, to let him know she was okay. And why wasn't she home yet? She'd been doing as her guides had instructed…maybe it wasn't working.

"It *is* working," Posie said, reaching around her and gently nudging the Earth viewing cloud away. "You know what happens before something big manifests?"

Katie shook her head as she wiped a tear away with her shirt sleeve.

"Absolutely nothing." Posie pulled her into a hug. "So you need to keep the faith. Stay positive, and *believe* it will happen. Now, I think we need to do something fun," Posie said. "How about a concert? Music is uplifting."

"You got that right." Black Eagle materialized a flute. He lifted it to his mouth and played a soft, lovely tune. He somehow played and sang at the same time, singing in a language Katie had never heard. Even though she didn't understand the words, the melody was beautiful and soothing.

She and Posie clapped when he had finished, and Black Eagle took a mock bow.

"Black Eagle loves his music." Posie winked at him, then turned to Katie. "So who do you want to see?"

"How about Jason Aldean? Cara and I love his music." Katie grinned. "And Cara says he's hot."

"She has excellent taste." Posie laughed. "Now there's a man who knows how to wear his Earth Suit."

Katie laughed, too.

"Well then, Jason Aldean it is." Posie waved Black Eagle and Bear over. "Let's go."

Katie angled her head. "Don't we have to wait for a concert?"

"I'll just find one from past or future." Posie closed her eyes for a long moment. When she opened her eyes, she snapped her fingers.

The sky turned midnight black as a swirling vortex lifted them up, then plunked them down on a large stage. It all happened in the blink of an eye. When they landed, Katie swayed, feeling like she'd just stepped off a boat. Extending her hands for balance, her body felt heavy, her energy dense.

Black Eagle rushed over and placed a palm on the small of her back, instantly grounding and steadying her. "You okay?"

Katie took in the bright lights, the massive crowd, and the loud music strumming through the speakers at the edge of the stage. "I guess," she said in a voice loud enough that Black Eagle could hear over the crowd. The show appeared to be in between sets. Still, she felt self-conscious up on the stage in front of what appeared to be a sold-out crowd.

"Where are we?" she asked.

"Bangor, Maine. Waterfront Pavilion," Black Eagle sang, his

voice pitched over the sounds of the crowd.

Katie's gaze zeroed in on two Security guards on the other side of the stage. They're going to kick us out, she thought, twirling a long strand of hair around her fingers.

"Don't worry." Posie put an arm around her shoulder. "They can't see us."

Posie sat on the edge of the stage, flinging her legs over the side. She patted the space next to her. "Come join me."

Katie perched next to Posie. Bear flopped down beside Katie and Black Eagle took the other side of Bear.

"Well, I guess I can sit—for a while anyway," Black Eagle said, his voice eager.

Posie turned to Katie. "Just a warning—Black Eagle will be all over the stage tonight—singing, dancing, playing."

Katie shook her head, a little dazed that she was an invisible guest at a Jason Aldean concert. "Who opened?"

"Hank Henley just finished," Posie said. "Guess we could have arrived in time to hear him play, too."

Katie looked out at the crowd. "I've never heard of him."

"He's up and coming. You'll hear about him next year Earth time."

Katie just laughed.

The lights dimmed and the audience roared in delight when Jason Aldean sprinted onto the stage. He wore tight Wrangler's, a blue and grey sleeveless plaid shirt and his trademark silver hoop earrings, leather bracelets, and cross necklace. His cowboy hat was Aldean style, positioned low, just above the rim of his eyes.

Posie was right on the mark. Jason Aldean looked *very* fine in his Earth Suit. Wait till Cara hears about this, she thought.

The band strummed the starting chords to "Big Green Tractor" and the crowd went wild. As Posie had predicted, Black Eagle partied all over the stage, clapping, dancing, singing. As the concert progressed, he took turns pulling her or Posie up to dance with him. While they were resting, Bear rocked with Black Eagle, and the two of them made Katie smile. She'd never had so much fun in all her life.

At the first strums to "My Kinda Party," Black Eagle snatched a guitar out of thin air and jammed right next to Jason.

"Black Eagle sure knows how to party!" she shouted over the speakers to Posie. She sang along too, thoroughly enjoying the concert from the best seats in the house. Jason played all of her favorites—"She's Country," "Tattoos on This Town," "Burnin' It Down."

Then he played a song Katie had never heard. Odd, she thought she knew *every* Jason Aldean song. "Is this a new song?" she asked, touching Posie's arm.

"No. Wait—yes. He hasn't written it yet."

For a moment, Katie breathed it all in, the concert, this incredulous time with her guides and her beloved Bear.

"When it's released in a couple of years you'll think of this concert," Posie said, giving Katie an angelic smile.

Katie put her head on Posie's shoulder. "I'll never forget it."

Black Eagle bopped over and pulled both of them up. Katie squealed when Jason started playing "Dirt Road Anthem." "I *love* this song!"

Apparently Black Eagle did, too. He burst into the refrain, belting it out right along with Jason. He had the rap part down too, clearly articulating each and every word.

"How does he know all the words?" she asked Posie. "Of every single song?"

Posie's lips curved. "He's a music man."

"Cara would love this concert," Katie said, all of a sudden feeling homesick.

Posie pulled her into a loving embrace. After, they returned to their seats at the edge of the stage. Near the end of the concert, humming along with the music, Katie perused the crowd, and then did a double take. The entire audience was enveloped in a luminous soft blue light. Glancing over her shoulder at the stage, she didn't see any special lighting.

"Where are the blue lights?" she asked her guide.

"Look closer," Posie said. "It's not lighting, it's energy."

Katie returned her gaze to the crowd. The sky-blue radiance—or energy—as Poise had called it, blurred people together making the audience appear as a continuum.

She stared in disbelief at what she saw with her own eyes. "But… what does it mean?"

"It shows how we're all connected, all a part of the same God energy." Posie fluttered a hand in front of them. "The blue hue is energy, vibrations uniting one being to another. If you look with your broad perspective, you can see the connected view, but if you focus in using your individual perspective, you will see the distinct beings within."

Katie closed her eyes and directed her mind toward the expansive. Blinking her eyes open, she marveled at the connectedness. Each person blurred into the next, into an integrated field of energy where no boundaries existed. She could no longer recognize individual arms, legs, faces, nor could she tell where one being ended and another began. They all blended together, one into the other like they were part of a single form. Then she thought about individual people and could once again make out separate forms. "Amazing," she whispered, in complete and utter awe.

"Most humans think they are separate beings," Posie said. "In reality, all people from all walks of life are connected. When humans embody this concept, resentment, hate, and negativity fade away."

If people understood this connectedness, the world would be a better place. There would be no war, no prejudices, no divisiveness. It would be a *New Earth*, Katie thought wistfully, where mankind would flourish in peace, love, and joy.

LIAM SHUFFLED into the hospital feeling more than a little nervous. Usually the shift prior to his was Jen's, but she had a date tonight so Katie's mother was there instead. Making his way to the ICU, he hoped Mitch wasn't there. He also wished that Katie's parents didn't hate him. Not that there was a hell of a lot he could do about it. He blew out a frustrated breath, squared his shoulders, and pushed through the door to Katie's room.

Carolyn was at Katie's side, tears streaming down her cheek. An ache rose in Liam's chest. He had no doubt that Carolyn loved her daughter...and that was the one and only thing they had in common.

"Evening, Carolyn," he said quietly.

Katie's mother lifted her head and wiped her cheek. "Liam, I didn't hear you come in."

"I can be stealthy." He stuffed his overnight bag underneath the bedside table, then on impulse stepped over and touched a hand to Carolyn's arm. "Thanks for being with Katie tonight. I've gotten behind at the shop and had to finish up some paperwork, otherwise I could've covered."

"It's not a problem." Rising, she finger-fluffed her silvery hair. "I appreciated the extra time with my daughter."

He nodded, then shifted his attention to Katie, his eyes roving down her body searching for any changes. Unfortunately, none were evident.

"Hi sweetie," he murmured, stepping over. He kissed Katie on the cheek.

Carolyn cleared her throat. "Well, I guess I'll be leaving."

He straightened and turned. "Thanks again for being here, and thanks for the time you're spending time with Cara, too. She's really enjoying it." Although he still wondered why after all these years.

"I'm doing it for Katie," Carolyn said, as if reading his mind.

Not for him. He got it, loud and clear. Still, he took the higher ground hoping that someday Carolyn would come around to him, too. "Cara's talked nonstop about going to the spa and having dinner with her grandma. You're the only one she has, so it was extra special."

Carolyn's features softened. "Honestly, I've enjoyed it, too. I'll call her in a couple of days so we can plan something else."

"That would be nice." When she turned to leave, Liam decided to go for the gold. The timing was ideal considering this was the first pleasant conversation he'd ever had with Katie's mother. "Carolyn?"

"Yes?"

"I know you and Mitch wish Katie hadn't married me. In some

ways, I even understand it. But know that I love your daughter more than life itself and I'd do absolutely anything for her."

A hint of a smile curved Carolyn's lips. "I'm beginning to see that."

After she left, he sat on the armchair and scooted it close to the bed. "Hope you had a good visit with your mom." He lifted Katie's hand and kissed it. "She's been warming up to Cara, and Cara's been loving it. Who knows, maybe I'll be next."

He rested his head against their clasped hands. "I miss you so much." So much that his chest hurt, a constant niggling pain he'd grown accustomed to. But that didn't make it any easier.

Drawing in a long breath, he dove into his usual chit-chat. It still felt a little crazy talking to Katie while she was in a coma. But if there was any truth to the medical studies that suggested coma patients had some level of consciousness, he was damn sure going to let Katie know he was with her, that he loved her. He also kept her abreast of the happenings at home so she would remember everything she had to come back to.

"Pan's still super-lonely. He wanted me to give you a kiss from him." He rose, brushed a long strand of hair away from her face, then kissed her cheek. Easing back onto the chair, he linked their fingers again. "Brandon asked Sabby out and she said yes." He let out a tight laugh. Hard to believe his second longest tenured guy at Callahan Cycles was dating their niece. "You'll never believe this, but Seth has a crush on Cara." He shook his head, let out another dry laugh. "Poor Seth. Cara seems to be clueless."

"Oh, I almost forgot." Reaching into his pocket, he pulled out a silver band. "I brought this in for you." He traced a finger across the inscription on the ring—*Mo Anam Cara*—Gaelic for 'my soul mate.' He'd given it to Katie on their first wedding anniversary. He slipped it onto Katie's right ring finger, then lifted her hand. The tiny diamond in the band sparkled as big and bright as his love for her. "Thought you might want this to remind you that you're still my always and forever. You make me insanely happy," he said, rubbing the ring. "Come back to me, Katie-Cat."

When he lowered Katie's hand, she linked her fingers with his.

CHAPTER ELEVEN

*A*nother week had passed with Katie still in the coma.
But hope had unfurled in Liam's chest and every time
his gaze darted to the soulmate ring he'd put on Katie's finger last
week, it expanded. Leaning against Katie's bed, he glanced at the
ring now, absently rubbing his fingers over the inscription as he
reflected on the events of the past week.

Earlier this evening, like last Sunday, Carolyn had covered the
shift before him. But this time, instead of running off as soon as he'd
arrived, she had greeted him warmly and the two of them had visited
with Katie together for a good hour. Before leaving, she had
surprised the hell out of him by kissing him on the cheek. Maybe
Katie's mother was warming up to him after all.

She sure had warmed up to Cara. On Wednesday, she had taken
Cara and Sabby on an all-day shopping trip in the D.C. area. Cara
had come home happy as a lark with handfuls of packages and just
as many G-Ma stories. Maybe after Katie woke up they could all go
out together. By *all*, he meant his family and Katie's mother…Katie's
father still hadn't come around, and Liam wasn't sure he ever would.

When Mitch had stopped by the hospital earlier in the week,
he'd been his usual dickhead self, grumbling over Katie marrying a

Catholic and someone beneath her stature. He'd rambled on about how she should've—and still could—marry some asshole Curt, who worked at Mitch's venture capital business. But he refused to let Mitch get to him. If Katie had wanted Curt, she would have gone out with him when her father had tried to fix them up before.

Besides, this week even Mitch Patterson couldn't rain on his parade. Liam gently caressed his fingers through Katie's hair, his heart spilling over with gratitude for the signs of life her body had shown over the past week. It had started last Sunday when he'd slipped the soulmate ring on her hand and she had responded by linking her fingers with his. After, little shifts here and there had evolved into a series of progressively larger movements throughout the week. Dr. Evans had surmised that her body was working its way out of the coma. After the doctor gave that prognosis, Liam had cried. Not baby-ass tears either, but full-fledged sobs of relief. Thankfully, only Shane had been around to hear his blubbering.

"Katie-Cat," he murmured, lowering to the chair and scooting it close to the bed. "I wish you'd wake up now." He pushed down the bed rail and smoothed a hand over the drab gray hospital sheets, and then covered Katie with the red plaid blanket he'd brought in. The blanket gave the space a kick of color, and also brought back memories of picnics he and Katie had taken at Rock Springs Park when they were dating.

"You know, I think your mom's starting to like me. Your dad, not so much." He rested his head on her mattress. "Even if he never comes around, I wouldn't have done a single thing differently. I love you so much…." His body grew heavy as he spoke, the toll of the last few weeks settling in. "I thank God every day for that charity motorcycle ride, for bringing you into my life." His last words slurred as his eyes blinked shut. With Katie's steady breathing lulling the ache in his heart, he drifted off thinking about the day he had met Katie at a bank-sponsored motorcycle ride.

He didn't know why he had signed up for the ride because his preference was to ride alone. But when his friend Doug had asked something deep inside him had urged him to say yes. That morning when Doug had a last-minute emergency, Liam had even agreed to serve as the ride's captain.

He jumped on his motorcycle, thankful for the warm, sunny day, and made his way to American Security Bank in Frederick. When he arrived, the parking lot was already inundated with bikes, so he pulled into the overflow lot. After removing his helmet, he climbed off his bike and ambled toward the check-in area.

He took his place in the long line and made his way toward the front. About halfway there, the woman behind the registration table looked out and caught his eye.

And time stood still.

Liam's heart thundered like the engine in his motorcycle. She was young, perky, and curvy, not model-thin like the women Shane dated. Dark wavy locks tumbled exotically to the middle of her back, ruffling in the light breeze.

But it was more than just her looks. There was something else too, something that touched him deeply. In that stolen moment, it was as if he'd glimpsed inside her soul and found the nurturing, caring woman he wanted by his side for the rest of his life.

He'd never had his head in the clouds. He was a practical man. A tough, strong biker. Yet these feelings were so intense that to deny them would be like denying his own existence. In a trance-like state he stepped forward, eyes glued on the captivating woman.

Was this love at first sight? The romantic notion he'd once mocked now seemed as real as the bright sun glistening overhead.

Moving along with the line, he studied the woman, who in a matter of seconds, had consumed every fiber of his being. Holding a clipboard, she bustled around behind the check-in desk, thanking participants, handing out T-shirts, flashing smiles. Every time she glanced his way, his heart skipped a beat...or two or three. Nothing like this had ever happened to him before. He barely even dated. After his volatile relationship with Rose, he simply hadn't been interested. Besides, as a single dad, he preferred spending his spare time with his daughter.

But deep in his soul, he recognized that this woman was different.

Finally, he reached the front of the line.

"Hi there," he mumbled unable to come up with anything dashing to say.

Staring into her milk chocolate eyes, he studied the contrasts—dark with flickers of light, kind with traces of secrets—and once again there seemed to be a tangible bond between the two of them. He cleared his throat, removed his ball cap and forced out words. "I'm Liam Callahan. Seems I was elected to fill in as ride captain."

"Katie Patterson," she said, shaking the hand he had extended. Her skin was soft, warm, and as he'd expected, stirring. She wore a white tank top that revealed real curves, making him wonder what her breasts would feel like naked and rubbing against his chest. "Thanks for filling in." She tossed back her long, wavy hair and flashed him a killer smile.

Picking up the clipboard, she shifted into business mode. "Thanks again for serving as the ride captain. This is one of our biggest fundraisers, and as you probably know, St. Paul's Children's Charity is a great cause." She asked for his shirt size, tossed him a T-shirt, and then leaned in to speak with the other girl behind the desk. Her tight blue jeans stretched as she bent down revealing more curves, and a scorching jolt shot straight to his groin.

"Tammy, can you cover for me? I need a break." she said to the blonde girl. After her helper agreed, she pivoted to him. "Have a minute?" Without waiting for an answer, she strode toward the other side of the parking lot, far away from the check-in table and the riding crowd.

He followed her to the other side of a small brick maintenance building where she leaned against the wall. He hovered in front of her, wondering what she wanted, having already decided on the walk over that he'd do whatever she asked.

"Do you have a rider?" she said.

"No."

"Want one?"

"Yes," he said, silently cursing himself for uttering single-word responses.

"I should warn you, I've never ridden." She twirled a long strand of hair around her fingers as she spoke. "But I thought maybe I should get into the spirit of it, you know, 'cause I'm in charge of our bank's community events, including this ride."

Shaking off the shock, Liam pulled himself together. "Not a problem. I brought my touring bike."

At her blank look, he clarified. "It's a big bike."

"Oh, um…okay." All of a sudden she sounded nervous and more than a little hesitant.

"There's nothing to it," he assured her, not wanting to lose his good fortune. "The back seat is big and comfortable. All you have to do is lean into the curves with me, and on straight-a-ways, just sit back and feel the breeze. You're gonna love it." He tapped his palms over his heart and put on his sexiest smile. "I promise."

She laughed, the sound soft and lyrical.

"I got a helmet yesterday." Her lips curved into that gorgeous smile as relief whooshed through him.

It had been a long time since he'd been with a woman. Over the years, he'd had his share of one-nighters, but he carefully selected partners who were looking for mutually satisfying sex and nothing more. Nothing he had ever experienced had prepared him for this intense pull, and although he and Katie clearly had chemistry, that was only part of her appeal.

He set off with Katie riding behind him, and led the long line of bikers through the Maryland countryside. Maneuvering his Harley was as natural as the air he breathed, but on this ride, he had to concentrate. With Katie's arms around his waist, her voluptuous breasts pressed against his back, he'd sported a hard-on since the get go. Even the rolling hills, covered bridges, and wide-open roads didn't capture his attention the way they normally did. When they passed by Dixon Park, he fantasized about peeling away from the ride and making love to Katie in the gazebo overlooking the pond. Considering the unlikeliness of her going along with the idea and because he was the ride captain, he instead steered the riders back to the bank with a tight chest. He didn't want his time with Katie to end. While he didn't know a single thing about her, his heart didn't want to let her go.

141

He hung around while she thanked riders and volunteers, collected proceeds and took her stuff into the bank building. When she had finished, he approached her. "Want to have dinner? I could take you out, or you could come over to my place." Maybe he shouldn't have asked her to his place seeing as they had just met. But he was a good cook, and he wanted the opportunity to dazzle her with his skills in the kitchen. Besides, it would be more intimate than eating out on a Saturday night and he'd have a better opportunity to learn more about this woman who had so quickly drawn him into her spell. "I'm a great cook," he said, sliding her a lazy grin.

"I'd like to, but...." Katie shuffled her feet on the pavement. "I'm just not sure."

When her soulful brown eyes raised and met his, she looked innocent...and *very, very* young.

"How old are you?" he asked, narrowing his eyes.

"Old enough." She raised her chin. "I'm twenty-three."

Damn. Old enough, but still plenty young. At eight years her senior, he had no business messing around with her. She should be with someone her own age. But his need didn't diminish and his heart told his head to shut-up.

He cleared his throat. "So, how 'bout it? Dinner at a location of your choice."

"Okay," she agreed, her lips curving into a slow smile. "Your place."

"You sure?" he asked, and then mentally kicked himself. What a dumbass question.

But she didn't back out as he had feared.

Instead, she nodded in agreement. "That's my car." She pointed at a sleek black Mazda. "I'll follow you."

On the drive to his place, Liam neurotically checked his mirrors to make sure Katie was still behind him. Each time he looked, there she was in her swanky RX-8 following him into the country.

As he shifted his thoughts to dinner, panic grabbed him by the balls. What the hell was he going to make? He *was* a great cook, but damn it, now he was under pressure to whip up an impressive meal.

Why hadn't he suggested they go to a nice restaurant instead? He couldn't even remember when he'd last been to the grocery store.

Turning onto his long driveway, he willed away his anxiety. It was just dinner. He'd figure something out and they'd have a nice meal, a nice conversation.

Jumping off the bike, he scurried over to the Mazda and opened the door for her. After helping her out, he gestured toward his two-story home. "Welcome to the Callahan's."

"It's nice," she said, taking in the stone house and mountain views. "You live here by yourself?"

"Just me and my daughter."

Katie's lashes flew up and her expression clouded. "Are you married?"

"What? No, my wife passed away over seven years ago."

"Oh." Katie's expression turned to sympathy. "I'm sorry."

A stab of guilt poked at his gut. He didn't deserve Katie's compassion considering he'd never experienced the kind of pain he should have felt over losing his wife. Instead, he'd mostly felt pain for Cara because she'd lost her mother.

"How old is your daughter?" Katie asked.

"She's ten." He took Katie's hand. "But she's with her uncle tonight." On the front porch, he pulled keys from his pocket and unlocked the door. "Make yourself at home," he said once they were inside. Swooping down, he picked up a trail of shoes and Cara's toys, giving her a sheepish grin. "Sorry, wasn't expecting company." He dropped the armful of stuff behind the couch, making her laugh, then made his way back.

She looked at him with surprise. "It's...your place is so inviting."

"Thanks." His insides warmed as he smiled at her. "Want a drink? I think I have beer, soda, and juice. I'll have to rummage around to see what I have in the 'fridge for dinner."

She didn't answer. Instead, eyes locked on his, she moved into his personal space and touched a hand to his chest.

What the fuck?

Heat smoldered where her palm touched. Was the heat his or hers? Was she sending him a signal, he wondered, or just giving a friendly pat. Since he wasn't one-hundred percent sure, he settled on the high road. "I'll just, uh, go…check the pantry…get us those drinks…."

His words trailed off when she palmed his chest, flipped back her hair, and tossed him a sultry look. Message received. He yanked her into his arms and kissed her. She was everything he imagined she would be. Soft, responsive, and so damn hot. Twining his fingers through her long curly hair, he deepened the kiss, drawing in her honey sweetness.

Katie molded herself against him, pressing her soft body along his hard planes. She was so different from the women he'd been with in the past. She had an almost-innocent quality, a girl-next-door manner, yet together they soldered into heat so hot it could weld parts together.

Even so, was he taking advantage of her? And what the hell, he never thought about shit like that, but something about her summoned his protective mode.

He drew back, lifted her chin, and studied her eyes. Chocolate pools of passion assured him that she wanted this every bit as much as he did. As further validation, she tugged his mouth back to hers and they went at it again. After a smoldering kiss that made him want to drop to his knees and thank God for creating this woman, he called on his self-control to slow it down a notch. He needed to give her time to make sure she knew what she was doing.

He pressed his lips across the nape of her neck and trailed open-mouthed kisses along her jaw and forehead. But Katie was a woman on a mission. Her hands flew wildly in all directions—rubbing his chest, massaging his biceps, squeezing his ass. As she touched him, she let out adorable whimpers of pleasure.

She wound a leg around his thigh and thrust her body against his thick erection. He slid his hands down, cupped her ass, and tugged her closer.

"Damn, Katie," he murmured. "You feel so good." And he wanted her more than he wanted his next breath. While their chemistry was clearly off-the-charts, this was more than just the physical. He had deep feelings for her that didn't seem possible on such short acquaintance, but they had slipped into his heart anyway, making their connection even more magical.

He pulled off her T-shirt and then his own. Entwined with her, he kicked the front door closed with his boot. Stumbling, they staggered back a few steps.

She still had on the white tank top so he slid a hand underneath and found that her large breasts fit perfectly in the palms of his hands. A hiss of satisfaction escaped him as he circled a nipple with his thumb. Lowering his head, he sucked her bud through the thin material of her shirt while he massaged her other breast with his hand.

When he lifted the tank over her head, his breath caught. She had on a plain white bra, the material thin and worn, and her generous breasts nearly spilled out of the cups. He'd never seen anything that turned him on more.

"You're beautiful," he said quietly.

Katie gaped at him, her expression rife with disbelief. "No one's ever said that before," she whispered.

What the hell was wrong with the men she'd dated?

She pulled the band out of his hair, ran her fingers through its length, and then scraped her fingernails down his back. When her hands circled around to his navel, his blood hammered in anticipation.

He grabbed her hand, led her through the living room and toward the stairs. When she lunged against him, they fell onto the landing of the wooden staircase.

"You okay?" he managed between uneven breaths.

"Yes," she whispered.

Cupping her chin, he looked her directly in the eye. "You sure about this? Say the word and we'll stop."

"A hundred ten percent," she said, pulling him back for a knock-him-on-his-ass kiss.

He flicked off her bra, groaning when her breasts pressed against his chest. Leaning down, he ran his tongue over a nipple. She moaned, such a beautiful sound, and he did it again and again, before drawing a breast into his mouth and sucking gently.

All the while he remained alert, listening for Katie's reactions to his touch. She felt so fucking good, he could have thrust into her now and taken her hot and hard. But she brought out his protective instincts, and instead he found himself in unchartered waters. Loving her slowly, gently, tenderly.

But she didn't make it easy. Digging her nails into his back, murmuring soft pleasures, she nibbled on his ear and wiggled and writhed beneath him.

Still, he stayed the course taking his sweet time. Using his mouth and tongue, hands and fingers, he lavished her lush body with attention. Kissing, licking, massaging. Savoring her wholesome scent—lavender and vanilla was his guess—he feathered his fingers through long strands of hair that cascaded down her back.

She stroked his bulge through the denim. It thumped back at her, with heat and desire. Yanking open the button of his jeans, she freed him. His muscles tensed at her soft touch on his most sensitive flesh.

He pulled in a long steadying breath. "This is all I've thought about since the moment I laid eyes on you." He traced his thumb over her lower lip. "This has never happened to me before."

"Me either," she said in a shaky voice as her hands continued to stroke him.

While Katie's actions were bold, her expression was wide-eyed and innocent. "Are you sure?" he asked, his voice gravelly. "I know I already asked, but I want you to be sure." He rubbed a strand of her hair between his fingers. "After this, I'm not sure I'll be able to stop."

"I'm sure," she said without hesitation. "Very sure."

Relief coursed through him, followed by a longing so intense it made his heart ache. When he recovered, his mouth went to work on her trembling, nearly naked, body. "Katie," he whispered, nuzzling her hair. "I've never wanted anyone the way I want you."

"Me too," she said, her voice low and sexy. "So have me."

In a split second, he found his jeans—gave silent thanks for the condom that was still in his wallet—and sheathed himself. In a frenzy, they tugged, tossed, and slipped away the rest of their clothes.

Holding her gaze, he pushed inside her, and it was like he'd entered heaven on earth. He moved with care, treating Katie like the precious jewel that she was.

As he slowly moved inside her, he framed his hands around her face. "You stagger me."

She once again looked surprised. He took her hand and pressed it against his heart so she could feel the chaos she caused inside him. She batted her lashes, looking pleased as hell.

Together, they danced in a rhythm old as time. While the act itself was familiar, everything about it was different. Because Katie was different. In that moment, Liam realized he'd had plenty of sex, but he'd never made love.

Until her.

As he moved with slow, sensual strokes, he lost himself in her. In her eyes, her body, her breath. He kissed her forehead and temple, and then returned to her lips. Hovering just above her mouth, he closed his lids for a beat to absorb the bliss of being inside her. When he opened his eyes, he kissed her adoringly and his heart tumbled. She dredged up powerful feelings that had been buried deep inside him, awakening needs he hadn't known existed.

Katie wrapped her legs around his waist and pulled him in deeper, and all of his emotions fused with the physical as they rode each other faster. Sweat beaded on his chest, but even as his body shifted into overdrive, an overwhelming tenderness arose. The material world faded and boundaries became ambiguous. A cohesiveness appeared everywhere their bodies were joined. When his breath blended with hers, the oneness of their connection was all that existed.

When Katie began to tremor, consciousness returned to Liam's body. He pressed his hands into the thick waves of her hair, and then cupped her chin so he could gaze into her eyes.

One look was all it took for him to fall. He'd never been in love before. Even so, he knew without a single doubt. Feelings this intense, this powerful couldn't be anything else.

He pressed a soft kiss against her forehead, reveling in the ecstasy. Friction mounted as they continued the dance, and he savored every action, every reaction. When her tremors eventually turned into quakes, he let himself go along with her. Together they climaxed in a sensual rush that turned his world upside down.

After a few long moments he caught his breath and stole a glance at her. A large, dark bruise marred her perfect skin.

"God." Embarrassed and pissed over what he'd done, he slid his gaze to the wall. "I'm so sorry."

"For what?" she asked, her voice breathy.

He gently touched the dark circle on the back of her thigh.

She choked out a laugh. "You probably have a few of those, too."

He ran a hand through his hair, relieved that she didn't seem to be the least bit put out. Still he was frustrated with himself. "I could have at least taken you upstairs to bed."

Their eyes caught and held.

"Why don't you take me there now?" she suggested.

He gave her a long appreciative look before scooping her up. Leaving clothes and shoes scattered along the steps, he carried her up the stairs and down the hall. Stepping into his bedroom with her wrapped around him, he was certain his life would never be the same.

An hour later after another very hot bout of love-making, Liam stirred and stretched, feeling a contentment he'd never known.

Katie sprawled along his side with her head nestled against his chest.

Are you sorry?" he asked, half afraid of the answer, but needing to know.

"No." She shook her head. "Maybe I should be, but I'm not." She rose into a seated position, seemingly unashamed of her nakedness. "I…it's been a really long time. But something about you spoke to me." She trailed a finger down his tattooed arm. "You're all bad-boy, yet I can see your kindness. And we obviously have chemistry."

"Off-the-charts," he said and couldn't help the shit-eating grin. "How long has it been?"

Katie hesitated, tracing a finger over the comforter. He wasn't sure if she was going to answer.

"Six years, give or take."

He quickly calculated the math, then quietly swore under his breath. He'd been the first man she'd been with since she was seventeen. That explained the innocence. "Holy hell." He glanced over at her. "Why? I mean you're super-hot."

She wore a sad—maybe embarrassed—expression. "To be honest, I had a hard time my last couple years of high school, and after the drama, I shied away from men." Her mouth curved into a sexy smile. "Well, until now."

He touched a hand to her cheek. "I'm honored you chose me to come out of your hiatus with. And, Katie?"

"Yeah?"

"Whenever you want to do that again—" he gave her a mock salute "—I'm at your service."

She laughed. "Well, I should be good for a while now."

"This wasn't a one-time deal," he said, his voice sounding unnerved, which was exactly how he felt. He put his hands on her shoulders. "This wasn't just sex, at least not for me."

She bit her lower lip and didn't answer for several seconds. Liam's heart stopped while he waited for her to respond.

"It wasn't for me either," she finally admitted. "Even though I wanted it to be."

He wondered why she wanted it to be a one-time deal. She obviously wasn't a woman who slept around, nor was she into one-night stands. But he didn't want to press his luck, and he wasn't sure he wanted the answer anyway. Instead of asking, he leaned in and rested his forehead against hers until his heartbeat returned to normal. "You hungry?" he asked a minute or so later.

"I should probably get going."

Hell no. He pulled her over and scooped her onto his lap. "But I promised you dinner." Circling his arms around her back, he kissed the top of her head. "I'm a man of my word. You gonna make me break my promise?"

She stayed.

He gave her a beer and she sat at the table and chatted with him while he whipped up Fettuccini Alfredo and a tossed salad.

Over dinner, he asked her how she had liked riding.

"I loved it." Twirling the pasta on her fork, Katie gave him a smile that warmed his insides like a shot of bourbon. "Being on a motorcycle is so different. I loved the open air and feeling like a part of nature."

"There's a solitude in riding that you can't get any other way," he said, ridiculously pleased that she had loved it. "What made you want to ride?"

"Well, I was the ride chairwoman and since my bank sponsored the ride...." She put down her fork as her words trailed off. "You want to know the truth?"

Placing a hand over hers, he nodded.

"I had no intention of riding until yesterday when I was talking with my dad." The lines across her forehead creased making him think it had either been a difficult conversation or her dad wasn't a very nice guy. She took a couple gulps of her beer. "He was pissed that I couldn't make it to his cocktail party last night to meet some guy who works at his venture capital company." She let out a huff of frustration. "Curt's a mini version of my father. No thanks. Besides, I was getting things ready for the ride. When I told my dad, he misunderstood my role." She took another slug of beer. "I got one of his infamous lectures. Riding's low-class, blue-class, I was brought up better...blah, blah, blah." She gave him an impish grin. "So I ran out and bought a helmet just to prove my independence. I had no intention of riding until I saw you. Then—I know this is gonna sound stupid—but after we connected, it seemed like the helmet purchase had been part of a grander scheme."

Liam wasn't sure what would happen next. It appeared that Katie came from a well-to-do, pretentious family. She was too young for him and clearly out of his league. Despite all of this, he wasn't willing to walk away. What existed between the two of them felt so real it was as if his life before her had been a long dream and he had finally awakened.

CHAPTER TWELVE

*I*t was unlike any place Katie had ever been. "It's beautiful," she murmured, digging her feet into the warm, powdery sand. Her guides had told her they had a surprise, but this was—wow! The sand had a mystical reddish glow. The nighttime sky glistened with stars, planets, and orange luminescent bodies while two massive full moons sparkled light on the ocean. Taking it all in, Katie was filled with wonder. The stars were big and bright. Orange dots—maybe stars?—traveled in groups, shooting across the sky and trailing orange specks in their wake.

"What are those?" she asked, pointing at the orange clusters.

"Which ones?" Black Eagle's gaze followed her finger.

"The shimmering ones…they look like orange fairy dust."

"Fairy dust." Black Eagle chuckled. "I like that. Those are new universes. The fairy dust, as you call it, is energy emanating from each newly formed cosmos." Staring up at the starry expanse, a sense of wonder filled Katie. New life was being birthed before her very eyes. Black Eagle looped his arm in hers. "My dear, we brought you here for the beauty but also because it provides an ideal backdrop to talk about connections."

Posie joined them on her other side, and the three of them

strolled along the moonlit beach. "When you return to Earth," Posie said, "remember all you have learned here. Follow your heart, make your intentions clear, and believe that your dreams will come true."

"It works for any desire, large or small." Black Eagle patted her arm. "When you don't know what you want or when you're unsure whether something is right for you, attune with your feelings or take the time to quiet your mind and ask for guidance."

Bear sprinted over with his toy, and Katie bent down to rub his head.

"Know you are not in this alone. We—" Posie gestured between her, Black Eagle, and Bear "—will be with you. Always."

Katie nodded, overcome with love, positive energy, and hope. Was she on her way back to Earth? Thinking of reuniting with Liam and Cara she was overcome with a sense of elation, but at the same time, she felt a twinge of sadness. She would miss her beautiful guides and her sweet Bear.

"And that's not all," Posie said. "You're also connected to God, connected to everything that exists."

Black Eagle led her to the edge of the water where waves tumbled onto the shore. They waded into the white foam as Bear sprinted off, gleefully diving into the ocean.

"Look out there and you see a collective body of water." Black Eagle bent down and scooped up a handful of liquid. He extended his cupped hands toward her. "But this is now separate." Pulling his hands apart, the water fell back into the ocean. "Each drop of water is individual, yet at the same time, a part of the whole. You cannot separate the droplet any more than you can separate the scoop. Even when the smallest drop is removed, it is still a part of the ocean."

When he stepped out of the water, Bear sprinted over with his stuffed toy. Black Eagle took it and tossed it toward the ocean. Bear took off after it, and this time returned to drop the toy at her feet.

She picked up the stuffed puppy imbued with so many happy memories, rubbed its ear, and then hurled it toward the water.

"It's the same up there," Posie said, pointing at the sky. "Each star, planet, universe is individual yet still a part of the broader multiverse. It's like that with you as well, Katie. You're an individual speck, a separate soul, but you are also eternally connected to God. All that you do—every thought, every action—impacts the whole."

Katie drank in every detail—the astonishing beauty that surrounded her, the concept of connectedness—as an overwhelming sense of awe swept through her. She'd felt this connection before. Watching the sun sink into the mountains, gazing in Pan's eyes, riding their motorcycle through a canopy of bright fall-colored trees. But she hadn't fully understood what it meant—that she was an actual part of that which was greater than herself.

Black Eagle snapped his fingers and a bonfire appeared on the sand along with cushioned lounge chairs. He extended a hand. "Shall we?"

They ambled over and climbed onto the loungers. A few minutes later, Bear joined them, flopping onto the shorter but wider chair.

"I never grow tired of this magnificence." Posie leaned back on her lounger, then glanced over at Katie. "Are you comfortable?"

Katie adjusted her pillow. "Very."

"We've talked about vibration," Black Eagle said. "Remember that every thought and action causes an effect in the universe's vibrational fabric. When you have positive thoughts, it creates positive ripples in the universe and positive things return to you. Many humans don't understand cause and effect, because it's not the *exact* feeling or circumstance that comes back, but something on the same vibratory scale."

Katie toyed with this idea. How often had she woken up feeling joyful and then noticed all of the goodness that occurred throughout her day? Big and small things, each of them positive. A friend unexpectedly showed up to take her out to lunch, she garnered a smile from her typically cranky boss, flowers were delivered from Liam for no particular reason. It worked the opposite way on days when she woke up irritable.

"It's the same concept with negativity," Posie said picking up on her train of thought. "If you're feeling angry or depressed, matching vibrations return to you. Remember that thoughts are powerful.

There've been many studies that demonstrate that positive thoughts —like appreciation and gratitude—can change molecular structure. Focusing on the positive directly impacts your mind, your body, your overall wellbeing."

Katie took a long moment to digest this information. A few years ago, she'd read an article about a Japanese scientist who had observed the effect of thoughts and words on water. When he had happy thoughts and said nice things, the water crystals were symmetric, light, beautiful. But when his words were negative, the water crystals turned dark and sickly. When she'd first read the article, she had dismissed it as new-age propaganda, but this seemed to be exactly what her guides were saying. If thoughts had that kind of impact on *water*, they would surely have an impact on her mind, body, and spirit. And since she was connected to the whole, maybe they could even impact the environment around her.

"You've got it, Katie," Black Eagle said. "Now, let's kick it up a notch." He steepled his fingers. "As an individual, your thoughts also contribute to the whole, affecting the collective consciousness of the universe. If your thoughts are positive and loving, that's what you share with the universe."

Posie leaned up on her elbows. "You see this play out whenever beings bond together to support and love one another whether in friendships and families or across different countries and cultures, different religions and political leanings. But when there is more negative than positive, you see that outcome instead. It ebbs and flows throughout history—wars, acts of violence, famine, natural disasters."

"It's like biofeedback on a cosmic scale," Black Eagle added. "When enough positive vibration is contributed, a critical mass is achieved, collective consciousness rises, and the universe shifts for the benefit of all humanity."

Katie put her arms behind her head and gazed up at the night-time sky, contemplating the incredible idea that the individual could impact the whole. "So little 'ol me can really help all of humanity?" It was a hard concept for her to grasp. Even if she was connected to everyone else, her life was one out of nearly eight billion on planet

Earth. How could her insignificant daily existence possibly contribute to the collective consciousness in a meaningful way?

"You *do* contribute." Sitting upright, Posie gave her a knowing smile. "Humanity evolves individual by individual as each is connected to the whole. Individuals who share peace, love, and light contribute positivity to the collective. Actions work the same as thoughts. If your actions come from a place of love you will contribute to your soul's highest growth and to that of others. What humans don't always realize is the extent to which their actions impact others. Most understand if they do something good, it may benefit another. What they don't see is the infinite downstream impacts, the connection to the broader universe. Black Eagle, maybe you could show Katie. That's really your forte."

Black Eagle chuckled. "I love illustration. Let's see...." Black Eagle sat cross-legged on his lounger, and rubbed his hands together. "Remember the movie *It's a Wonderful Life?*"

Katie sat upright. "I watch it every Christmas."

"Remember how Clarence showed George the impact to the community and to George's loved ones had he never been born?"

Katie nodded. That was the most heartwarming part.

"That's exactly how it works. Cause and effect on an individual level triggers downstream cause and effect. Every action causes an infinite number of reactions and each becomes a thread in the tapestry of the universe."

As Katie contemplated, Black Eagle drew a viewing square. She lifted her head to look at the screen, surprised to see scenes from her own life. The little girl whose name she'd drawn from the Angel Tree, and that girl's joyful Christmas morning as she opened her stocking and the gifts Katie had purchased.

Black Eagle touched a finger to the screen and it froze on a clip of the girl's parents. "Your gift not only touched Julia, but her parents, Jack and Ellen, too," Black Eagle said. Katie leaned in to get a closer look at them. Both were smiling. Ellen's hand rested on Jack's arm as he gazed up at her with caring eyes. "Julia's parents had both been laid off from their jobs. They had been stressed about Christmas and fighting regularly." He tipped his head toward the screen. "That Christmas gave Ellen and Jack some much needed peace, joy, and hope. Jack found a job the week after Christmas, and Ellen, two months later. As Julia grew, her parents taught her the importance of giving back." Black Eagle made a fist. When he opened it, a small river stone sat on the palm of his hand. "Good deeds are like skipping pebbles in a pond. It's not just the single ripple that is affected, but the multiple rings radiating outward, bumping into one another and intersecting, all a part of the downstream impacts from that one small pebble."

Katie gaped at Black Eagle in amazement. She'd never thought of it like that or considered the many ripples that occurred from a simple benevolent act.

Black Eagle's smile expanded. "We're just getting started." He waved a hand in front of the screen and new clips streamed. Ellen and Jack selecting names from an Angel Tree, and as Julia got older, her participation in the Christmas giving. A homeless man Katie had given money to used the money to buy a warm meal. While dining, the man met the restaurant's owner who hired him on the spot and helped him get back on his feet. Katie's heart tugged watching the formerly homeless man reunite with his adult son.

The next scene showed the son visiting an older woman. Posie tapped the screen and Katie studied the clip of him hugging a woman with the same robin-blue eyes. "Not only did Donnie's dad get his life back on track, but Donnie progressed as well," Posie said. "He had blamed his mother for his father's situation, and for many years, Donnie had been estranged from both of his parents. Through his father's growth, Donnie put aside his past hostilities and fostered new relationships with his father *and* his mother."

The episodes of Katie's life flew by like images on a movie screen. A kind word, a smile, a helping hand. Gifts, large and small, material and intangible, all influencing lives. Examples continued to stream, one after the other depicting cause and effect and the countless succeeding impacts. Katie watched as Donnie's young children met their grandpa, and later their grandma, for the very first time. She saw Julia, the young girl from the Angel tree, go to college and become a teacher. An amazing, extraordinary teacher who worked in a

Title 1 school. Over the years, Julia touched the lives of hundreds of low-income students. Observing the downstream impacts in each of those children's lives, and the lives they subsequently touched, was nothing short of mind-boggling. One saved lives after a boating accident. Another became a doctor, also saving lives. But what really struck Katie was the impact from those who led seemingly ordinary lives. Their simple, day-to-day acts—a smile, words of encouragement, a kind gesture—in turn caused another positive action which like ripples in the pond, caused another and then another, until they all merged into bigger turning points in the lives of the recipients. *That* was how little 'ol her could make a difference. Perhaps it wasn't the grand gestures, but instead, the small acts of compassion that made the greatest impact in people's lives, and thus generated the greatest contribution to the collective.

The next scene showed a down and out woman. It took Katie a minute to realize it was *Jen*. Only her best friend didn't look at all like herself. She looked tired, disheveled, depressed. Katie gasped as Jen took a handful of pills and raised them to her mouth.

"Wait!" Katie shouted and the screen froze. She pushed a palm to her chest to stop her heart from thumping. "That can't be Jen. She's beautiful and happy." Katie had never felt so far away, so helpless. "When did this happen? Can't you help her?"

"It *didn't* happen." Posie slipped over next to her, and put an arm around her shoulder. "Keep watching."

Black Eagle sat on her other side. He tapped the screen and it showed Katie meeting Jen, shortly after Jen had lost her parents. The next scene was of Katie talking Jen through a dark day, then Katie, Jen, and Cara roller skating, and Jen having dinner with Katie and Liam.

"It never happened because you were there for Jen," Black Eagle said. Katie breathed a sigh of relief, grateful that her friend was okay. "You listened and gave Jen a shoulder to cry on. You hung out with her and made her feel comfortable with your family. It's not always the big things that make the big differences. More often, it's the small day to day acts of kindness," he said, confirming Katie's earlier thoughts.

"You see, Katie, the smallest things can make all the difference," Posie said in a quiet recap before she and Black Eagle returned to their own chairs.

"Connections," Katie murmured, growing weary. "I've got to get home. For Liam and Cara, and to connect with Savannah."

Katie fell asleep under the star-studded sky reflecting on small acts of kindness and the infinite downstream impacts. When she awoke, she was back on the big, fluffy cloud, snuggled next to Bear.

She stretched, then shifted into a seated position. Her limbs were tense, her body heavy, and her mind pensive. Her intuition, which had grown by leaps and bounds during the time she'd been in Tranquility, advised change was imminent.

Bear rustled and gazed up her. His knowing expression was the same as it had been during their last few minutes together on Earth.

"I'm not sure what's happening, Bear." She cupped her hands around his fuzzy face, her chest heavy with the same piercing grief she'd experienced when Bear had gotten sick and died in her arms on Earth. "If I'm on my way back, know that I love you so very much."

Posie and Black Eagle appeared, one on each side of her.

"What's happening?" she asked, rising. An onslaught of emotions whirled through her—uncertainty and hope, joy and sadness. "Am I on my way home?"

"The power to go home has always been within you," Posie said. "Early on, you made your intentions clear. Now that you've started to *believe*, your desires are materializing. Your body is reconnecting with the physical and your mind is returning to your Earth state."

Joy bubbled in Katie's heart even as a blue sorrow blanketed her chest. She was *finally* going home to reunite with Liam, Cara, and Pan, but she would miss her guides and her sweet Bear so much.

"Remember all that we've taught you." Black Eagle put a hand on Katie's shoulder, and warm vibrations danced up and down her body. "Follow your heart, believe in your ability to make your dreams come true, and remember the ripples. You can, and you *do*, make a difference."

A lump grew in Katie's throat as a tear slid down her cheek.

Black Eagle brushed the tear away with his thumb. "How can I be happy and sad at the same time?" Sniffling, she shook her head. "I'm going to miss you—" she glanced around their circle, her gaze connecting with Black Eagle, Posie, and Bear "—*all* of you so very much."

"Don't think of this as goodbye." Posie leaned in and kissed her cheek. "You'll *feel* our presence when you get back to Earth. We'll be with you there, always have been, always will be."

Katie pulled her beautiful guide into a hug and held on tight. "Still, I'll miss being with you *like this*." She rested her head on Posie's shoulder and soaked in her guide's love. "I'll miss your friendship, your kindness, your angelic smile. And all of your wisdom."

"Oh, we'll still impart wisdom," Posie said drawing back and giving Katie her trademark smile. Posie touched a soft hand to Katie's cheek and then stepped aside to allow Katie to say goodbye to Black Eagle.

Black Eagle enfolded Katie in his arms.

"How I'll miss you," Katie said, her voice breaking. "Your sense of humor, your music, your soothing voice." She pressed a kiss to his chest. "Everything you've taught me."

"We'll still be with you," Black Eagle said, parroting Posie's words. "One more thing, when you get back to Earth find an energy practitioner."

"A what?"

Black Eagle chuckled. "A Reiki practitioner or energy healer. Don't worry, we'll guide you to the right one." He kissed the top of Katie's head. "She'll help your body heal. She can also teach you to quiet your mind and look for guidance within."

"Okay. Thank you." She hugged him again. "For everything."

Bear was last. She sat down, touched her head to his, then wiped away another tear. "Oh, Bear. How can I say goodbye to you *again?*" Sniffling, she tossed a few white puffs onto his back. "I'll miss this and I'll miss you. Bye for now, my sweet boy." She kissed the top of his curly head. "Don't be a stranger."

As much as Katie wanted to go home, she would miss Posie, Black Eagle, and Bear more than she'd ever thought possible. Her chest squeezed as the uncomfortable mix of joy and sorrow pricked at her insides all over again. With a guide on each side of her and Bear on her lap, Katie closed her eyes and sought comfort in their loving embrace.

But even as she snuggled deeper and deeper into the cloud, she couldn't get comfortable. Her fluffy atmosphere thinned and hardened. Her body weakened and her right side began to throb. Rolling to her side, she got tangled. Jerking upright, she opened her eyes and found an IV tube attached to her arm. Disentangling from the tube, she took in her immediate surroundings.

She was back in the hospital.

Awed and amazed that she was back on Earth, Katie lifted her left hand, then her right, and then moved her fingers. They all worked. She lifted her legs, wiggled her toes, then followed the same process working her way up and down her body. Other than the pain that extended from her ribs to her toes on the right side of her body, she was seemingly okay. What a miracle. *A miracle resulting from your intention*, Black Eagle's voice said in her head. She closed her eyes for a long moment to give thanks for her well-being and for the magical adventure she'd just had in the clouds.

When she opened her eyes, she surveyed the room. Her chest kicked at the sight of Liam curled up in a chair in the corner. Seeing him in the flesh brought more tears to her eyes. "Liam?" she squeaked, her voice small and crackly.

She cleared her throat and tried again. "Liam." This time, it came out stronger and louder.

Liam flew out of the chair, rushed to the bed, and threw his arms around her neck. "Katie, you're back!" He planted noisy kisses all over her face.

With a low laugh, she cupped her hands around his cheeks. It was hard to believe she was back. It felt good to touch him, good to hear his voice. "Oh, Liam."

"I've missed you so much, baby." Liam rested his forehead against hers, relief shuddering through him and into her. Feeling his unending love, Katie melted into it and a few more tears fell.

Liam wiped them away with his thumb just as Black Eagle had done a few minutes ago. "You okay?"

Nodding, she smoothed her palm up his arm. "Just happy to be back."

"God, me too." Liam let out a long breath, then put his hands on her shoulders and looked her up and down. "Are you sure you're okay? How do you feel? We've been with you this whole time. Do you remember anything?"

"I feel pretty good, all things considered. I missed you, too. But…." She raised her gaze to meet his. "I just had the most amazing journey."

CHAPTER THIRTEEN

*S*unlight streamed from above, blanketing the mountains in a celestial-like radiance. Fluffy white wisps danced across the blue summer sky, reminding Katie of her time in the clouds.

Leaning against the front porch column, she sighed wistfully as she rubbed Pan's head. Her dog hadn't strayed from her side since she had returned home from the hospital a few days ago.

Bending down she fluffed Pan's ears and kissed the top of his head. "You're my best buddy, aren't you?"

Pan's tail thumped zealously.

When she rose, her gaze slid across the yard toward the Callahan's and Patterson's, family and friends, mixing and mingling in celebration of her homecoming. That is, most were socializing. Her father stood off to one side brooding, but at least he'd come, and that was a major step in the right direction.

The past week had been a crazy, joyful blur. She'd woken from the coma on Sunday and had been released from the hospital on Tuesday evening.

Warm arms wrapped around her from behind. She pivoted, and smiled up at Liam.

"Have I told you how grateful I am that you're home?" He kissed her forehead. "And how very much I love you?"

Her smile widened. He had told her—many, many times. But she didn't mind the repetition. She loved hearing the words, and she loved being home, too.

"Get used to it," Liam said, twirling his fingers through the loose tendrils of hair framing her face.

As a homecoming gift, her hairdresser and close friend, Jon, had stopped by to help her get ready, styling her hair in an elaborate updo and fussing over her makeup. Touching a hand to her hair, she had to admit she felt like a million bucks. The pretty white sundress she and Jen had purchased expressly for this event was stylish. According to Jen, it also showcased her post-hospital fit figure.

As if one with her thoughts, Liam gently rubbed his knuckles over her cheek. "You're so beautiful," he whispered. "I missed you so much, Katie-Cat."

She pulled Liam's face to hers for a long, passionate kiss. When Liam's hands lowered to cup her butt, she had the strong urge to thrust her hips against his belly, but she reluctantly drew back. She could have spent the entire evening making up for lost time with her sweet hubby. But they had guests. She smiled up at Liam. "Thanks for the party," she said, linking her hand with his. "C'mon. Let's go mingle."

Throughout the evening, Katie visited with her guests. She talked about the accident, her coma, her ongoing recovery. She didn't talk about her time in the clouds, except for a few snippets she had shared with Liam.

Because, really—*had* she spent time in the clouds or had it all been an amazing, larger than life dream? Almost a week after waking, she still wasn't sure.

Her time in Tranquility had seemed so real. Even now when she closed her eyes she could see Posie's angelic smile and hear Black Eagle's calming voice. At times, her bed felt as soft as the cloud, and the other day when she searched Pan's eyes, she would've sworn it was Bear staring back at her.

Circling the house, she made her way up the stairs onto the back deck. Leaning against the rail, her gaze skimmed the evening sky as a mammoth cumulus cloud floated overhead. She smiled, knowing—dream or reality—she'd never think about clouds in the same way again. A strong, sweet scent directed her attention to the flower garden where streams of light shone on a stunning white bloom.

The shimmering flower radiated strength. Drawing in the sweet fragrance, Katie resolved to tell Liam about Savannah. *Tonight.*

She had to tell him soon because she needed to call Gwen's attorney. Savannah's school year would be ending in a few weeks. She tried to remember the exact date but came up blank. She had trouble remembering the details from her discussion with Mr. Loncar because of everything that had occurred since their brief conversation.

Smoothing down the material of her dress, Katie's gaze scanned the back yard looking for Liam. A lot had happened while she had been in the coma. She smiled at Sabby and Brandon who ambled by holding hands. They were dating now, even though it was long distance since Liz and Sabby had moved back to Georgetown. Liz and Shane had also dated. But after Katie came out of the coma, Liz had broken up with Shane indicating she didn't believe in long-distance romance. Shane claimed he didn't care, but he had moped around all week. Tonight, both he and Liz had gone out of their way to avoid each other.

Pan edged closer and nuzzled her leg. She squatted down to rub his ears. "Still my little shadow," she cooed.

"I would be too if I could get away with it," Liam said, approaching.

Laughing, she lowered to the deck stairs. Liam and Pan sat on each side of her.

Liam scrutinized her. "You doing okay?"

She was starting to feel tired, but she wasn't about to tell Liam that, especially after he and Shane had gone to all the effort to throw her this great party. Besides, Liam had worried endlessly about her ever since she got out of the hospital. Sure, her body was still weak and she moved around slower than she had before the accident. Her mind wasn't as sharp either, but she was hoping all of that would return to normal soon. Her doctors hadn't found anything medically wrong, although they were keeping a close eye on her. Maybe the burden of the impending discussion about Savannah was weighing her down, too.

"I'm fine," she said, and then remembered that Black Eagle had said something about going to see a healer and that he would guide her to the right person. She was waiting and watching for that guidance, and hoped it would come soon.

"Liam?" Biting her lower lip, she twirled a strand of hair around her index finger. "Do you think I'm crazy? You know about my dream...or whatever."

"Not at all." Liam grazed his lips over her hair. "Something obviously happened while you were gone. You've told me bits and pieces, but sometime soon I want the whole story."

"Okay." She rested her head against his solid chest, appreciating his support. "It all seemed so real. But, well...I guess it was probably a dream."

"Does it really matter?" he asked, gently rubbing her thigh. "If it was planted in your mind as a dream, does that make it any less real?"

"I guess you're right." When had her husband become so wise? Drawing in a long inhale, she took his hand. "I'm glad you feel that way because there's something else I need to tell you."

"Great, and there's something I need to tell you too."

"You go first," she said, relieved for the pass. She shifted so she was facing him.

"I had a lot of time to think while you were in the hospital. I was so afraid I might lose you," Liam said, his voice thick with emotion. "But the coma put things in perspective. I promised myself after you came back we wouldn't fight anymore."

He wrapped his arms around her. "The last thing I want to do is spend our precious time fighting." He nuzzled his face in her hair. "I love you, Katie, and I promise that from now on I'll support your decisions. Whatever kind of job you want, *wherever* you want to work, I'm good with it."

She had Liam's full support for whatever career she desired. That was exactly what she'd wanted before the coma. But in the clouds, she'd gained more perspective, too. "I appreciate that. A lot." She rubbed a hand on his arm. "But I've done a lot of thinking, too, and I'm not sure I know what I want. Posie and Black Eagle taught me to stop thinking about what everyone else wants, and focus on what *I* want. They said if I tune into my feelings that I'd figure out what is right for me."

"That sounds about right." Liam gently pressed her head against his chest. "And I'm gonna support whatever you decide."

Resting her head against Liam, gratitude swelled in her heart and seeped into her soul. She prayed that her husband's unwavering support would carry over to the moment when she found the courage to tell him about Savannah.

THE NEXT MORNING, Katie paced the living room floor, her stomach queasy despite the great night she'd had. Her homecoming party had been the first time she'd celebrated—or had done anything, for that matter—with her *entire* family. Her parents had come to her and Liam's home for the very first time. Liam had offered his full support for whatever she decided to do career-wise. In spite of those positives, she was irked with herself because she had yet to tell Liam about Savannah.

Racked with guilt, she slowly paced back and forth, twirling strands of hair around her fingers until it turned into a knotted mess. On her umpteenth rotation, she ran into Liam.

"What's wrong?" He slid his hands around her waist and tugged her in close. "I thought you'd be happy this morning after your party. Half the town was here, not to mention your family, even your father."

Katie burrowed her head into the hollow of Liam's shoulder. "I know." She had so much to be thankful for, but that only increased her shame. "I know," she repeated.

"What is it then?" Liam drew back and lifted her chin. "Is this about Shane and Liz? I know Shane's been a bear, but he'll get over it. He always does. Is that why you're upset?"

"Yeah." The agreement just popped out as she took a pass yet again. The guilt in her gut enlarged.

"Hey, now." Liam kissed her cheek. "Don't worry, sweetie. I'll talk to Shane, tell him to snap out of it."

Katie blew out a breath. Damn it, she was a strong woman. Okay, maybe she *hadn't* been recently...but that was going to end.

Unease rooted in her stomach like a honeysuckle vine, growing fast as a weed, waiting for her to tend to it. "Liam, we need to talk." She forced the words out quickly before she could change her mind. Once she did, she drew in the sweet honey scent of honesty.

Liam's face paled and his forehead creased, but he took her hand and led her to the sofa. After they were settled, he looked her in the eye. "Tell me what's wrong. Whatever it is, I'll fix it, okay?"

She nodded, feeling a sense of relief even before she told him. Liam had always been there for her, solid and steady as a rock.

"I should've told you this before but I just found out right before the accident." She pulled in a long breath. "Remember the call I got the day before the accident?" After he nodded, she continued. "I was gonna tell you after our ride, but then we had the accident...."

As her words drifted off, Liam's arms wrapped around her. "What is it? Tell me now."

"The call was from my cousin Gwen Shelton's attorney," she said, nuzzling her head against his heart. "She's the one who lived in Texas."

"I know who she is." Liam put his hands on her arms and pulled back slightly. "But it's hard to understand when you're talking into my chest."

Katie swallowed hard, then blurted the rest of it out. "Gwen died and left me custody of her daughter, Savannah."

"Okay." Liam's eyes widened but otherwise he showed no evidence of the shock he must have felt. "I didn't think you knew her well. Were you and Gwen close when you were young?"

"No. I only met Gwen once. But that's not the point...there's more." Katie nervously twisted her hands on her lap. "I should've told you this a long time ago." She peered up at her husband. "Savannah's my daughter."

Shock registered in Liam's expression. "What? How?" he asked, his voice thick. "You're gonna have to back up and start at the beginning."

Her long-held secret was finally out. Liam seemed surprised, but not at all mad. Relief washed through her like a soft summer rain. "I will. But first I'm sorry I didn't tell you before. I almost told you a bunch of times, but you're such a devoted dad, a *real* family man, I was afraid of what you'd think of me."

"Damn, Katie." Liam let out a dry laugh. "I appreciate the thought and these days I sure try. But I was a complete fuck-up when my parents were alive and your parents still think I am so don't put me on a family values pedestal." He brushed his knuckles over her cheek. "But you...you're an amazing, loving, giving person. You have nothing to be ashamed of."

Sitting a little straighter, Katie squared her shoulders as the weight of the world lifted from her back.

"You must have been so young, so scared," Liam said. "How old were you when you had Savannah?"

"Seventeen," she whispered, throwing her arms around Liam's shoulders. She had wanted Liam to forgive her for giving away her child. But he'd done even better. He hadn't judged her in the first place. Now she needed to stop judging herself. She held him tight, wondering why she had ever doubted his support.

After several long moments, she drew back. "Savannah is twelve now." She proceeded to tell Liam about spending her junior year of high school as an exchange student. Finding out she was pregnant shortly after settling in with her host family, giving birth to Savannah while in Belize, and her dad arranging for the adoption.

Liam squeezed her in closer. "Well that explains some things, too."

She didn't need to ask what he meant by that. She had never thought about it before, but perhaps part of her father's hold over her was tied to their shared secret. Other than marrying Liam, she usually acquiesced to her father's wishes. Now that she'd confided in Liam, her father's power over her had lost its impact.

"Tonight is ours," Liam said, referring to their overnight get-away, "but when we get home, why don't you call Gwen's attorney and make arrangements for us to go get Savannah?"

Straightening, Katie gaped at her husband. "Just like that?" She'd known she'd had Liam's backing, but how could he be so easy and accepting about adding another child to their family? They hadn't yet talked about logistics, finances, how Savannah would fit into their family.

"Just like that." Liam pulled her back into his arms. "She's your daughter. Of course we'll make her a part of the Callahan family."

∿

KATIE WAITED on the front porch swing for Liz and Sabby to arrive. She and Liam were going on an overnight get-away so Liz was house-sitting. When she pulled into the drive, Katie walked down to greet them.

Sabby opened her door, then peeled off her shirt to reveal an itty-bitty bikini. While it was probably suitable attire for the pool party that she and Cara were going to this afternoon, she wondered if it would have killed Sabby to keep her shirt on until she actually reached the pool.

"Hi, Aunt Katie." Sabby adjusted the strap on the ridiculously small patch of material covering her breasts.

"Hi, Sabby."

Liz scowled at her daughter. "Why did you take off your new cover-up?"

"Mom, no one covers at a pool party." Sabby crossed her arms.

Sighing, Liz spun toward her. "You gotta love teenagers."

Katie lifted the corners of her mouth in commiseration, even though Cara was thankfully a little more conservative than her cousin. "Thanks for coming." She gave Liz a quick hug.

"Anytime, especially when that sweet husband of yours is whisking you off to the Inn at Little River," Liz said.

Katie grinned. "I've been wanting to go there."

"I wanna go, too," Sabby whined. "I hear it's the bomb." When Liz pinned a look on her, Sabby rolled her eyes. "The *spa*, Mom." She rounded the hood of the Mercedes and slid behind the driver's seat. "Cara's friend, Lindsey, gets her toes done at the Inn."

"Liam scheduled a facial and pedicure appointment for me later today." Katie sighed happily. "He's so thoughtful."

Cara rushed out, dressed in shorts and, God bless her, a tank hoody cover-up. "Hey, Liz. Hey, Katie. Hope you and Dad have fun tonight."

"Thanks, Cara." She hugged her step-daughter. "You and Sabby have a good time, too. We'll see you in the morning."

" 'Kay, love yah," Cara said slipping into the car.

"Love you too. Have fun, and be good, girls," she added inanely. But it was her routine with Cara.

"See ya'll later," Sabby hollered as she peeled out of the drive.

"Crazy girl." Liz shook her head. "I don't know why I let her drive my Mercedes."

Katie laughed. "Because you love her." She linked her arm with Liz's. "C'mon, let's have lunch while Liam finishes up in the shop. We have an hour to catch up before he'll be ready and I have some news to share."

Liz gave her a curious look. "Do tell."

Katie wasn't about to have this conversation in the front yard. More importantly, she needed a few minutes to gather her courage. Liam had been the hardest to tell, yet his reaction had buoyed her. Shane had been an easy conversation, but he didn't count because he thought she walked on water. It would be harder to tell her sister. Even though Liz had traveled a lot when Katie was a teenager, Liz had always been supportive of her. Looking back, she had no idea why she hadn't reached out to her sister at the time. "Let's get lunch ready first."

Inside, Liz set the table and poured two glasses of iced tea, while Katie pulled containers from the refrigerator.

"Is this your homemade chicken-walnut salad?" Liz asked, eyeing the glass bowl.

"Yep."

"Yum." Liz patted her belly making Katie laugh.

Katie added a scoop of chicken salad on top of the tossed salads, and carried the plates to the table. As soon as she and Liz were seated, she forced herself to broach the subject of her daughter before she lost what little nerve she had amassed. "I have a daughter," she said matter-of-factly, taking a bite of her chicken salad.

Liz gave her a sidelong look. "Yeah, so do I…."

"No, not Cara." She put down her fork. "I have *another* daughter, a child I had when I was seventeen."

"Are you serious?" Liz's head jerked up, and her eyes popped. "Why didn't you tell me? Where is she?"

"I'm sorry I didn't tell you before," she said, taking in her sister's hurt look. "But I was young and embarrassed."

"Okay." Liz wiped the corner of her mouth with a napkin, then placed it on her lap. "I'm gonna need some details."

Katie filled her sister in on the call from Gwen's attorney and the subsequent discussion with their father confirming that Savannah was her daughter.

"Wow!" Liz took a gulp of her iced tea. "How do you feel about this? What does Liam think?"

"I'm scared, thrilled, grateful. Liam's been amazing. Shane's been great, too. He bought open tickets for Liam and I to fly to Texas as soon as I can make arrangements. I'm beyond excited." She took a drink of her tea. "By the way, I haven't told Cara yet so don't say anything. I'm going to tell her after we get back tomorrow." Katie put a hand over her sister's. "You should give Shane another chance. He's a sweetheart."

"No arguments there." Liz sighed. "But I've been around the block and I know better than to try to sustain a long-distance relationship."

"It's only an hour drive to Georgetown," she countered.

Liz stabbed a forkful of chicken salad. "Two in traffic."

"But you really liked him." Then it dawned on Katie. *That* was the problem. Her highly independent sister *really* liked Shane.

171

Liz waved her off. "Let's get back to you. Savannah is the big news here. How old is she?"

"Twelve."

"And why didn't I know about her?" Liz asked.

Katie lifted a shoulder. "I had Savannah when I was in Belize."

"So you got pregnant there or had the baby there?" Liz leaned toward her. "I'm sorry you had to go through that alone, but tell me why Dad knew and I didn't?"

"I had the baby in Belize. Dad knew because my exchange dad called him. Then, he arranged for the adoption so fast it made my head spin, but I never knew it was with Gwen." She let out a long exhale. "After I got home I was ashamed so it was easy to follow Dad's directive and brush it under the rug. But I never forgot." Her heart tugged as her mind flashed to the sweet baby girl she'd held in her arms way too briefly. "I've thought about Savannah every day since I gave her up."

"Oh, Katie," Liz said, her voice sympathetic. "What about her father?"

"He told me to eff off." Katie stared at her clasped hands. "He didn't want anything to do with our baby. Actually, he didn't want anything to do with me either after we did it the one time."

"What a jerk." Liz's brows creased. "But I would have been there for you, Katie. I can't imagine going through that alone, especially at seventeen."

"I know but you were on assignment. Australia, I think." She twirled a strand of hair around two fingers. "It's hardly a conversation to have over the phone. Besides, you couldn't have done anything from half way across the world."

Liz rested her head on her palm. "I'm a horrible big sister."

Katie nudged her sister from across the table. "You are not."

"I'll make it up to you." Liz flashed a smile. "I'm gonna be a kick ass aunt."

"You already are. You're a great aunt to Cara."

"Well, I'm gonna be even better—for Cara and for Savannah. Now that I'm not traveling as much, I'll be around a lot more."

Katie smiled at her sister. "I like having you around."

"Me too." Liz rose, took their plates to the sink, and rinsed them. "Guess you'll be heading out soon."

Katie glanced at her watch. "Liam should be here any minute." She took their glasses and put them in the dishwasher, then stacked the plates that Liz handed to her. "I'm gonna grab my bag so I'm ready when he gets here."

"Did I hear my name?" Liam asked, stepping into the kitchen.

"You didn't tell me *she* was here," Shane grumbled, rounding the corner behind Liam.

Liam gave his brother an innocent shrug, then turned to her and Liz. "Hi, Katie, Liz. Great news, Shane agreed to stay overnight to keep an eye on Cara."

"Hi, Shane." Katie kissed her brother-in-law on the cheek, then looked at Liam. "I'm confused. Liz drove down to stay with Cara. Remember? Sabby and Cara went to Abigal's pool party today."

"Huh. Sorry." But he didn't look sorry; he looked almost gleeful as he scratched his chin. "Guess I'm getting old. But Shane's here, too," he said, grinning. "How 'bout that? So you about ready to go, babe?"

A glint appeared in Liam's eye and she caught on. They needed to get out of dodge to force Shane and Liz into time alone.

"Let me grab my bag and we'll be off," she said, and then shifted toward Liz. "Thanks for being here."

"Have fun." Liz hugged her. "But no sense in me staying if Shane's here."

"But Sabby has a date with Brandon tonight. It's ridiculous for you to drive home, then drive back in the morning." Katie slid her gaze between grumpy looking Shane and frustrated Liz. "It'll save you time, not to mention gas. You couldn't go until later tonight when Sabby gets back with the car, anyway."

"Guess I'll be leaving then," Shane said. "If Liz stays with Cara and Sabby, they don't need me."

Arms crossed, Liam leaned against the door frame and shot Shane a smug look. "Cara's been talking about your Canasta match all morning. You don't want to let her down, do you? Especially since Sabby has a date tonight."

Shane frowned.

A twinge of guilt flitted into Katie's chest, but she ignored it. Her and Liam's meddling was for a good cause. "Then it's settled," she said a little too cheerfully. "Shane and Liz can *both* stay. Come on, Liam, let's rock and roll."

~

AFTER KATIE AND LIAM LEFT, Liz gave Shane a frosty look. "That was *so* staged."

"I had nothing to do with it." A muscle in Shane's jaw twitched as he lifted his hands in the air. "I can leave and come back after Cara gets home."

"Don't be ridiculous," she said. Although whether she could handle being in close proximity with the man who had consumed her every thought over the last week was yet to be determined. "We're both adults," she said, reminding herself along with Shane.

"That we are," he agreed in a husky voice.

His navy fitted T-shirt did nothing to hide the bulging and flexing of his muscles as he made his way over. But it would be downright weak, not to mention mean, to send him away simply because he was too sexy. She let out a resigned breath. "I'm sure we can manage a few hours together before Cara gets home." She put a hand on her hip, flustered at her body's quick reaction to Shane, annoyed at being played. "But when did your brother become Mr. Matchmaker?"

Shane leaned his hot body against the kitchen counter, drawing her attention to his sinewy biceps. "Maybe Katie put him up to it."

She snorted. "Why would Katie do that?"

"Maybe she thinks you missed all of this," he said, waving a hand around his body and giving her a cocky grin.

A laugh tumbled out of her. Shaking her head, Liz pushed off the counter and moved to the wine rack. "Modesty is one of the things I love most about you." Remembering Shane's preference for red, she grabbed a bottle of Cab and extended it toward him. God knew, she could use a drink to help her get through the afternoon.

Shane shrugged. "Why not?" He grabbed wine glasses and a corkscrew, then followed her into the living room where he popped the cork and poured the wine.

Pan trotted over and flopped on the floor in front of them.

"Hey, buddy." Shane reached down to pet the dog. As Shane stroked Pan, her eyes zeroed in on his large hands. Hands that had capably worshiped her body before they'd been busted. She wondered what those hands would feel like on her naked body. Too bad they had never gotten the opportunity.

Now it was too late. They had separate lives and they lived too far apart to make a go of it. Knowing this, she tried for ambivalence, but her body flushed and her breasts heated despite her best efforts.

Straightening, Shane picked up his glass. "How've you been, Liz?"

She let out a tight laugh. "We saw each other yesterday."

"*Saw* being the operative word." Shane took a slow sip of his wine. "We didn't speak other than a curt hello." He put his glass on the table and slid closer. "As a matter of fact, I think you went out of your way to avoid being near me."

Liz's heart hammered in her chest and she had the overwhelming urge to throw herself at Shane. He wasn't making it easy, sitting in such close proximity with heat practically radiating from his body. And he stared at her lips as if he wanted to devour them.

Damn the man.

He put a hand on her leg. Why had she worn a short dress today of all days, she wondered? When his fingers caressed her bare flesh, her breath hitched.

Look away, she told herself. Look away and pretend it's not happening. She shifted her gaze, but when she did, Shane moved in even closer. Now his body brushed against hers and those clever fingers traced tiny designs up her thigh.

He took her glass and placed it on the table. To escape his irresistible appeal, she continued to stare in the other direction. But Shane wouldn't be put off. He put his hands around her face and gently angled it toward him, then skimmed his thumb over her lower lip.

"I wonder why that is," he murmured, his mouth mere inches from hers.

Why what? She couldn't think about anything other than his mouth hovering close to hers. When she drew in his exotic, earthy scent, her resolve began to crumble.

His bottom lip touched hers. "What do you think?"

Now, she couldn't think at all. She wasn't sure she was even breathing, her awareness was so completely focused on Shane's devastating presence.

He sucked on her lower lip, and her body rocked with sweet anticipation. At any moment, she would surely lose it. As if he could sense her vulnerability, he shifted and touched his chest to hers. Her breasts quivered and her belly fluttered as if in harmony with his advancing.

Sighing, she yanked Shane's head to hers and claimed those tempting lips. The kiss spun out, urgent, needy, and delicious.

When they eased back, lust flickered in Shane's eyes. His fingers moved up her leg and under the hem of her dress. "Maybe we should give this another go," he said. "I've missed you."

KATIE AMBLED through the gardens feeling light as the breeze that gently brushed through the summer blooms. Her face was tingly clean after the exfoliation and moisturizer, her feet soft as a baby's bottom after her pedicure. Wriggling toes the color of cotton candy, she wound her way through the inn's pebble footpaths on her way back to her and Liam's room.

She found Liam sprawled on the side of the bed, phone in hand. He sat up when she entered, a grin covering his entire face. "Hey, baby, how was the spa?"

"Amazing. Thank you." She sat down next to him and kissed his cheek. "It was a really nice gift."

"I'm glad you liked it. You deserve to be pampered." Still grinning, he handed her his cell. "Take a look at this."

She read the text message from Shane: *Liz and I are giving it another go*, followed by a smiley face emoji.

"Nice." Her lips curved up. "Looks like your nefarious plan worked."

"Yeah, how 'bout that? I like the two of them together. Shane needs a mature, confident woman."

She slid over so her body rubbed against Liam's. "Maybe we should spend the evening getting back together, too." She batted her lashes. "If you know what I mean."

Liam's eyes widened. Desire sparked, and then just as quickly clouded. "Today is about pampering you." He kissed the top of her head. "To help you relax and get your strength back."

She brushed her right breast against Liam's arm, and he let out a low groan. "I feel really good now," she whispered.

Liam tugged her onto his lap. But instead of drawing her into a passionate embrace, he pressed her head against his shoulder and gently stroked her hair. "It's too soon," he said, his voice heavy with regret.

"But I've been out of the coma for over a week."

"Too soon," he repeated as he caressed her hair.

Sinking her head into the hollow of his chest, she sighed, half in frustration, half in pleasure. His hands were rough, but his touch soothing. She gave in to it and soon after, her eyes grew heavy.

Sometime later, she awoke face down on the bed. Liam was next to her, gently rubbing her body. She rolled over to face him.

He brushed a long strand of hair away from her face. "Did you have a good nap?"

The concern in his voice staggered her. She touched a hand to his cheek. "It was good. I'm fine, Liam. Really."

She sat and stretched.

"You hungry?"

Her stomach growled. "I guess I am."

"When you're ready, we can eat here at the inn," he said. "I walked around earlier while you were at the spa. The restaurant smells great and they have tables overlooking the river."

"Sounds good." She rose. "I'll just freshen up, then we can head over."

"Okay. Hey, baby, why don't you call Gwen's attorney now instead of waiting till tomorrow?" He glanced at his watch. "It's only 4:00 in Amarillo." "Make the call, Katie-Cat," he said, after he drew back. "Then we can make plans over dinner."

"That's a great idea." As her stomach clenched with excitement, Katie searched her purse for her cell phone. After she found it, she located Mr. Loncar's number in the history log and hit call. The receptionist answered, and a moment later put her through.

"Loncar," the attorney said in way of greeting.

"Hi. It's Katie Callahan. I'm calling about Gwen Shelton's will and Savannah."

There was a brief pause, then Mr. Loncar cleared his throat. "Yes, Ms. Callahan, I expected to hear from you weeks ago."

"I know. I'm sorry. I was in an accident, but I'm better now," she said. "I want to make arrangements to see Savannah and to pick her up after her school session ends."

The attorney sighed. "Custody has already been awarded." Katie sucked in a sharp breath. "When you didn't call in the stipulated timeframe, custody was awarded to Gwen's brother, Warren." Katie slumped onto the bed as her heart shattered into tiny pieces. "Those were the terms of Ms. Shelton's will."

Katie's phone slipped from her fingers as tears streamed down her cheeks.

"What's wrong?" Liam asked crouching in front of her.

She tried to tell him what Mr. Loncar had said but the words got jumbled with her sobs and came out as gibberish. Liam wrapped his arms around her and held her tight. But even his strength did nothing to console her. She had lost her one opportunity to gain custody of her daughter. Sorrow tore at her insides as a deep, dark pain unfurled in her chest. Stupid accident, stupid coma, stupid her. Why had she waited so long to tell Liam about Savannah? If she had told him right after her initial conversation with Mr. Loncar, Liam would have called while she was in the coma and probably could have gotten an extension on the timeline.

As she sobbed, some of her sorrow morphed into anger—at herself, at God, at her guides. In the clouds, Posie and Black Eagle had taught her that she just needed to put her desires out there and believe in them. They'd said if she did that her wishes would come true…they'd said it was universal law.

But that was exactly what she had done, yet instead of making her dreams come true, the very thing she had wanted the most—to reunite with her daughter—had been cruelly ripped away.

Her head sank into Liam's chest as the anger inside her whipped and whirled into a dark tornado of depression.

CHAPTER FOURTEEN

*L*iam grabbed a bottle of water, lit a Marlboro, and plopped down in front of his desk. He needed to quit smoking one day, but today sure as hell wasn't that day. Booting up his PC, he took a long drag, chugged water…and worried about Katie.

She had been depressed and pessimistic ever since the call with Loncar a few days back.

With forced concentration, Liam worked through the morning's emails, made an update to the company website, and paid bills. He still had an hour before his team would arrive so he made his way into the bay area to work on a few bikes. The physical labor fed his body in a way his earlier gym workout hadn't. When his team shuffled in, he headed back to the house to check on Katie.

She was awake, but still dejected. "Why bother?" she muttered when he suggested she get out of bed. Thankfully, Pan seemed to understand. While Liam sat on one side of bed stroking Katie's hair, Pan snuggled next to her on the other side. He kissed Katie's forehead, and then locked eyes with the dog. "You look out for her, Pan," he said, rubbing the dog's ears. When he pushed up to a standing position, Pan rested his head on Katie's shoulder and gave him an *I-got-this* look.

The hopelessness in Katie's eyes kicked at Liam's chest. His heart ached for her, for her loss. Overwhelmed and not knowing what else to do, he headed downstairs and called Shane to ask for help. Even though he *never* asked for help.

Strong and independent, Liam took care of his family on his own. But nothing he had tried had worked with Katie, so he swallowed his pride and called in additional reinforcements—Liz and Carolyn.

He had surprised Carolyn—and himself—by calling her. But dire times called for dire measures. Katie had made it through the accident and the coma. Now, he was damn well going to do everything in his power to help her regain her strength—physically and emotionally.

Calls made, he grabbed a Coke and waited on the front porch for everyone to arrive.

Shane showed up first, and gave him a half hug. "How's our Katie?"

"Not well." He pressed a hand to the back of his neck to ease the tension coiled there. "Cara's upstairs with her now, but, I'm worried."

Carolyn pulled into the drive next and made her way to the porch. "Liam, Shane."

Liam hugged his mother-in-law. "Thanks for coming."

"I appreciate you calling," she said. "I just found out about Savannah—and from Liz, at that!" Liam understood the irritation he detected in Carolyn's voice. Mitch should have told her about Katie's child, especially considering his role in the adoption. "Anyway, thanks for including me. I'll do whatever I can to help."

When Liz arrived half an hour later, Shane made a pot of coffee and they gathered in the dining room. Taking a seat at the head of the table, Liam brushed a hand over the walnut finish. The table had been in his family for generations, hand-crafted by his great, great grandfather. Someday it would go to Cara, Savannah, or to a yet to be conceived child he and Katie would have together.

When a soft hand touched his shoulder, he turned to find Cara behind him.

"Katie's sleeping," she said.

"Thanks, sweetie." He tipped his head toward the others. "We're having a family meeting. Sit, join us."

Cara greeted Shane, Liz, and Carolyn, and then took a seat.

Liam added cream and sugar to his coffee, took a long sip, and then looked around the table. "Thanks for coming. Katie's really down." He took another sip of coffee, and the caffeine gave him a much-needed jolt of energy. "I've never seen her like this."

"Just tell me what I can do," Carolyn said.

"Me too, Dad," Cara put in. "I wanna help, too."

Liz leaned in close to Shane, rubbing a hand up and down his arm. Carolyn raised a brow but Liz either didn't notice or chose to ignore her mother's unspoken question. Instead, she looked directly at him. "Us, too."

"You know it," Shane said. "We're all here for Katie."

Liam nodded, appreciation welling in his chest. "She was just starting to regain her strength, but after the call with Loncar, she hasn't even tried. The last few days she's barely gotten out of bed. She says, 'why bother?' "

Liz pressed her lips together. "That's so unlike Katie."

"She thinks she blew her only chance for custody. But even before that, she was pretending she was okay even though she's still weak from the coma." He ran a hand over his cheek. "And she's been beating herself up over not having a job. We're doing just fine so I don't know why she's so worried."

He clasped his hands in front of him, feeling completely overwhelmed. Shane must have picked up on it, because he leaned forward and put a hand over his. "We're all gonna help, bro. Let's save the discussion about Savannah for last—it'll take the longest—but we'll fight for custody."

For once, instead of resenting Shane's offer to help, Liam was grateful.

"One step at a time," Liz said, drumming her fingers on the table. "First, the job." Liz's brows creased. "Do you know why she's so concerned about not having a job right now?"

"It's your father," Carolyn said, surprising Liam with her honesty.

"He means well, but he needs to back off. Katie has enough to deal with." She reached over and patted his hand. "I've got this."

If Mitch stopped pushing Katie, she could stop her incessant worrying and focus on taking care of herself. That is, once he got her out of bed. "You could do that?" he asked, allowing a smidgeon of hope to unfurl in his chest.

"Of course." Carolyn's eyes flashed determination. "Mitch usually calls the shots, but when I take a stand, he knows I mean business."

He nodded. "That would be helpful."

"You could ask Katie to help out at Callahan Cycles," Shane suggested. "It would give her something productive to do which might lessen her worries."

Liam had been thinking the same thing. "It would help my business too," he said, "and she could work limited hours."

"I'll talk with her," Liz offered. "Play up her marketing expertise."

"That would be great." It would probably be better coming from Liz so Katie didn't feel pressured. "Getting Katie's strength back is priority, so I'm taking her to see an energy healer tomorrow," he said. When he had taken Katie to the Inn, she'd told him about her time in the clouds and what her guides had taught her. She'd also shared that Black Eagle had suggested she see a healer and that he would help her find the right one. When Liam saw the ad in this morning's paper, he had taken it as a sign. "That is, assuming she wants to go." He hoped that she would. He also hoped the energy healer could not only help Katie get her strength back, but her positive outlook, too.

"I can cook," Cara said. "It'll be one less thing for Katie to do. Besides, she's been talking about going vegetarian, so I can cook veggie dishes for me and Katie and toss on a chunk of meat for you."

He let out a quick laugh. "Thanks, sweetie."

"Now let's talk about Savannah," Shane said, glancing across the table at Cara. "You know about her, right?"

"Duh, you just talked about her." Cara rolled her eyes and then grinned. "But, yay!" She traced hearts on the table with her finger. "I have a little sister."

"Figured you'd be excited," Shane said, and then shifted toward Liam. "We can use my attorney. I already called Ken and gave him the lowdown." Shane shared his attorney's suggested strategy, including a court request that would allow Liam and Katie to visit Savannah while the legal issues were under review.

"Thank you," Liam said, feeling a deep sense of gratitude. He rotated his gaze to connect with everyone at the table. "I appreciate the support."

"We're family," Carolyn said. "That's what family does."

Katie's mother's full support and unexpected words of solidarity filled Liam with renewed hope for a positive relationship between the two of them. He appreciated *all* of their support, and because of it, he now had positive updates to share with Katie, especially the attorney's strategy. This was exactly what he needed to nudge Katie out of her depression.

KATIE PEERED out the bedroom window, ashamed of her inability to pull herself out of her funk. Considering that Shane, Liz, and her mother had all left the house at the same time, she could only assume that they'd had some kind of gathering to talk about her and her many issues. That irked her, although she wasn't sure whether she was irritated at them for talking about her as if she were a child or at herself for acting like a child.

Sighing, she flopped onto the bed. Pan hopped up and scooted next to her as she curled into a ball. "May as well take another nap," she mumbled. "Maybe I'll wake up in a better mood."

Pan tipped his head to one side as if questioning the validity of her statement. "I know, buddy, I don't really believe it either," she said, as a new wave of hopelessness swept through her.

Pan, her ever loyal companion, snuggled next to her and licked her face. At least that made her smile. "Thanks, Pan," she said, then sat up when the bedroom door opened.

Liam strolled in and sat beside her on the edge of the bed. He leaned in and kissed the top of her head which annoyed her because that was how he often greeted Cara. Stop acting like a child, said a voice in her head, and everyone will stop treating you like one.

Sighing, she glanced over at Liam. He had been nothing but sweet and kind and she had been acting like an ungrateful child.

"How are you?" he asked, with genuine concern in his voice.

She wanted to say she was fine. She desperately needed to climb out of her pit of despair. But how? She blew out a long breath. "About the same," she answered honestly.

"We're gonna fight Warren for custody," Liam said, gently tipping her head toward him. "Shane's already talked to his attorney and he's put together a solid plan." Katie's heart thumped hopefully even though the situation still seemed pretty darn bleak. Custody had already been awarded to Warren.

"We're gonna fight hard and we're going to win." Liam took her hand. "But sweetie, you need to do your part, too."

She scrunched her lips together. "What do you mean?"

"When we were at the Inn, you told me the whole story of your time in the clouds," he said. "You shared what your guides taught you. You need to remember all of that now, and you need to *believe* that we'll get custody."

She studied the gold flecks gleaming in Liam's eyes. His expression was sincere, positive, and determined.

She so wanted to believe. But she'd lost her faith. What Posie and Black Eagle had taught her *hadn't* worked. "How can I after what happened?"

Liam leaned in and rubbed his palm over the top of her hand. "Based on what you shared, your guides didn't tell you it would be easy or that you'd never have obstacles." He pressed his lips to her forehead. "They didn't say every request would happen quickly. They said to believe and it would happen." He moved a hand through her hair. "So you need to keep believing. Not just in God, the universe, and your guides, but in your family, too. We're all standing with you, Katie. One day, mark my words, Savannah will be with us."

"Oh, Liam." Katie's heart flooded with love and gratitude for her amazing husband. When she was weak, he was strong. When she

185

was spirtless, he was filled with faith. When she lacked courage, he was brave. She appreciated his strength and unwavering confidence now more than ever.

And he was right; she needed to find a way to believe. But life had a way of taking its toll. Her mind had been trapped in the proverbial 'what if's,' and the 'what if's' terrified her. What if Warren was a great uncle and Savannah was better off with him? What if they fought Warren and lost? What if she had missed her only shot at reuniting with her daughter?

But Liam's recap of what Posie and Black Eagle had taught her had been spot on. In Tranquility, she had learned that things happen for a reason. Everything—the motorcycle accident, her coma, her time in the clouds. Maybe all of it had happened to help her through this very situation. A glimmer of light appeared in the recesses of her mind.

Liam smiled. "I haven't seen that sparkle in a while." He rubbed his hand on her thigh. "I've missed it." He leaned in and kissed her, this time on the lips. When he drew back, he touched a hand to her cheek. "Everything's going to work out, but we need to be strong."

Katie nodded. Maybe she could draw on some of his strength until she rebuilt her own.

Liam pulled a newspaper clipping out of his back pocket. "I saw this earlier." He handed her the paper. It was an advertisement for Simone's Energy Healing Center in Frederick. Goosebumps pricked along her arm. "This ad was in today's paper," he said. "Our *local* paper. I think it's the sign you've been waiting for from Black Eagle."

Her hand trembled as she passed the paper back to Liam. She nodded in agreement, drawing in a lungful of relief. Maybe her guides hadn't failed her, after all.

THE NEXT MORNING Liam drove Katie to her energy healing appointment. She felt badly for pulling him away from work just because she was feeling down. She glanced at his profile as he pulled into the parking lot following the instructions on her phone's GPS.

"I could've driven myself," she said, wincing at her words as she climbed out of the truck. She hadn't meant to sound so snotty.

But Liam didn't take offense. "I know, baby, but Seth has things covered at the shop." He hustled around the hood of the truck. "I wanted to be with you." He linked her hand with his.

"Thanks, Liam." She kissed his stubbly cheek. "I'm glad you're with me. I'm a little nervous." She let out a shaky breath. "I don't know why. This is supposed to be relaxing."

"It will be." Liam pulled her into his arms. "Everything's a little overwhelming right now, but we'll work it all out."

Katie snuggled into Liam's embrace, appreciating everything he was doing to make her feel better. Last night, Liz and Shane had come over for dinner. After eating a delicious vegetable cashew casserole that Cara had made, they'd talked about the custody case and Ken's ideas. For the first time since her conversation with Mr. Loncar, Katie felt real hope. She took a long moment to focus on the positives in her life, including all of the love and support from her family.

Drawing back, she took Liam's hand. "C'mon, let's go see what this is all about." They made the short walk to the strip mall and located the door to Simone's Energy Healing Center.

Inside, a receptionist gave her a clipboard with paperwork. While she completed the forms, Liam lightly scratched her back. As she signed the last page, a petite woman with short blonde hair and sharp emerald eyes emerged.

"You must be Katie. I'm Simone." Katie shook the woman's extended hand.

"And you are?" Simone asked looking at Liam.

"Katie's husband, Liam." They shook hands.

"Why don't you both come back for our pre-session discussion?" Simone suggested. "If that's okay with you, Katie."

Katie nodded, ridiculously pleased that Liam could be with her. They followed Simone into a bright room at the end of the hallway. Sunlight filtered through a wall of floor-to-ceiling glass. Tall, lush greenery lined the windows and water trickled from a fountain in the middle of the foliage.

Simone gestured toward a set of plush chairs. "Make yourselves comfortable."

Katie and Liam took a seat. Simone picked up the clipboard and eased onto a rolling chair across from them.

"An accident and a coma, wow." Simone looked at her with warm eyes. "Glad you're here." She glanced down at the papers again studying what Katie had written. "I can definitely help with your healing process. So, how did you hear about us?"

"We saw your ad, but also…well…." Katie found herself at a loss for words.

"Katie had an encounter while she was in the coma," Liam said, taking her hand. "Her spirit guides suggested she see an energy healing practitioner."

"One day I'd like to hear more about that." Simone smiled at Katie. "Now tell me what you know about energy healing."

"To be honest, nothing." Katie twirled a strand of hair around her fingers.

Nodding, Simone placed the clipboard aside. "Let's start with the basics. Forget the labels—whether you call it Reiki, chi, or universal energy—it all refers to the life force energy that flows through the universe. Using a form of healing that's thousands of years old, practitioners like me simply tap into that vital energy," she said. "Using our hands and intent, we promote healing and balance in the body, and we can also assist with specific issues. Besides helping you regain your strength, is there anything else you'd like to focus on?"

Biting her lower lip, Katie toyed with her hair. Liam squeezed her hand. "We're trying to win custody of Katie's daughter and we've also been trying to get pregnant."

"I see." Simone's green eyes lit with compassion. "We'll focus on those as well."

Believe. Katie felt a tingling sensation in her right shoulder, then it spread throughout her body. As she sensed her cloud guide's presence, her entire body was enveloped in love. Black Eagle's calming voice entered her awareness first. *Let go, Katie.* Posie's soft voice followed. *Let go and believe.*

Katie did just that, and an hour later, she left the healing center feeling markedly lighter. Outside, Liam pulled her into his arms. "You look amazing. Happy, carefree."

"That's how I feel, too."

Cupping his hands around her face, Liam kissed her. Long, slow, and tender. After, he walked her to the truck.

"I made some decisions while I was in there," she said before climbing into the cab.

Liam raised a brow. "Such as?"

"I'm gonna take time off from my job search like you and Liz suggested. I'm going to focus on getting my strength back and on getting Savannah. Maybe we can also work on trying to get me pregnant." Sighing contentedly, she rubbed her hands up and down Liam's arms, tracing her fingers over the tattoos on his right arm. "I can help out some in the shop, too. Then I'll figure out what I want to do career-wise later. Okay?"

Liam's lips curved up. "You just made my day, baby."

She laughed. "I'm gonna come back next week to see Simone again. After a few energy sessions, she's going to teach me mediation. She said it would help me sustain my calm or something like that. She also said it'll help me tap into my inner wisdom…maybe even help us get pregnant." She let out a long breath as her gaze lifted to Liam's. "I know this sounds crazy, but I felt Posie and Black Eagle in there, and I think they're helping, too."

"Not crazy," Liam said pressing a kiss to the top of her head.

"I'm excited," she said, taking pride in her leap from depressed to hopeful, even if she did have a little help from her friends above.

Liam pulled her back in his arms and hugged her tight. "That's my girl."

TIME FLEW and by the following Friday night Shane was ready for relaxation and a little romance. The last week had been busy but rewarding.

After the family meeting at Liam's, Shane had his attorney put together a strategy for the custody case. Ken had also secured a court order allowing Liam and Katie to visit Savannah. They were in Texas now, and Shane was house-sitting for the weekend.

Over the last week, he, Liam, and Liz had all spent quality time with Katie, and she had, for the most part, returned to her former optimistic self.

To top off his spectacular week, the markets had continued their bullish trend, and yesterday he took time to analyze the boatload of money his funds had already generated this year for his clients. The results had been staggering, even for him. He leaned against the front porch column, thumbs hooked in his jean tabs, soaking in heat from the summer sun, basking in his successes.

Cara ambled out, and leaned against the porch column across from him. "When's Liz and Sab gonna be here?" she asked, smoothing down her long hair.

"Anytime now."

"Does Liz know about the chef?"

"Nope." Shane stuffed his hands in his pockets. "It's our secret for now, okay?"

Cara shrugged. "Sure. Thanks for getting a limo for me and my girls."

Cara had talked him in to letting her have a sleepover with Sabby and two other friends. He agreed, but had quickly arranged for an outing—dinner and movies, with limo service. With the girls out, he planned on dazzling Liz with a cozy chef-prepared meal.

Cara hung out with him on the porch until Liz and Sabby arrived at the same time as Cara's other friends. After the girls scampered off to primp for their evening, he yanked Liz inside and into his arms.

"Hi there," he whispered before kissing her. "I've missed you," he said when they came up for air.

Liz let out a breathy laugh. "How've you been the last two days?" They'd seen each other on Wednesday night when he'd driven up to Georgetown to take her and Sabby out to dinner at an upscale restaurant.

"Missing you." His lips touched hers as he spoke, and this time when he lowered his mouth, he kissed Liz with a sweetness he hadn't expected.

The effect was unnerving. Desire shot through him like a bullet —fast, piercing, and surprising. He expected it with the heat, but not after a tender moment. Damn, was he getting soft? Then Liz slid him a come-get-me look and he didn't care. He reached for her again, but was interrupted when a knock sounded at the door.

He ran a hand through his hair. "That would be my surprise." He pulled the door open and shook his friend's hand. Jacques Pierre looked like a stereotypical chef in his white double-breasted jacket and tall hat. "Please come in. JP, meet Liz."

His friend patted him on the back, then took Liz's hand, raised it to his mouth, and kissed it.

"Elle est plus chaud que vous avez dit," JP said. *She's as hot as you said.*

Shane grinned. She was indeed.

"Merci mais il est Juillet. Bien sûr, il fait chaud," Liz responded. *Thank you, but it's July. Of course it's hot.*

Shane winced as Liz replied in French. She had lived in Paris for two years; of course she spoke the language. But JP wasn't embarrassed. Instead, he threw his head back and laughed.

Shane quickly changed the subject. "JP is here to cook for us tonight. He owns, and is head chef, at Chez Pierre in D.C."

Liz's mouth fell open as her hand flew to her chest. "You're *the* Jacques Pierre?"

"Oui, oui, my cherie." JP gave a mock bow. "Guilty as charged."

Liz laughed. "It's harder to get dinner reservations at your place than at the White House."

"You are too kind," JP said.

Liz was laying it on thick. "You're too much," Shane said, taking her hand.

"I'm serious." Liz smiled at JP. "I've been to dinner at the White House. But I've never gotten in to Jacques' place."

Damn, she hadn't been kidding. Shane knew his friend's restaurant did well, but he hadn't realized it was *that* popular. He'd have to finagle an invite so he could take Liz there.

"I will make one of my most popular dishes for you tonight. I promise I will not disappoint." JP smiled at Liz before turning to him. "Lead the way."

Shane escorted them to the kitchen where his friend studied Liam's modern appliances.

"This will do just fine," JP said, patting the stove. "I'll go grab my supplies."

"Do you need help?" Shane asked.

"No thanks. Open a bottle of wine or make out with your beautiful lady."

When JP left, Liz turned to him. "Thank you, Shane. This is a wonderful surprise."

He'd planned to keep his hands off her because it wouldn't take JP long to get his stuff. But Liz lunged at him, and his best efforts collapsed like Black Tuesday on Wall Street. Spinning her around, he pressed her against the kitchen counter, and skimmed open-mouthed kisses along the neckline of her dress. When she let out a needy whimper, it hit him straight in the groin.

Desire shot through him again, but this time it branched out and intensified, making its way frighteningly close to his chest. Despite the short period of time he'd been dating Liz, his feelings for her were deeper than he'd felt for any other woman...even Jana. Another caution flag waved in his head, but before he could think about it, JP returned.

"I see you opted for the latter," his friend said, chuckling. "Now about that wine...."

Shane held Liz's gaze for a long beat. She looked beautifully disheveled with mussed up hair and her sexy brown dress a little crooked. Her blue eyes sparked and blazed, drawing him in like a moth to a flame. When JP cleared his throat, it still took a concerted effort for him to step away. Blowing out a breath, he moved to the counter where two bottles of wine were open and breathing. He poured three glasses and handed them out. "This Bordeaux is from your neck of the woods," he said, looking at JP. "Cheers."

"What region are you from?" Liz asked his friend.

"I'm from Aquitaine, it's in the southwest corner of France, a—"

"I know exactly where it is," Liz said. "My daughter Sabby and I vacationed there when we lived in Paris."

"Ah, grand Paris. That explains your impeccable French." JP grinned at Liz as he turned on the oven. "Did you enjoy Aquitaine?"

Liz sighed. "Picturesque villages, gourmet cuisine, beautiful beaches."

"I'll take that as a yes," JP said, standing taller.

"I've never been to that region." Shane swirled the wine in his glass as he caught Liz's gaze. "Maybe we should fly over for a weekend get-a-way."

Liz's eyes brightened even as she shook her head. "No one goes to France *for a weekend*."

"Don't underestimate my man," JP said as he bustled around the kitchen. "Shane is the master of spontaneity."

"Damn straight." Shane wiggled his eyebrows and gave Liz his best *ooh-la-la* look.

Liz laughed.

"I've arranged for a fun night for the girls too," he told her. "Dinner and a movie, limo style."

"You're too good to them." Liz gave him a sweet, almost shy look, and then took a sip of her wine. "How do you two know each other?"

JP glanced over from the stove. "Shane has handled my investment portfolio for many years. He's made me a wealthy man."

Before Shane could respond, Cara, Sabby, Tiffany, and Abigail invaded the kitchen, and he made introductions.

"Smells good," Cara said.

"Steak au Poivre," Jacques said.

"Yummy." Sabby lifted her nose in the air to draw in the various scents.

"Sab, Jacques is the chef and owner of Chez Pierre," Liz said.

"Shut up!" Sabby spun around to gape at JP. "That's like eight blocks from our place. Not that we've ever been there."

"I can certainly fix that." JP winked at Sabby.

Sabby bounced up and down, then threw her arms around JP's neck, making him laugh.

The girls snapped pictures of each other with the famous chef. When the limo arrived, they took more shots inside the spacious vehicle.

A few minutes later, back in the kitchen Liz nudged him and extended her cell. "Sabby's Facebook page."

Shane studied the phone, chuckled, then handed it to JP.

"I am most humbled," JP said after studying the picture of him and Sabby in front of the stove. He glanced at Liz. "Your daughter is sweet. Smart, too, like her mama."

"Comme c'est gentil." *How kind.* "Tell me, how is such an outgoing chef so elusive?"

"What do you mean, my cherie?"

"You've never given an interview." Liz tossed her hair back. "Ever."

"Oh, that." JP waved her comment off with the wooden spoon in his hand. "I don't trust reporters."

Shane coughed. "Foot in mouth."

Tipping his head, JP raised a brow.

"No worries," Liz said. "I'm not easily insulted."

"Liz is a reporter," he told his friend.

"Je m'excuse." *I apologize.* "I had a bad experience with a reporter in my younger days. Who do you work for?"

"Occasionally the Post, but I mostly do freelance work for magazines."

"Liz is big time," Shane said, with unexpected pride in his voice. "She's written for the major periodicals. *Time. National Geographic* —" he glanced her way and winked "—*Playboy*…you name it."

"I read religiously. It's my guilty pleasure." JP sprinkled herbs over the green beans. "What's your pen name?"

"I use my own name. Liz Patterson."

"Ma chère." Jacques sailed over to Liz, took her hand, and kissed it noisily. "I didn't know you were *that* Liz Patterson! You wrote an article on the orphans in my birthplace, Rio de Janeiro. Your article was real, moving, brilliant. You treated the children with great dignity and respect. You, my dear, are a talented writer."

Liz's cheeks pinkened, but her eyes sparkled with delight.

"Tell me about the rest of your work. Maybe I've read other pieces, too," JP urged.

Shane had planned a romantic dinner that entailed his buddy making a quick exit after preparing their meal. But considering how Liz lit up while talking with him, Shane invited JP to stay. His friend initially declined, but he gave in after Liz added her plea.

The three of them leisurely feasted on mussels, steak, truffle potatoes, and herbed green beans while polishing off the two bottles of French wine. Liz stroked JP's ego by declaring it the best meal she had ever eaten.

Dessert was even better, considering the orgasmic sounds Liz made while biting into the fancy French pastries. Just thinking about the things they could do with the chocolate topping and fresh cream had they been alone made Shane's chest break out in a sweat.

"Isn't that great?" Liz leaned over and touched a hand to his arm, drawing him out of his erotic daydream.

"Sure." He smiled at Liz and hoped it was convincing.

Thankfully, JP clarified. "If you'd prefer to come to my restaurant at a different time, just let me know."

"No, that works. Thanks." Shane made a mental note to call his friend later to get details.

After they'd finished eating dessert, JP rose. "I must be off," he said as he gathered his supplies. "Shane, it's always a pleasure." Reaching into his bag, he retrieved a business card and handed it to Liz. "*You* I trust. Give me a call next week and we'll schedule time for an interview."

By the time JP departed, the girls had already returned from the movies. It wasn't the evening Shane had planned, but when Liz called it 'her best night ever,' he figured he could've done worse.

CHAPTER FIFTEEN

*S*itting on the long wooden bench in the lobby of Big Randy's, a legendary Amarillo steakhouse, Katie twirled her hair around her fingers as nerves tapped inside her chest. Tonight, she would meet her daughter for the first time.

Liam pulled her fingers out of her hair, and held her hands on his lap.

"Everything's going to be fine," he said. "We're just two relatives who flew out for a visit."

"I'm still nervous." She puffed out a breath. "And why isn't Warren coming?" Gwen's brother had declined their dinner invitation at the last minute.

Liam shrugged. "Maybe he had plans." He squeezed their hands together. "Savannah's grandparents are coming, that's good enough."

"I'm nervous about meeting them, too." She pressed a hand to her belly which was now drumming with anxiety in tandem with her chest. "Won't they think it odd that we're showing up now? I don't think they know—" her eyes darted to the nearby patrons as she lowered her voice "—that I'm Savannah's mother."

"After Gwen's passing, they're probably happy to spend time with other family members, especially for Savannah's sake." Liam gently rubbed his fingers on her thigh. "Let's just enjoy the evening."

"You're right." She managed a smile as her eyes scanned Liam's attire—black jeans, a plaid shirt and cowboy boots. Uncustomary attire for him, but he had taken her shopping earlier in the week, insisting that they dress the part while in Texas. She had on western wear, too—an orange sundress with a denim jacket and, of course, cowgirl boots.

"We're in this together, Katie-Cat."

The muscles in Katie's face relaxed as she took comfort in Liam's support. She pressed her palm over his plaid shirt, squeezing his hard muscles. "Have I told you lately that you're my rock?"

Liam kissed her temple. "And you're my goddess...and I think they might be here."

Her head whirled around in time to see Savannah step inside the restaurant. As she let out a quiet gasp, the older couple faded into the background. Her heart caught in her throat as she scrutinized her beautiful daughter. Savannah was tall and thin with long wavy hair the same texture and sandy brown color as her own. Rising, she could do nothing more than stare, caught off guard by the instant connection and maternal bond that suffused her being.

Liam took her hand. "C'mon, let's go meet them," he whispered. "Sweetie, Savannah's stunning. She looks just like you."

In a daze, Katie followed Liam to the front entrance where he made introductions. Savannah's grandparents, Colt and Deb, greeted them warmly but Savannah was more reserved.

Katie was acting the same way. She'd done nothing more than utter polite pleasantries. At the hostess station, she lectured herself. *Snap out of it! You only have one chance to make a good first impression.*

She envied, but at the same time was grateful for Liam's laid-back nature. He could talk to anyone, anywhere, and had a knack for making people feel at ease. That is, when he wanted to. And he obviously wanted to with Savannah. As they were ushered to the back of the restaurant, he joked with her about the cowboy pictures hanging on the walls.

"Think I could do that?" he asked, pointing at a picture of a rancher herding cows.

Savannah gave him a look that said she wasn't sure what to make of him.

"What about this one?" Liam pointed at a picture of a cowhand lassoing a horse, and he struck a similar pose.

"I don't know." Savannah's lips twitched as she put a hand over her mouth. "Have you done it before?"

"Nah, but how hard can it be?"

Savannah giggled.

Once they were seated, a waitress promptly took their drink order. After she left, Katie finally found her voice. "What grade are you in, Savannah?"

"Seventh."

"Middle school." Katie scrunched her nose. "Fun."

"Savannah's a straight A student." Deb and her granddaughter exchanged a look of whole-hearted love. Envy pulled at Katie's gut, making her feel like a loser. She wanted her daughter to have an abundance of love in her life. Besides, she shouldn't be jealous of Savannah's grandmother. Breathing into her abdomen, she pushed aside her undesirable thoughts.

"She loves school." Colt winked at his granddaughter. "Isn't that right, pumpkin?"

Savannah relaxed visibly, and Katie did, too. Her daughter was clearly loved.

"Yeah, and I like seeing all of my friends too." Sipping her sweet tea, Savannah squinted across the table at Katie. "I love your jacket."

"Thanks." Katie glanced down at her outfit. "Liam insisted we go shopping before coming here. You know, so we could look all Texan."

Savannah laughed, and it pulled at Katie's heart. It was hard to believe she was sitting across the table from her daughter. She was awestruck by how much Savannah looked like her when she had been a young girl.

"Well, you kids did good." Colt's smile covered his entire face and the corners of his eyes crinkled.

"I love shopping." Savannah bit her lower lip. "Ma and I had a big shopping trip planned for this summer," she said, her voice full of sorrow.

Deb put an arm around Savannah's shoulder and hugged her.

Katie's heart hurt over the pain in her daughter's voice and over the anguish Savannah must have felt after losing the only mother she had known. At the same time, Katie experienced a fresh pang of grief over her decision to give her daughter up for adoption and for missing Savannah's childhood. Regardless of what happened with the custody case, she would never get that time back.

Their waitress appeared and took their dinner order. After she bustled away, Liam continued the same conversation, probably trying to make Savannah feel better.

"Maybe your uncle can take you shopping over the summer," he suggested.

Savannah's face scrunched and tightened. Apparently, shopping wasn't Warren's thing.

Katie turned to Liam. *They* could take Savannah shopping. As if one with her thoughts, Liam took her hand under the table and squeezed it.

She slid her gaze to Savannah. "Maybe Liam and I could take you shopping tomorrow."

Savannah glanced at the floor. "Well...."

Deb leaned in close to her granddaughter. "Go ahead, honey. You'll have fun."

Savannah lifted her head, and gave Katie a shy smile. "Maybe I could get a couple of new outfits and something to wear to Sally Ann's end of semester party."

"Of course. I love to shop." Katie's lips curved up. "It's a date then. That is, as long as your uncle doesn't mind."

"Oh, he won't mind." Savannah slurped the last of her drink. "He's always busy. Granma says if he were any busier he'd be twins."

A light flush crept into Deb's cheeks. "Oh, sweetie, you shouldn't quote your 'ol grandma."

"Pshaw." Colt waved off his wife's concern. "Everyone knows our boy has a hole in the screen door. He's out more than he's in."

Katie respected Colt's honesty, but her image of Warren diminished by the second. Did he do *anything* with Savannah? If he was out all of the time, who looked after her daughter?

Over dinner, they talked about life in Texas and Maryland, Savannah's school and Liam's business. Savannah took part in all of their conversations. Even through she'd been through so much heartache, she was polite, charming, and fun. The evening passed by way too quickly and as Liam paid the bill, Katie longed for more time with her daughter. At least they had a shopping date set for tomorrow.

In the parking lot, Deb surprised her and Liam with an invitation to their place for a nightcap. After accepting, they followed the older couple to drop Savannah off so they could talk with Warren about taking Savannah shopping.

When they pulled into the drive of the stucco and brick one-story home, a man—presumably Warren—stepped onto the front porch. As Katie climbed out of the rental car, she took a closer look.

Tall and blond, he had a boyishly-handsome face and seemed to be in good shape other than the slight pooch around his belly. As she and Liam followed Deb, Colt, and Savannah up the front walk, a scantily clad brunette burst through the front door and wrapped herself around Warren.

"Hey, ya'll!" Warren said, glancing at each of them before shifting his gaze back to Savannah. "This is Timber."

Savannah mumbled hello to the other woman before making introductions. "Uncle Warren, this is Katie and Liam. They wanna take me shopping tomorrow, okay?"

Swaying on his feet, Warren glanced in their direction. Katie caught the faint scent of whiskey in the air. Was he drunk, she wondered, as anger coiled inside her. How could he care for Savannah in that condition?

"Hey, ya'll," he repeated. "You wanna take Savannah to the mall, fine by me. Maybe you could swing by early." He squeezed the brunette in close. "Timber here's gonna spend the night."

He had women whom Savannah had never met spending the night? And *her*? The woman was dressed like a Dallas Cowboy cheerleader, not exactly a great role model for Savannah. Katie's anger expanded, roaring through her system as she tried to think of something to say to Warren other than the foul words that had formed on her lips.

Thankfully, Liam beat her to it. Ignoring Warren, he turned to address Savannah directly. "What time works for you, sweetie?" he asked. "We could take you out for breakfast too, if you want."

"Yes, please." Savannah nodded enthusiastically. "How 'bout eight?"

"What the hell," Katie said once she and Liam were back in their rental car. Every muscle in her body constricted as resentment unfurled in her gut. *That* man was mothering Savannah instead of her?

"Tell me about it." Backing out of the drive, Liam's mouth was tight and grim.

"Poor Savannah. Wonder how *that man* got to be second on Gwen's list. He'd be last on mine."

"Seriously." Liam's irritation somehow comforted Katie. She put a hand on his leg, touched that he seemed to be every bit as incensed as she was. But maybe the situation wasn't as bad as it seemed. They would get a better feel tomorrow when they spent the day with Savannah. She shifted her thoughts to Deb and Colt. "Why do you think the Shelton's asked us over? I got the impression they want to talk."

"Yeah, me too."

"Makes me a little nervous."

Liam put his hand over hers. "We're in this together." At the next red light, he turned toward her. "After meeting that fuck-head Warren, we'll do whatever it takes to get custody of Savannah."

She nodded in agreement, incredibly grateful for Liam's support.

"Nice place," she said when Liam pulled into the curved drive in front of a large white plantation-style home. As they made their way up the long walkway toward the house, Katie took in the large, freshly cut yard and the massive oak trees. One of the trees had a tire swing attached to it. She smiled thinking about Savannah playing in the yard, swinging on the tire swing.

The Shelton's greeted them on the porch and quickly ushered them inside. The entrance was grand, with an all-white traditional foyer, two-story coffered ceilings, and pristine tile flooring. It was also warm and inviting, in part due to the large arched windows above the front door and the skylights that flooded the area with light.

Deb escorted them to the drawing room, an inviting space with sweeping ceilings and beige furniture accented by bright orange and purple toss pillows and a large multi-colored area rug. "Please make yourselves at home," Deb said, gesturing toward the love seat.

"I'll whip us up some Texan Classics." Colt moved behind the bar. "It's my own recipe—a mix of bourbon, grapefruit juice, and a sweet syrup," he said as he pulled out the ingredients. "You're gonna love it."

Katie and Liam settled on the love seat while Deb sat in an upholstered chair across from them. They made small talk until Colt returned, passed out drinks, and sat next to Deb.

"Thanks for coming to visit." Deb lifted her drink toward Katie and Liam. "I know Savannah appreciates it. The last couple of months have been hard on her."

Deb's blue-green eyes clouded with concern, and Colt reached for her hand. Based on appearances, the two were an unlikely pair. Colt towered over Deb, his massive frame an extreme contrast to her petite figure, yet the large man was like a teddy bear when interacting with his wife.

"She's fine, honey." Colt rubbed Deb's arm. "She's been through a lot since Gwen's heart attack. We've got to expect ups and downs but our little pumpkin will bounce back. She comes from hearty stock." He patted both hands on his round belly.

"I suppose," Deb said, brushing back a strand of her short gray hair. "Sometimes I wish we'd taken custody of Savannah. I love my son, but bless his heart, until recently he's never been around kids much." She took a sip of her drink. "Gwen updated her will a few years ago. We assured her we'd always look after Savannah, but...."

When Deb's words drifted off, Colt finished her sentence. "We're in our late seventies. We'll be watching our granddaughter's college graduation from the big blue sky."

"I understand," Katie said softly. That explained why Warren was next on Gwen's list. He was the only family left.

"I'm gonna cut to the chase here, because I'm fond of the two of you." Deb tossed back another swig of her drink, then moved her gaze to Katie. "We know that you're Savannah's biological mother."

Katie's belly twisted in surprise and rolled with unease. She studied Deb's face, but couldn't read the older woman's expression. Fidgeting with her hands, she couldn't come up with an appropriate response so she simply nodded.

Liam took her hand, and a tingly warmth flooded her body similar to the energy she'd felt when she'd been with Black Eagle. She sensed his presence now. With Liam and Black Eagle on each side of her, she lifted her chin, feeling safe, strong, and confident...like she could take on the world.

"We didn't find out until recently," Deb continued. "When Gwen adopted Savannah, she arranged it on her own. To be honest, we were surprised." She let out a half laugh. "We had hoped she'd find a husband, get married, and *then* have kids. But after a tough break-up, our independent girl decided she didn't need a man to start her family. Next thing we know Savannah shows up." Deb's lips curved into a smile. "Colt and I fell for her on the spot."

"Gwen told us about you when she was in the hospital," Colt said, puffing out his cheeks. "I guess she knew she was in bad shape." He dipped his head and Deb picked up the conversation.

"She asked us to touch base with you," Deb said leaning toward Katie, "should she not make it." She grabbed a tissue to wipe her eye. "But Mr. Loncar beat us to it. When we didn't hear back...."

"Look, I'm gonna be direct too," Liam said before Katie could respond. "Katie and I both want Savannah, so please don't think we're not interested."

"Then why didn't you let Mr. Loncar know?" Deb asked.

"We were in a motorcycle accident right after he called," Katie said.

Liam squeezed her hand. "Then Katie was in a coma for several weeks after. I didn't know about Savannah until a few days ago, or I would have called myself."

Colt and Deb exchanged a look, and then Colt blew out a long breath. "That could change everything."

~

"It's beautiful here." Katie sipped her sweet tea as she gazed out the windows of Buck's Diner. Tall sandstone and red rocks colored the landscape, so different from the rolling green hills of Maryland. "Nice pick," she said, looking across the table at Savannah.

"Thanks. And thanks for taking me to breakfast." Savannah bounced up and down in her seat. "And shopping, especially the shopping."

Katie had been worried that Savannah may not be comfortable spending the day with her and Liam, but her fears had quickly been put to rest. Even though they'd only been together for an hour, Savannah was sunny, energetic, and clearly excited about their outing.

"We should do some tourist stuff, too." Savannah stuffed a bite of salsa baked eggs in her mouth. "You know, *after* we go shopping."

Katie laughed. "Don't worry, we'll go shopping first. What do tourists do here?"

"There's the Big Texan Steak Ranch and Cadillac Ranch."

"Tell us about them," Liam said, cutting into his steak.

"The Big Texan is a restaurant where you go to eat a really big steak, like seventy-two ounces. But you gotta do it in an hour or less to get it for free. If not, you gotta pay seventy-two bucks." She gave them an impish grin. "They give you a bucket to puke in too. What d'you think?"

"Ugh." Katie scrunched her nose.

Savannah giggled. "But everyone in Texas eats big steaks."

"I could probably do it." When Liam beat his fists on his chest, Savannah burst into laughter. "But Katie's been eating vegetarian. What's this Cadillac Ranch all about?"

"We should totally go there...you know, *after* shopping."

Savannah took a heaping bite of cheddar grits, her plate nearly clean. "They have Cadillacs painted in funky colors. They're half stuffed in the ground angled like the pyramids."

"Sounds like fun," Katie said, polishing off her veggie scramble.

"Let's do it." Liam winked at Savannah. "You know, after we take you shopping."

On the drive to the mall, Katie looked over her shoulder at Savannah. "We brought some stuff you might want before we hit the mall." She handed her daughter three cards. "From Cara, Sabby, and Shane." She and Liam had shown Savannah pictures of the girls, Shane, Pan, and their place in Maryland over breakfast.

"Awesome-sauce." Savannah opened the cards, and a few minutes later glanced up wide-eyed. All three had included gift cards to stores Cara and Sabby had deemed hip. Katie hadn't planned on taking Savannah shopping during their weekend visit, but since they were currently headed to the mall, the gifts had been perfect. "But they don't even know me," Savannah said, her voice filled with awe.

"We're family," Liam said, glancing in the rearview mirror. "Family takes care of family."

"Tell them thanks." Savannah clutched the cards close to her chest. "Maybe I can meet them one day."

Katie's heart danced with joy. She wanted Savannah to meet the rest of the family, and she wanted to show her their home and take her around Gem Valley. "We'd love that." Katie smiled at her daughter, already plotting trip ideas in her head.

Three hours later they were eating again, a late lunch on the way to Cadillac Ranch. After shopping for hours, Savannah had left the mall with bags of new outfits—vintage tops and skinny jeans from American Eagle, shorts and tees from Hollister, and a ribbed dress from Charlotte Russe that she'd changed into before they had left the mall. She looked adorable in the short red dress with the distressed brown leather cowgirl boots Liam had insisted on buying.

"I love my new stuff." Savannah's lips curved into a sweet smile. "Thanks for taking me shopping. And don't forget to thank my cousins and Shane, too."

"We will," Liam promised, biting into his Texas-sized burger.

"We'll show them the pictures we took, too." Katie tapped her phone. She'd taken countless shots so she could keep Savannah close to her heart even after they returned home. "So what do you do for fun?"

"Mostly just hang out." Savannah slurped up the last drop of her watermelon lemonade, and the friendly, big-haired waitress swooped over to replace it with another.

"Ma and I used to go to baseball games," Savannah said, her voice hitching. "We had field seats to see the Thunderheads."

Savannah's sadness sliced at Katie's chest. She was so young to have experienced such great loss, although it was because of that loss that Katie now had the opportunity to get to know her daughter. She wanted to pull Savannah into her arms and hang on tight, but it was too soon. Instead, she placed a hand over Savannah's. "I'm sorry about your mom."

Savannah nodded solemnly.

"Does Warren like baseball?" Liam asked, presumably in an attempt to lift Savannah's spirits. Her husband, a major baseball fan, had once declared it un-American to dislike baseball.

But his plan backfired.

"No." Savannah sighed. "He doesn't have time for games, plus he hates baseball."

"What does your uncle like to do?" Katie asked with forced cheerfulness.

"Drinkin' and datin'," was Savannah's response. "That's what G.P. says anyway."

"G.P.?" Liam lifted a brow.

"You know, Grandpa."

Good 'ol Colt. Katie ducked her head to hide her grin. From the little bit that she knew about Colt, that sounded like something he would say. He reminded her of Shane—direct and quick-draw, but inside, a sweet teddy bear.

Last night after she and Liam had shared the details of the accident and her coma, Colt and Deb had been nothing but kind. Maybe in a way, they had been comforted, too. Prior to that conversation, they had assumed that she and Liam weren't interested in

Savannah. Once the facts were out in the open, Deb had assured them that she wanted whatever was best for Savannah. Colt had agreed, and had hemmed and hawed around the notion that Warren probably wasn't 'the best.'

She and Liam were meeting with Warren later in the evening to talk. Hopefully, it would be a quick and easy conversation because Warren didn't appear to have much interest in his niece.

At seven o'clock, Katie and Liam met Warren at the Red Barn. Liam had selected the restaurant because of their farm-to-table concept and healthier dining choices, which was her preference over one of the area's plentiful steakhouses. That was her Liam, so thoughtful.

Warren turned out to be the opposite. Although they had been seated for less than thirty minutes, he had just ordered drink number three, and he was becoming more obnoxious with each. While she and Liam attempted to make polite conversation, he seemed mostly interested in his alcohol and the cute red-headed bartender who was personally delivering his drinks.

"Warren, you're looking extra handsome this evening," Laura had said after dropping off his first drink. "Sugar-pie, I'll take care of you tonight," after the second.

Delivering Warren's third drink, Laura brushed her right thigh against Warren's shoulder. "We had so much fun last weekend. When are we gonna do it again?" Bending down, she whispered loudly in Warren's ear. Something about a present out back.

"What the fuck?" Liam demanded when Warren strutted off with Laura.

Katie couldn't help but laugh. "He's got issues," she said, shaking her head.

"You aren't kidding. Listen, babe, let's not waste all night with this loser." Liam took a sip from his mug, still nursing his first draft beer. "Why don't I change our order to have appetizers here and dinner to go? When Warren comes back, we'll cut to the chase. It's obvious he isn't interested in Savannah. Every time we mention her name, he changes the subject."

"Works for me, and agreed." Katie twirled a strand of hair around her fingers. "But after hearing Savannah talk about him yesterday, I think he does care about Gwen's money."

"Let him keep the damn money," Liam huffed. "We do okay."

Katie gaped at her husband in surprise. "Really?"

"Of course, whatever it takes."

She had known she'd had Liam's support, but she hadn't realized the extent of it until that very moment. He didn't blink an eye over waving off money that could help feed and clothe Savannah, money that could send her to college. He only cared about doing the right thing for her daughter. Katie's chest swelled as she blinked up at him. "I love you so much."

"Anything to make you happy." He cupped his hands around her face and drew her in for a sweet, tender kiss. After, he rested his head against her forehead. "I want to do the right thing for Savannah, too. Whatever it takes," he repeated.

When Warren returned, she and Liam were digging in to their bruschetta and tomato-mozzarella caprese.

"Help yourself," she offered, waving a hand over the food.

"No thanks." Warren tapped his glass. "This here's my appetizer."

Liam slapped his napkin onto the table, with more force than he had probably intended. Glasses shook and Katie's knife flew to the floor.

"Whoa, dude, chill." Warren spoke with a slur but managed to raise his hands in the air, no doubt intimidated by Liam who was clearly the stronger man.

"Let's get to the *real* reason why we're here," Liam said, linking fingers with hers under the table. "Gwen left custody of Savannah to Katie and we want to work out the details with you."

"Katie had her chance," Warren said, then tossed back the contents of his drink.

Katie sucked in a wounded breath as despair crushed her chest, squeezing out all hope that Warren would play nice in the sandbox.

She glared at him, but Warren wouldn't look at her. Instead, he motioned to the bartender, waving his glass in the air. Just what he needed—another drink. Was he an alcoholic, she wondered? At least Savannah was with her grandparents for the night.

"We were in an accident," Liam said tersely. "I believe your folks told you about it earlier today. They were also going to share that Katie is Savannah's birth mother."

Warren shrugged, then swayed, nearly falling out of his seat.

The vein under Liam's eye pulsed. "It's obvious you don't want Savannah."

"Never said that." Warren looked across the table at her and then Liam. "Gwen wanted me to have her."

"No, Gwen wanted *Katie* to have her." Liam's jaw clenched. "I get that you want the money. You can keep the caretaker's fund. We don't give a damn about the money."

"Wha...I...hmm." For once, Warren seemed to be at a loss for words. After a long moment, he cleared his throat. "Is this a trick?"

After Laura dropped off Warren's drink and practically gave him a lap dance, Liam scowled.

"It's not a trick," Katie said, finally finding her own voice to weigh in. "I just want my daughter."

Warren's pupils brightened like beady little pots of gold, then dulled just as quickly. "Doesn't matter," he said. "Whoever gets the money gets the kid. That's what the will says, so she's stayin' with me."

Rising, Liam slapped his palms on the table. As silverware flew to the floor, he leaned in close to Warren. "We'll fuckin' see about that."

CHAPTER SIXTEEN

"You okay?" Liam asked, glancing over at Katie as he pulled into the Shelton's drive on Sunday morning.

"Not really." Katie blew out a long breath. "I wish last night had gone better."

Liam summoned an outer calm for Katie, but inside he was seething. Warren was a shithead who didn't give a damn about his niece. Last night after he had blown up, he'd regained his composure in order to try again. But their second round of discussions with Warren hadn't gone any better than the first, and he and Katie had stormed out after Warren's phone call with Timber. It was painfully evident that Warren wanted his sister's money and he was using Savannah as his pawn. What the hell had Gwen been thinking?

Putting the car in park, he conceded that Katie's cousin had had little choice. She hadn't given custody to Deb and Colt because of their age and she had offered Katie first rights. After Katie, Warren was the only family left, so Gwen hadn't chosen him as much as she had used him as her last resort. Something he intended to change as soon as possible.

This morning he planned to meet with Colt in private for a man to man talk. Colt seemed to have a soft spot for his granddaughter and Liam intended to use that to his full advantage.

He rounded the hood of the car and opened Katie's door. "Me too, but don't worry. We're gonna fight for Savannah and we're going to win."

"I don't know what I'd do without you," Katie said, slipping out of the rental and into his arms.

"Good thing you'll never have to know." He brushed his lips over hers, then rested his cheek against her head for a long moment. "C'mon, let's go inside and have a nice visit before we fly home."

As they made their way up the walkway, Savannah burst through the front door and raced toward them.

"Look, another new outfit." She spun around showing off her stone-washed jeans, flowery top, and leather boots.

"You look beautiful," Katie said, and Savannah hugged her.

"Very hip," Liam put in, which got him a hug, too.

"C'mon, Granma's in the kitchen." Savannah waved them inside and led them to the back of the house where Deb was fussing at the stove.

"You're here." Deb wiped her hands on a towel. "Didn't hear you come in. Colt, they're here," she called out.

"Good to see you," she said approaching them. "Savannah's been talking up a storm about your shopping trip." Deb pulled Katie into a hug first, and then him.

"We had a lot of fun." Katie smiled at Deb. "We're hoping Savannah will visit us sometime over the summer. When we called home yesterday, Cara, our daughter, and Shane, Liam's brother, talked up our hometown."

"I wanna go," Savannah said, spinning on her heels. "Cara said we could go shopping in Washington, D.C. and they have huge malls. Then *Uncle* Shane—he said I could call him that—he said we could all go to a Nationals game. Can you imagine—the majors!"

Savannah's enthusiasm was written all over her face. Katie's delight was too, intensifying Liam's resolve to make it happen. "We'll get you up for a visit," he told Savannah. "We just have to work out the dates with your uncle."

"He won't care." Savannah twirled in a circle. "Let's do it soon."

Colt appeared and greeted them.

"I should get back to making breakfast so we can eat," Deb said.

"Katie and I can help." Savannah grabbed Katie's hand. When she and Katie followed Deb into the kitchen leaving him alone with Colt, Liam's plan fell into place perfectly.

"You smoke cigars?" Colt asked.

"Yes sir."

Colt patted him on the back. "I got some beauts in my den." The older man gestured for him to follow.

Colt escorted him down a long hallway to a room on the right.

"Have a seat." Colt waved at the burgundy leather sofa in the center of the room.

Liam eased onto the sofa, his gaze taking in the wall of windows and the large patio and yard outside.

Colt went behind his desk and pulled out a humidor. Returning, he sat on an adjacent chair and handed Liam a cigar.

"Thanks." Liam lifted the Cohiba to his nose, drawing in the rich tobacco scent. "Nice."

Colt removed a cutter from a drawer in the end table. After snipping his cigar, he passed the cutter and lighter to Liam.

"Thanks again." Liam cut and lit his cigar, then glanced around the room. "Nice place."

"Been here for most of our married life," Colt said. "Our Gwen tried to get us to move into one of those fancy ranches she bought and flipped, but Deb and I love it here."

Liam took a puff of his cigar. "Gwen was in real estate?"

"Yep. She made a fortune in it. Our girl was sharp as a nail and she loved everything about fixing and turning homes." Colt smiled nostalgically. "When she was little, she helped me with house projects. When she got older, our projects got bigger. Built that deck together," he said, pointing out the window. "Guess it stuck. She knew how to find the right deals, and she knew when to sell them, too."

"You must be proud," he said.

Colt nodded, and then turned quiet.

Liam gave the older man a long moment before he spoke. "I'm sorry about your loss." He put his cigar in the ashtray. "I couldn't imagine losing my Cara."

"It was tough," Colt said, his voice uneven. "And unexpected." He clasped his hands in his lap and tipped his head back. "I believe things happen for a reason but sometimes it's sure hard to understand."

Liam nodded. "Doesn't make it any easier for loved ones left behind."

"That's the truth." Colt lowered his head and puffed out a breath. "But on to happier topics. Did you enjoy your day with our granddaughter? She was full of herself this morning."

"She's a great kid. Katie and I had fun, and I think Savannah did, too."

"It's all she's talked about." Colt took a long puff from his cigar. "Now, my boy Warren…well I love him, but…."

When Colt's sentence trailed off, Liam looked him in the eye. "May I be honest, sir?"

"I wish you would."

"I'm not entirely convinced that Warren's interested in being a father-figure for Savannah."

"That's hardly a news flash," Colt said, shocking Liam even though he appreciated the older man's blatant honesty.

"It's a big adjustment for Savannah." Colt puffed on his cigar. "Gwen was a great mama, so attentive. Warren…well, he's trying."

Trying my ass. It was time to lay his cards on the table. "Is he?" Liam challenged.

Colt put down his cigar. "What are you sayin'?"

"Warren doesn't seem to spend much time with Savannah or pay attention to what she's doing. She's at a pivotal age where she needs parental guidance." Liam knew all too well how easily kids could get on the wrong track. *He* had gotten on the wrong track despite the fact that his parents *had* paid attention to what he did. Damned if he'd let sweet Savannah fall through the cracks because Warren was a self-indulgent dickwad. "He also seems to drink—a lot." The lines on Colt's face had tightened, but Liam continued, fueled by the irritation jabbing at his gut over Warren's piss-poor parenting skills. "He has a steady stream of women in and out of the house. None of that is a good influence on Savannah."

Colt rubbed his hands on his lap. "I'll give you the drinking part, and that woman hanging on his arm Friday night sure was something. Deb and I figured her spending the night while Savannah was there was a one-time lack of judgement. We know he dates a lot, but we expect him to be discrete around Savannah."

A muscle in Liam's jaw twitched. Warren was the opposite of discrete. "It was the same deal with the bartender Warren was with last night."

Colt sighed. "He has some work to do, but I still think he's trying." The older man raised his cigar, took another long draw. "But now that you and Katie are interested, we'll have to figure out what's best for Savannah." Colt put down his Cohiba. "Deb and I talked last night and we want to honor our daughter's wishes."

Relief rushed through Liam. That was much easier than he had anticipated. Katie was going to be thrilled....

"Except now we have our son to consider, too," Colt said, crushing Liam's inner triumph.

Damn it. He hadn't wanted to share what he had learned last night, but now he had no choice. "I know I'm biased, but I don't think staying with Warren is what's best for Savannah." He ran a hand down his ponytail. "I'm not sure whether I should share this or not because maybe I misunderstood...."

"Just spit it out," Colt said tersely.

"After Warren made a date with Laura, the bartender, Timber called. He tried to talk in whispers, but he'd had a lot to drink. Warren made plans with her, too." Liam blew out a breath, then met Colt's gaze straight on. "He told Timber it would be easier for them to get together after he sent Savannah to boarding school in the fall."

Colt's face turned brick red. "He's not sending my grand-daughter to boarding school. What the hell's he thinking?" He slammed a fist on the end table. "Why would he even consider such a thing?"

"Like I said, sir, I'm not sure Warren's interested in being a father to Savannah."

Liam hesitated again. Even though Warren was Captain Asshole, he was still Colt's son. But in order to get Colt's support he needed to be completely honest. "Last night I reiterated that Katie and I want custody and that we want Savannah to live with us so there was no need for boarding school. When he mentioned Gwen's money, I told him we didn't care about the money; that he could keep the caretaker's fund as long as he gave us custody." Liam's blood boiled just thinking about Warren's response. He pulled in another long breath and mustered up every ounce of self-control in order to maintain a composed voice. "Warren said the will states that *the kid*—Warren's words, not mine—goes where the money goes, so he'll keep *the kid.*"

Colt let out a long stream of curses, including words and combinations Liam had never heard before. When the older man had finished, he picked up his cigar and took a long inhale. "You let me know what I can do to help."

Two weeks later on the drive home from church, Liam's gaze gravitated to the passenger seat. He had taken Katie to Saturday evening mass in hopes of lifting her spirits. It had, but after, she'd fallen asleep within seconds of climbing into the truck.

Reaching over, he brushed a strand of hair away from her face. Katie had been tired and stressed ever since they'd returned home from Texas. He empathized. While Katie worried non-stop about Savannah's wellbeing, he worried about her and the strain of the custody battle on her mind, body, and spirit, all still fragile from the accident.

At least she wasn't depressed like she had been when they'd learned that custody had been granted to Warren. But she'd had her share of ups and downs over the last couple of weeks. She took comfort in the fact that Colt and Deb seemed to be on their side, but then she'd think about battling it out with Warren in court or about Savannah's welfare, and despite her best efforts to stay positive, she'd end up frazzled.

When he turned right onto Main Street, Katie stretched and yawned. "We almost home?" she asked, her words sleepy and slurred.

"Almost." Reaching over, he gently scratched the back of her neck. "You hungry?"

"Mmm hmm."

"Good, 'cause your mom and Liz are making dinner." He pulled into their long driveway.

Katie straightened and rubbed her eyes.

He hopped out and rounded the hood of the truck. After opening Katie's door, he helped her down, then held her hand as they walked to the house.

Pan rushed outside to greet them. Katie squatted down and cupped the dog's face. "How's my sweet little muffin cake?" she cooed as Pan wiggled and wagged in response.

Liam chuckled. Katie always called Pan her sweet *little* this and sweet *little* that, even though the *little* dog weighed seventy-five pounds.

"You're back. Hope you two are hungry," Carolyn said, after they stepped inside. "We have enough food to feed an army."

They made their way to the dining room, greeting Shane, Liz, Cara, and Sabby along the way. Mealtime topics ranged from weather to shopping, Callahan Cycles to Liz's latest article.

"This casserole is delicious." Katie spooned up a second serving.

"I helped make it," Cara said. "I'm glad you're eating vegetarian with me. About time we had another non-carnivore in the house."

Liam shrugged off his daughter's comment, and even though the tomato and corn casserole wasn't bad, he slid another piece of grilled chicken onto his plate when Cara wasn't looking.

"Sab and I have ice cream dates tonight," Cara said. "Perry's Creamery is all the rage."

"It's *the* place to be on Saturday night," Sabby put in.

"Brandon," he said, nodding at Sabby, and just to mess with Cara, he turned to her. "Who are you going out with tonight?"

"Josh." Cara huffed. "Duh, Dad—we've been dating for almost two months."

"Huh." He scratched his chin, and then stuffed a large piece of chicken in his mouth. He knew damn well who Cara had been dating, but he didn't have to acknowledge it. Especially considering in all that time, the little weasel had yet to come by the house to meet him.

"Are Brandon and Josh friends?" Shane asked.

"Brandon doesn't like Josh." Sabby took a swig of her sweet tea. "I'm not sure why."

Liam knew why. Brandon was friends with Seth who had a major crush on Cara. But he wisely kept his mouth shut.

"Hashtag—whatever." Cara lifted a shoulder. "Brandon has to deal 'cause Sabby's my cousin and my BFF."

"Simone wants me to try meditation," Katie said, changing the subject. "She says it'll reduce my stress."

"Can't hurt," Carolyn said, surprising Liam. Katie's mother didn't strike him as someone who believed in that kind of thing. On the other hand, he'd caught glimpses of a whole different side of her recently. "You know Betsie?" she asked Katie.

"Your neighbor?"

"Yes." Carolyn smiled at Katie. "She meditates daily, and she's about the least stressed woman I know."

"I'll do it with you," Cara said, clasping her hands together.

"Me three." Sabby flipped back the single strand of burgundy in her dark hair, then grabbed another piece of chicken. "Mom, we should move up here so we can do all this stuff." Grinning, she took a bite of her biscuit. "And so I could be close to Brandon."

Sabby pinned a look on her mother and she wasn't the only one. Shane's hopeful eyes were glued on Liz, too. For a self-proclaimed lifetime bachelor, Shane sure seemed to have it bad for Katie's sister.

But Liz brushed Sabby's comment away. "We can't just pick up and move, but we can drive up so you can meditate." Her lashes fluttered as her gaze slid across the table toward Shane. "I'm sure I can find something to do to entertain myself."

Shortly after they'd finished eating, Katie announced she was tired. He and Liz talked her into going to bed. Walking her upstairs, Liam silently prayed that she'd get her energy back soon. Katie had always been strong and vivacious, he hated seeing her so sapped. He also hated the helpless feeling in the pit of his stomach. He wanted to fix this for her, but he didn't know how.

He and Pan waited for her to change. When she came out of the bathroom in her short, tight pajamas, the evening sun cast golden light around her beautiful, curvy body, making her look like a hot angel. His body reacted, but he attempted to will away his bulge. Katie didn't need that added pressure. Blowing out a breath, he strode over and pulled her into his arms. He held her to the side so she wouldn't feel his desire, but she saw right through him.

"Sorry I'm tired all the time," she whispered.

"I'm just grateful you're here," he said, ushering her over to their king-sized bed. Tucking her in, he pulled the blanket up to her chin and kissed her cheek. "I'll check on you in a little bit, Katie-Cat." When Pan nestled in close to her side, he scratched the dog's ears. At the door, he paused. "I love you, baby," he said, his voice a little unsteady.

"Love you, too," Katie said, her voice sleepy.

Downstairs, he found Liz and Carolyn in the kitchen finishing the dishes.

"I didn't expect you to do clean-up," he said, approaching them. "You two cooked."

Although it was just the dishes, his heart flooded with appreciation. Katie's health and the custody fight for Savannah weighed heavy on him too, not that he'd admit it to anyone other than himself.

"You've got enough going on," Liz said, drying a pot. "You keep taking care of my sister and I can certainly help with the dishes."

He kissed Liz on the cheek, and then on impulse gave Carolyn a peck, too.

Carolyn placed her towel on the drying rack, leaned against the counter, and looked him in the eye. "I know I haven't given you much credit in the past. But I want you to know how much I appreciate the care you're giving to my daughter."

She stepped over and patted his shoulder. "You're a good man, Liam."

"Thanks." He felt like he should say more, but he didn't know what else to say. Still his chest swelled, absurdly pleased with Carolyn's praise.

He grabbed a couple of beers from the refrigerator and found Shane on the front porch. He sat next to his brother, then handed him a beer.

"I wonder what Liz could do to occupy her time while Sabby's here practicing Om's," he said, nudging Shane. "Does my baby brother have a girlfriend?"

Grinning, Shane took a swig of beer. "Just trying to fuck with the Pattersons."

Liam raised a brow. It was obvious that there were real feelings between Shane and Liz.

Shane shrugged and, as was his norm, dodged the topic he didn't want to discuss. "How's our Katie *really* doing?"

"She's tired." Liam took a long pull from his beer. "And stressed over Savannah. I wish we could've gotten a hold of Loncar sooner, then Savannah would be with us now." Regret chewed at his gut. Why hadn't he insisted that Katie tell him what was wrong the day she had received the call? Had he known, he would have called Loncar after the accident and asked for an extension. Instead, Savannah had been left with an unfit guardian who was fighting them for custody because he wanted the money that came along with it. Liam ground his jaw. "I understand Katie's concerns. Warren's a real fuckhead." His temples throbbed with rage as he thought about Warren's irresponsible ways. "He doesn't give Savannah the time of day. He's in it for the money and she's his meal ticket."

"I'll call Ken first thing on Monday," Shane said. "See if we can speed things up.

He's a damn good attorney. He'll get it done for us."

Liam nodded. "I appreciate it."

"Is Savannah out of school for the summer?" Shane asked, sipping his beer.

"Yep." Liam pulled a cigarette out of his shirt pocket and lit it. "That's what upset Katie most recently."

Shane tipped his head.

Liam took a long drag of his cigarette. "As part of Gwen's will Katie was supposed to get custody of Savannah right after her school semester ended."

"Then let's fly Savannah up for a visit," Shane suggested. "That would lift Katie's spirits."

ON SUNDAY MORNING, Katie awoke feeling as light and wispy as the air blowing through her open window.

For two weeks, she'd been trying to snap out of her roller-coaster mindset. But she would take two steps forward, then one step back. In the clouds, she had learned that she needed to be positive in order to attract positive vibrations. Even though she understood and believed in that premise, it took a conscious effort and strength that she didn't always have to stay positive on a *consistent* basis. Since they'd returned from Texas, every time she got herself in a good place, she'd think about Warren and poor Savannah, who was stuck living with him, and she'd get frustrated all over again.

Last night she'd asked for help and her grandmother had visited her in a dream. Stretching, she reflected on their conversation.

"But how do I believe when things are so sucky for Savannah?" she'd asked. "How do I pretend everything's okay when it's not? When Warren is such a jerk, and yet he's the one who has custody of my daughter."

"I'm not saying to pretend it doesn't suck," Grammie had said, making Katie giggle over her grandmother's use of the word 'suck.' "Acknowledge your feelings, *accept* them, and then redirect your thoughts to something happy."

"I could do that." She had been buoyed by her grandmother's suggestion. If she didn't have to pretend things were great when they really weren't, it would make her quest to maintain positivity easier. There were countless positives in her life. If she thought about Pan,

Liam, vacation, or any other happy memory whenever her mind started to stray to the dark side, she was confident she could flip it back to the positive.

"It's all about choice," Grammie had said. "Knowing about the Law of Attraction, do you really want to choose negative thoughts and emotions when you know it will only attract more of the same?"

Of course that wasn't what she wanted. "Thanks, Grammie," she had said. When she'd rolled over, she had found Posie and Black Eagle on the other side of her bed. Her guides had given her a refresher on the Law of Attraction, stressing her internal power to attract her desires along with the importance of believing that they would come true. When she woke up, Posie's and Black Eagle's voices lingered in her head. *Be positive and believe. You have a huge support team cheering you on—in the clouds and on Earth.*

With Grammie, Posie, and Black Eagle's guidance, determination unfurled and settled in Katie's chest. She had allowed her faith to falter once again. But going forward she would be stronger. She would stay positive and believe. Maybe it really was that simple. It was what had gotten her home, after all. She'd believed until it had happened.

After showering and dressing, she headed downstairs in search of Liam. She found him watching sports highlights in the living room with Shane.

When he spotted her, he dashed over. "Hey, baby. How did you sleep?"

"Really well." Taking Liam's hands, she let out a happy sigh.

"Hey there." Shane waved at her from across the room.

"Hi, Shane," she called out, then smiled up at Liam. "I'm gonna head to the shop." When Pan rubbed against her leg, she squatted down to kiss his nose. "And Pan, too." She nuzzled her face against his head. "Are you gonna work with me today, my little buddy?" Pan thumped his tail on the floor.

When she rose, Liam's eyes narrowed. But before he could protest, she continued. "I'm gonna finish the invoicing, then play around with some marketing ideas," she said. "It'll be quiet today since you only have a couple of guys working. Can I use your office?"

Liam looked her up and down. "Sure you're up to it?"

"I'm fine, other than needing something productive to keep me occupied."

Liam stared at her for another moment. "Promise you won't overdue it."

She put a hand over her heart. "I promise."

"Okay." He grazed his lips over hers. "But first, Shane and I have a surprise for you."

"What is it?"

"You tell her," Liam called out to Shane. "You arranged it."

Rising, Shane grinned. "The Shelton's are coming to visit. Savannah, Deb, and Colt will all be here on Friday."

Katie's heart swelled with joy as big and bright as the August sun. She hadn't thought she'd get to see Savannah again so quickly. Bubbling with excitement, she squealed, raced over, and threw her arms around Shane's neck. "Thank you so much." She kissed his cheek. "This is so exciting. Thank you, thank you, thank you."

Shane laughed. "Anything for you, Katie."

She spun around and hugged Liam, then plastered kisses up and down his cheek. "So exciting," she repeated.

His whiskey-colored eyes twinkled. "We thought it would make you happy."

"Oh yeah!" She rubbed her hands together. "We've got to plan what we're gonna do. We need to go grocery shopping, plan meals. And come up with stuff Savannah would enjoy. I want her to have a great time."

"Don't worry, we'll figure it out," Liam said. "Shane's getting tickets for a National's game next weekend."

She smiled. "Savannah will love that."

"We can talk through other ideas over dinner." Liam pressed a kiss to her forehead. "Okay?"

"Sounds great. Hey…." She turned toward Shane. "Why don't you come over for dinner? Then we can all talk about the trip."

"No can do." Shane's face split into a whopper-sized grin. "Liz, Sabby, and Cara are coming to *my* place tonight."

"Really?" Katie raised a brow. It would be her sister's first trip to Shane's home. She found it odd that Shane hadn't invited Liz before, but then again, he seemed to be trying a new approach with her.

Shane shrugged nonchalantly even as excitement teemed in his eyes. "We're having a movie marathon, then a sleepover."

Now Shane caught Liam's attention, too. "They're *all* staying the night with you?"

"In separate rooms." Shane stuffed his hands in his pockets. "At least as far as the girls are concerned."

CHAPTER SEVENTEEN

On Saturday evening, Liz waited for Shane on Katie and Liam's front porch. He pulled into the drive at six o'clock sharp. Prompt, as usual, a trait she appreciated in a man.

She made her way down the steps as he jumped out of his Hummer. He looked all kinds of handsome in dark gray khakis and a white shirt. Her eyes lingered on the shirt and how well he filled it out. As he moved toward her his muscles bunched and tightened, stretching the shirt and causing her breath to quicken. She had the maddening urge to launch herself against him and press her chest along those hard muscles.

Lifting her gaze, she found him standing in front of her with a cocky grin. A twinge of embarrassment slipped into her belly but it melted with the heat that sizzled in the space between them. Once again all she could think about was pressing her body against his... and maybe shedding a few articles of clothing.

When he leaned in, her eyelids fluttered shut, but they flew open when Cara and Sabby noisily rushed toward them. She stepped aside so Shane could greet the girls.

Shane hugged Cara, then pulled Sabby in, even as his sexy eyes held hers. His lips lifted into a slow, sultry smile that made her entire body thrum with want. After he released the girls, they scampered off and climbed into the Hummer.

He closed the space between them and tugged her into his arms. He gave her a quick hug, and then took a half step back. Her body sighed in disappointment even as her mind applauded his restraint. Of course he had to keep it casual considering the teenage eyes that were peering at them.

But she was wrong.

Even though he kept his body a slight distance away, he slid a hand behind her neck and drew her into a long, passionate kiss.

Giggling ensued, followed by a "Way to go, Uncle Shane," from Cara.

Shane pulled back, but his eyes held hers for a long, heated moment. "Until later," he whispered, his voice rough.

He offered his hand and escorted her to the passenger side of his vehicle. After she was settled, he climbed into the driver's seat and started the Hummer.

"Are you two a thing now?" Sabby asked.

Liz and Shane both replied at the same time. Her with, "It's complicated," while he answered, "Yes."

Sabby ignored her response and patted Shane's shoulder as if he had made some kind of accomplishment. "That's awesome," she said. "*Finally*, my mother dates a guy I like."

Then she disappeared into the back, and she and Cara were in their own world again, discussing the pros and cons of each movie on their potential watch list.

"Wait!" Sabby hollered as Shane backed out of the drive, causing him to slam on the breaks.

The girls giggled.

"Mom, Brandon texted to see if Cara and I can meet him tomorrow for breakfast. Can I drive your car over?" Sabby asked.

After Liz agreed, Shane put the Hummer in park. Sabby and Cara hopped out, chatting about breakfast and whether Josh would actually show up. Once they were alone, Liz glanced at Shane. They were a 'thing' now? She wasn't even sure what that meant in teen speak. It probably meant that she and Shane were in a relationship…and despite her best efforts, she supposed that they were.

Shane's lips curved into a lazy smile.

She gazed out the window as they made their way to his place, taking in the rise of the mountain and the dense green forest. Before long, Shane turned up a steep, winding drive. When they rounded the corner, an enormous wood home with an A-Frame center appeared. Tall windows overlooked a picturesque valley, and a multi-level deck extended the gargantuan length of the house.

Sabby and Cara pulled into the drive behind them along with another car.

"This is your *little* place in the hills?" she asked with more than a *little* shock in her voice. The place had to be worth millions.

"Yep." Shane jumped out of the Hummer, appeared on her side and opened the door. She stepped down, still gaping at the house.

Sabby trotted over. "Sweet, huh Mom?"

Cara tugged at Liz's arm. "Come on, Liz, Sab, I'll give you the tour. Wait till you see the movie room!"

Shane started after them, but then he noticed the older woman who had climbed out of the Ford Fiesta that had pulled in behind the girls. "Give me just a minute," he said to Liz, and then trotted toward the woman. "Hi, Kay, didn't expect to see you today."

"You're never at home anymore, young man," she said. "I need fifteen minutes of your time." She wagged her index finger at him. "I shouldn't have to drive over on my day off to get it."

As Shane apologized to Kay, Liz wondered who the older woman was.

"Come on, this way," Cara sang out as she sprinted toward the house.

"Who's Kay?" Liz asked after catching up with Cara.

"Uncle Shane's housekeeper."

Inside, she and Sabby followed Cara around Shane's massive home. Along the way, she peppered Cara with questions because her niece was a cornucopia of information. She learned about Shane's housekeeper, gardeners, and the pool help. In the enormous garage, she found a shiny red BMW; a few muscle cars Cara said he'd gotten from Barrett-Jackson, an expensive auto auction company Liz had seen on TV. Her pulse shot into overdrive when she spotted the Harley Davidson in which she and Shane had ridden together.

Down the hall was the movie room complete with six reclining leather chairs, a theatre-sized screen, and a popcorn and soda bar. Next was a game room, and on the other side, an indoor pool. There were private dressing areas, showers, and a steam room. After, Cara gestured in the direction of the expansive wine cellar. "It's nothing exciting," Cara said, "just bottles and bottles of wine," and then she moved them along.

Before the house tour, Liz had already come to the conclusion that Shane didn't have to worry about money. But she had had no idea he was this well to do…the man was downright rich. Frankly, it was a bit intimidating and a threat to her independence. She didn't need a man to pay her way or to take care of her. She might not be in the same league of wealth as her father or as Shane, but she made plenty to take care of her and Sabby.

"Mom, look at this awesome pool!" Sabby hovered in the open French doors, waving her over.

Liz followed her daughter onto the deck and admired the outdoor pool. Large, as seemed to be Shane's style, the curved shape allowed for a seating area where the pool narrowed and a grilling area on the more spacious side. It was surrounded by natural beauty— rocks, greenery and bursts of color in the flower gardens. At the edge of the pool, water tumbled down from the rocks above. Curved stairs led to an upper deck where a hot-tub bubbled in the corner.

Shane caught up with them and drew her into his arms.

Sabby and Cara alternated between kissy sounds and pretend gagging.

"C'mon, Sab," Cara said. "Let's take your stuff upstairs. You can stay with me in my room. It's huge. Besides, your mom and Uncle Shane obviously need some alone time."

" 'Kay 'Kay. I'm coming," Sabby said, then she and Cara scampered off snickering.

Shane leaned in for a soft kiss. "What do you think of the house?"

Disoriented from the kiss, it took her a moment to get her bearings. The house. His richness. She tried not to judge, but honestly, she would have preferred it if he were a little less loaded. She'd grown up with wealth, but this place made her parents' home seem like a shack. While she'd certainly reaped the benefits of her father's net worth, she had also seen first-hand how men with significant wealth treated women. Her father still pulled her mother's puppet strings.

"It's nice," she said.

Shane cocked his head to one side. "Just nice?"

She crossed her arms. She supposed most of his women went gaga over this ginormous place, maybe even found his extreme wealth to be an aphrodisiac. But she wasn't like those women. She cared about who he was on the inside, not about his material belongings. "Yes, just nice," she repeated, refusing to coddle him like he had clearly expected.

"What am I gonna do with you?" Shane said, in a light-hearted voice. As he put an arm around her shoulder, she told herself to lighten up. He was still the same man she had grown fond of, and even though he was wealthy, he had never tried to control her the way her father controlled her mother.

Shane escorted her to the main level and into a large family room that had gorgeous views of the valley and the mountains. "Would you like a glass of wine?" he asked as she settled on the plush sofa. "I have a nice bottle of Cab open. And a bottle of Montrachet of Cote de Beaune chilling in the wine fridge."

She had no idea what Montrachet was, but knowing Shane it was excellent wine. "I'll take the Montrachet please," she said, smoothing a hand down her knit skirt.

"Be right back." Shane winked at her. "I have a couple of surprises for you."

She didn't have a good feeling about his surprises although she had no idea what brought on her trepidation. Usually, she was open and adventurous.

She made her way to the expansive windows and looked out at the large inviting deck, and beneath it, the turquoise pool and colorful gardens. All this overlooking a valley of rolling green hills, backdropped by blue mountains. She could admit that the house was beautiful. It would be nice to have use of a pool year-round. She could envision herself soaking in the hot tub in the winter, over-looking the picturesque valley as snowflakes danced around her.

Even so, the place was mammoth. Did Shane like living here by himself, she wondered? She'd be lonely in this large palace with no one to enjoy it with.

Shane returned and handed her a glass of wine.

"Thanks." She took the glass, and nodded toward the windows. "Gorgeous views."

Shane's lips curved up slowly. "Do you like the wine?"

She took a sip. It was intense, complex, and truly delicious. "It's okay," she teased.

Shane shook his head. "You're a hard woman to impress, Liz Patterson." He gestured toward the couch. "Have a seat. I'm gonna go get your surprises."

Liz's gaze trailed Shane as he made his way upstairs. Even the stairs were impressive, big and wide, graciously curving to the second level. Sighing, she sat on the couch and sipped her wine.

A few minutes later, he trotted down the stairs carrying a large picture. It was turned toward him, making her curious. When he lifted it to the window ledge and turned it toward her, she gasped. She rose, stepped over, and ran a finger along the frame as she studied the piece. A beautiful iconic Georgetown view of Key Bridge and Georgetown University from the Potomac River. In the paint-ing, the sun dipped below the trees and behind the bridge, streaking hues of orange and pink across the water. Antoine Minett's *George-town at Dusk*.

"I picked this up for you," Shane said, grinning. "You mentioned you loved this piece."

She gaped at Shane for a long moment, shocked that he had remembered. She'd mentioned it when they had strolled through Georgetown and she'd seen the print in a store window. She appreci-ated Shane's remembrance, especially since it had only been a passing comment.

It was a thoughtful gift, but way too expensive. She had ogled the painting at an art exhibition last year, and had nearly fallen over after she'd glanced at the price tag of a hundred grand. The hair on the back of her neck bristled. Why would he buy her such an expensive gift? Her father had bought her expensive things too, but afterward he would demand something in return or use the gift to manipulate her. As a young girl, she'd wanted an American Girl doll with all of the accessories. Her father had purchased everything she had requested, but in return he'd made her enter a beauty pageant that his company had sponsored. When she'd turned sixteen and had begged for a trip to Paris he'd delivered, but it had cost her a summer of babysitting for his secretary's kids, a commitment he'd neglected to mention until she had returned. She pressed a hand to her neck, calling on her logic. Shane had bought her a nice gift. It had cost too much, but it was sweet nonetheless, and he hadn't asked anything of her. At least not yet.

"Do you like it?" Shane asked.

"It's lovely and it's very sweet," she said. "But way too expensive."

Shane's expression was out-and-out hurt. She tried to push aside the spasm of guilt in the pit of her belly. She hadn't meant to make him feel bad, but she needed to establish boundaries. No expensive gifts and no strings or demands.

Shane reached behind the picture and pulled out a manila envelope. "Maybe this will make you happier," he said, handing it to her.

Unease settled around her like a low-hanging fog as she wondered what it was. She'd had enough surprises for one day. "What is it?"

"Just open it." A smile tugged at his lips.

She opened the envelope, removed a small stack of papers, and skimmed through them. From what she could gather, it was a lease. With *her* name on it. Confused, she glanced over at Shane. "What is this?"

His smile broadened. "It's a lease for a big house just up the road."

"I don't understand," she said. "Why would I need another house?" Irritation swelled inside her. "And why would you do this without even talking with me?"

Shane's body tensed and his eyes widened as if he were surprised by her reaction. "I thought you'd like it."

How dare he rent a house for her without so much as a single conversation? She couldn't help but wonder if this was what he had wanted in exchange for the painting—to put her up like some kind of mistress and expect her to be at his beck and call? Her jaw clenched as anger coiled in her gut. This was the same pattern she'd experienced with her father. He would give her a lavish gift or give in to one of her requests, but there was always a string attached. Like the time he let her take in a stray cat, then after she'd fallen in love with Twinkle, he'd demanded that she attend finance camp over summer vacation in order to keep the cat. When she'd been comparing colleges, he'd bought her a brand-new sports car. As he'd handed her the keys, he had *suggested* that she attend his alma mater.

Shane stuffed his hands in his pockets. "I thought you might want to be closer. You said the commute was tough and you didn't get to see Katie as much as you wanted." His hurt expression returned. "And I thought you might want to be closer to me, too."

The commute was long especially in the endless D.C. traffic, and she didn't get to spend as much time with Katie as much as she would like. But she lived in Georgetown. It was presumptuous for him to think that she and Sabby would uproot their lives and move up the street without a discussion. Guilt for not appreciating Shane's gesture flashed for a single beat, but it was quickly shoved aside by frustration. When had Shane become her father? She put a hand on her hip. "Did you ever stop to think that I have commitments in Georgetown, and Sabby is settled in school there?"

"I thought you had some here too," he said quietly.

The guilt in her gut intensified, but so did her frustration. She was sorry that she'd hurt his feelings, but he was way out of line. She wasn't going to cave to his sad puppy-dog expression. Expensive gifts, renting a house for her. They had only been dating for a couple of months. These were things people in relationships talked about. Not that she or Shane had much experience with *real* relationships. Her earlier fears and doubts bubbled to the surface. She and Shane lived very different lives, and they lived in different towns. Apparently, she wasn't the only one who had a problem with their geographic distance. But she had work to do in D.C. She lifted her gaze to meet his. "I have an article series on the most popular bars in D.C."

"That seems beneath your talent," Shane said.

Her father used to say the same thing about her writing. Her asshole ex had as well. She'd thought Shane was different, that he respected her work. Granted, this series wouldn't be her most prestigious, but it was a job. Sometimes she had to take the ordinary in between the extraordinary. To keep her contacts, to pay her mortgage. "Some of us need to pay the bills," she spat out, still annoyed that Shane appeared to be more like her father than she had initially thought. Buying expensive gifts, making decisions on her behalf. She didn't want that kind of help from her dad, and she didn't want it from Shane, either.

Shane rubbed a hand on his cheek. "If you're only doing it for the money, I could give you what you'd make for that series."

Shane probably thought he was being helpful, but so had her father. Throughout her life, her dad had been there to help when she'd needed it. But the help, like the gifts, had always come at a cost. After he'd hired a nanny for Sabby, he had insisted that she date some stuffy young executive at his venture capital company. Her father had paid for her college education—for one measly year. After she had changed her major from finance to journalism, he'd informed her that he would no longer pay if she was going to "waste her time with words." She'd taken out student loans and had spent the next eight years paying them off. When Sabby was four, he'd offered to buy them a luxury townhome. She'd been uber-excited until she had learned what he'd wanted in return. This time he had wanted to buy Sabby. He'd wanted Sabby to go to *his* church, join DAFT (Daughters of Financial Titans) when she came of age, and send her to a prestigious boarding school so she'd be ready for the right colleges. When Liz had tried to negotiate, he'd told her it was his way or the highway. She had chosen the highway then, and she would choose it now, too.

"Who the hell do you think you are?" she asked Shane, quivering with indignation. "I don't know what kind of women you're used to, but you can't buy me."

"I wasn't—"

She raised a hand. "Don't waste your breath. We're done."

"I can't believe I'm here!" Savannah squealed. The excitement in her daughter's voice suffused Katie in a soft, maternal glow.

Cara and Sabby were on each side of Savannah. The three of them had been inseparable ever since Savannah had arrived earlier in the day.

"Look Katie!" Savannah scurried over, extending her right arm. "We made *sister* bracelets."

"It's beautiful," Katie said, grateful that Cara and Sabby had been so welcoming to Savannah.

"I know, right?" Savannah beamed up at her.

Katie touched a finger to Savannah's bracelet. "I especially like the sparkly blue stones."

Large chocolate brown eyes—a replica of Katie's—flitted a curious glance at her. Katie's womb fluttered as she stared at the spitting image of her younger self. How had she given up this precious child?

Time stilled as she and Savannah scrutinized each other. They had the same the same eyes, the same oval shaped face, the same straight-edged nose. Was Savannah noticing their likenesses too, she wondered?

Savannah grabbed a long strand of dark, wavy hair and twirled it around her fingers. Katie smiled. It was a gesture she caught herself doing on a regular basis. A motherly ache pinged deep inside her. The desire to tell her daughter the truth was almost unbearable. She pulled in a steadying breath, reminding herself of the conversation she and Liam had had with Deb and Colt. After talking it through, they'd agreed it would be better to work through custody first. Afterward, and regardless of the outcome, the four of them would tell Savannah together.

Tilting her head to one side, Savannah's eyes narrowed and sharpened. Katie held her breath. Had Savannah made the connection?

But the moment was lost when Deb approached. The older woman oohed and ahhed over Savannah's bracelet, and then smiled at Katie. "We're so happy to be here." She patted Katie's arm. Thanks for putting us up."

"We're happy to have you."

"Food's on the table," Katie's mother called out. A couple of hours earlier, after Katie and the girls had returned from taking Pan for a walk, she'd peeked into the kitchen and had been surprised to find her mother cooking alongside Liam and Shane. She had offered to help but Liam had urged her to play hostess instead. Even though she'd felt guilty, she had enjoyed visiting with Deb and Colt.

They all made their way to the dining room. Liam sat next to Katie, and Shane on the other side of Liam. Shane slid her a smile as he passed, but the smile didn't reach his eyes.

The Shelton's had taken the red-eye flight into Dulles, and she and Liam had picked them up at eight that morning. They'd all spent the day together visiting...everyone except for Liz who had dropped Sabby off and then driven off, insisting she had something important to do.

Shane was a little rusty when it came to long-term relationships. He hadn't been in one in over six years. He dated regularly, but until Liz, hadn't been interested in anything more. Now, he looked at Liz as if she were the only person in the world who mattered. Though Liz would never admit it, she looked at Shane the same way.

Even though Liz had told Katie bits and pieces about what had happened, she still didn't understand why her sister was so riled. The lease Shane had surprised her with seemed to be part of it, but based on Liz's mutterings over their father, it appeared that Liz had been comparing the two men. Which was ridiculous. The only thing their father and Shane had in common was their wealth.

Katie had yet to make the connection as to why Liz was upset over the picture. Shane had bought her a beautiful oil painting of Georgetown from an artist that Liz loved. Why that irked her sister was beyond Katie. But she could concede that Shane may have crossed the line with the lease. Even so, his heart had been in the right place. The Callahan brothers were fixers. When Shane had heard Liz lament about not being around enough, he found a place where she and Sabby could crash when they didn't want to drive back to Georgetown. He hadn't wanted her to feel pressured to stay with him if she wasn't ready to do so. That seemed like a *nice* gesture to Katie. Even so, he probably should have talked with Liz first, but Shane had said he'd wanted to surprise her.

"It was beautiful flying into Dulles," Deb said, drawing Katie back. "I love our desert landscape, but it was nice seeing all that green."

Colt grabbed a chicken breast, then turned to Liam. "I enjoyed seeing your shop earlier today."

"Me too!" Savannah grinned at Liam. "Cool motorcycles."

"Maybe Dad or Uncle Shane will take you for a spin," Cara suggested.

"I wanna go riding." Savannah's head snapped between Liam and Shane. "Will you take me?"

Liam and Shane answered at the same time, both with affirmative responses.

"That is, if it's okay with your grandparents," Liam added.

"Fine by me." Colt winked at his granddaughter.

"My Colt used to ride." A smile curved Deb's lips. "He had an old Indian, and lord have mercy he ran that bike into the ground. I rode with him a few times, but he was a little too fast and a little too wild in those days."

Colt laughed. "Good times. But then we had Gwen and I gave it up. Still miss it sometimes."

"I miss riding, too," Katie said, surprising herself. She hadn't realized how much she had missed being on the back of a motorcycle until that very moment.

"Really?" Liam eyes brightened as he stretched his arm across the back of her seat. "I have the insurance money so we can get a new bike anytime," he said quietly. "I just wasn't sure…."

Katie inched over, her stomach clenching with excitement. "I definitely wanna ride."

Liam touched his forehead to hers. "Then we'll go shopping soon," he whispered.

She nodded, then reluctantly pulled back because they had guests at the table. Even so, she could barely contain her elation. There had been so much going on with her doctor's appointments and healing sessions, Savannah and the custody case, that she and Liam hadn't gotten back to their normal routines—long walks with Pan, riding their motorcycle, making love. This past week they'd begun walking again and now they were going to buy a motorcycle. The only thing left was lovemaking.

Before the accident, she and Liam had enjoyed an active love life. What was the problem now, she wondered? She had been tired and stressed after the coma, but she was fine now. Even so, Liam hesitated. He stroked her and spooned her every night, but whenever she tried to initiate something more, he'd say, "you need rest," and then he'd scratch her back or feather his fingers through her hair until she fell asleep.

"Hey, Savannah." Cara's words drew Katie's attention back to conversations at the table. "Me and Sab are going to Beaver Falls on Monday. Wanna come?"

"It's a cool waterfall," Sabby said. "There's a rec center too, with go-carts and arcade games."

"Yeah." Wide-eyed, Savannah turned to her grandparents. "Can I?"

"Of course, sugar," Deb said.

"Awesome." Laughing, Savannah reached under the table. "Pan's licking my leg. I wish I had a dog. I love him so much."

"You don't have a dog?" Liam tipped his head. "Every kid needs a dog."

"I know, right? Mama and I dog sat for Lina—Ma's friend—for like six months while she was away. Then we were gonna get our own dog." Savannah's smile faded and her eyes dulled. "But Uncle Warren says no way."

Katie's chest pinched at the sorrow in Savannah's eyes. "You can come visit us and Pan anytime."

"*Anytime*," Liam echoed. "Pan seems to have taken a real liking to you. He's usually only that kind of affectionate with Katie."

Savannah grinned.

Conversation shifted to talk about Texas and then the differences between Texas and Maryland. Eventually, they circled around to their plans for the week. Everyone was super excited about next weekend's ballgame. Like Savannah, Colt and Deb were major baseball fans, and Shane had secured a suite for next Saturday's Nationals game in D.C. They were going to D.C. tomorrow too, for sightseeing—the Washington monument, the Mall, maybe a few museums.

"Take some pictures for me," Shane told Savannah. "You can wow me over dinner tomorrow night."

"What?" Katie leaned around Liam to gape at her brother-in-law. "You're not coming?"

Shane wouldn't look at her as he responded. "Nah. I have...uh, something going on."

He sounded exactly like Liz. Katie's jaw tightened. "C'mon, Shane. It'll be fun."

"Yeah, Uncle Shane," Sabby said.

Cara joined in on the begging too. "Pleeease Uncle Shane."

Looking ruffled, Shane took a long moment before he responded. "D.C. is Liz's thing. She should take this trip."

"Oh, for God's sake." Katie tossed her napkin on the table. "You two are grown adults. You can't be in D.C. together?"

Savannah's eyebrows squished together as she glanced across the table at Shane. "You and Liz don't like each other?"

"Oh, he likes her," Sabby said before Shane could respond. "And she likes him, too." She flashed Shane an encouraging smile. "They're just having a little disagreement."

CHAPTER EIGHTEEN

*T*hroughout the week, Liz had accompanied the family on sightseeing and shopping trips while Shane had joined them at the local carnival. He had also hosted a pool and movie party at his place. Liz had had dinner with them on Sunday and Wednesday night; Shane on Monday and Thursday. It was stupid and childish and Katie was determined to put an end to it.

If Liz and Shane weren't going to make up, they could at least be friends. Their families were too close for anything less. But what Katie really wanted was for them to get back together because they had *both* been happier as a couple.

Thus, she decided *both* Liz and Shane would attend the ballgame on Saturday.

She'd called her sister and had laid on the guilt trip. It wasn't something she did often, nor was she particularly proud of it, but it was for a good cause. Maybe if Liz and Shane were in the same space, they'd have an actual conversation. Besides, Savannah, Colt, and Deb were leaving on Sunday, and she wanted their last night together to be perfect.

As a result, on Saturday afternoon they all met up at Nationals Park in the large suite Shane had secured. Liz *and* Shane and *both* of her parents were there. Katie wasn't sure what had convinced her father. It could have been her call, (she had laid the guilt trip on him too,) the opportunity to spend time with his cousin Colt, or simply the chance to see his favorite team play. It was the first time he had attended any event with her and Liam. While she was thrilled, Liam seemed anxious, and her father didn't help with his standoffish manner. Still, they were all together which was a major step in the right direction.

She gave her dad credit for coming, even though his priorities were still screwed up. He'd grunted hello to Liam, but had greeted Shane warmly. Her father equated money with a man's worth, and as usual, Shane had come through in a big way. They had an extravagant suite with a large selection of food and drinks. Shane had also arranged for a fleet of limos to drive them to the game. Shane was a great guy and generous to a fault. What her father had neglected to notice was that *both* Shane and Liam were caring, good-hearted, salt-of-the-earth men.

Maybe someday, she thought, refusing to give up hope on her father. She made her way to the buffet and filled a plate with fresh fruits and vegetables, hummus, and various appetizers. Shane had hired a catering firm that offered a wide selection, including vegetarian fare for her and Cara and Maryland specialties like crab cakes, Old Bay fries, and pit beef sandwiches.

Grabbing a bottle of water and a wedge of lime, she strolled over to Liz who was sitting by herself at the far end of the suite.

"Want some company?" she asked.

"Sure." Liz patted the space next to her and Katie sat.

Liz reached over, grabbed a piece of celery from Katie's plate, and dipped it in the hummus. "Yummy."

"Yep. Shane outdid himself today." Katie popped an apple slice in her mouth. "Then again, he always does."

Sighing, Liz stared out at the bleachers.

"The girls look like they're having fun," Katie said, changing the subject to draw Liz in.

Liz glanced at Cara, Sabby, and Savannah and smiled. "They've really bonded over the last week."

"Look at how cute they are," Katie said. The three girls were dressed alike, all wearing Nationals T-shirts, skinny jean shorts, and Sperry sneakers, outfits they'd purchased during their D.C. shopping trip.

"Any news on the custody case?" Liz asked.

Katie took a sip of her Perrier. "Our attorney thinks it'll be a slam dunk. I sure hope so. I hate Savannah going back to life with Warren." She popped a carrot in her mouth, then extended the plate to Liz.

"What do Deb and Colt think?" Liz asked, grabbing a mini spinach wrap.

Appreciation warmed Katie's chest. "They've been very supportive."

"Good. You'll let me know if I can do anything?"

She nodded. "You betcha. Now back to the subject of Shane."

Liz pressed her lips together.

"Come on." Katie nibbled on a piece of celery. "Shane might have been a little over zealous with the lease but his heart was in the right place."

"Maybe. But I refuse to end up with someone like Dad." Liz lifted her chin. "I love Dad, but no way am I having a man tell me what to do."

Katie couldn't help but laugh. Shane was the most generous man she knew and he never asked for anything in return. "I'm not sure we're talking about the same man."

"He leased a house for me," Liz said, her voice pure frustration. "It's classic Dad."

Katie pushed her plate aside. "It's *nothing* like Dad. Dad would have dangled the house while telling you what he wanted in return. Or he'd give you the house and later demand something after you'd already fallen in love with it." She leaned toward Liz. "Tell me, what did Shane ask of you?"

Liz opened her mouth to speak, then closed it. Her shoulders sagged a little. "I didn't give him enough time to ask."

"So you *assumed* he wanted something in return, but you never asked?"

Liz sighed. "Maybe I should have asked."

Katie put a hand on her sister's knee. "It's how we were raised, but Shane's not like that."

Liz's head dipped. "How do I know?"

"Shane's been in my life for over five years," Katie said. "Cara has him wrapped around her little finger. He gives in to her every whim —whether it's an ask for a few bucks or a movie night or an expensive trip. He's never asked a single thing of her. He's always there when I need him and he's never asked anything of me, either. He's always trying to pay Liam back for putting him through college, but my stubborn hubby won't let him."

A myriad of emotions ran through Liz's eyes. Confusion, shame, and a flicker of hope that she quickly veiled. "Neither Shane or I do relationships." Liz's gaze wandered to the field. "It's better this way," she said, but her voice was unconvincing.

"Really?" Katie's eyes remained fixed on her sister. "Then why are you both so miserable?"

Liz spotted Shane slumped against the wall in the corner of the suite. His head was turned toward the game, but his expression was an empty stare. Guilt squeezed her lungs, making it hard to breathe. She made her way toward him slowly, her heart heavy with regret over her behavior. While she held firm in not wanting to be with a man who was like her father, she owed Shane the benefit of a conversation. Katie had painted Shane as laid-back, loyal, and giving and that's how he'd been around her as well. Katie had shared that Shane had done a lot for her and Cara over the last five years and that he'd never asked for a single thing in return.

After talking with Katie and thinking through her points, Liz wondered if she had overreacted. In truth, she'd been wondering that all week. She had been miserable, missing Shane like crazy. Her gut told her she'd been wrong, and Katie had pretty much said the same. Damn it, she shouldn't have jumped to the conclusion that he had wanted something in return for the painting. And she shouldn't have flipped out over the lease. Maybe, it had simply been a kind gesture.

Glancing across the ballfield, the truth hit her bright as the sun and clear as the baby blue sky. She had linked Shane with her father because she'd been afraid of her growing feelings for him. After Phillip, she'd sworn off long-term relationships, vowing she'd never again be controlled by a man. But she was willing to concede, as Katie had suggested, that not every man was like her ex or her father. Her father had been shamelessly open with his manipulation. His motto—he held the purse strings, so he made the rules. Phillip had been subtler with his controlling ways. Like when he'd tell her what kind of work she should take or decline. He would say they were just *suggestions*, but whenever she didn't do what he had *suggested*, he'd bitch and moan until she got so tired of hearing it, she would cave.

She drew in a deep breath to calm the anxious waves in her stomach. Approaching Shane, she lifted her chin to fake poise and confidence.

"Liz." Shane's greeting was a husky whisper. As he leaned against the wall, his arm muscles bulged and Liz felt a zap of awareness low in her belly. He looked uber-hot in cowboy boots, dark blue jeans, and a grayish-blue shirt that brought out the same unique color in his eyes.

"Shane—" she began, but he held up a hand.

"Can we find a private place to talk?" he asked, glancing at the others milling about around them.

Relief filled her as she nodded in agreement. It would be much better to have this discussion in private. "Sounds good."

Shane placed a hand in the small of her back and led her out of the suite. In the main corridor, he called over a staff member and produced a hundred-dollar bill. They were quickly ushered to a smaller room next door.

After they were settled on a cushioned bench facing the ballfield, Shane took her hand. His palm was large, warm, and comforting. She glanced down at their linked fingers, realizing how much she'd missed his touch.

"I'm sorry," he said. "I didn't mean to overstep my bounds."

Surprised by Shane's ready apology, Liz slowly lifted her gaze. His gray-blue eyes shone sexy, seductive…and genuinely sorry.

"I was trying to be helpful," he continued, "but after I thought about it, I saw your point." He traced circles on her hand, causing shivers to race up her arm. "I should have talked with you before getting the lease. I should have asked what *you* wanted."

Shane's apology humbled Liz. It appeared he really had gotten the lease just to make it easy for her. He hadn't asked for anything in return—then or now. She was the one who had overreacted and yet he was the one apologizing. The guilt she'd felt earlier resurfaced and amplified. "I'm sorry too," she said. "I overreacted."

Shane lowered his head. "I made you feel uncomfortable. I know this may sound bad, but I'm not good at relationships or communication." He let out a low laugh. "Guess I need practice." He slowly lifted his gaze to meet hers. "But I want to be better—for you Liz."

Shane's unexpected words moved her. Her chest opened and the tightness dissipated. In its place was a soft, fuzzy sensation. "That's very sweet." She had called him presumptuous, but it may have been *her* who had presumed. But she needed to be sure. "I need to ask you something."

Shane rubbed his thumb over the top of her hand. "Anything."

"Why did you get the lease?" Katie had offered her perspective but she needed to hear it from Shane.

"Because you said you wanted to be here more often and that the commute was becoming a hassle." Shane held her gaze. "You and Sabby are more than welcome to stay at my place, but I thought if I suggested that I might be pushing my luck."

She sighed. "So you didn't want anything from me in return?"

Shane lifted her hand to his mouth and took his time pressing soft kisses across her palm. "Yeah, I want something." Her heart stopped beating until he flashed a quick, teasing grin. "I want you to give us another chance."

A laugh rushed out of her. She wanted to be with him, too. But before she could commit, she needed to be one hundred percent sure there had been no strings attached. She blew out a breath, puffing her bangs. "I mean before. You know for giving me the picture and the lease."

Shane's brows creased. "Why would I give you a gift and then ask something of you?"

She wasn't sure how to respond but as it turned out, she didn't need to. Shane shifted toward her, his jaw tight, his eyes compassionate. "I'm not your father," he said. "I gave you the picture because you mentioned Minett was your favorite artist. I got the lease because I thought it might make life easier for you."

She dipped her chin to her chest as guilt and shame washed through her. She'd assumed the worst and she'd maligned him. She wrapped her arms around his neck. "I'm so sorry. I shouldn't have jumped to that conclusion."

"Apology accepted." Shane lifted her chin and looked into her eyes. "I've never given a gift with an ulterior motive and I'm not about to start now. When I give you a gift, know it's because I want you to have it."

"Thank you," she said quietly as relief swam through her veins. That wasn't how she'd seen it work, but she understood that was how it *should* work.

She was grateful that Shane hadn't wanted anything in return for his gifts. Even so, she needed to set some ground rules. She didn't want Shane spending oodles of money on her. Or Sabby either, although her daughter didn't seem to have issues with accepting Shane's gifts. Over the past week, Sabby had come home with new clothes, a new iPad, and a new hairdo from the trendiest salon in D.C. which had cost more than the rest of her gifts combined. "We should talk about spending limits."

"Why?" Shane drew back, his expression so befuddled that it made her laugh.

" 'Cause it's not appropriate for you to buy me—or Sabby—expensive things."

"That's ridiculous," he said. "I have plenty. What good is it to have money if I can't spend it on those I care for?"

Moved by his words, by the confirmation that he was *nothing* like her father, Liz's heart tugged and swelled.

"I care about you," Shane said, tucking a strand of hair behind her ear. "A lot. This past week has been empty without you." Liz's belly did a happy dance as Shane cupped his hands around her face. "I hope you'll give us another shot." He gave her the lazy grin she found so hard to resist. "You know the old saying—third time's a charm."

Joy filled her insides like sunshine. It was time to stop running scared, time to put on her big girl panties and see where this might go. She leaned in and grazed her lips over his, taking delight in the shivers that shot out in all directions. "I'd like that."

THROUGHOUT THE DAY, Liam had chatted with Liz, hung out with Shane, and watched part of the game holding hands with Katie. He'd played trivia with the girls, smoked cigars with Colt, and had bonded with Deb and Carolyn over a shared piece of chocolate cake. The one person he hadn't spent any time with was Mitch Patterson.

So what if he'd avoided Katie's father today? He doubted that anyone would blame him. Mitch had never been shy about his ardent dislike of him, or his disapproval over his marriage to Katie. Liam swallowed the familiar hurt that had lodged in his throat and reminded himself that he didn't give a shit. But deep down the knowledge that he *did* care persisted, and it wasn't all on Katie's father. *He* needed to step up his game instead of going out of his way to avoid Mitch like a damn pansy.

It was true Mitch had unfairly judged and convicted him, without even giving him a chance. It made him feel small, like he was still the fucked-up asshole he'd been as a teenager. After all these years, it was disappointing that Katie's father hadn't come around. But it pissed him off, too. He took good care of Katie, he made her happy. What the hell did the old man want?

Whatever it was Mitch wanted from him, Liam wished for a better relationship between the two of them.

He grabbed a beer, drew in a long breath, then strode across the suite to join Mitch and Carolyn who were engrossed in conversation with Colt and Deb.

Colt noticed him first and waved him over. "Liam, come join us."

"Thanks." Liam had quickly grown fond of Colt. He appreciated the older man's warmth and friendliness. Entering their circle, he nodded at the rest of the group. "Howdy."

"Hi, Liam." Carolyn gave him a bright smile. "This has been a nice day and I'm not even a baseball fan."

"I'm glad you're having a good time," he said, feeling a little burst of satisfaction over his budding relationship with Katie's mother.

"It's been a great day," Deb said. "And I'm a huge fan. Thanks for inviting us."

Liam smiled at Deb, whom he'd grown fond of too. "It's our pleasure."

"Savannah has had a ball." Deb laughed at her own joke. "Pun intended. And she had fun playing trivia with you earlier. You have a way with her."

"Thanks." A small tug of pride unfurled in Liam's chest. "Savannah's a sweetheart." He glanced over at Mitch hoping for a reaction, but Katie's dad looked like his stoic, poker-faced self.

"How's the custody case progressing?" Colt asked.

"Moving forward." Liam took a sip of his Corona. "Our attorney thinks it'll be quick. Katie and I sure hope so."

"We'll miss Savannah when she moves here," Colt said, pleasing Liam with his assumption that the case would be resolved in their favor. "But we want what's best for her." He patted Liam on the back. "Clearly, that's you and Katie."

Liam put down his beer. "That means a lot." Receiving the compliment in front of Mitch was damn nice, too. "We meant what we told you," Liam said, making eye contact with Colt, "you and Deb are welcome to visit anytime. Let's plan on a lot more ballgames in the future."

"Sounds great." Colt slapped him on the back.

Standing taller, Liam hooked his thumbs in his belt loops and soaked in Colt's endorsement. Based on prior conversations, he had understood that they'd had Colt and Deb's backing. But this was the first time he'd received public praise and respect from parental figures other than his own.

When the crowd thundered, all of their attention shifted to the field. Higgins slammed in a homer for two runs and a win for the Nationals. Liam's thoughts filtered back to a pivotal game in high school when he'd hit a grand slam for the game win, securing the state championship. For a moment, he relived the adrenaline rush, thrill, and gratification he'd felt over leading his team to an important victory.

"Looks like my boys got another win," Mitch said, rubbing his hands together. When Katie's father glanced his way, every muscle in Liam's body tensed.

Mitch's gaze zeroed in on Liam's arm. Both of his arms were intricately tattooed from shoulder to wrist. At least Mitch had zeroed in on his left arm, the tamer Irish side, including a Celtic cross bearing Katie and Cara's names. Underneath the cross was a flaming shamrock, a leprechaun with raised fists, and the phrase *Pog Mo Thoin*—Gaelic for *Kiss My Ass*—a phrase that was on the tip of his tongue at this very moment.

"Hope you're successful in the custody case," Mitch said.

Even though Liam had only had two beers all day long, he was sure he had to be hallucinating. His expression must have looked as shocked as he felt because Mitch lifted a shoulder. "For Kate." Mitch had finally stopped calling Katie 'Kathryn,' but he didn't like the nickname 'Katie.' It was too juvenile, or so Mitch claimed. "Savannah should be with her birth mother, and Kate should be with her child."

There was the Mitch he knew. *It's not for you, Liam, you shithead, it's for Katie.*

"What?" Savannah shrieked, and all eyes turned to her. She had apparently slipped into their circle unnoticed. "Kate?" she said, her voice puzzled. As she spun toward Deb, her eyes widened. "Katie? Katie's my birth mother?" she asked in a high-pitched voice.

She didn't wait for a response. Instead, Savannah sprinted across the floor and threw herself at Katie.

Katie wrapped her arms around Savannah and quiet words were exchanged. Afterward, Cara and Sabby leaned in for a group hug. Relief poured through Liam like a heavy rain. Katie had been worried over how Savannah would feel when she learned that Katie was her mother. Would she be mad and resentful...or accepting, maybe even happy? Katie no longer had to fret; Savannah looked delighted.

As Katie talked and laughed with the three girls, Liam could feel their elation from across the room. When her gaze lifted to meet his, her expression was pure joy, and Liam's resolve to win custody of Savannah increased ten-fold.

CHAPTER NINETEEN

*K*atie was grateful that Savannah finally knew she was her biological mother. She had prepared herself for a multitude of emotions, including hurt, anger, and resentment. She'd prayed and asked Posie and Black Eagle for assistance. At the ballgame last weekend, Savannah had said two beautiful angels—a light-haired female and a dark-haired male—had visited her in a dream and promised to reunite her with her birth mother. They'd assured her that she would be welcomed and loved and that she would be happy in her new home. After the angels had visited, Savannah had dreamed about Katie.

Once again, Posie and Black Eagle had come through. Katie had been utterly relieved to find nothing but joy in Savannah's reaction to the news. Now that Savannah knew she was her mother, the two of them had been talking on the phone or FaceTiming a couple of times a day.

The custody case had been progressing well, and while they still had to go through the last legal motions, according to Ken, it was a slam dunk. All of this good news had Katie's spirits flying high as she, Cara, and Savannah shopped for Savannah's room accessories.

She and Liam wanted to have her bedroom ready so Savannah could move in as soon as custody had been resolved.

They already had new furniture thanks to Shane, who had paid a ridiculously high fee for rush delivery. Now they were shopping for window treatments and bedding. Tonight, they would clean and paint the room, then pull it all together tomorrow.

They'd purchased the paint—a light teal which was Savannah's favorite color—and were now searching for the perfect comforter, toss pillows, and curtains.

"What about this?" Sabby asked, holding up a bright pink Hello Kitty comforter.

"She's not five," Cara snapped with a roll of her eyes.

"Jeez, I was kidding!" Sabby shook her head.

When Sabby shuffled to another aisle, Katie sidled up to Cara. "What's wrong, sweetie?"

"I guess I'm just in a mood today," Cara said with a lift of her shoulder.

Katie knew her step-daughter well enough to wait it out. Sure enough, a few aisles later, Cara slapped her hands on her hips.

"It's stupid Josh, and bowling with Sab and Savannah."

Katie wasn't sure what the issue was. Cara and Sabby had taken Savannah bowling last weekend, and Savannah had come home all kinds of excited. "What happened? Savannah said she had a good time."

"Well, it ended up being nice," Cara said in an irritated voice, "but Josh wouldn't come."

"I thought you took Savannah along on your double date." Katie held up a blanket as she spoke, glancing at Cara for her opinion. When Cara scrunched her nose, Katie put the blanket down.

"That's what was *supposed* to happen," Cara said. "But Josh said he had better stuff to do than hang out with a twelve-year old, then we got into a fight."

Sabby joined them and gave Cara a sympathetic look. "Josh was pretty lame."

"So, *her* boyfriend showed up," Cara said, thumbing at Sabby, "and I looked stupid and dateless."

Katie took Cara's hand. "Sweetie, Savannah doesn't think you're stupid. She adores you." Katie smiled at Sabby. "And Sabby, too."

"I guess." As they walked down the aisle, Cara ran her fingers over the bedspreads. "But I expected more from Josh. Brandon was really good with Savannah."

"He was." Sabby's lips curved up. "Seth, too."

"Yeah." Cara tugged a comforter off the bottom shelf. "Savannah loved spending time with Seth at the shop. He showed her all of the bikes and even took her on a ride up and down the driveway."

A warm glow swept through Katie as she remembered Rose's visit in the clouds, and her observation that Seth would be good for Cara. "Savannah was smitten with Seth, that's for sure." She tipped her head at the comforter Cara had selected. It had a white background with a flight of colorful butterflies twisting through the center. "Very nice."

"It's perfect," Sabby said. "Savannah will love it."

"Sold!" Katie took the comforter and grabbed a few matching pillows.

"So you guys don't think I should be mad at Josh?" Cara asked as they made their way toward the counter.

"Never said that." Sabby smoothed down a strand of her newly styled hair. "I'd be mad all right. He's an asshat." As soon as the words popped out, she covered her mouth. "Oops, sorry Aunt Katie."

Katie suppressed her snicker. While the language was inappropriate, she tended to agree with Sabby's assessment. She nodded at her niece to acknowledge the apology.

"Do you think I should be mad?" Cara asked, linking arms with her.

"I don't think you should be mad, that's just wasted energy." Katie rubbed Cara's arm. "Instead, you should think about what qualities you want in a boyfriend and then consider whether Josh has what you're looking for."

∽

On Sunday, Katie took Pan for a walk at sunrise and then got ready for her appointment with Simone. In the driveway, she leaned against her car, taking a moment to appreciate the flowers blooming in a riot of color in the cottage garden she'd planted last year. Overhead, a yellow sun glimmered in a breathtaking blue sky as white puffy clouds hugged the purple mountains. She whimsically blew a kiss toward the heavens, calling out a greeting to Posie, Black Eagle, and Bear, and then got into her car.

With the radio blaring and fresh air wafting through the open window, she took delight in the half hour drive through the countryside. Before she knew it, she'd arrived at her destination.

This was the last of her healing sessions, although she had joined Simone's weekly meditation class. She was appreciative of her energy healer's help, physically, mentally, and spiritually. Simone had not only helped her body heal, but she had also reinforced what Katie had learned in the clouds. She'd stressed the importance of putting out positive thought vibrations and positive actions in order to receive positivity back, reiterating what Posie and Black Eagle had taught her.

The healing session went by quickly, and as Katie made her way home, appreciation bloomed in her chest bright as the flowers in her garden. She thanked her guides—in the clouds and on Earth—for all of their help. She had come such a long way since the accident. She felt amazingly well, and she was stronger, wiser and more positive than ever before.

Back at the house, a Mediterranean salad was waiting for her. She ate with Shane, Liam, Cara, and Sabby. Sabby had been staying with them during Liz's business trip on the west coast, and would be staying for one more night so Shane and Liz could get some much needed alone time. After lunch, Cara and Sabby tugged Katie upstairs to show her Savannah's room.

When Sabby pushed open the door, Katie lifted a hand to her mouth. "It's so beautiful!" She stepped inside, and whirled around to take in every detail. "You girls did a great job finishing," she said, and then pulled Cara and Sabby into a hug.

The room was spacious, even with the maple furniture they'd

painstakingly selected. The queen-sized bed easily fit against the teal wall, and the butterfly bedspread and bold toss pillows added spark. Pendant lights hung from a track over the bed, and inspirational framed posters covered the walls. She loved the picture of the single white dandelion with its seeds blowing in the wind. The message read: Some see a weed, some see a wish. Katie put her hands over her heart. "Savannah's going to love it."

"We had a little help from Dad and Uncle Shane," Cara said with a big grin. "Our pre-teen contemporary funk design is all that."

Sabby fluffed the pillows on the bed. "Yeah, we killed it."

"You sure did," Katie agreed. "Sabby, I'm glad you stayed to help. Thank you both, it's amazing! We should call Savannah and show her."

Cara ran off to grab her iPad, and a few minutes later they Face-Timed with Savannah, showing her every detail in a three-hundred-sixty-degree narrated tour.

"Thank you, thank you, thank you." Savannah clapped her hands together and squealed at every detail. "OMG, it's the coolest room ever!" she said, shoving her face close to her iPad, giving them a closeup view of her face.

As Katie took in Savannah's milk chocolate eyes, long wavy hair, and sweet smile, her heart ached with the need to be with her daughter.

"I love it so much. It's awesome!" Tears trembled on Savannah's lashes. "I can't wait to move." She tipped her head to one side. "Do you know when?"

"Not yet, but we should have an update in a few days." Katie's gaze flicked to the dandelion seeds on the wall as she set her intention that the custody case would be settled in their favor soon.

"When you come back, Seth said he'd take you on another motorcycle ride," Cara said, smiling at Savannah. "He said he'd make it longer this time."

"Awesome!" As Savannah bounced up and down, her image blurred on the iPad. "I heart him. Tell him that, 'kay? Maybe he can come bowling with us next time."

"Maybe," Cara murmured. When she stared off into space, Sabby grabbed the iPad to chat with Savannah.

Katie stepped over to Cara. "You okay?"

"Yeah." Cara ran a finger over the butterflies on the new comforter. "Just thinking about what you said."

Katie wasn't sure what Cara was referring to—maybe her suggestion that Cara think about what she wanted in a boyfriend? "I'm here if you want to talk."

"Thanks, Katie." Cara hugged her. "Love you."

The girls left shortly after finishing their conversation with Savannah to go to the carnival to meet Brandon, but not Josh. Interesting....

Katie headed upstairs to practice the new mediation methods that she, Cara, and Sabby had learned in class on Tuesday evening. She had dabbled with it a couple of times since, but this afternoon she was taking it to the next level. A long bubble bath with flickering candles and then after she was relaxed, she'd rest in silence.

She dimmed the lights, lit candles, and drew her bath. She'd put one foot in the hot, foamy water when Liam appeared. He gently nudged her into the water and gave her a back and shoulder rub. Afterward, he surprised her by stripping and stepping into the tub.

"How did this happen?" Liam teased as he lowered into the water behind her.

Katie's heart thumped in anticipation as Liam grazed his lips through her hair and skimmed his hands along the curves of her body.

Even though Liam was tall, they had plenty of room in the oversized Jacuzzi that Shane had gifted her a few birthdays back. She'd made good use of the tub, but this was the first time Liam had joined her. He wasn't a tub kind of guy, he'd told her.

"I love you so much, baby," he said. "I'm gonna cherish you every moment of every day." She rested her head against his chest, melting into him as she treasured his sweet words. "We're gonna grow old together, spend our elder years rocking on the porch swing surrounded by Cara, Savannah, and our other kids. And all of our grandkids, of course."

Envisioning it, Katie's belly fluttered with excitement. "Sounds perfect," she said, drawing in his earthy, male scent.

"I'm gonna love you till the day we die, and then some," he said quietly, resting his forehead against hers. "Your coma scared the shit out of me."

It had her, too. It had also caused her to think about what was most important in her life, and she was now more focused than ever on what she wanted. Liam. Savannah. More kids. A united family.

"I'm gonna tell you how much I love and adore you every single day." Liam pressed his lips to her temple.

Her chest reeled at Liam's romantic words and the intensity behind them. Didn't he know he'd always made her feel that way? It was one of the things she appreciated most about him. "Oh, Liam. I love you, too." She lightly scratched her nails up and down his thigh. "I thought about you every day, practically every moment I was away." To show him how much she loved him, she pressed her butt against his growing erection.

Over the last couple of months, Liam had treated her with kid gloves. She'd pushed the topic earlier in the week and he had admitted that he didn't want to take any chances with her still recovering body.

But she felt great now, and today she taking matters into her own hands.

"I'm feeling good—" she wriggled her butt on his lap "—really, *really* good." When she shifted from side to side, Liam let out a low growl. As pleasure tingled through her body, she spun around and slid her legs around his waist. Running her hands up his muscular arms, she traced her tongue over his shamrock tattoo.

"God, Katie, you have no idea what you do to me."

"There's more things I could do, you know," she said, need bunching in her belly.

His eyes smoldered, but he quickly concealed his desire. "I don't want to take any chances. Getting your full-strength back is too important."

"I asked Dr. Bradley." She had inquired during her check-up on

Friday and had been looking for the right opportunity to share the news with Liam.

Liam's head snapped to attention. He tucked two fingers under her chin, lifted it, and looked her in the eye. "And his response was?"

"He said it was fine, that it might even be beneficial. It releases...."

Her words were lost when Liam swooped in and kissed her with such sweet passion that her entire body quivered. As he pressed kisses along her jawline and down her neck, the water in the tub cooled but the air around them heated. A hot ache formed in her throat. It had been so long and she was so ready. Liam's roughened hands gently caressed her breasts and her nipples hardened in delicious expectation.

"Katie," he said in a ragged voice, "I've missed this. I want you so much."

She'd missed it too, so much that she had been dreaming about feeling him inside her. A frantic need quivered in the pit of her stomach. "Then have me," she said, scooting back and spreading her legs.

Liam's eyes turned dark and he was on her in a flash, his thick erection thumping wildly against her belly.

Pulling the band out of his hair, she twined her fingers through its thickness. Wet heat wrapped around them as she pulled his mouth back to hers for a sizzling hot kiss.

"Are you sure?" he whispered when they came up for air. "You sure you're ready?"

It had been over two months and her mind burned with memories of their mindboggling lovemaking. Her breasts were heavy, her nipples hard, and need pooled between her legs like hot molten lava.

Instead of answering, she slid her hands down the long length of him and led him home.

LIZ WOUND her way up the steep drive to Shane's home, white-knuckling the steering wheel as nerves whirled in her chest. She and

Shane had been dating for months now, albeit with a few stops and starts. But, tonight they would finally be alone.

Pushing her anxiety aside, she parked, grabbed her bags and ambled toward the house taking in the gorgeous views of the valley below. When she reached the front door, before she could even knock, Shane yanked it open and tugged her into his arms.

"I've been waiting for this all week," he said.

She'd been counting down the days, too. "I know what you mean."

Shane drew back and stared at her with eyes that resembled the morning sky after fog had lifted from the mountain tops, still a little sleepy, but oh-so-sexy.

He led her inside the house, took her purse and overnight bag and placed them on a nearby table, then leaned in and brushed his lips over hers in a kiss that was soft, slow, and magical. Both of them were a little breathy when he finally pulled back.

"Hi, there," he said, his voice raspy.

"Hello, Shane."

He had on faded blue jeans and a brown shirt. Casual, yet somehow Shane still managed to look like he'd just stepped off the cover of GQ magazine. She longed to reach out and touch the soft shirt and rub her hands all over the hard muscles underneath, but she supposed there would be plenty of time for that later.

Shane took her hand and led her to the kitchen where he grabbed a Killian's Irish Red from the refrigerator. "Can I interest you in a drink? Beer? Wine?" he asked, with his head still in the fridge.

But she'd wandered over to the small white ramekins on cooling racks on the dark marble countertops. "Mmm—is this crème brulee?" She drew in the sweet, sugary scent. "I rarely have dessert, but I can't resist crème brulee."

"That's why they're here."

Touched, she pivoted toward him. "How did you know?"

Leaning against the wall, Shane popped the top from the bottle as he slid her a lazy grin. "Badgered it out of Sabby."

How thoughtful. She stared at him for a long moment before

returning her attention to the dessert cups. "What kind?" she asked, eyeing the custard. Two had red swirls, two brown.

"Vanilla bean with raspberry and vanilla-caramel-chocolate," he said, stuffing his hands in his pockets. "I wasn't sure what kind you like."

"Both sound delicious." She gave him an appreciative smile. "Did you make them?"

"My culinary talents don't run that deep." Winking at her, he angled the dark bottle in her direction. "Want one?"

She shrugged. "Sure, why not?"

Shane handed her the Killian's, then returned to the fridge to grab another.

He had gone to a lot of trouble to make this night special. She took a long sip of beer to soothe the nerves that had once again tangled in her chest.

"I thought we'd throw some steaks on the grill. Have a nice meal and then—" his lips ticked up into a wolfish grin "—*whatever.*"

Air heavy with tension, she lifted her gaze to find Shane studying her intently, his blue-gray eyes on a slow simmer. They had waited for so achingly long yet they still had dinner to get through and all of the niceties that went along with it.

Or did they, she wondered? There was no rule that said they had to eat first. She was beyond ready. Her breasts burned with yearning and her legs physically shook with need. "I want you, Shane," she whispered.

His eyes widened and darkened, then he staggered back a few steps. *Staggered.* He put his bottle on the counter and leaned against it as if he needed its support to keep him upright.

His reaction fueled her confidence. She had an urgent need to be naked, and she wanted him naked, too. The tension that had built up between them over the last couple of months was about to detonate. She only needed to strike the match.

Did she dare?

Not one to walk away from a challenge—even if it had been conjured up in her own mind—she lifted the black summer dress over her head and tossed it to the floor. "Why don't we start with the *whatever*?" she asked in a sultry voice.

For a few seconds, Shane didn't move. Had she not heard his sharp intake of breath, she would have wondered if she'd made a mistake.

She had very little on now—a skimpy black push-up bra, a matching thong, and spiky open-toed heels. Going for the gold, she spun around to give Shane the complete view, laughing when he sucked in another breath and raised a hand to his heart.

Stepping over, she pulled his face to hers and indulged in a smoking hot kiss. "So, how 'bout it, big boy?"

"Hell yeah," he said, his voice gravelly. Then they were all over each other...lips locked, tongues tangling, bodies pulsating. She splayed her hands over the toned muscles of his chest while his hands trailed along her curves, ultimately dropping to squeeze her butt.

They were *finally* doing this. They'd been so close so often, yet they hadn't had the chance to see it through. The long, excruciating anticipation made her want him so much that her entire body was vibrating with need.

Shane tugged off his shirt, and she kicked off her heels. He pitched his boots aside and they made their way, twisting and turning, through the great room, past the massive A-frame windows and toward the stairway, kissing, touching, meshing.

"You're so fucking hot," he murmured, running his hands through the layers of her hair as he seared hot kisses up and down the nape of her neck.

A ripple of excitement fluttered through her body. At the same time, panic formed low in her gut and skittered out in every direction following the goosebumps that prickled her flesh after each brush of Shane's lips.

What was she thinking? She was about to make love with a man that she was falling for, *really* falling for. She should step back, take a breath, think. She needed time to construct walls around her heart before they moved past the point of no return.

Both she and Shane had awful track records when it came to

relationships, so theirs was surely doomed to fail. She hesitated fleetingly, considering how easily she could get hurt, but when Shane began trailing kisses through her hair, down her arm, and across her fingertips, she decided she would think about it later. After he'd kissed every part of her upper body into a tingling frenzy, she lost all rational thought.

Halfway up the stairs, Shane spun her against the wall and gazed into her eyes. "You okay?"

Shane's hand shook, and even though it was slight, it made her realize he was nervous too. Moving to intimacy in a relationship where they cared deeply for each other was new territory for both of them. Shane's nerves gave her a new bout of certainty.

"I'm good." Eyes glued to his, she walked her fingers down to the waistline of his jeans, then trekked further south. She traced a circle around the button of his jeans, then pressed her palm along the zipper, shivering at his hardness. A male groan made its way out of Shane, and when she tugged down the zipper, it turned into a growl. As his jeans dropped to the stairs, her lips lifted into a smile. He wore nothing underneath—no boxers, no briefs—just Shane in the flesh, his want for her glaringly evident.

Shane shrugged adorably, then flicked open her bra and tossed it aside. Scooping her into his arms, he sprinted up the rest of the stairs, down the hall, and into the massive master suite.

She let out an eager whimper when he lowered her to the bed. Sliding in next to her, he claimed her lips, surprising her with a deep tenderness. After, he showered tiny kisses on her forehead, temple, and cheeks which did nothing to stop her from falling for him.

A soft whimper slipped from her lips, and Shane's mouth turned needy. She rubbed her body against his hot, hard chest. His hands dropped to her breasts, then his tongue traced along the same path. When he pulled a nipple into his mouth, she gasped in sheer delight. He caressed and licked one, then the other, and her nipples quickly tightened in response. Her breasts quivered, the space between her legs turned slick, and she grew hotter and hungrier by the second.

"More, Shane." She tugged off her thong and pitched it over the bed. Murmuring his name like a chant, she yanked him against her, and they were all over each other again, rolling back and forth across his king-sized bed. When they paused to take a breath, she ended up on top. Wriggling against him, she found herself on the edge of desperation.

"Now," she demanded, feeling ravenous to her core. She *needed* to feel him inside her. "Now, Shane," she repeated, her voice urgent.

"Patience," he said, rolling to his side beside her. Capturing her gaze, Shane moved his thumb to her center and stroked in a light, circular motion.

"Shane." She raised her head. "You're making me crazy."

He slid two fingers inside of her. "That's the general idea," he said giving her a cocky smile.

She groaned out his name as his fingers caressed her. Wet and wanting, she moved in rhythm with him, allowing herself to revel in the erotic sensations. Shane slowly shifted lower until his face reached her core. His breath whispered against her swollen flesh, and her entire body quivered in response. He removed his fingers and his mouth took over, kissing her slowly and thoroughly. Just as she was sinking into the pure pleasure, he slipped his tongue inside.

She didn't know how much more she could take. Her body pulsed and hummed, racing faster than the high speed on her bullet vibrator. As heat shot through her like a wildfire, she instinctively spread her legs wider. Shane licked and stroked, and quickly had her teetering on the brink. He kept going like the energizer bunny, hot and unrelenting, until she finally spiraled out of control.

Her orgasm hit like a force of nature with tremors slicing and jagging through her like an earthquake. After the very last quiver, Shane cocked his head and searched her eyes. "You okay?"

When she nodded—she was way more than okay—he reached across the bed and grabbed a condom from the nightstand.

She took it from him, rolled it on, and climbed on top of him.

"An on-the-top kind of gal," he said in an amused voice.

She splayed her hands over his chest. "Got a problem with that?"

"Hell, no."

She tossed back her hair, lifted her thighs, and slowly lowered down onto him. She held her breath, feeling every single inch of him sliding into her. It had never been like this before, a blinding pleasure so intense it left her dazed and speechless.

Shane must have sensed her pause because he moved with slow, measured strokes. When she finally gathered herself, and pressed down to take him deeper, his tempo increased.

"You feel so right," he said, stroking a hand through her hair. "It's just like I thought it would be." Contentment flickered in his eyes as the color deepened to a cobalt blue.

"It's even better than I imagined," she admitted. He was everything she had expected, and so much more.

Grinning, Shane skillfully flipped her underneath him. Still inside her, his grin turned smug. He shifted into high gear, driving with long powerful thrusts that had her whimpering out her bliss.

Her insides tingled, and tremors started to erupt all over again.

"Look at me, Liz," he said.

His movements ceased until she lifted her gaze. When she searched his eyes, she found something deep and enduring, and it moved her all the way to her soul.

She tried to hold on to that precious moment, but couldn't. She tumbled over the edge crying out his name. He let himself go along with her, and then they collapsed side by side, hearts racing in the breathless afterglow.

Rolling to his side, Shane drew her close and spooned her. Contentment swirled in her chest as he possessively wrapped his arms around her belly. But panic followed, unfurling slowly, like a murky, low-lying fog. She had crossed the line of no return. She'd given Shane not only her body, but her heart as well.

CHAPTER TWENTY

*L*iam found Katie in the living room ready for their date, even though Shane and Liz weren't due for another twenty minutes. "A double date with my brother and your sister," he said approaching her. "Who would've thought?"

Katie laughed. "I know." With a happy sigh, she leaned against the couch. "I'm excited to go out with Liz and Shane, and I've wanted to go to Orchid Bistro for a long time."

Shane had talked them into going to the Orchid, an extravagant place in Frederick for lunch. Liam would have been happier grabbing a burger or eating at the Gem Valley diner. High-end establishments made him feel out of place, but he'd agreed because Katie had wanted to go.

Shane had advised that the place was exclusive—Liam would call it stuffy, but tomato, tomahto—thus they had to dress accordingly. Who the hell dressed up to go to *lunch*? But here he was wearing dark khakis and a button-down shirt.

Katie had on the new dress she'd purchased during her weekend shopping trip with Liz and Jen. Katie called it a sundress, but it looked pretty fancy to him. The light gray top was form-fitted and molded to her generous curves. The bottom was loose with colorful flowers reaching toward her waist. The dress ended mid-thigh making her legs appear to go on endlessly. And those silver high-heeled sandals could bring a man to his knees.

"Damn, you look good," he told her.

Katie beamed, and did a little spin.

She was killing him.

He moved his hand down the length of her dress as he pressed kisses across her face. When he dipped his fingers under the hem, her lips lifted to his.

He took what she offered, kissing her with all he had. "You got me worked up again, baby." After their lovemaking in the tub last weekend, they couldn't seem to get enough of each other. Making up for lost time, he supposed. Not that he was complaining.

"They'll be here any minute," Katie said. Although, based on the way she leaned into him and rubbed her breasts against his chest, he wasn't sure if she was reminding herself or him.

"We just need a few minutes," he said, wiggling his brows. But as soon as he slid his hands underneath the dress to cup her ass and swooped in for another kiss, the front door swung open.

"Hey y'all, let's hit it," Shane said, chuckling as Liam and Katie flew apart, adjusting their clothes and hair.

"Shane, we interrupted," Liz said shifting her gaze between Liam and Katie. "Let's go away and come back later."

"No can do," Shane said as Liam muttered curses under his breath. "Sorry, bro, but we have reservations."

Who the hell made reservations for *lunch*, Liam thought grumpily.

Shane stepped over and kissed Katie's cheek. "You're looking mighty beautiful today."

She gave him a mock curtsy. "And you Shane Callahan are quite the flatterer. But you look very nice, too."

"You lovebirds ready?" Shane asked, glancing at him.

Liam blew out a breath and nodded, then they headed out. While they made small talk with Shane and Liz, he couldn't stop his hand from moving up Katie's thigh. He took satisfaction in her sharp intakes of breath and the looks she gave him that indicated she'd like to be at home in bed with him.

The restaurant was everything he had expected…and everything he hated. Fancy, snobby, and ridiculously expensive based on a glimpse of the menu he caught on the outside wall. Thirty bucks for a lunch entree was highway robbery. He didn't frequent places like this, nor was it his idea of fun. It was ultra-expensive—his and Katie's lunch would cost seventy-five dollars or more—and he could think of countless other things he'd rather do with his money.

Shane, on the other hand, was a regular. This was one of the places he used to impress the ladies. When they made their way to the hostess station, he was greeted warmly, and they were quickly ushered to *his* table in the back corner.

"Pretty snazzy," Katie whispered in his ear as they passed tables with white tablecloths and black linens and wait staff dressed to the nines. Pretty snazzy, indeed.

While he'd rather be just about anywhere else, he'd bring Katie here every week if she wanted. Liam put an arm around her shoulder. "We could come here more often if you want."

Katie slid her hands up his arm. "I'm glad we're here today." She flashed an appreciative smile. "It's nice to do something different once in a while. But this seems like more of a special-occasion kind of place."

Liam sighed in relief. "Okay, but if you change your mind, let me know."

Katie reached up on her tippy-toes and kissed his cheek. "You're sweet, but I love our life. I wouldn't change a single thing, including the places we usually go."

God, he loved her.

After they were seated, they were quickly attended to by Amanda, a waitress whom Shane seemed to know. Drinks arrived within minutes of being seated, then they placed their meal order. He ordered a burger after all, even though he had choked on the twenty-five-dollar cost.

"Lighten up," Shane said, kicking him under the table.

He started to scowl, but forced it away. Shane was right. They were here and Katie was happy. He put his arm around Katie and joined the table conversation.

A short while later, Shane's phone chimed. He pulled it out of his pocket and glanced at the screen. "It's Ken. Let me grab this." Rising, he answered the phone, then asked Ken to give him a minute. He bent down and kissed Liz on the cheek. "Grab me another drink, okay, sweetie?"

Liam grinned. He'd never heard Shane call any woman 'sweetie,' and he and Katie had been on plenty of double-dates with Shane and whoever. Pre-Liz, Shane had been polite but aloof, and terms of endearment had been on his forbidden list.

The waitress stopped by and Liz ordered another round of drinks, but Shane returned before she had finished.

"Cancel that," Shane barked. Then he drew in a long breath. "Can you put this on my tab, Amanda?" he asked in a calm voice that sounded forced. What the hell was going on? "We need to head out."

"What about lunch?" Liz asked.

"We'll eat at home," Shane said tersely. He pulled a few large bills from his pocket and pressed them into the blonde waitress's hand. "For you."

After Amanda left, Shane turned to face them, looking like a steamed beet. "We need to head home. We can regroup there."

"What the hell?" Liam demanded. If Shane was this worked up, it had to be something bad. He glanced at Katie and her pale face suggested she was thinking the same thing. Ken had just told them the case would be a slam dunk. What could have changed over the last few days?

"We need to go," Shane repeated, reaching for Liz's hand. He glanced in their direction, but wouldn't look him or Katie in the eye. "We have a problem."

Liam took Katie's hand. "Whatever this is, we'll fix it. Okay?"

She nodded, but he didn't miss the tears swimming in her eyes. He and Katie rose and they all made their way out of the restaurant.

Outside, he inched up to Shane. "What's going on?"

Shane's cheeks were still flushed and the muscles in his face were tighter than the strings on a guitar. "We have a fight on our hands."

"What kind of fight?" An ominous feeling slammed into Liam's gut and twisted into a lump of anxiety. He hoped this wasn't about *his* past. But, it couldn't be. His issues with the law had occurred nearly two decades ago. "Damn it, tell us what's going on."

Shane glanced at him, then Katie. "We'll discuss it at home," he said, and then stalked into the parking lot leaving Liam, Katie, and Liz behind.

Liz let out a huff. "Someone's a little grumpy."

Katie linked one arm with him, the other with Liz. "Liam's right," she said. The resolve in her voice made Liam glance over. The tears in her eyes were gone. They'd been replaced by an expression of sheer grit. "We're gonna fix whatever this is. We have to stay positive."

Shane had just told them they had a fight on their hands. Why was Katie being all Zen? How could she not be at least a little worried, he wondered? Regardless, he sure as hell wasn't going to question it, so he shoved his own worries deep inside as they walked toward the Hummer.

The twenty-minute drive home passed in a long, uncomfortable silence. While Shane stewed, Liam quietly ruminated on the situation. Things had been moving along well in the custody case. What was going on, he wondered, and why wouldn't Shane tell them? Had it been just him and his brother, he would have forced the issue. But he suspected Shane held off to protect Katie, so he let it go. He would have it out with Shane at the house.

As soon as they got home, Liz made her way to the kitchen. "I'll make coffee," she said.

"Thanks," Katie said. "Can you make mine a latte, please?" She smiled at Liz. *Smiled.* "I'll set up in the living room."

Liam gaped at Katie. She was still calm, and her calm was genuine. How was she so unruffled while he was freaking out? It was as if they had reversed roles. But he couldn't seem to help himself. The anxiety in his gut had grown during the drive home, molding into an omen that had put him on high alert. As Katie gathered mugs, sugar, and cream, he left in search of Shane.

He found his brother on the front porch pacing back and forth.

He held out a palm to stop Shane. His brother stopped in his tracks but wouldn't look up at him.

"What the hell's going on?" he demanded. "No more stalling."

"It's fucking Warren," Shane whispered angrily as his eyes flitted toward the house. "You aren't going to like it."

"What is it?" Liam asked, the muscles in his body constricting at the mention of Warren's name.

Shane slammed his fist against the wall, spewing out curses.

He grabbed Shane's arm. "Just tell me."

Shane shook him off, but after a long moment, he let out a heavy breath. "Warren found out about your arrest." He slumped onto a porch chair. "He got a copy of your record and filed it with the court."

"Fuck!" Liam kicked the wall with his boot. "I knew my past would come back to bite me in the ass." Like a gray cloud shadowing his otherwise bright existence, his long-ago arrest hovered over him, dark and menacing. After lingering for nearly two-decades, it had finally caught up with him, a twister eager to wreak havoc on his life. At sixteen, Shane had yet to develop the muscles he sported today. Jim Ledford, a stocky twenty-year-old, had been pushing Shane around for weeks. Liam had initially tried to let the situation work itself out like he'd learned in parenting class. But after some chick had broken up with Jim to date Shane, Jim had punched Shane in the face. Liam had tracked Jim down, told him pick on someone his own age, and had proceeded to beat the shit out of him.

He and Shane had tried to explain what had happened to the judge. But Jim had given an entirely different story and his record had been clean while Liam had had his share of drug and alcohol related trouble. Liam had a felony because of it, but at the time he'd felt lucky. He'd retained custody of Shane, and probably because of his brother, he'd been sentenced to two years of probation instead of jail time.

Now the judge presiding over the custody case with Savannah

would see his record. And Deb and Colt would hear about it, too. Would they think less of him, he wondered. How could they not? Unfortunately, the assault wasn't the only blemish on his record. He had other charges too, like misdemeanors for possession of weed and a DUI.

He sagged against the wall. His past was now standing in the way of Katie getting custody of her daughter. He shoved a hand through his hair. She didn't deserve this shit. Maybe her father had been right all along. He *was* bad for her.

"You didn't do anything wrong," Shane said, his voice low and tight. "You were defending me."

He *had* been defending Shane. But he'd had a record before the assault incident. If he'd had his shit together, the judge may have listened to him instead of Jim.

What would *Katie* think? He had told her about his possession and DUI misdemeanors, but he'd never shared his assault conviction. He had hoped he could keep that ugliness where it belonged— in the past. But over the years, guilt had nipped at his insides. He should have told Katie *before* he'd asked her to marry him. Now, when so much was at stake, was a hell of a time to fess up. But he wouldn't let her lose custody. Katie deserved better, and so did Savannah.

"Damn it." He squeezed his fists together. "I'm not taking Katie down. There's got to be a way." Forcing a composure he didn't feel, he sat next to Shane. Clasping his hands together, he took a good look at his brother. Shane was fidgeting and clearly still holding back. "What did Ken say?"

"We'll figure it out," Shane said, avoiding his question.

Liz poked her head out the front door. "You guys ready?"

"No," Shane snapped.

"Well you don't need to be an ass about it," was her reply.

Blowing out a breath, Shane rose. "Be right back." Liam heard him whispering sweetly to Liz on the other side of the door.

When Shane returned, Liam crossed his arms and gave him a don't-fuck-with-me look. "What did Ken suggest?"

Shane ran a hand over his short hair. "It's a shitty idea."

"Shane, I swear to God—"

"Okay." Shane lifted a palm to stop his rant. "He said this is really bad and that the court would take the assault conviction seriously even though it happened a long time ago. And when a child is involved…." A muscle in Shane's jaw twitched.

"What did he suggest?" Liam repeated through clenched teeth. He needed to know even though he had a bad feeling he wasn't going to like the answer.

"He said you and Katie could get a legal separation." Shane's face tensed, and deep lines creased his forehead. "It's a stupid idea."

"It may not be." Liam's chest tightened, his heart hurt. But he wouldn't hold Katie back, and he wouldn't let her lose her daughter.

"What the hell?" Shane's head jerked toward him. "That's ridiculous, and Katie won't want that any more than you do."

"We may not have a choice," he said in dejected resignation. "Come on. Let's go tell Katie what's going on."

Liam made his way to the living room like a convict on death row. There was no solution in sight that didn't involve loss. How could he give Katie up and yet how could he not? He loved her too much to do anything other than help her reunite with her daughter.

Trudging toward the living room he combed his brain for other ideas, but came up blank. A fist gripped his heart, squeezing out the last remnants of hope.

Maybe he and Katie could get back together after she'd been awarded custody of Savannah and the lawsuit dust had settled. Unless his presence in Katie's life would forever put her at risk. His heart sank. After two decades of positive transformation, the past had ripped the floor from beneath his feet and he'd fallen back to feeling like the unworthy screw-up that he no longer wished to be.

He pushed aside the dull ache in his head, the dark hole in his heart. With an unwavering determination to do the right thing for his wife, he lumbered into the living room and lowered himself to the sofa next to Katie.

Even though she had to be anxious to hear what Shane had learned, her lips curved into a half smile as she glanced over. He soaked in her smile, considering he might not see it again for a really long time.

How would he survive without Katie in his daily life? He pressed a fist against his heart to stop the physical ache.

Katie took a sip of her latte, then tipped her head to one side. "What's going on?"

Shane started to speak, but Liam interrupted. This was his fuck-up and he needed to man up.

He told Katie everything. His arrest, his record, Warren's filing with the court. As he spoke, Katie sipped her drink, unnervingly quiet. Her expression was cautiously neutral, and for the first time since they'd been together, he was unable to read her. Feeling nauseous, he shifted uncomfortably, wondering what was she thinking, wishing she would say something—anything. The silence was killing him.

Shane, undoubtedly reading *his* glum expression, pressed a mug of coffee into his hands. He took a couple of gulps, then put his mug down and took Katie's hand. "I can't begin to tell you how sorry I am."

He glanced at Shane and Liz before continuing. Shane's brows were furrowed and his eyes shot sparks of indignation. While Liam appreciated Shane's support, he'd expected it. Shane always had his back. But Liz surprised him. He had expected at least a little scorn— he had a felony for God's sake—but her expression mirrored his brother's.

"You know this isn't your fault, right?" Liz asked.

He shook his head, unable to find words to convey what her encouragement meant. Even so, it really was his fault, hence the felony.

"Thanks, but it's on my record," he managed. He dipped his head before turning back to Katie. "It's a big deal, and a deal break-er." Still holding Katie's hand, he let out a long, slow exhale. "Ken says the only way you have a shot at getting custody is if we get a legal separation."

He heard Liz's quick intake of breath and Shane grumble, "dum-bass idea." But his focus remained one-hundred percent on Katie.

He'd been staring at their clasped hands but he finally gathered the courage to glance up at her, preparing himself for disappointment and hopelessness.

He found nothing but compassion and determination. Squaring her shoulders, Katie put her hands on his arms. "Liz is right. This isn't your fault."

"Rat bastard, Warren," Liz muttered, followed by a string of highly descriptive and creative curses that could easily rival his and Shane's.

Moved by Katie and Liz's unequivocal support, he didn't immediately respond.

Katie touched a hand to his chest. "You're a good man." She brushed her fingers over his heart, and the friction was like a salve to his bruised soul. "This won't stop us from getting Savannah."

"It could." Remorse and fear clogged his head and his heart. "We can't take that chance."

"I believe in you," she said, and some of his fear washed away, creating an opening for something positive. Sure enough, a smidgen of hope trickled into his chest. "I believe in us." Katie tipped her head toward Shane and Liz. "In *all* of us. I believe, Liam. I believe the right thing will come to be. How can I not, after everything we've been through?"

Relief gushed through Liam's entire being and most of his fear washed away with it. He let out a long breath, and then rested his forehead against Katie's. Unease still kicked around in his gut, but it probably wouldn't go away completely until they had been granted custody of Savannah. Even so, it wasn't as great as it had been because hope had taken root in his heart.

When he drew back, Katie linked her hands with his. "I need to ask one thing of you."

By now, she had to know his love knew no bounds, that he'd do anything she asked of him. "Anything."

"We need to let Shane help." She squeezed their joined hands. "Financially too, if needed."

His chest tightened as reluctance set in. Damn it, anything but that. Asking his little brother for help made him feel inadequate. He was a proud man, and he took great satisfaction in taking care of his family without handouts. But that wasn't the only reason he wouldn't let Shane help. He hated his brother's I-owe-you-conundrum. Shane didn't owe him for the past. He'd been a minor and Liam's baby brother; it had been Liam's responsibility to take care of him. But Shane had never bought into that.

Shane had offered monetary assistance countless times in the past as he clearly had the resources. Liam had never accepted, and in allegiance with him, neither had Katie, not even in their early days when money had been tight.

But this time, it was different. This time it was for Katie. And it was for Savannah.

Resigned, he swallowed his pride and gave a single nod of concurrence.

Afterward, Katie turned to Shane. "I need you to fix this," she said. "Whatever it takes."

AFTER THEY'D RECEIVED the bad news from Ken on Monday, Liz had invited Shane to her place in Georgetown for a change of pace and to get their minds off the dismal turn in the custody case. The next day, Shane had taken her, Sabby, and Brandon to dinner at JP's restaurant. Though they hadn't planned on it, Shane had ended up staying for several days, with the two of them working side-by-side out of her large home office on Tuesday and Wednesday. He'd headed home on Wednesday night, but only after making her and Sabby promise they'd spend the weekend, which Shane claimed started on Thursday, in Gem Valley. So, she and Sabby had driven up yesterday and she'd spent the night at Shane's while Sabby had stayed with Cara after a double date.

She was probably spending way too much time with Shane. It was certainly more than she'd given to any other man since the end of her marriage. But it was so easy with him. Sabby adored Shane, and the three of them went out together frequently. Besides, spending extra time in Gem Valley gave her the opportunity to be around Katie more often, and after the coma, she appreciated her sister time more than ever.

Despite her deepening feelings for Shane, she refused to give up her independence. But Shane wasn't at all controlling and hadn't impinged on her independence. Maybe, she would rethink her ban on commitment.

Although, it didn't really matter because Shane wasn't looking for a commitment. While he wanted to be with her for absurd amounts of time, he never asked for anything more.

Now they were headed to Frederick for a meeting with Ken Anderson. Initially, Shane had suggested that she wait at his house while he met with the attorney. But she had sweet-talked—or more accurately, she'd *sex-talked*—him into bringing her, promising all kinds of naughty acts when they got home if he did. She wasn't ashamed of it either, because it had worked.

"We're here," Shane announced, pulling into a parking space behind a tall red-brick building with large two-story windows. They walked inside in silence and took the elevator to the loft.

"Nice building," she said, taking in every detail as they stepped out of the elevator. According to the plaque out front, it had been constructed in 1862, but the pristine interior suggested it had been fully renovated.

Shane muttered an agreement and took her hand. The poor guy was still grumpy over the custody situation. He and Ken hadn't come up with any solutions during their meeting on Wednesday so he had scheduled another touch base for the two of them this morning. And now, with her as well, she thought smugly.

"We're gonna figure this out," she said, leaning over to give him a peck on the cheek.

Shane ran a hand over the top of his head and then surprised her by tugging her against him right there in the middle of the hallway. People eyed them in passing, but she didn't care.

"Thanks," he said quietly. "Sorry I've been a bit on edge."

Then he kissed her, and it wasn't a quick peck. It was a full graze of his lips over hers, then he drew her into a soft kiss. She lost herself in the sweet, tender side of Shane as the kiss spun out for a sinfully long time. Shane pulled back when she felt his bulge twitch against her belly.

"Damn it," he muttered, sliding her a dazed look. "Sorry."

She laughed. "You never have to apologize for *that*, Shane."

He took her hand again, and they made their way down the short hallway to Ken's office. After greetings and beverages— sparkling water for her, a Coke for Shane and Ken—they got right to the heart of the matter.

"I'm gonna be honest," Ken said, taking a sip of his Coke. "Warren has a real case now. His two key points—one, Katie gave up rights to her child when she was seventeen, and two, Liam has a history that includes an assault conviction, are both factual." He guzzled more Coke. "Unfortunately, both are compelling points. While the judge may be convinced to overlook the first given Katie's age and the circumstances, the assault evidence is hard to overcome."

"Damn it, Ken," Shane said in a clearly frustrated tone. "It was a misdemeanor that happened over eighteen years ago."

"I understand," Ken said patiently. "Even so, the legal system takes assault convictions seriously, especially in cases regarding a child's welfare." Ken put his elbows on his desk and clasped his hands together. "At risk of raising a sensitive topic, why didn't Liam take care of this before? Based on what you told me, any attorney worth his beans could have gotten the charges dismissed, especially since Liam's skirmish was in response to an assault of a minor."

Shane sighed. "We were dirt poor, we didn't have money for an attorney."

"Okay." Ken nodded. "Then why didn't Liam take care of it later?"

"Why would he?" Shane demanded, his voice full of piss and vinegar. Liz could tell this was highly personal for Shane, and why wouldn't it be? This new trouble was all because Liam had defended Shane's honor all those years ago.

"He started his motorcycle business and all was forgotten." Shane took a gulp of his soda, then narrowed his eyes at Ken. "Can you take care of it now?"

"Sure," Ken said, making a note on his legal pad. "But it doesn't fix the custody challenge. Warren's attorney already submitted Liam's record."

"Can we make it about the money?" Liz suggested, squeezing Shane's hand under the desk. "That's what Warren cares about."

"I like it." Shane shifted his gaze between her and Ken. "What do you think?"

Ken shook his head. "Gwen's will stipulates that the caretakers' fund goes to the caretaker. If Katie gets custody of Savannah, the fund would move to her. The money was earmarked for the welfare of the child so I doubt the judge would be willing to modify that. It all goes to Savannah after she turns twenty-one, anyway."

"Well, shit." Shane huffed out a breath. "What now? We gotta come up with something else."

"It may be difficult," Ken said, "but our best shot may be to go after Warren's credibility. We could attempt to prove that he's an unfit caretaker. Do you think his parents would testify against him? We'd need their help if we take this approach."

Shane was silent for a long moment, then he rose with a dogged look on his face. "Fuck this noise. I'm taking care of this the Shane Callahan way."

CHAPTER TWENTY-ONE

*A*fter spending the morning welding parts on a custom cycle, Liam made his way to the office. He preferred hands-on maintenance work and designing custom bikes, but office work was a critical part of running his business. Even so, it was one of those things he had to force himself to do. He grabbed a Coke and sat behind his desk. When he opened the inventory app on his computer, he was surprised to find that the inventory had already been completed.

Linking his hands behind his head, he reclined. Earlier in the week, Katie had finished the payroll and invoicing. She'd also created a kick-ass advertising campaign, and Liz had managed to secure half-price rates at *The Washington Post*. If the *Post* ad generated the level of new business he anticipated, he'd have to add another employee or two.

He took a sip of his soda, ordered a few custom parts, then glanced out at the bay area where motorcycles were being serviced. He'd built a solid servicing business, but over the last couple of years his custom business, turning motorcycles into trikes or choppers, had really taken off. He and Seth handled most of that side of the business, but Brandon was learning quickly. Liam would probably have to hire a welder soon, so he and Seth could spend more time on design details. Sighing in satisfaction, he turned back to his computer to finish emails so he could cut out early.

But before he had responded to the first one, Shane walked into his office. Good timing, because getting a custody update from his brother had been on his to-do list.

"Hey, bro," Shane greeted, grabbing a Coke from the corner fridge.

"How's it goin' ?" Liam gestured for Shane to have a seat.

"Great." Shane eased himself onto one of the chairs, then popped the top on his Coke. "Liz is at the house visiting with Katie. We're gonna go away for the weekend, so Sab's gonna stay here. That okay?"

"Sure. Sabby's always welcome here." Liam eyed his brother. "Where you going?"

"Doesn't really matter," Shane said.

Liam shook his head. That translated into Shane didn't have a damn clue. His brother was a seat-of-the-pants kind of guy. "What's going on with the custody case? Katie's been in a great mood all week. I want to keep it that way, but we're both worried about Savannah."

Shane drummed his fingers together. "Here's the thing. I met with Ken, like I promised. He's got some ideas, I've got some ideas. I don't have anything definitive, but things are moving forward."

Unease surfaced in Liam's gut. "What do you mean things are moving forward? You don't have an update?"

Shane blew out a breath. "You're gonna have to trust me on this one."

Anxiety clogged Liam's throat. What was he supposed to tell Katie? He swallowed hard, then glowered at Shane. "Damn it, I can't give Katie that kind of BS."

Shane leaned across the desk toward him. "Do you trust me, Liam?"

Shane had no update. Liam wanted to demand something more. But, he did trust Shane. He'd trust his brother with his life...and with Katie's and Savannah's. "You know I do."

Shane left a few minutes later, promising solid information early next week. Shifting, Liam faced his computer, determined to finish up for the day so he could take Katie out to dinner. He quickly finished the emails, then sent progress reports to his two custom clients.

Now he could focus on Katie. After doing a quick search for restaurants, he clicked on the website of a new bistro located in between Gem Valley and Frederick. These days he had to plan ahead of time to make sure he took Katie to places that offered vegetarian food options. But before the menu loaded on the screen, Cara stormed into his office.

"Josh broke off our date!" Blinking through her tears, she slapped her hands on her hips. "What the hell?"

Given his daughter's distressed state, he overlooked her language. He rose, rounded the desk, and pulled her into his arms. "What happened, sweetie?"

"He *said* he was sick," she said in between sniffles. Liam lowered to look in her eyes and was pleased to find more mad than hurt. "We were supposed to go to the movies tonight with Sab and Brandon. He's not really sick, so I guess it's just me."

"Of course it's not you," he said inanely. He had no damn idea, but Josh was a complete dumbass regardless. "How do you know he's not sick?"

" 'Cause Courtney Phillip's Facebook page says he's at her place." Cara sniffled dramatically. "That's just wrong."

"I told you he wasn't good enough for you," Liam grumbled, suppressing the desire to drive over to Courtney's and kick Josh in his cheating ass. "Don't you worry, sweetie, one of these days you'll find someone who deserves you."

"But I *really* wanted to go to the movies tonight," Cara whined. "I'm tired of being a third wheel with Sab and Brandon."

"You're not a third wheel. Sabby's your best friend, and you know Brandon adores you."

"It's not the same. I'm a dateless loser." Cara positioned her thumb and index finger into an 'L' and touched it to her forehead.

"You're not a loser." He dragged her fingers away from her face.

Sighing, Cara grabbed a tissue.

Out of the corner of his eye, Liam watched Seth lumber back and forth outside his office. Cara wasn't soft spoken when she was provoked, so Seth had likely overheard everything. *Come in, Seth*, he silently willed.

Seth walked past the door again, then spun around and retraced his steps.

"You can come in, Seth," he said. "We were just having a moment."

Seth stepped inside. He nodded at Liam in greeting, inhaled deeply, then turned to face Cara. "I'll take you to the movies tonight."

As Cara gaped at Seth, a series of emotions flitted through her eyes—disbelief, surprise and then…was that *interest*?

Cara glanced up at Liam, presumably looking for approval.

He nodded.

"Okay," she said softly, and Seth's face split into a foolish grin. "We were gonna go out with Sabby and Brandon." A half smile played at Cara's mouth. "Brandon never liked Josh anyway."

"Yeah? Me either," Seth said, still grinning like a loon. "How 'bout I pick you up at six so we can grab something to eat first? I'll work it out with Brandon."

" 'Kay." Cara looked up at Liam. "See ya, Dad. Love you." Then she turned to Seth. "See you at six," she said, then sauntered off.

Seth glanced over at Liam. His eyes glowed happiness, but it was impossible to mistake the look of concern on his face. "This okay with you?"

"It is." Liam slapped Seth on the back. "Now get back to work."

Seth raced out the door and into the bay area. A few seconds later, Brandon and Seth high-fived.

Booting down his computer, Liam called out to his team, "I'm outta here. Seth's in charge." Glancing at the guys circled around Seth, he chuckled. "Since it's apparently date night, you can all head home early."

He was pretty confident they wouldn't get anything more done today anyway.

~

Shane tossed clothes into the suitcase feeling a keen sense of satisfaction. He'd put the *Shane Callahan* plan into motion right after leaving Ken's office and it had been progressing flawlessly ever since. He had already arranged for a private flight to Amarillo and had picked up the legal paperwork he'd requested. He'd also called Deb and Colt and had secured their support.

A couple of hours later, he and Liz were in the air. He had to give Liz credit for spontaneity. She hadn't even blinked when he'd shown up with their bags packed and had sprung the idea of the trip on her. Even though she didn't know any of the details, she'd been all in. That had pleased him greatly. He'd never met a woman who shared his sense of impulsiveness, but he'd met his match in Liz.

During the flight, he shared the details of his plan with her. While Ken had given lukewarm support, Liz had fully endorsed his idea. It *was* brilliant, he thought, slinging an arm around her.

He closed his eyes for the remainder of the flight, thinking about winning custody for Katie. He walked through every detail in his mind, making a few adjustments now that he was including Liz in the meeting with Warren.

He'd initially planned to meet with Warren alone, but Liz had easily talked him into taking her along. She had promised him wild and crazy sex if he took her, and if last time had been any indication, including her would be well worth the reward. But, after thinking it through, he would have taken her regardless. Liz was smart, crafty, and highly successful at getting her way. That asshole Warren didn't stand a chance against the two of them.

After they landed, they quickly made their way through the airport and the rental car counter, then he whisked Liz off to the Bed and Breakfast he had reserved. Deb and Colt had offered a bedroom at their place, but he wanted privacy. This was his first trip with Liz. While it was for a specific purpose, he still wanted to show her a good time, so he'd booked a secluded bungalow tucked in the woods of a sixty-acre B & B.

Liz's eyes sparkled with excitement as they drove deep into the

281

woods. Their log cabin appeared at the next turn, and he parked in the gravel driveway.

"This is lovely," Liz said, jumping out of the car and rushing toward the front porch.

Inside, the Great Room had beautiful hardwood floors and a large stone fireplace. He tucked their luggage in an entry-way closet while Liz dropped her bag on the coffee table, then made her way to the French doors on the other side of the room. She opened them and stepped outside. "Oh, Shane, it's perfect."

He joined her on the back deck. It was dark outside, but they could hear water trickling in a nearby creek. Pulling Liz into his arms, he pressed his lips to her forehead. "You're perfect," he whispered.

Liz put her hands on his chest and lightly massaged his muscles. "Your sweet talk has improved considerably since we've started dating," she teased. "I must be good for you."

"You're damn good for me," he said, his voice more ragged than he'd intended.

"Well, then...." Liz tugged his shirt over his head and dropped it to the deck. "How about I make good on my bribe?" She pulled off her own shirt, followed by her bra, and tossed both aside. "There's no reason to wait...I can trust you to keep our deal, can't I?"

Moonlight glimmered over Liz's body and her nipples tightened as if in anticipation. As she waited for him to respond, she caressed his erection.

All he could do was nod. "Uh, you want to go inside?" he finally managed.

Liz opened the button on his jeans, pulled down the zipper. Rubbing her bare chest against his, she batted her lashes up at him. An indecent glint flickered in her eyes, and his dick throbbed with powerful want. He'd never been this needy. He and Liz had just made love last night, but he couldn't seem to get enough of her.

"No," she said, tugging down his jeans. "Here."

Lust hit him like a punch to the gut.

"I could get a blanket..." he offered, but his words trailed off when Liz dropped to her knees and took him into her mouth.

He staggered back a step and gripped the deck rails. A burning sensation as if he'd just tossed back a shot of whiskey worked its way down his throat. The hot sensation moved into his gut, then slid further south to where Liz was lavishing him with her lips, mouth, and tongue.

"I. Can. Handle. It." Liz purred out each word in between pulling him in and out of her mouth.

And damned if she didn't.

THE NEXT MORNING, Shane stepped onto the deck as an assortment of warm muffins, freshly squeezed orange juice, and coffee was delivered. Liz joined him a few minutes later and after a sweet kiss, they settled at the cozy table overlooking the woods and a gurgling creek.

"Did I earn my way into our meeting tonight?" she asked, her voice tinged with smugness, and deservedly so. He felt smug, too. People who had shared the pleasures they had experienced last night ought to feel smug.

He poured two cups of coffee and slid one over to Liz.

She smiled at him, drawing his attention to her beautiful, full lips. He sighed in contentment thinking about the way those lips had gratified him last night. Afterward, they'd tumbled onto the deck and she'd ridden him like a wild bronco. A bottle of wine and a blanket later, they had made love again, assuming positions he'd never before considered.

"Oh, you earned it all right." He gave her a lazy smile. "You keep doing that stuff, and you can have whatever you want."

Liz tipped her head and shot him a sultry look as she plastered her blueberry muffin with butter. "Then I guess I should plan on becoming one spoiled woman."

Desire zapped in his groin. "Damn, Liz, you keep talking like that, and I'm not gonna want to leave the cabin."

Popping a piece of muffin in her mouth, Liz glanced at her

watch. "Then hurry up and eat, and we'll have just enough time for a quickie before we have to head out."

After making love and showering, they made it to Deb and Colt's only a few minutes late. They had a nice conversation with Savannah's grandparents, and because they all assumed Warren would accept Shane's proposal, they made plans for family get-togethers in both Maryland and Texas over the next several months. Before long, Savannah came down to join them, and he and Liz spent the rest of the day shopping with her.

Later that evening, he drove to Warren's with a mixture of anxiety and hope. His plan was solid, but he didn't know Warren well enough to predict his reaction. Shane hoped that tonight they would get this situation taken care of, once and for all. He parked the rental in front of Warren's stucco and brick ranch and turned toward Liz. "Ready to do this?"

Liz took his hand and lifted her chin. "Let's go kick some ass."

A woman after his heart. "You got that right."

Warren pulled open the door, looking disheveled in a rumpled T-shirt and torn-up jeans. Then again, maybe he dressed that way all the time. Shane neither knew nor cared. After they sealed the deal, he didn't plan on ever seeing the dickwad again.

"What do you want?" Warren demanded as they approached. Not "Hey," or "Come on in," or any of the usual southern niceties. Under other circumstances, Shane would have appreciated the man's direct nature.

But not tonight. And certainly not with Warren. Had he forgotten that they'd scheduled this meeting, Shane wondered? "You in a rush?" he asked Warren. "Got a date?"

"Not that it's any of your business, but yes," Warren said, swaying a little. The man's breath reeked of alcohol. "Don't have much time."

"Well then, we better get started," Liz said in a sugar-sweet tone, then she stepped inside the house uninvited. Impressed, Shane followed, as did Warren. "We won't take much of your time, but how about we go in there—" Liz pointed toward the dining room "—so we can sit down and have an *adult* conversation?"

Warren missed the ding, but Shane didn't. When Warren lumbered into the dining room, Shane planted a quiet kiss on Liz's cheek.

Once they were all settled around the table, Shane pulled a folder out of his leather briefcase. "I'm gonna cut to the chase here." He glanced across the table at Warren. "I'm prepared to make you a financial deal to wrap up our custody battle, but you need to listen up because I'm only going to make this offer once."

Warren rolled his eyes. "Liam already offered me the caretaker's fund. I doubled checked after he left, but my attorney said it can't be changed. Whoever gets the kid, gets the money."

The muscles in Shane's body tensed. *The kid?* What the hell?

Liz leaned toward Warren, and the dickhead's eyes drifted to her chest. Not that Shane could blame him. She was wearing a brown v-neck dress that hugged her curves and offered just enough cleavage to peak a man's interest. Still, it was a matter of principle. He started to rise, but Liz was already taking care of the situation.

"Eyes up here," she said, tapping her temples.

Warren shrugged, but his eyes returned to Liz's face.

"The kid has a name," Liz said, "so stop talking about her like she's a *thing*." Her contemptuous tone made Shane proud. "And let me give you a little tip—Shane means what he says. So unless you wanna miss the deal of a lifetime, I'd suggest you get yourself a cup of coffee so you can sober up and pay attention."

Reaching into her bag, Liz pulled out an iPad. After punching a few buttons, she pushed the tablet across the table to Warren. "I just Googled Shane Callahan." Surprised, Shane glanced over at her. He hadn't known she was planning this gambit, but it was really, really good. Showing Warren that Shane could walk the talk would help him close the deal. Why hadn't he thought of that, he wondered? He smiled at Liz, pleased they were in this together.

She winked at him in response, then turned back to Warren. "Take a look at any of the articles in *Investor's Daily*," she said. "You can find information on the success Shane has had on Wall Street and an overview of his portfolios. This one—" Liz tapped a nail over an icon on the screen, "—alludes to his net worth. If I were you, Warren, I'd wise up and pay attention."

Grumbling, Warren pulled up one of the documents and squinted at the iPad. A few minutes later, his eyes popped. He gaped at the screen for a few long moments, then pushed back from the table. "Excuse me."

When Warren returned, he had a Pepsi in hand. He flopped down, guzzled soda, then placed the can on the table in front of him. "What's your offer," he asked, turning his attention to Shane. "And why are you doing this?"

"I'll answer your last question first." Shane clasped his hands on the table in front of him. "Katie wants her child, and I'd do anything to make my sister-in-law happy. Also, she and Liam will be far better parents than you can ever hope to be." Warren didn't even flinch at Shane's remark, reinforcing the fact that he had no desire to be a parent himself. "I've grown fond of Savannah and I want what's best for her. Regarding the offer—" Shane tapped a large manila envelope "—I'll get to it in a minute, but first we need to establish what you're currently receiving so you'll have a comparison. My offer is a good deal, but I'm only going to offer it once. If you don't accept my offer tonight, I'll fight you in court and I'll fight long and hard. As Liz just pointed out, I can afford it. Not sure you can say the same, my friend." He raised a brow and let his observation sink in. "I've had my attorney review the caretaker's fund. All that you stand to receive is the *interest* on the five million dollars from the fund."

"Yeah, but that's a decent amount of money," Warren said, glancing at the clock on the wall.

"Not really," Liz countered. "Have you calculated the amount?"

Warren's brows furrowed but he didn't answer Liz's question.

Shane pulled a copy of Gwen's will from his briefcase. He flipped to the flagged page, then pointed to the appropriate section. "When Savannah turns twenty-one, the entire fund goes to her. The only money you get is the interest on it between now and then."

Shane pushed the document toward Warren to give him the opportunity to read it for himself.

Warren didn't look at the page. Instead, he crossed his arms and narrowed his bloodshot eyes. "Tell me something I don't already know."

Irked, Shane yanked the document back. "Let me lay it out for you," he said, attempting to keep his voice calm. "The caretaker's fund is invested in U.S. treasuries, which don't offer a hell of a lot of interest. Using a rate of one percent, which is generous, you'd get fifty thousand per year for the next nine years."

Warren comically tried to do the math in his head. When the dolt began counting on his fingers, Shane did it for him. "It's four-hundred-fifty thousand at the end of nine years, assuming you're saving it all."

A muscle in Warren's jaw twitched and his lips moved into a scowl. Now he was getting it.

"I'm guessing you're not saving," Shane said, making an effort to hide his knowing smile. "After nine years, it's nada."

"Not the deal you thought, huh?" Liz asked, raising an eyebrow.

Warren guzzled the rest of his soda.

"So, here's the deal." Shane pulled a folder out of the manila envelope and placed it on the table. "I'm willing to offer you six-hundred thousand right now if you turn over custody of Savannah. I have all the paperwork in here—" he tapped his index finger on the folder "—and I have a cashier's check in my car with your name on it. All you have to do is say yes and sign the papers." Shane removed papers from the folder and pushed them toward Warren.

"I'll give you a little time to think about it. Think long and hard," he said, rising. Liz rose and stood beside him and he felt powered by their united front. Even so, nervous tension swirled through him. Would Warren take the deal? It *was* a good deal, but Warren wasn't the brightest crayon in the box, so it could go either way. Regardless, there wasn't much more he could do here. "It's a good deal, Warren," he reiterated. "It's more than you'll get from the caretaker's fund and you won't have to spend a cent raising a child. But take or leave it tonight. If you pass, I'll fight you in court till it comes out my way."

Liz linked her hand with his. "We're gonna take off," she said. "And give you time to review the paperwork."

Shane was actually enjoying this tag-team deal. Who would have thought? He gave Warren one last look. "What I spelled out is all in there, minus the check. We'll be back in one hour, so have your decision ready."

They made their way to the foyer, but just as Shane's hand touched the doorknob, Warren called out. "Wait!"

Shane and Liz stopped and turned.

"Don't go," Warren said. "I accept."

CHAPTER TWENTY-TWO

Katie peered out the front window for the umpteenth time. "Where are they?" Shane had texted Liam to advise that he and Liz were on their way over with news, and the anticipation was killing her.

Liam wrapped his arms around her. "They'll be here soon." He brushed a kiss over the top of her head. "Don't worry, sweetie. He said the news was good."

"I know, but I'm still anxious." Drawing back, Katie twirled a long strand of hair around her fingers. Had Shane and Liz found a way to turn the custody case to their favor once again? Maybe Ken had gotten Liam's record cleared, or had somehow removed the evidence Warren had submitted. *Good* news could mean any number of things. While she was more than ready for some good news, nothing would fully satisfy her until she heard the words "you've been granted custody of your daughter."

"Let's wait in the living room," Liam suggested, taking her hand.

"Sure." Staring out the window wouldn't get Shane and Liz over any sooner.

Liam grabbed a couple of Cokes, then sat down beside her on the couch. He asked about enrolling Savannah in school, and suggested they get season tickets to the Nationals after Savannah moved in with them. Katie knew what he was doing—talking as if Savannah moving in with them was a done deal. It reminded her of Posie and Black Eagle and what they had taught her about the Law of Attraction. When she'd been in the clouds and had wanted to return home, Posie had taught her to visualize being home. Liam was doing the same thing now. Acting as if custody had already been decided in their favor put out positive thoughts, and therefore positive vibrations, to attract that outcome.

She leaned in and planted a kiss on Liam's cheek. "How did you get to be so smart?"

Liam answered with a kiss, but just as his lips locked with hers, the front door opened.

"Honey, we're home!" Shane called out in a teasing voice.

Katie flew off the couch and rushed to the foyer. She threw her arms around both Shane and Liz. "Hi! I want to hear all about your trip—wherever you two went—but first what's your news?"

Liam strolled over and gave Liz a kiss on the cheek, and Shane a half hug. "Come on in. As you can see, we're a bit anxious to hear the news."

"We were in Texas," Liz said as they made their way to the living room.

Katie stopped and grabbed her sister's arm. "In Amarillo?"

"Yep," Shane said, flashing a grin. "We met with Warren and wrapped things up." His eyes sparkled as he hooked his thumbs in his belt loops.

A surge of hope rushed into Katie's chest. Wrapped up sounded really, really good, but what exactly did it mean?

"Wrapped up how?" Liam asked, as if reading her mind.

"I made a financial deal with Warren," Shane said, shifting his gaze between Liam and Katie. He lifted up on his heels and turned toward Katie. "He's giving up the custody fight."

Wave after wave of shock gushed through Katie. That would be amazing, but it sounded too good to be true. "Are you sure?" she asked, not wanting to get her hopes up prematurely. She wanted that to be the case, but she didn't trust Warren. "How do you know he won't back out?"

"It's a signed deal," Liz said, rubbing a hand over Katie's arm.

"I had legal papers drawn up and Warren signed them," Shane said with a cocky grin. "He can't back out now."

Liam let out a happy whoop as Katie threw her arms around Shane's neck. "It's really done?" she asked, as tears of joy rolled down her cheeks.

"It's really done," Shane confirmed.

"Thank you." She hugged Shane again. "How can I ever thank you?"

"Just be happy," Shane said. It was a typical, unassuming response from her generous brother-in-law. He was so good to her, to all of them. While Shane readily brushed off compliments, she hoped he knew how much she appreciated him.

She kissed his cheek. "Don't know what we'd do without you."

"Congratulations," Liz said, handing her a tissue, and pulling her into a hug. "You too, Liam," Liz said after she released Katie.

As Liz hugged Liam, Katie dabbed at her cheeks. Her heart was so full of joy she thought it might burst. She was going to be reunited with her daughter. After all of their challenges, it was finally going to happen. She had put out her intention and she had believed, even when their obstacles had seemed insurmountable. And once again, it had worked.

"Damn good job," Liam said, sliding his gaze between Shane and Liz. "Both of you." Then he stepped over and scooped Katie into his arms. "Congratulations, baby!"

Ask and it is given, just as Posie and Black Eagle had promised, she thought happily, as Liam spun her in a circle.

A WEEK LATER, Savannah moved in with them. Katie had invited Deb and Colt too, and they had not only helped Savannah move, but they'd stayed all week. It had helped ease Savannah's transition and it had allowed Deb and Colt to be a part of their granddaughter's firsts in Maryland—her first day of school, her first A, her first friend. Deb and Colt were flying back to Texas tomorrow, but not until they'd experienced yet another first—a barbecue at Katie's parents.

Sighing contentedly, Katie leaned against her favorite maple tree in her parents' back yard. As a kid, she'd climbed this tree and had swung on it. As she'd grown older, she'd marveled at its beauty. Now, the tree was just beginning its transition into fall glory, with a few orange leaves poking here and there in between the green. Her family was in transition, too. Like the tree shedding its leaves, they were getting rid of their old ways. Case in point, today's barbecue included Liam and Shane for the first time ever. She couldn't have been more thrilled over this transformation, and it couldn't have come at a better time. After the motorcycle accident, Katie's mother had started to bond with Cara, and her dad had come around, too. Now Savannah would have the same opportunity, and another set of grandparents to spoil her.

She shifted her gaze to the softball game where the entire crew other than her and her mother were playing. Her mom didn't like to play sports, and besides she had their meal to attend to. Katie had bowed out because she'd been feeling a little lightheaded. It was probably because of the giddiness associated with Savannah's move.

For the game, they had split into two teams. Liam had surprised Katie by agreeing to coach one of the teams, especially since her father had volunteered to coach the other. She'd expected a big rivalry and at least a little contention—because that's how her dad played—but from what she could tell, the game was affable with both teams cheering the other on. It appeared that her father and Liam had even exchanged friendly conversation.

Katie cheered as Savannah scored a run. She was so immersed in the game, she didn't notice her mother approach until she pressed a glass of lemonade into her hands.

"Thanks," Katie said, accepting the glass and taking a long sip.

"Good game." Her mother nodded toward the makeshift field where players were still congratulating Savannah. "You think Seth dropped that ball on purpose?"

Katie smiled. "Oh yeah."

"Me too." Her mother's lips curved up as she touched a hand to Katie's forehead.

"How are you feeling?"

"I'm fine." She was feeling better. Standing in the shade and drinking the cool lemonade had helped. Even though it was late September, it was a warm day and the sun was bright and strong.

"Why don't you come sit with me on the patio?" her mom suggested. "The game should be ending in a few minutes anyway."

By the time she and her mother had reached the patio, the game had ended.

"We won!" Savannah said, sprinting over. "By two runs." She beamed at Liam who trailed behind her.

"Great job, kiddo," he said, ruffling Savannah's hair.

"We kicked butt, sis," Cara said, high-fiving with Savannah.

Katie's dad approached. "Good game," he told Liam, then shook Liam's hand. "Congrats on the win."

Pleased with her father's good-natured approach, Katie winked at him when he glanced over. The rest of the crew moseyed in, grabbed drinks, and bantered over highlights from the game.

A short while later, Mitch and Colt fired up the grills while Katie, Liam, Shane, Liz, Deb, and Savannah sat at the table.

"I love softball," Savannah said on a sigh.

Katie assumed it was a happy sigh until she noticed Savannah's bottom lip protruding. "What's wrong, sweetie?"

"I want to play softball here," Savannah said. "You know, in school. I was really good on my old team."

"That she was," Deb agreed with pride in her voice.

"Then you should play." Katie shifted to study her daughter. She wasn't sure what the problem was.

"Gem Valley used to have a great girls' softball team," Shane put in from her other side.

"I used to play softball in school." Liz smiled nostalgically. "Of course, that was a very long time ago."

"We don't have a team anymore." Savannah pressed her lips together. " 'Cause they don't have a coach."

Katie, Shane, and Liz all turned to look at Liam.

"Okay, okay." Liam lifted his hands in the air. "I'll call the school."

"Really?" Katie gaped at her husband. In the past, Liam had declined at least three coaching opportunities. She'd always figured it had something to do with his lack of faith in himself as a role model, which she had never understood. Sure, his parents had passed while he was an eighteen-year-old who had yet to pull his life together, but these days, he was the best dad, the best husband —really, the best man she knew. Katie rested a hand on Liam's arm.

Liam grinned at his wife. He knew what she was thinking —*about time*! And it was. He was more than ready to let go of the guilt that had been weighing him down—and holding him back— ever since his teenage years. "Sure, why not?"

"Liam used to be the best ball player in high school," Shane told Savannah. "He's been asked to coach before, but he's always said no." Shane glanced at Liam in bafflement.

Liam understood his brother's confusion. He had declined many coaching requests. But he no longer felt unworthy. Besides, this was for Savannah. He tipped his head toward her. "I'm doing it for Savannah."

Savannah's face lit up. "You're really gonna coach?" She clasped her hands over her heart. "For me?"

If he hadn't already been convinced, Savannah's sweet, hopeful expression would have won him over. He leaned in and kissed the top of her head.

"Anything for you. I'll call the school on Monday."

"Cool, thanks!" Savannah whipped out her iPhone. "I gotta text Grace. We were just talking about softball. She's gonna be so excited!" She quickly typed a message, then put the phone on her lap with a sigh. "I wish we could start before spring."

There was no reason why they couldn't. "We could get a training camp going this fall," he said. "Since there hasn't been a team in a couple of years, it'll make for a good start. It'll be like spring training except in the fall."

"That'd be great." Beaming, Savannah picked up her cell again. "I'm gonna tell Grace that, too."

Katie nudged him. "Come help me with the appetizers."

He rose and followed Katie inside the house. But instead of going to the kitchen as he had expected, she pulled him into a formal room off the main hallway. Then she looked up at him with narrowed eyes.

"What?" He stuffed his hands in his jean pockets as post-game excitement raced through him like it had when he'd played in high school. Damn, he'd missed it.

"I'm surprised you offered to coach the girls' softball team."

"Oh that." He shrugged. "It'll make Savannah happy. And that'll make you happy." He grinned, feeling pretty happy himself. "Besides, it's time to get over my hang ups."

Katie smiled up at him. "What made you change your mind?"

Liam returned her smile. "I guess I'm feeling more confident these days. Maybe it's the support your mom's given me. Colt and Deb, too. Hell, your dad's even coming around a little." Scrubbing a hand over his cheek, he rocked back on his heels. "To be honest, I also had a dream where my parents visited. They said they've been watching over me, cheering me on. They said they're proud of how I raised Shane, Cara, and Seth." His chest swelled with pride as he took Katie's hand. "I guess I needed to hear that."

Katie lifted up on her tippy-toes and kissed his cheek. "I'm proud of you, too."

His insides warmed at her words and his chest puffed even more as they made their way to the kitchen to retrieve chips, dips, and a veggie tray.

When they returned to the patio, Savannah and Shane were still talking about his offer to coach. "Liam was big stuff in high school," Shane bragged. "Colleges were hot on his trail, asking him to play for them."

Savannah glanced up at him. "Did you play in college?"

Liam put the food on the table. "Nah."

"Why not?" she wanted to know.

He and Shane exchanged a look and Liam felt a change in their dynamic. Normally, he would refuse to be the center of attention and Shane would insist on giving it to him. In the past, it had been a back-and-forth play that left no one satisfied. But today they both seemed content.

"Not what I wanted to do," he said. "I loved playing ball, but I loved working on motorcycles more, so I stayed here and started a business."

"Oh, Callahan Cycles," Savannah said. "Your business is so cool."

As his lips curved up, he and Shane exchanged another congenial look. Liam had finally figured out that Shane had *needed* the opportunity to pay him back for putting him through college. Liam and Shane had always been close, but their bond had strengthened even more after Liam had put aside his need to handle everything himself. Glancing at Katie, then at Savannah, and taking in their happiness, Liam was grateful he had given Shane the chance to assist with the custody case. Getting a little help hadn't made him a lesser man as he had once feared. Instead, it had made them all stronger.

Katie strolled down the long drive to Callahan Cycles excited to share her news with Liam. Along the way, she delighted in the colors of the new autumn garden Cara and Savannah had helped her plant last weekend. The three of them had also made the adorable doggie scarecrow.

She stepped into Liam's office at the same time as Cole, Callahan Cycle's newest employee.

"Hey, Liam, Katie." Cole removed his baseball cap and nodded at her.

"Hi, Cole," she said, smiling at Liam's new fabricator.

Liam circled around his desk, patted Cole on the back, then gave her a peck on the cheek.

"Sorry to interrupt," Cole said, turning toward Liam. "But can you check my work on the Army bike when you have a minute?"

"Let's do it now." Katie rubbed her hands together. I'd love to see the progress." One of Liam's current custom orders was a military-themed bike for a retired Army sergeant. She was already thinking about how to market it, including sending a press release to the DC military publications.

"Sure." Liam slung an arm around her shoulder as they followed Cole to the far bay. Along the way, Katie greeted the other guys.

When they reached the bike, she let out a soft gasp. Big, long, and sleek, painted Army green, it resembled a high-tech tank.

"Damn," Liam said, his voice full of admiration. A smile formed, and it expanded as he made his way around the motorcycle.

The stars had been shining on Liam the day he'd found Cole. The experienced fabricator had relocated to Gem Valley to look after his grandmother the same day Liam had placed his help wanted ad. Katie had deemed it 'perfect universal synchronicity,' laughing when she'd heard Black Eagle's voice uttering the exact same words in her head. She gave Cole a smile. "Where are the wires?"

"Running through the handlebars into the frame." Cole's lips curved up as he ran a hand along the front of the bike. "You'll never see them."

"Great job, Cole," Liam said. "I wouldn't change a thing." As Liam chatted with his employee, Katie wandered into the hallway, taking in the sights, the sounds, the positive energy. The camaraderie and enthusiasm of the team at Callahan Cycles was uplifting. It was a stark contrast to the tense, competitive environment of her last job, and this realization had led her to her recent career epiphany.

A few minutes later, Liam caught up with her. "I can't wait to see that bike after Doug airbrushes a screaming eagle on the gas tank." Grinning, he took her hand. "We're gonna have to market the hell out of that one."

"I already have ideas," she said and as they ambled toward Liam's office, she shared her idea about the military publications.

"Great. I hope you know how much I appreciate your help here." Liam tugged her into his office and in one smooth move pushed the door closed and pinned her against it. His lips claimed hers in a kiss that was both passionate and appreciative.

When Liam drew back, she laughed. "If that's all it takes, I can toss out a few more ideas."

Liam shifted to give her space, leaning against the door as his expression turned serious. "I mean it, Katie. I don't know what I'd've done without you over the last month. Business continues to grow from your Post ad. You've done all the invoicing and payroll—work I despise. And, I've never had the time or the expertise to do marketing. Now we're sponsoring Savannah's softball team, hosting a poker run for the Humane Society, and damn, getting us a spotlight in Iron Steed's "Builders to Watch" article—that's golden."

"I'm having fun." She took Liam's hand. "This is what I want, Liam. I want to keep working here."

Liam went still for a moment. "You mean work here...like full time?"

She nodded, feeling more certain than ever. She was using her skills and making a difference. For Callahan Cycle customers, for the community, for *their* family. Sales from two custom orders they'd gotten from the *Post* ad would generate more revenue than her annual salary at the bank, and she was just getting started.

"Are you sure?" Liam's voice was hopeful as his gaze pinned hers. "This is really what you want to do?"

"I minored in Marketing in college," she said, "but I never got to use it. I'm good at it. I enjoy it. A couple of weeks ago I realized I didn't dread Monday mornings anymore, I actually like coming to work here." She flashed a bright smile. "Yeah, I'm sure."

"Woo-hoo!" Liam wrapped his arms around her neck and pulled her into a long, passionate kiss. "That's the best news you could have given me."

She laughed. "I'm glad you're happy, but that's not all."

"What could be better than this?" Liam asked, his face stretched into a grin.

"Have you heard of *Cold Steel on Two Wheels*?"

"Who hasn't? It's the most popular biker build-off competition on TV." Liam cocked his head. "Why? You want to start watching the show with me?"

Squeezing her hands together, Katie could barely contain her excitement. "I got you a spot on next season's show."

Liam's jaw dropped as his eyes widened. "You're joking."

She shook her head. "I entered pictures of the Americana bike and the Dukes of Hazzard chopper," she said bouncing on her heels. "It's a done deal. That is, if you want it."

"Damn straight I do." Liam pulled her into his arms and planted sloppy kisses up and down her face. "Do you know what this means? Everyone who's ever been on that show has made it big...*every builder*, not just the winner." His eyes sparkled as he spoke. "I'm gonna have to hire more guys." The corner of his eyes crinkled as his smile spread. "We're gonna have to expand. We'll need another bay, maybe two more."

"Sounds good," she said, smiling at her success and at making her husband deliriously happy. "While you're at it, you can build an office for me, too. I just promoted myself to Chief Marketing Officer."

CHAPTER TWENTY-THREE

"*I* can't believe you're taking me to Paris for *a weekend*," Liz said as their plane descended into Charles de Gaulle Airport. "A first-class flight, champagne, a weekend in Paris. Not to mention the interview with JP. Editors are fighting over my article as we speak." She pressed her lips together as her stomach clenched with excitement. The piece had turned out exceptionally well, and it would be a boon to her writing career. All because of Shane. She shifted and smiled at him. "You're spoiling me, Shane."

"Anything for my Liz," he said, taking her hand.

She wasn't the only one Shane enjoyed spoiling. Last week, he'd practically bought out Best Buy after Sabby had whined about Cara and Savannah's new electronics. And in anticipation of Katie's upcoming birthday, he already had a crew starting work on her present—an in-ground heated pool and a hot tub—which had delighted Katie *and* her family.

Shane could be cranky and contentious, but he was also the most generous man Liz had ever met. And even better, he gave freely. Sighing happily, she gazed out the window, taking in the timeless familiarity of the grand city she'd once called home.

They went through a VIP process at the airport and zipped

through quicker than Liz had ever experienced at an international airport. After, they were greeted by the car service Shane had secured. She had never experienced this kind of first-class service, but had to admit that she liked it.

They were whisked to one of her favorite parts of the city—St. Germain-des-Pres, a classy Parisian district that was home to authentic 17th century buildings and apartments, trendy boutiques, upscale art galleries, and atmospheric restaurants. The historic streets in the area were made for strolling.

The area had once been home to Monet, Renoir, Picasso, and Hemmingway. The artistic history and positive energy appealed to her creative side. When she'd lived in Paris, she had ambled down the ancient roads countless times to spur her muse. She hadn't lived in that region because the neighborhood was out of her price range, but it had been fun to visit.

The driver stopped the car in front of a charming multi-story white building.

"Here we are," Shane said.

Her mouth dropped open as Shane climbed out of the car. They were staying in St. Germain-des-Pres? Shane circled around the trunk and opened the door for her.

Stepping out of the car, she gaped at him. "*This* is where we're staying?"

"I thought you might like it," he said, pulling his wallet out of his back pocket.

Like it? She took in the historic building, the lovely terraces, the intricate architectural details. "Shane, this is amazing!"

Shane settled with the driver, then grabbed their bags and ushered her toward the building. They took the elevator to the top floor where Shane pulled out a key to open the only door.

She stepped inside and took it all in—the large entrance gallery, the living room with its soaring ceilings and modern furnishings, and the oversized balcony with spectacular views of the bustling city. "I can't believe you found a place to rent here. I thought these apartments were all exclusively owned."

Shane lifted a shoulder. "It made me think of you."

"Thank you, Shane." He was so thoughtful.

"Do you wanna rest for a while?" he asked. "Then we can freshen up and head out to dinner."

A few hours later, after a long, decadent afternoon nap and a refreshing shower, Liz fixed her hair and make-up, then changed into a black sheath dress with a cowl neck. Pulling the thin leather belt around her waist, she checked herself out in the mirror. Not bad. The belt emphasized her hourglass shape, which is what she was going for. She wanted to look extra nice for Shane. It was the least she could do considering he had brought her to Paris and had found a place to rent in St. Germain-des-Pres.

She grabbed her evening bag and made her way to the living room, expecting Shane to bustle her out post-haste. They hadn't eaten since breakfast, and he'd risen from the nap before her and had been ready for at least an hour. When she walked into the living room, Shane was pacing the dark hardwood floors.

Concerned, she made her way over. His body was stiff, his forehead puckered.

"Everything okay?"

His eyes roamed her figure. "Liz, you're stunning."

She was pleased by the compliment, but waved it off as nerves sparked in her gut. He wasn't acting at all like the Shane she knew.

"You're looking very handsome yourself." She stepped closer to adjust his tie. "There," she said, patting his chest. "You clean up well, Shane Callahan. Now, why don't you take me out to a wonderful bistro?"

"Not yet," he said, his voice rough. Twisting the watch on his wrist, he glanced at her for a split second and then his gaze darted around the room.

What was going on? Was he breaking up with her? Her nerves threatened to charge full force into panic, but she talked herself down. *Get a grip, Liz. The man didn't bring you to Paris to break up with you.*

Still, the momentary alarm caught her off guard. She cared for Shane...a lot. With that thought, reality slammed into her like a French freight train, and she sucked in a gulp of air. She hadn't fallen *a little* as she had previously convinced herself, she'd fallen madly and deeply in love with him.

Holy shit.

Now *she* felt nervous, and a little nauseous, too.

"I need to talk with you for a few minutes before we go," he said.

She drew in a long, fretful breath. Nothing good ever came from that phrase.

"I'm not good at this." Shane fidgeted with his fingers. "The whole communication thing." He clutched his hands together. "You know."

Despite her anxiety, she choked out a laugh. "You're getting better."

Shane's lips curved up, and he slid a hand over his short golden hair. "I'm trying." He took her hand and led her to the French doors that opened to the terrace, but he didn't step outside. Instead, he turned to face her holding both of her hands.

"I've enjoyed the four months we've spent together."

Well, damn. Maybe he *was* breaking up with her. Her heart stopped beating.

"But it's not enough," he said. "I want more."

Her heart sprang to life, this time thumping in hopeful anticipation. Was he suggesting what she thought he was?

"I know you think you don't want a relationship."

"Shane, I—"

He leaned in to kiss her, a soft, tender kiss filled with hope and promise, and she completely forgot what she had been about to say.

"I'm not a controlling man," he said after he drew back. "I'll never try to dominate you and I won't let anyone else try to control you either."

Thoughtful words, but she already knew that. He had *shown* her, which was even better than the words. She drew in a calming breath. Where was he going with this, she wondered?

"I love who you are…your strength, your independence. You can keep all of that and still be with me. So…." Shane rubbed his thumb over the top of her hand. "I bought this place."

Her breath caught. "You bought this?" Her gaze took in the gorgeous space. It must have cost a fortune.

"You said you wanted to come back to Paris, maybe work here a couple of months a year," he said, squeezing her hand. "I figured it would be good to have a home base. You know, for you and Sabby."

Now she was confused. Touched, but completely and thoroughly confused. "You bought this apartment for me?"

"I'm fucking this up." Shane dipped his head. "I'm not good at this," he muttered, then lifted his gaze to meet hers. "I bought it for *us*. I want to give you the world, Liz, if you'll let me. Starting with this apartment."

Her heart did a slow, happy roll in her chest. He wasn't breaking up with her at all. He wanted them to be together and that was exactly what she wanted, too.

Shane dropped to one knee, and her hand flew to her mouth. Astonishment and joy did a rumba in her belly. But a smidgen of skepticism waltzed in, too. Was he really proposing, or did he have lint on his pant leg?

When he pulled a blue Tiffany box from his jacket pocket, her disbelief fluttered into elation.

Shane flipped the velvet box open. "Marry me, Liz."

Inside was the biggest diamond she had ever seen, shimmering in the late afternoon sun. She hadn't expected this. But she hadn't expected to fall wildly in love either.

"Yes." Joy swelled in her chest bright as the rays of light shining through the veranda windows. "Yes, I'll marry you." She'd never expected to say those words again, but they felt so very right.

Shane slipped the ring on her finger. He rose, lifted her in the air, and spun her in circles. "I'll make you the happiest woman on Earth," he said when her feet finally touched the ground.

"Oh, Shane." She rested her forehead on his. "You already have."

KATIE LEANED against her favorite maple tree, watching the last inning of the softball game in her parents' back yard. Once again, she and her mom had elected to sit out. Katie hadn't played because she'd felt a little queasy earlier and she hadn't wanted to press her luck. Her mother had wanted the extra time to fuss over Katie's birthday cake.

Katie didn't mind being on the sidelines. It was fun watching Liam coach, and seeing the camaraderie between he and Colt who was also coaching. Today, Savannah was on Liam's team, and Cara on Colt's, although both Liam and Colt seemed to be offering extra help to *their* girls.

Earlier, Colt had helped Savannah position herself in the outfield, even though she was on Liam's team. Now, Savannah was at bat and Liam was showing her how to swing through the pitch. It must have helped since she hit a double. But the next two batters got outs—Deb struck out and Jen grounded to first base. Liam's team moved to the field, and Colt's team was at bat with Cara up first. After she swung and missed on the first pitch, Liam jogged over to help her even though she was on Colt's team. She fouled on the next pitch, and Colt made his way to home plate. He and Cara had a lengthy conversation, and after, Cara hit a home run.

Katie cheered for Cara, then rested against the maple tree admiring the leaves in dazzling hues of red and orange. As a child, she had secretly believed this tree was magical. She'd made many wishes under the tree and most of them had come true. Now she understood that her wishes had simply been her setting forth intentions and her childlike expectation had put out positive vibrations which had in turn attracted that which she'd desired.

When Liam's strong arms wrapped around her from behind, she let out a quiet hum. Immersed in her thoughts, she hadn't noticed the game had ended. She pivoted to face him. "Hi there."

"Hello." Liam skimmed his lips over hers. "I've been to your parents' place three times over the last month." His lips ticked upward. "Never thought I'd see the day."

"Me either." But she couldn't have been more thrilled over Liam's growing relationship with her parents. Sighing happily, she smoothed down her burgundy-lace dress. Her outfit, which included an AEO jean jacket and denim wedge sandals, had been a gift from Jen.

Liam gave her the once over. "You look beautiful," he said, then leaned in and kissed her.

"Cut it out, you two lovebirds," Shane said as he approached with his arm around Liz.

Laughing, Katie elbowed Shane. "Like you have a lot of room to talk."

He grinned, then hugged her. "Happy birthday, sis."

"Thank you. And thanks again for the pool and hot-tub, you crazy man." It was an overly generous gift, but she couldn't wait to swim in the heated pool and sit in the hot tub during the first snow.

Shane shrugged it off like he always did, but the glint in his eye indicated he recognized her deep appreciation.

Liz moved in next and pulled her into a hug. "Happy birthday, Katie."

"Thank you. Now...." She lifted her sister's left hand. "Let me look at this big rock again." Liz's diamond sparkled, enormous and flawless. "Not too shabby."

Liz was all smiles. Katie couldn't remember ever seeing her sister this happy. She smiled back, thrilled that her sister and brother-in-law had fallen in love.

"When are you two tying the knot?" Liam asked.

"Sabby wants us to do it tomorrow." Liz half laughed, half groaned. "Because she wants to move here as soon as possible. But I need a little time to pack."

"It'll be soon," Shane said with a quick grin. "We're gonna keep Liz's place in Georgetown." He took Liz's hand. "So really, sweetie, you only need to pack your clothes and personal stuff."

"I've already started." Liz slid Shane a smile, then turned toward Katie. "We wanted to check with you before we finalize our wedding plans. We're thinking of flying to the Galapagos Islands," she said, bouncing on her toes.

"Just a simple ceremony on the beach," Shane added. "Maybe next month."

Katie was surprised. She would have guessed a large ceremony, which tended to be Shane's style. She assumed he was yielding to Liz who had simpler tastes. But next month? "Wow—that's soon."

"Next month," Shane repeated. "I'm not giving Liz time to change her mind."

Liz playfully swatted at Shane, making Katie and Liam laugh.

"We're having a short guest list. Sabby's coming of course," Shane said. "Carolyn and Mitch, and Deb and Colt. We want you guys, Cara, and Savannah to come, too."

"We're thinking Thanksgiving week," Liz said, her voice eager. "I checked the school calendar. Cara and Savannah have a few days off, and Sabby has the whole week off from community college. Would that work?" she asked, clasping her hands together.

"I can probably talk my boss into giving me time off," Katie said, nudging Liam. While she was just teasing, she realized it would be easier to take time off now that she was working for Callahan Cycles.

Liam winked at her. "We're in."

"It sounds perfect." Katie pulled her sister in for another hug. "Congrats again," she whispered. "Shane's a good man."

"Don't I know it," Liz whispered back.

"Time for cake," Katie's mother hollered from across the lawn.

Katie, Liam, Shane, and Liz made their way over to the stone patio where a giant cake with oodles of candles was positioned in the middle of the table.

"Jeez." Eying the cake, Katie laughed. "Did you really put thirty candles on it?"

"Of course," her mother said, standing tall.

"Let's see you blow all those out." Katie's dad gave her a double wink like he used to do when she was younger. "Make a good wish."

Her wish was that she would continue to absorb—and *apply*—everything she had learned in the clouds. She blew out all of the candles, then tugged Liam close.

"We have news to share. But, first, I want you all to know how much it means to have *all* of my family and friends together in one place." She made eye contact with every person around the table.

"It's the perfect gift. But I had another gift this week too that I—" she glanced up at Liam "—that *we* want to share."

Liam smiled at her adoringly. She appreciated him so much. He always made her feel treasured. He was her rock, her cheerleader. He had believed in their dreams even when she hadn't. She suspected his belief, his positive energy, had carried them forward when her faith had floundered. "Why don't you do the honors?" she suggested.

Liam's face stretched into a wide grin. "We're gonna have a baby!"

Cheers and congratulations broke out around the table. Cara and Savannah squealed and clapped along with everyone else even though they were already in the know. Katie and Liam had shared the happy news with them yesterday, right after Katie's doctor had confirmed. Both girls had been thrilled.

"How wonderful!" Katie's mother threw her arms around Katie, and then Liam.

Katie's dad hugged her next. "Happy for you, Kate." Her brows went up when he released her and stepped over to extend a hand to Liam. "Congratulations." Her father shook Liam's hand. "I'm happy for both of you."

After Katie and Liam had been congratulated, hugged, and kissed by every person there, Carolyn picked up the knife. "First piece of cake for you, Katie."

Friendly bickering ensued over the sex of the baby. Cara, Sabby, and Savannah insisted it would be another girl, but Shane and Katie's father predicted a son. Resting a hand on her belly, Katie smiled. She didn't care whether their baby was a boy or a girl. The intention she'd set forth was that he or she was happy and healthy.

After Katie opened her presents, she slipped outside with Pan. Allowing Pan to come to her parents' home had been a nice birthday surprise. In the past, her folks had been firm on their no dog policy. She squatted down and rubbed Pan's head. "You're such a good boy," she cooed. "Now that they've seen what a sweet little muffin-pie you are, they'll have you over more often." She kissed the top of his head, then tossed the ball.

As Pan raced off to retrieve it, Seth sidled up to her.

"Hey, Katie, congratulations again." He grinned. "I'm really happy for you and Liam." He handed her a bag. "One more present, but I wanted to give it to you in private."

Katie reached into the bag and pulled out a black shirt with the word 'believe' scribed in turquoise letters. She slid her finger over the words. It was a perfect gift. She wondered if Liam had mentioned her cloud experience to Seth because it was also a perfect reminder to believe in her dreams. "Thank you." She hugged him. "I love it!"

"I saw it and thought of you," he said, shuffling his foot on the grass. "You and Liam believed in me and gave me a second chance. I wanted to say thanks for believing, for making me believe in myself."

"Oh, Seth." She rubbed his arm. "You're an amazing young man. Don't you ever forget that."

"Happy Birthday, Katie." Seth's gaze cut across the lawn to Cara. "Uh, I gotta run."

"Go on, and have fun."

When Seth trotted off, Liam took his place.

"I love you, baby," he said, brushing a strand of hair away from her face.

"Love you, too." She lifted up on her tiptoes and pressed her lips to Liam's. He drew her in for a dreamy kiss that made her tingle from her head to her toes. After, he took her hand and they leaned against the fence in a compatible silence.

Seth's gift had reminded her of the power of believing. She had easily encouraged Seth through his teenage years, but somewhere along her own path obstacles and insecurities had set in, making it hard to believe in *her* dreams. With a little help from above, she had learned the Law of Attraction and rediscovered her faith, and an abundance of goodness had followed. She'd made her way out of the coma, gained custody of Savannah, found an exciting career, and had gotten pregnant after years of trying. And, her entire family had finally bonded together.

Now her life was full, her heart light, and happiness flowed through her like sunshine. She gazed up at the painstakingly blue sky. In the air, an eagle flapped its powerful wings. *Black Eagle.* A loving vibration touched her right shoulder, and warmth spread through her body. *Posie.*

A puffy cloud floated overhead and whispered in the wind—*The power to manifest your desires comes from within.*

The End

ABOUT THE AUTHOR

Author Sedona Hutton finds inspiration in the beautiful Smoky Mountains of Tennessee, where she lives with her husband and curly-coated retriever. In addition to writing, she's a Reiki Master and a certified Chopra Center Meditation instructor. She enjoys reading, yoga, gardening, playing with her dog, and riding motorcycles.

Visit her at www.SedonaHutton.com

 facebook.com/SedonaHuttonAuthor

twitter.com/SedonaHutton

READING GROUP GUIDE

1. Do you think Katie was in the clouds in an alternate dimension or was it all in her head?
2. Bear telepathically communicated with Katie, and she and Pan had a particularly close relationship. Do you think dogs, cats, and other animals, are more intuitive than humans?
3. Do you believe in love at first sight? Why or why not?
4. Do you think Liam's parents visited him or was it just a dream?
5. Some people believe that dream consciousness is every bit as real as waking consciousness but it takes place in a different dimension. What do you think?
6. Liz is highly independent. Do you think her father's controlling nature contributed to her desire to handle everything on her own? How do our parents, teachers, church, and society influence our lives?
7. What impact do you think Katie's stress had on her inability to get pregnant? Do you think her guilt over giving up Savannah contributed as well?
8. What do you think would have happened to Seth had